I0657293

Memoryblock

Who is John Normal

Suspicion and Curiosity

Ben Dolphijn

Chapter 1

A gentle shake moved his shoulder. He slowly woke
up. What happened. Where was he. He tried to
open his eyes but that was a problem. Automatically
he swapped his eyes with his hand. He was
shocked. It hurt terribly. His hand was taken by
somebody and put back on the ground beside him.
On the ground? Yes, he was on the ground. He felt
the ground. A concrete floor with many loose sandy
crap. He felt further by moving his hand over the
floor. More sandy concrete.
" Yes, you are on the ground and you are hurt," a
friendly lady-voice informed him.
"Please try to get up and sit. I will try to clean your
wounds."
He understood what she mend and tried to get
seated. He stretched his arm and pushed himself
calm and slowly up. His back hurt terribly but he
pushed through it and got seated. He stretched his
back and the pain level lowered.
"Great, very good !" the ladyvoice called out.
Another voice, a young man's voice sounded.
"So, he is alive. He even moves. Great. He can be
of help. So we are with four. So there are options.
Can he talk?"
"Easy, easy," the lady voice reacted. "First his
wounds and his eyes, than we talk. "

"You have a big bleu aria on your back. That will hurt you when you move. Further you have a large headwound. The blood is all over your face so I don't know how your eyes are under all that blood. I will now first clean your headwound and next your face and your eyes. I hope they are not damaged but we will see."

He felt water on his head. She was very gentle with her towel when cleaning. He felt the water on his forehead and in the end on his eyes. That hurt badly. He kept his eyes strongly closed. That hurt as well. The lady tried to clean his left eyelid. He accepted that it made him shiver. Again when she cleaned the other eyelid. She went on till she was satisfied.

"Try to open your eyes. Don't shake of wat you see. It is a horrible mess. Be careful, your eyelids are scratched, I guess that your eyes will be clean."

Slowly he tried to open his eyes. Both at the same time. His eyelids scrammed, but he went on. He had to see where he was and wat had happened. It was rather dark in the room where he was.

He saw a terrible mess. Large pieces of concrete were smashed on the floor. All kind of materials were lying around. Papers, broken chairs, parts of tables, cupboards, broken walls, the gates were scrambled. The gates ? Wat was that. Was he in a prison? He looked up. The ceiling was broken down partly. The store above had come down also partly. He could see open air through the holes in the ceiling above him. There must have been an enormous explosion to get this kind of damage. He saw a young man standing at the other site of the room, looking away from him. He was looking through the exploded wall and the scrambled gate. Next to him stood a solid woman. She had her hands on the scrambled gate and also looked into the hallway, he presumed. He looked a site to the gentle lady that had cleaned his head and eyes. She was beautiful but still very young. He estimated her a year of sixteen. Long blond hear and a small but sportive body and a very friendly face. She smiled at him and it made him feel good.

"Good," she said and stood up. "Come on John, how are you doing? I am "Marion", the young man is "Rico", the lady is "Mindy", do you remember? "

He nodded and tried carefully to get up. He was not disappointed. His back protested, but he knew, it were only bruises, so he got on. He got up and was not unsatisfied about his condition.

"So, my name is John" he proclaimed. He looked around. Nothing was familiar. Where was he, where was this. What did he do here. How did he came here, wat was he doing here? He looked at Marion. She saw his reaction.

"This location is a research centre. We, anyway Marion, Rico and I, were captured, kidnapped and transported to this location to be used for tests. We were lucky that someone has blown the building as you can see, one day after our arrival. We were in

4

the cells next to yours. They are all blown away, your cell was there, at the end of the hall. Do you remember when you came here? Do you remember what has happened with you before this all exploded?" Marion looked hopefully to John.
John tried to remember but nothing came up. Slowly his head seemed to clear up. He thought he remembered that he was brought here some time ago. He was drugged and did not precisely knew what had happened to him. He pulled up his sleeves and looked at his arms. He saw several injection points. Marion looked with him at the points on his arms. It was clear. He was a victim too.
Rico looked back at John and Marion.
"I think we better try to leave. Come on, let 's go."
He stepped over a part of the gate that was lying partly on the floor and walked into the hallway.
Mindy also looked back and followed Rico. Marion also followed and John started slowly up with walking. It worked. He followed the others calm and slow to test his moving's. He stepped over the gate and walked into the hallway.
Some ten meters in front of him the others were gathered. John saw a stairway, heavily damaged but still partly usable.
Rico started to step down the stairs.
John followed the group. They were only one level up, so they were quickly on the ground floor. The whole building was four stocks high. John looked back at the building. It was a total disaster. The

whole building was collapsed. He must have been very lucky to be one of the survivors. He looked along the building. Several people were running away from the building. Rico pointed to a jeep that was standing on a parking place some twenty meters away from them. Rico spurted immediately towards the car.

John tried to speed up his moves. That worked ok. He followed the others and finished his run in the truck, next to Marion at the back. Rico did something under the dashboard and the jeep started. He drove quickly away from the building. He seemed to know where he had to go to. He drove the area out through a large open gate and followed a broad avenue.

John had no idea where they were. He asked Marion. She seemed a little bit surprised.

"This is Bopol, we all lived in this city. Where did you live? "

John had no feelings by a city called "Bopol". He did not know the name. Vaguely he had the idea that his hometown was called something like "Jury". He told Marion wat he though.

She reacted that she did not know that town.

John looked around to get an impression from this city. It seemed all very organised.

Rico drove through a large city centre and followed the road a very long time. He drove about an hour.

Finally the petrol was finished so Rico dropped the jeep on a large parking area at the site of an enormous museum.

He told the others that he lived about three blocks away. He wanted to collect some clothes and things because the government would very likely try to arrest him again and send him to another forbidden area. They wanted to get rid of him.

John looked surprised at him. "What do you mean, "arrested"."

Rico smiled at him "Does not matter, " he simply stated and wanted to walk away.

Mindy shacked her head. " No, Rico. Don't go back. Come with me, I have an apartment in this area they do not know a thing about. It is a secret hiding place, come on." She started to walk towards the museum.

John could not follow the discussion. "Secret hiding places, they do not know about? Were they all convicted criminals? Was he a criminal too? The thought astonished him. Who was he. He had to get his memory back. Nothing was more frustrating than not knowing who he was and what had happened in the past. He must be realistic. If all those other three were judged convicted criminals, than he must be a judged criminal too. It seemed logic. Why was he in that building where they were held. What had he done to be convicted? What did he actually remember.

John puzzled about his memory. The group followed Mindy. She knew where to go. They passed the museum and walked into an area with very small walkthrough ports and gates and narrow streets. No cars could ride here, the streets were too small for that. After several turns and very small squares Mindy finally stopped in one of those narrow streets. She looked scary up and down the road. She than looked at Rico and John and kicked with her foot against a stone in de wall, a little bit above street level. The stone gave a click and turned towards the street. Mindy went quickly on her knees and picked up something from behind the stone. She immediately locked back the stone in its former position. Again she looked up and down the street and also to Rico and John. She got up and walked, all the time looking around, at least ten houses with front doors further. There, at house number 587, she stopped.

John saw the number on the wall beside the door. Mindy opened a small window in the door with her hand and put her hand in the gate of the little window. She knew where to look for and John heard a load click and the door opened.

Immediately Mindy pulled her hand out and pushed the door open. Again she looked up and down the road and stepped through the door. She made clear to the others to enter quickly. Behind the door was a very small hallway, leading to a very small staircase. Mindy closed the front door and walked to the staircase. She went up and the others followed her. John was in no hurry and followed as the last one. They went up two long stairs. The stairs went on but Mindy got to a door on the hallway.

John just came at the top of the stairs on that floor when Mindy suddenly stepped aside of the door and pressed her back against the wall. Rico and Marion followed immediately her example. John looked surprised at them. Marion made clear to him that he had to come to her and stand on her site with his back to the wall.

John did what she asked without words.

John heard a key being turned around and with a load click the door was unlocked. The door was opened from the inside. Mindy seemed to stretch herself out. She looked all of a sudden quite different, stronger, taller.

John wandered wat was happening to her.

"Hallo Rosemary, happy to meet again. Won 't you come in and introduce your comrades," a heavy voice stated.

"Hallo Ross, how are you doing. What are you doing in my house," Mindy replied. She stayed at her spot. Probably she did not trust this "Ross". John realised that Ross had called her "Rosemary". Another surprise? Another name for each case? "Rosemary, Rosemary, somewhere the name sounded familiar. "Rosemary Flame?" Rico whispered, staring at Mindy with big brown eyes.

Marion sighed, "I already suspected something like this. "

Ross answered with a smile in his voice. "Your house Rosemary? It is a house of the company. I saw it standing on the list of buildings owned by the company. I expected you to come here if you had survived the explosions on the Experimental Prison. But please come in. I am very glad that you survived the explosion. Perhaps you can tell me more about what has happened there. Did you place the explosives?"

Just before Ross had finished his speech, Mindy jumped through the door, rolled immediately over her shoulder and jumped up to see where Ross was standing. At that same moment a shot was heart. A bullet hit the wall above the staircase. It was clearly mend to hit Mindy.

John looked surprised to what was happening. This was dangerous. A serious yell from Ross made clear that Mindy was far too close to him to mis him. A tough blow was heard and a body slammed against the floor. Something was hit by the falling body because John heard timber being cracked or Mindy had hit Ross again with a chair.

Mindy came through the door and invited them in. They all came in. Mindy closed the door behind John and turned the key so the door was locked again.

John did not feel very well with that idea. He could not leave when he wanted. The door was locked, though he saw that the key was still in the door. He lost the closed up feeling.

Suddenly Mindy sussed and put her finger for her lips, asking for silence. They all stared at her.

Mindy looked at a door in the back of the room. She focussed and walked towards the door. Again she made the sign for silence and felt on the door handle. She listened on the door. Nothing was heart. She slowly put down the handle and swept the door open, at the same time she bended through her knees and jumped very low into the room. She rolled over her shoulder and wanted to give a tough kick against a figure that was sitting there in a chair.

She stopped her action and gave a heavy yell. She fell tough against the sitting person and fell together with her forwards with chair and all on the floor.

Rico jumped immediately into the other room and saw what had happened. He stopped. Also Marion and John came into the room.

Before them Mindy was busy getting up. On the floor with her back against the chair on the floor a very young girl was sitting in the chair, completely tight up with thick cables and with a prop in her mouth with a handkerchief bound around it, so she could not make any sound.

John walked to her and released her from the handkerchief and the prop in her mouth. She inhaled relieved and took several deep breaths.

"Thank you" she mumbled while John tried to get rid of the ropes. Rico helped him and John got the chairs right up. The girl got out of her chair and tried to get her blood to recycle again. Marion started to massage her arms and after that her legs. The girl liked it.

Mindy went back to the other room to look at the state of Ross. But she was too late. Ross had just opened the door and ran out of the front door.

Mindy sight and said, "Oh, let him go." She closed the door and locked it. This time she took the key with her.

John did not liked that idea and asked her to put the key back in the door.

To John's surprise she refused.

The little girl reacted symbolically.

"Don't you trust anyone of us? Are we now your prisoners? "She looked fearless to Mindy.

Mindy stretch her body out again and seemed to change . "This is my house. I keep the key to myself. Who are you little girl? Instead of being positive because I liberated you, you decide that other interests are more important? "

"My name is Rosemary". Just like you. I know you. You were in a way famous and in another way a criminal. You are a good fighter for a lady of your age. You used to be a boxing champion but you choose the wrong way." She looked sharp at Mindy. Nobody doubted her words.

Mindy smiled." You know everything about right and wrong, I understand. How come you are here. Were you kidnapped for a ransom by that dumbo Ross?"
"Right, you know about this sort of business. Kidnap a child and you get money from the parents, if they love their child. "
"And your parents did not wanted to pay, right?" Rico responded.
Rosemary turned shocked around to Rico and kicked him against his left leg.
"Au," Rico yelled. "Why is that!"
"I understand that your parents never loved you and I can understand why. No, Ross was so stupid that he was not able to collect the money twice. The first time he was too late. He missed the bus to get there in time. The second time he was at the wrong place. He is not only simple but also very stupid. I am glad that Mindy, you call her, hit him firmly on his head. Maybe his brain got the right hustle. By the way. Will he return with his gang members?" Rosemary looked at Mindy.
Mindy nodded. "That is very likely, so we better leave. "Mindy walked to the left wall, took the painting from the wall . A safe came visible. She put her hand on the lock. A small camera came forward and verified her eyes. The door opened with a heavy click.
Everybody looked surprised at the big bundles of money in the safe. Mindy got to the kitchen and came back with a big bag. She dropped all of the

money in het bag. But left five bundles on the shell. She put all the other things, small boxes also in het bag. The bag was heavily filled. She closed the bag with a zap. She picked up the last bundles of money and gave each of the persons, including Rosemary and herself a bundle.

"Come let us go. Ross will be back soon, we must be far away by then."

Mindy unlocked the front door, let them all out and closed the door behind them. They walked out of the building. Mindy was bearing the heavy bag but it seemed as if she did not notice the weight.

John concluded that she must certainly be a strong women.

Rosemary came walking next to John. Mindy got upfront and Rico and Marion where at the back. They left the small street.

A sudden yell from shortly behind them made clear that they were spotted. A big guy came towards Rico and Marion. Rico stepped before Marion but Marion just swopped him aside. She even stepped towards the big man.

The giant was surprised but laughed happily with this nice change to prove himself. Before he noticed he had a big blow in his face and a big bleu eye was created. The next moment he had a heavy kick against his left knee and before he notice it, his left shoulder received a heavy blow. He sacked through his knee and was totally disconnected.

Marion looked to the falling giant, giggled and turned back to the others.

"Come let us go on", she stated and walked on. Everyone was still being confused about her fighting technics, but followed her quickly.

Little Madeleine asked the question. "Where did you learn to fight like that. I want to learn that too, will you learn me that?"

"O, maybe, we will see later. First we have to find a new shelter." Marion answered.

"Well I think I have the right place. I will keep it a secret who you are but I have to inform my parents that I am free again. You liberated me so I am very grateful about that. Come, I will show you were to go.

Everybody looked surprised to Rosemary but followed her without any protest. They did not know where she would bring them but they all seemed to trust her.

Chapter 2

Rosemary got the hand of John and walked together with him at the front of the group. Mindy and Marion followed and Rico closed the group. They walked quite a long time through small streets, than a serial of larger streets followed and, it already started to get dark, they came in the richer area of the city.

On a large avenue Rosemary turned to a huge and very high building. She walked to the front door, put her hand on a tableau and the door opened. She winked them in and walked to the elevator. She pushed the button for the elevator to go up and waited.

The grownups looked around. This was really very exclusive. Rosemary 's parents must have a lot of money to have such a residence as a sort of extra city spot.

The elevator brought them to the twelfth store. They stepped out and Rosemary opened the front door, One of the three doors on this stock, by using her eyes before a scan device. It was a giant apartment. It even had four bedrooms. Rosemary pointed them all to the kitchen to prepare some food. She first of all wanted to call her parent to tell that she was all right.

John went along with her to the phone on the desk and stayed with her while she was calling.

Rosemary's parents were very glad that she was free. Rosemary told her parents that she was now in their apartment in the city with her liberators. They would like to stay in the apartment for a while, a couple of days, than they would all be going their own way again.

Her parents were very happy. They would talk to the police but would not tell were Rosemary and her liberators were staying. They themselves would come tomorrow to meet everyone and to thank them for their input.

Rosemary was happy to see them the next day. They went to the kitchen and John asked Rosemary to tell them wat she had appointed with her parents. Everybody was happy.

In the meantime Mindy and Marion had taken a shower in the two bathrooms. Rosemary and Rico were next and John was last.

John was happy with the large shower. He felt dirty and he felt a lot better after the shower. During the shower he looked at his body. He looked pretty strong, reasonable trained. He should find out wat he could handle in a gym. Rosemary had found clothes for everybody but for John the clothes were a little bit small. He pressed himself in the pants and the shirt and promised himself to buy clothes as soon as it was possible.

Everybody got hungry so they plundered the kitchen.

There was a lot to eat in the kitchen. They all eat very much and very good. Somethings were made warm in the oven, other things were eaten cold. John finished with a good cup of coffee. He took it with him to the livingroom. There was an overwhelming sightseeing option. The city was great and good to oversee from a huge balcony. Marion had been looking at the television. Their prison was repeatedly on the news. They all looked at the information. The mayor was totally flabbergasted by what had happened. The prison was totally destroyed, not only the building itself but also the total entrance site. The entrance gate and the building next to it, were blown away. Only a ruin remained. It was unclear how it could have happened. So many explosives could only look at a terroristic act, but the target did not really gave any indication in that direction. Also unclear was how, whoever had done this, could have had the option to place all these explosives. It was almost impossible to get such a job done. As far as was known at the moment three people lost their lives by this incident, seventy persons were wounded in hospital of which three seriously wounded. Eighty prisoners were escaped. It was not known whether there were casualties among these prisoners. Images of the damage were shown. It was really impressive. Some commentators on the subject mend that this could only be done by a criminal organisation. Not was clear whether they wanted to kill somebody who was in the prison or that they wanted to punish the system.

Others mend that some heavy criminals happened to have put in yale on this location only one day before. This was very peculiar. The four criminals that were put behind bars the day before were very, really very heavy criminals. First of all Rosemary Steils, famous leader of the Flamengo group, specialists in robbery of banks and gold transports. As known she was arrested based on an anonymous tip about her location and proves. Further Rico Grambous, leader of the Stuffers, active in gambling, Marion Strong, fighting machine who almost killed a policeman in a bold moment and Tremous Gaglaro, drugs. In all cases they showed pictures of the persons they were talking about. All three were shown, Mindy, Rico and Marion. The fourth person was unknown by the group.

John was not completely but still a little bit surprised that Marion was a fightingmachine. He had seen what she did with the giant guy that followed them on the way through town. She hurt him heavily in a slit second. She really was dangerous, if she was against you.

Nothing about John.

It was suggested that the drugscriminal was one of the persons that was killed. That could have been quiet well the reason for the explosions. The

drugsworld was very violent, also against each other. Drugswars were always very bloody.
Rosemary looked at John, she had to laugh. He looked as if he got blown up and his clothes did not grow with him. She promised to get better clothes for him. The shop stayed open till late at night and Rosemary promised to go out and get better clothes for them all. Because the others could not get outside because they might be recognized and John did not look very decent dressed, she had to go alone.
Mindy did not wanted her to go alone. They decided that John had to go with her so he could try to keep his new clothes on.
It took them one hour to collect the right clothes for everyone. They all got redressed. John had bought a double set for himself. One set he already wore, the other set he kept in his bedroom. The three ladies would sleep in one room with three beds and Rico and John had their own room with each one single bed.
Rosemary went to sleep. She was very tired after three stressful days.
The others followed her not long thereafter. They all had had busy days.

John slept deep and long. He felt reborn when he woke up. He took a shower and got dressed. In the kitchen Mindy already finished het breakfast. Rico was on the balcony, watching the traffic in the city.

Mindy finished her breakfast and went to her sleeping room to awaken Marion and Rosemary. They gathered in the livingroom and discussed what to do. John asked if there was an internetcafé nearby. He wanted to find out more about himself. Rosemary thought that there was one three blocks away. To come back into the apartment again he had to use the outdoorbel.

John decided to go there. Mindy asked him to buy some extra food for the coming days. Rosemary would accompany him, she knew where the shops were to buy the food.

They left and walked through the large boulevard. They actually found the internetcafé and John bought an hour internettime.

He made a picture from himself with the computer and used this as a surge option. The system needed some time to start searching.

Suddenly a list of options appeared. He started with the first. There were several pictures of faces that did look like him but it was not him. Rosemary looked with him to the photos.

"No," she said, "the next".

They looked for almost an hour before they seemed to have a first result. They found a picture in a paper that did look like John. It was a very bad photo so they were not convinced that it actually was his photo. It was a story about the sun of some important person that was disappeared. It was a story from more than six months ago. The father was interviewed. He expected the kidnappers to contact him to buy his son free. They surged for more pictures of the same story to see whether they could get a better photo. They actually found two more stories with a picture. One only had a picture of the father, the other made it clear that the sun was or anyway looked a lot younger than John. John was a lot stronger and more muscular than the boy on the picture. Rosemary suggested that a lot could change in six months in an experimental prison. John printed the picture out and they left the café.

Rosemary knew where the supermarket was and they bought a lot of fruits, meat and vegetables. John paid with the money he had become from Mindy. There was not much left after the clothes they had bought yesterday and the food they had bought today. John carried the bags and Rosemary complimented him with his strong body.

When they were back, the parents of Rosemary where present. They welcomed Rosemary. They were extreme happy to have her back.

Rosemary's father did have a problem. He made clear that he could not formally give shelter to escaped prisoners, escaped convicted criminals. He would give then one more day. He was very grateful that they saved their little girl but he also had to think about his reputation. He was prepared to give them some money for the coming period but they had to leave the apartment.

Mindy and Rico understood the point.

They promised to leave the next day direct after lunchtime. They had to find out where to go. John and Marion accepted the proposal also.

Rosemary 's father asked John his name. In a way he looked familiar to him but not completely. He puzzled about this point.

Rosemary told his father about the things that had happened in the prison. It could be possible that John had changed under the influence of the experiments that had taken place in the prison. Experiments on people, on convicted criminals.

John asked him where he was thinking of.

Rosemary 's father told him that some six months ago a young man was kidnapped. His parents paid for the release but their son was never brought back.

The kidnapper was caught a month later, through the money that he wanted to open an account with at a bank.

The kidnapper only laughed. He had fun because, as he stated "he had received double money, because he sold the boy twice."

Nobody understood what he stated but they concluded that he had sold the boy to somebody else instead of returning him back to his parents. He found that John did look like that boy, but he had never met the young man in person.

John asked for the name and the address of the parents, perhaps he could remember more of his past when he could talk to them.

Rosemary's father informed him about this and also wrote the name and the address on a small paper and gave it to John.

Rosemary's father knew these people. He wished it to be the truth, so the episode could be completed happily.

Rosemary and her parents said goodbye and left the apartment.

Rico wanted to leave immediately. What would withheld the parents of Rosemary to inform the police at this very moment.

Mindy and Marion did agree. They picked up their clothes and said to John that it was better for him not to accompany them any longer. In principle he had nothing to fear from the police if his story was the truth.

John agreed. He did not had the idea that he was a criminal, though he was in prison. Could he have been sold to the experimental prison? He did not know, he tried to remember more about his parents but he could not remember a thing.

He said goodbye to the others, thanking them for accompanying him the last days and wishing them a nice and prosperous future.

They left, he was alone. He returned to the balcony and looked over the city. How could he loosen up his memory, how could he open the doors of his memory. It was hopeless. He could not find a single clough.

He just stood there on the balcony, watching the city rushing around. There was a lot of traffic.

Suddenly he felt a nasty stitch in his neck.

Immediately he felt and found a kind of stich. He lost contact and fainted.

Chapter 3

Slowly John awakened. He felt his neck but could not find anything. His head was clear. He had expected some pain or pressure but he seemed to feel all right. He opened his eyes. He was laying on a crib in a cell, a prisoncell.

He came up in a sitting position. He looked around. It was a prisoncell indeed. He looked through the gate. Opposite to him was, after a small hallway another cell. The cell was empty. He stood up and did the one step to the gate. He looked along the hallway. All he could see were more cells, though the hallway was everywhere a lot broader than for his cell.

Suddenly a soft signal sounded. The gate of his cell started to move sidewards. He stepped back. The gate rolled away, all the way. John stepped forward and walked into the hallway. He looked to the right. The hallway ended with a cell. He looked to the left. There the hall seemed to end with a door. Calmly he started to walk to the door. Above the door he saw a camera. He was being watched. When he approached the door, it opened in front of him. As far as he could notice there was nobody in one of the cells he had passed.

This was all at least peculiar. Was this all real or just suggestion. He knew this was an option. He remembered a test after an experiment. He had to tell what he had experienced. He did not remember

the test or what he had experienced. He only remembered that he had to tell his experience. Was this a similar situation? If so, what should he tell? He entered a small room with no other door than the door through which he had entered the room.
In the middle of the room there was a chair, a reasonable comfortable chair. John looked at the chair. He did not had the intention to sit down. He walked around the room. Looking for something that would come to his attention. He looked up and down. He noticed a small mark on the bottom in one of the corners. To re-orientate he looked back to where he expected the door to be. He missed it. He stood up and looked around. No, no more door at all. He was sure that the door was on that site. He looked at the chair, it was no longer on the same spot, it moved slowly away from the middle. Now he was sure. They were testing him. Again or were these new. He walked to the place where he knew the door was and sat down on the ground. It was now up to them to decide about the next step in this happening. He relaxed and waited. Calm and easy breathing, he waited and waited.
The door opened in front of him. He stood up and walked back to his cell. He calmly seated on his stretcher and waited again.
The total surrounding changed. The walls disappeared. A large room was created. A large bank with two great seats appeared. A large window seemed to give a view over a big city.

John got up and sat down in one of the big fauteuils. He calmly looked around and waited.

A door behind him was opened and someone came in. A middle-aged man approached him and introduced himself. He wore a luxe suit with a formal ty all in a kind of wooden colour, a sort brown and green. It all seemed to fit pretty well. The man called himself "Trestan Grout".

It did not ring a bell. John had never seen this man before as far as he knew.

"We have tried" the man started " to read out your memory. I do not like to say so, but we failed. This is out of order. Wat is wrong with you?"

John smiled. "My memory has been blocked. Try to find out how and open it again for me, and for me only." He was curious about the reaction. He also was curious to find out how they could have tried to read out his memory. Did they have a special computer for that. He waited for an answer.

Trestan sight deeply. "We tried, we failed. We have a special computer that can read the minds and the memories of people. We may only use that if we think that criminal actions have taken place. You escaped from the Prison after the explosions but we could not find a file over your case. " He looked at John, hoping to get answers from his site.

"Is it possible that I was never convicted but through criminals brought there for money. Drugged and sold. I don't know, I have no memory reachable at the moment."

"Not very likely. These kind of practices are not allowed in any prison, certainly not in this special prison. Though it was a special prison they had no allowance for experiments on people. They only were allowed to experiment with mental promotions, without the option to use any drug or other chemicals on people. So only mental training. " John looked at the man. Could he be trained to lock away his memory. For wat reason. Why should he have to do so. What purpose would it surf.

"John, " his opponent tried to get his attention.

" It is not impossible that they have learned you to lock your memory away. If they have bad intentions they could hypnotise you and have you for instant, commit a murder, when they want it, on their mark. They decide, not you. Though I still do not believe that they tried this kind of experiences in that prison. It is continuously controlled by us. This kind of experiments did not happen."

"How do you explain my memoryblock" John asked.

"We cannot. This is impossible. "

"You seem to be very qualified to manipulate the mind through the eyes. Is this only by handling the air or do you also use a interaction with the eyes?" John asked interested in the technical view.

"I am sorry, I cannot answer your questions."

"Can you than tell me something about the organisation you belong to, Who are you ?" John hoped it was the police but he had his doubts. The police did not had this kind of specialistic knowledge.

"I am sorry, I may not answer your questions. I have to go." Trestan got up and walked calmly to the door and left.

John got up as well. He walked to the window, knowing that it could be a simulation. He looked through the window. He did not know this city, so he had nothing to recognize.

He was surprised to see a church that looked familiar. He looked if he could see any movements outside, cars that were riding or people that were walking. Noting seemed to move. He looked at the trees, no wind, nothing moved. Just a picture, no life vision. He turned around and looked at the door. He was not sure whether Trestan really existed or that he was just a visualisation of somebody. What organisation had this kind of knowledge. Governmental or private. He choose for private. Was it a criminal organisation or not. Criminal, he concluded. Why should a private organisation kidnap him. There was something peculiar about his situation. He had been present at the escape of the little girl, Rosemary. Her father looked like a well-respected businessman. Could he have tipped a criminal organisation. He found it not very likely but there was no other explanation why he was kidnapped shortly after he had left the apartment of Rosemary.

If the father of Rosemary had criminal contacts then there were reasons why he would inform these contacts about him. What did that mean for his position. Could this mean that he was of interest for a criminal organisation. He wished he knew why , for what reason. They had tried to read his memory. They must have very advanced technical experiences to be able to do that. What would a criminal organisation do with this kind of knowledge. Stealing knowledge from someone's mind is only useful if you have somebody that can understand that knowledge. The only knowledge that everybody understands is information about daily affairs. Did you kill that man or where did you hide the money from the bankrobbery. Right, that is useful information for criminals.

Following this line the question was, wat they might have thought that he could give wat kind of information. About what could he possibly inform them. Perhaps they thought he knew more about Rico, Mindy or Marion.

Ok, John thought. What could he do about his present situation. He could wait but he did not liked waiting for someone else to decide what was going to happen. He preferred to be in the lead. He started to look around to find clues about the way they used the air with lights and possibly signals to manipulate the eyes.

He started to control the clothes that he wore. There was nothing in his pockets. He wore a one-unit sort of gardentrousers and a simple shirt. He sat down and picked up his shoes. He looked at his socks but found nothing special. He tried to move the bottom of the shoe but nothing seemed movable. He put them on again and looked around in the room.

At that moment the door appeared again and Trestan came in again, now accompanied with a large table with a lot of good looking food on it. "Your lunch," he simply said. He left the table after six meters, turned around and left.

John had hoped for this moment. He took a superquick rush and followed Trestan through the door. Trestan did not react on the presence of John. He simply disappeared in the air after three meters. John looked around. He saw nobody. In front of him was another door, a door of glass. He could look through it. A long corridor was behind it. John immediately jumped through that door and ran through the corridor.

He notice a staircase and jumped down the stairs. In front of the stairs there were windows. He quickly looked outside. It was dark outside. He was surprised. They brough him his lunch. Did they wanted to find out what he felt about his day and night schedule. It did not matter. He saw that he had a long way to go down. At least eight stocks he had to go down. He speeded on. He saw nobody. Suddenly he heard some noises from upstairs. He decided to leave the stairs. He still had two stocks to go but he ran through a hallway. He understood that the way he was dressed was to special. He looked for a kind of storageroom, hoping that he would find other cloths there. He thought to see one. He stopped and opened the door. De door was not locked, he was lucky. The light went on and he looked around. There were lockers and cupboards. He tried a cupboard and again he was lucky. He found a pair of trousers and a shirt, both in dark blue. He also found socks and shoes. The clothes were rather large and big but that did not troubled him at all, better than too small, he thought. He left his own clothes in the cupboard, closed the door and left the room. He calmly walked further through the hallway. He suggested that there would also be a stairway on the other site of the hallway. Indeed he was right. He found the stairway and calmly walked down. He finished in a large entrance area. He easily walked to the frontdoor. A man, sitting behind his desk, looked at him and called to him. John waived to the man and left the building. Outside he immediately crossed the road, there was hardly any traffic. On the opposite side was a park and John entered the park straight away. He walked through the park. He followed the road when he came through the park and kept on walking. He did not run. He did not wanted to draw any attention. He wondered what he would do. He did not know the city or at least he did not remember anything about it. At a busstop he found a map of the city. He found a streetname that sounded familiar. How could the streetname sound familiar, he wandered. Than he remembered that the father of Rosemary had mentioned the name of the street of the people that could be his parents. He also wrote it down, but he lost the paper in his clothes that were taken from him. He tried to remember the housenumber. He thought Rosemary 's father had mentioned housenumber 76.

John looked at the map. It would be a long walk. He started to walk.

He had plenty of time to look around and get some impression of the city. It was a clean city. There was plenty of green everywhere. He liked it. There were plenty of squares with large historical buildings. Every half hour he looked for a busstop to verify that he still walked the right way. Twice he had to correct his direction but after some hours he reached the road where he wanted to go to. The sun came up and he looked down the road. He decided to walk on the side of the even numbers and to look along the broad avenue to the houses on the other site. He calmly walked the road. This was an area for the superrich. The houses were huge. It was calm in the street. It was still very early. House number 76 was just like the other houses, huge. He walked on. He had the feeling that he was being watched. He carefully looked around but could not find any clue how or in what way he was followed. He walked on. He came on a small square with some banks on it. He decided to take his time and to wait until the traffic was more intensive. He had in a way a bad feeling about this. Why was Rosemary kidnapped. Right, of course for a large ransom. Just for the money? Why did Ross, being the kidnapper, missed the payment appointments. Twice, as Rosemary stated. He could not understand this kind of behaviour. He was very surprised that there was only one kidnapper. How was the girl kidnapped. John did not know. He realised that he had not tried to find out. He and none of the others had asked it. On itself that was peculiar. He took his time to think through all the unanswered questions but did not find any solution.

The sun was rising and he had to make a decision. Would he simply call on the frontdoor and asked the opener if he could be their lost sun? What else could he do. He could not find any alternative.

Chapter 4

John simply walked on the right site of the road and walked to housenumber 76. He hesitated. Were there really no alternatives. He sight, he looked at the huge house and stepped up to the road to the house. The road was about fifty meters long to finish at a great plateau in front of the entrancedoor. He stepped up the plateau and ringed the doorbell. A young man in uniform opened the door. The assistantbutler John expected.

"Hallo My name is John, I think," he started. "I would like to see the master and or mistress of this house. I lost my memory but it could be so that I am their lost sun. " He did not know what else to say. He would probably being kicked away as a cheat or idiot.

The young man looked at him. "I must admit that you do look like him, but not completely. Just a moment I will inform the housemaster. Please wait." He closed the door.

John had no alternative than to wait.

The door was rushed open and a woman looked at him.

"Theodore !!! " she yelled out and embraced him. John was surprised. Could this be his mother. He did not really felt anything. He embraced her too but more reserved.

"Come in, come in, Tell me everything, I have to know, "she pulled him in.

John did not know what to say or what to do. He stepped inside and followed the lady. The assistantbutler followed John.

The lady of the house went to the left and walked into a small office. She pointed at a chair to John and took a chair for herself.

"Theodore, you said something about your memory to Geoffrey, our assistantbutler. Could you tell me more about that?"

"Of course mem." John decided to tell her his story, as far as he could remember. She calmly listened to him. He really told it all to her. It took him more than an hour. Geoffrey had served coffee and John took also two of the large cakes.

"So I do not know whether I am your sun but more than this I do not have" he finished his story.

"What do you think of your own story? "she asked interested, watching him closely.

"I understand that this is a crazy story. Completely unbelievably. But it is all I know," John said honestly.

"I think I know who the parents of Rosemary are," she said calm. "I can call them and ask them their story?"

"Please do, "John reacted immediately.

She only smiled.

"Well, you do have a special story. The facts fit together but it gives no information about you and your history. Would you allow us to take a bloodsample to find out whether your physical facts match with the historical information from our sun." John agreed. He wanted to know it also.

She immediately asked Geoffrey to get the testmaterial. Geoffrey went to a cupboard and got a bag out of the cupboard and handed it to his mistress. She knew what to do and took a bloodmonster from John and at the same time a small monster out his mouth for the DNA-test.

"Please accept for the time being to stay with us. We would like you to take a shower and get dressed in a proper way. Geoffrey will accompany you."

John looked surprised at her. "You mean that you really believe that my story could be true ?"

"No," she said " but I do not want to risk the change that you really are my sun. I must admit that I have a warm feeling for you. You do look like Theodore but you are far more muscled. If all kind of experiments have taken place on your body and your mind than everything is possible. Your blood shall not be changed, your DNA can not be changed. We will cheque these things. These are facts that cannot be changed. "

"Ok," John said. "Please do wat is necessary, I am probably just as curious as you are. "

Geoffrey was clearly instructed and John went together with him to the first floor. John did not recognize anything. Geoffrey showed him how the shower worked and showed him the clothes that were available. The clothes were by far too small,

John immediately noticed. He pointed this out to Geoffrey. Geoffrey accepted the correction and said that he would collect other clothes in the time that "John" as he wanted to be called, would take his shower.

John undressed and took a long and pretty hot shower. He liked it very much. His body relaxed under the hot waterstream. He washed his hear and cleaned his nails that were pretty dark and damaged. He felt strong. He would like to start training again. Again? He asked himself, what did he remember about training. His mind stayed empty. Though he liked the idea to strengthen his muscles. He also would like to find out how good the rest of his condition was, running, lifting weights spinning etc.

Geoffrey came back with larger clothes. He put it on, it fitted pretty good. He already felt a lot better. He went back to the office with Geoffrey. A man was there. He astonished stared at John.

"You really look like a better muscled Theodore," he sight. John introduced himself as "John", that was the only name he did remember.

"My name is "John", the man said. I could be your father.

John looked surprised at the man. He was small but friendly. He did not look like him at all. On the other hand he might have had a feeling about his name. John.

They friendly shaked hands.

"You do have had a pretty rough time in the last days. Though you do not look exhausted. You must have been in a very good shape," John sr. remarked.

"Well, I do not know," John hesitated. "I do not know how I am when I am in topcondition", he answered gently.

Geoffrey came in and invited them all for the lunch. They ate in the diningroom an extending lunch. John noticed that he was very hungry and he did eat a lot.

The man of the house told John and his wife about his coming appointments with several business people. Important people as the mayor and some investors in a dispute about a new project of his company. They also talked about all kind of appointments she had that afternoon.

John realised that they were both very busy businesspeople. There would be little time for him. At the end of the lunch Geoffrey came in with a printout on a service plate.

John senior thanked him and read the paper.

"Ok, I have the results of the bloodtest and the DNA test."

He turned to Geoffrey and made him a compliment about the very quick action he had taken.

John sr. looked at John. "These results are very clear. You are not our son. Your blood and your DNA are different from those of Theodore."

He looked at his wife who seemed pretty disappointed. Also John was surprised but he had kept his doubts all the time.

He stood up and apologised for the trouble he had caused. Of course he would leave the house immediately. He would go on with his search about himself. He thanked them both for the kind response he had found and asked if he could keep the clothes he was wearing.

John sr. was happy to give these to him.

John got up, stretch himself out. He had to accept the situation. Of course he was disappointed but this was the reality.

He walked to John sr. and shaked his hand, he did the same with his wife. He also thanked Geoffrey and walked out of the diningroom towards the hall to leave the house.

He left the house. He walked towards the square where he had started the day. He must admit that it had been a long day. He felt tired but not exhausted. Of course he was disappointed.

He walked back towards the citycentre and came through a big park. He saw some banks in a wide circle and sat on one of the banks. He had to think about the actions he wanted to take to go on.

He had no home, no money, so also no food and no place to stay.

He felt bad about his situation. He had no idea how to go on. Should he go on. Why. Ok, he wanted to find out who he really was. But how could he get any information about that.

An older lady stopped right in front of him.

"Do you always use the whole bank to sit?" she asked a little sharp.

John was so busy with his own thoughts that he had not noticed the lady. She leaned on her rollator and looked at him with a little bit an angry face.

John was shocked. He immediately apologised and got to the site on the bank to make place for the lady so she could get seated as well.

The lady thanked him and got heavily seated on the bank. She fell a little bit to the site. John picked her arm to keep her steady so she would not fall.

She rolled back towards him and thanked him. Suddenly she had a needle in her hand and put it in his arm, through his shirt. She injected him with something. John looked at his arm and looked surprised at the lady.

He felt that he was weakening and lost control over his body. Again others took over. It made him a little bit angry. Why? He looked at the lady and lost contact.

John noticed that he was sitting and could not move. He looked carefully to his hands. They were tied up. His legs also were tied at the chair, he presumed.

"I know you are awaken. I know you can hear me. Please stay calm. There are some things that did not happen. One of these things should have happened. Our boss is furious. He will be here soon. You better be prepared for his anger. I cannot say more. He will talk to you. Please try to stay calm. Accept his approach otherwise there could be an even bigger problem for you.

John stretch his body up and looked at her. He smiled. It was the lady from the bank.

"You again?" he stated. "What is your name?"

"My name is of no importance. Wat is your name?"

"I do not know. One of my problems. I call myself John". John looked at her, inviting her to tell something more. She looked a lot less cripple than in the park. He wondered how she had found him. Why was she looking for him. What did they want from him. What did she mention. Something did not happen that should have happened. Was he supposed to understand these mysterious words? John looked around. He was in an apartment. It looked like a livingroom, small but clean. The curtains were closed. The lights were on.

He could not see the entrancedoor.

Behind him some noise indicated that there was something happening there. He looked at the lady in front of him.

She stood up and stepped behind her chair. She looked at the direction of the noise.

The entrancedoor was kicked open and struck hard against the wall. A heavy voice laughed roughly.

"Hallo Adrana," he loudly called out.

"Hallo Grob" she answered politely. She kept her face very closed with no expression. John saw fear in her eyes.

"Go," Grob said simply.

John heard Grob approach his chair from the left and he saw Adrana walk to the door along the other side.

A big, very strong muscled man approached in front of him. Grob stood behind the chair of Adrana. He crossed his arms and looked at John.

"Do you know who you are?" he started the conversation.

"No," John simply stated. "I call myself John".

John felt that he could touch the ground with his feet. He tapped on the ground and closely watched the reaction of Grob.

Grob watched the feet of John, surprised about its tapping on the ground. Than he smiled.

"Yes, "he concluded, you are sending signals to your liberators. Brilliant." He loudly laughed. He really seemed amused.

John looked at him and smiled. The big man told him that he made more noise with his laugh than John with his feet.

John carefully tried to move his arms. There seemed to be a little movement possible but that was all.

Grob saw what he was doing. "If you want something you will have to do a lot more than only a small innocent little tip. You have to be extraordinary strong to do something with those ropes. " He smiled and walked to the side of the room. He picked up another chair and put it with its back towards John. He immediately sat down having its arms on the topback of the chair.

"You are right, "John said. "Could you tell me the reason why I am here? "

"Oh, yes. You are a peculiar interesting person." He stared a little bit surprised at John as if he could not understand why.

"You seems to be worth a lot of money. " Grob looked sharp at John to see his reaction.

John looked astonished at Grob. He fronted his eyebrows. What had Grob said. He was worth a lot of money? From whom? Why? He stretched his body and stared at Grob.

"What do you mean?"

"Am I not clear ? ", Grob smiled. "I am going to sell you to the highest bidder. "

"You mean there are more buyers interested in me. This must be a mistake. Just mark my words. "John started to get angry, "I am not for sale !"

"Perfect, you are angry. I love you. You are going to make me happy. Just one small question, just curiousness from my site. Do you have any idea why you are so interesting? As far as we could find out, you were a criminal that did escape after the explosions in the prisonbuildings. That is all. Could you tell me more?"

"I am sorry, Grob, I do not understand what could be of interest about me. My memory is totally disturbed. I do not remember one thing of my life before I did escape out of the prison. " He looked at Grob. His memory was blocked, so he could not say more, even if he had wanted.

Grob did not liked the answer. "John," he said calm but with a dangerous undertone. "John, do not make me hurt you. I have to know why they want you." He looked at John .

John smiled at him. "I do not know. Even if you hurt me, I cannot tell you what I do not know myself," John calmly answered.

Grob sighed. He got up and put his chair back at the place where he picked it up earlier. He walked to John and said as a kind of apology: " You let me no choice. I need to know why they want you. Your value depends on this information."

Grob looked at John. He shaked his head and brought his righthand fist threatful backwards.

John looked at Grob, even if he wanted, he could not inform Grob. He put his feet as strongly as possible on the ground. If Grob really would try to hit him, he could try to push himself backwards. He bent a little bit foreword so he could also use his body to kick himself backwords to lower the blow of the hit. Grob was large and strong so a blow would come in firmly, certainly when it would come on his face.

Grob hit him heavily on his face. John pushed with his feet and his body at the same time backwards, hoping that his moves, together with the blow from Grob hit him including his chair backwords. He really was blown away. He flashed backwords against the floor with the chair. He immediately kicked with his legs backwards, hoping to break the legs of the chair. The back of the chair broke from its seat and also the legs broke down. Suddenly the chair was broken and John rolled away from the broken pieces of the chair. His arms were still bound by the chairarms. His legs still were bound by the legs of the chair but he could quickly stand up. He must make a small pass sidewards to keep his body straight up.

Grob looked surprised about what happened. His eyes blinked to the door, just beside John. John saw it and realised that he must try to get out. Grob was too quick for him. John tried to have his blood streamed but because his arms and legs were still bound by de ropes that did not work too well. He calmly got rid of the ropes among his arms, stepped back, away from the door where Grob had located himself and pushed the wooden parts of the chair from his legs. He stepped further backwards. He felt the curtains in front of the windows behind him. He pushed them away and looked out of the window. John was completely surprised. There was no window behind the curtains. There was only wall, concrete there. John, while moving his arms and after that his legs to try to better his bloodcirculation, turned around to the door where Grob, calmly looked at John.

John did not know what to do. He noticed that Grob quickly looked at his feet. He could not imagine why. He also looked down. Just his socks and shoes. Why would Grob look at his shoes. He leaned over against the wall and lifted his right foot and tried to move it a little piece of the bottom. Nothing. He quickly looked at Grob.

Grob looked along with him to his actions.

The second shoe gave a surprising result. John found an extra line in the site of the shoe. He crabbed it open and a small broadcaster fell out. John picked it up and looked at it. He through it on the ground an stepped on it. With a gentle crack the apparat broke. John looked at Grob.

Grob stared astonished to the broken signalbringer. John had the impression that this was new for him. Grob turned to the door, opened it and gave a loud yell. He closed the door again and waited. John understood that this was a new point reached in this case. This apparatus was not from Grob or his gang. Someone else had created this signalbringer. John immediately thought about the assistantbutler, Geoffrey. He had brought him his clothes. So he represented another organisation and had recognized him. Was it only Geoffrey or was there more? He hesitated.

Chapter 5

A knock on the door disturbed his thoughts. Grob stepped aside and the door was opened.
Immediately Grob was hit on his head by a young man that jumped through the door. Grob fell aside, knock out.
John stared at the young man. The man stretch himself out, waiting for John to come to him in his search for liberation. John did not. He just stood still and looked at the young man. The young man was dressed completely in black.
Suddenly the young man's eyes got great, got glazy and he sacked down on the ground.
John stared surprized, again. What was happening?
Adrana came in and looked around. She had some kind of special weapon in her hand. She quickly felt the neck of Grob. He was only knock out. She also felt the neck of the young man in black. The same. The weapon seemed to knock out its opponent from a distance.
Adrana looked at John. "What a mess !!"
She picked a phone out of her pocket and called somebody. In the meantime she directed her weapon on John.
John understood that he had to take action. He made a move to the left, jumped to the right and pushed Adrana hard aside. Adrana was just concentrated on her conversation on her phone and

only felt the push. She fell aside and John rushed through the door.

He came in a small corridor. He saw right in front of him a staircase going up. There was no staircase going down, so he must be in a cellar or something like that. He speeded up the stairs and came in a larger hallway. He stood in front of a door and opened the door immediately. He stepped through it and looked around. He was in a large open area on the ground floor of a large building. On the left he saw a street and walked towards that street. Several people walked with him and also a couple of them were going the other way.

John did not look around, he just walked with the group that walked with him to the street. All the people got a cart to get out. John saw it and decided to follow one of the persons, a young man closely, so he could get out without a card. He was lucky, the system accepted his quick departure. Out on the street he calmly followed the flow of the pedestrians. There were a lot of people out on the streets. It was extremely busy. He walked into a park following the stream of people. He stepped out of the flow and found a large bank and got seated. He looked at the flow going by. He heard pretty heavy music coming out of the direction most of the people were following. A music festival, he supposed. He could disappear there pretty good, he suggested. He got up and followed the sound of the music.

He came on a huge area where thousands of people already were present. He felt good. He walked calm and easy through the enormous number of music fans. He had the idea that he also liked music. He anyway liked the sound that he heard. He looked forward and saw an enormous large podium. A man stood in the middle, surrounded by a gigantic soundmachine. He liked the view and went forward. He was fascinated by the way the man created the music. The folks seemed to know the sound because they made sounds that looked like the melody. He felt more and more influenced by the music. Suddenly he stood right on the front of the podium.

The man behind the soundmachine waved at hem and invited him to come to him on the stage. John did not know what was happening. He looked around whether he understood it right, that the man waved at him. One of the stage officials came to him and gave him a hand so he could get up the stage.

John looked surprised but also excited at the man. He grabbed the hand and jumped up the stage. The man behind the soundmachine made a lot of noise towards the public. An enormous noise came from the people. John looked at the people and waved to them. What was he doing. He wanted to stay out of site. What happened. Why was he here. A certain sound was started by the man behind the soundmachine. The public went crazy. He felt that he changed. He turned to the man behind the soundmachine and the man stepped aside. He took over the total machine. He just played what he felt that he had to do. A sweet jumping sound started. The public fell still. This was totally new. John combined more and more sounds an created a smooth and sweet melody, filling in more and more instruments. At one moment he started to reduce the instruments and levelled up the rhythm. He finished with a super speed combination of the same basicsound. The melody fainted away. He raised his hand and the public exploded.

They started to yell, "More, more, more."

For John it was time to disappear again. He waved and left through the back of the podium. He was totally outraised. How was this possible. He must be well known otherwise the man behind the soundmachine would not have invited him to come up the stage. He must be well known, he was experienced with the music and certainly with the soundmachine. He used the machine as an experienced player.

He speeded away. He had to try to get some money to get something to eat.

Suddenly a young girl jumped in front of him. He could not help it but banged directly against her. They both fell and John started to apologise for his unattended behaviour.

The girl smiled at him. They both got up.

"He wild man, you owe me something. You cannot just bump into a girl, without a reason. Do you like me? Well? You lost your tongue?"

John was totally overbluffed. He did not know how to react.

"Ok, ok, "she started to talk again "I must admit that I deliberately banged into you. I like you, would you like to eat something, together with me. I buy this time? "John was not yet recovered from the quick statements this girl made. She deliberately banged into him. She liked him. Did he wanted to eat something.? Yes he was hungry. He confirmed her invitation by moving his head in a positive reaction.

"You did lose your tongue, did not you?" She laughed happily. My name is Lia, short for Odsylia." She laughed again about her own joke.

John smiled. She was nice and looked good.

"I am John" he said with a gentle voice. He listened surprised to his own voice. His voice sounded different. It sounded a bit softer and sweeter.

Lia did not stop talking. She probably felt better when she talked.

John had no problem with her talking, he liked it to listed. She constantly commented her colleagues at the ballet. They were all jealous over her. She really could dance extraordinary good. She now was the leaddancer. Ok, the group was still very unknown but their new performance, the new ballet would beat everybody's head of. She had a whole day free," she explained, "therefor she was in town. She needed to relax regularly and she did. "

Lia walked to a large shoppingcentre. John found it pretty imposing. It really was huge.

They simply entered through the frontgate. All alarmbells went on.

John looked surprised.

Lia found it super. She walked out and in again. The alarmbells kept on ringing. She picked John's hand and pulled him out. The alarmbells stopped.

"It is you!!!, She yelled gloriously. She pulled him in again and the alarmbells went on again.

"Yes, it really is you, come on. I have to search you to find out on what you made the alarmbells going on !!"

She pulled him to a small square with some banks. She put him on a bank and started to touch his hears, felt the skin.

Suddenly she burst out in a heavy laugh. "We do look like monkey's, look at us. How are your flees doing, I have a problem, I cannot find it. "

She came sitting on the bank.

"John, can you tell me wat is wrong with you? Why are you not allowed in the shoppingcentre? "

John could only whisper that he did not know. He had no idea.

"Perhaps I am wired!!!"he suddenly expressed. It surprised him as well as Lia. If he was wired, they, whoever they were could always find him. The alarmbells would also react on the signal he was sending. He felt in his neck but did not find anything. His shoulders, may be that was an option. He asked Lia to control his shoulders at the back of his body. He explained his thoughts to Lia and asked her to look for something hard at his back, probably at his shoulders.

Lia smiled at him.

"Of course, you are a spy. The contra-espionage has caught you and now you are wired so they can find you anywhere. Right?"

John got up. "Sorry for bothering you. I do not want you to be involved in my problems. Thank you for your company, I enjoyed your present enormously. I really would like to stay with you but it might be dangerous for you. I am very sorry. "

"O, since when is it up to you to decide about my involvement. You do not even know me. Come here. Sit !! Sit!!" she repeated.

John smiled she was nice. She was the first really nice person he had met as far as he could remember. Ok, the escape group was friendly but only for the time being. This girl was great company. He sat down. She turned him a little bit away and started to feel his back through his shirt.

"Yes" she said suddenly. "I do feel something , here. She wagered on Johns back. She lifted his jack and felt on his naked skin. "Here, do you feel it as well? " John confirmed it. "Can you take it out? "he asked.

"How tough are you, it might hurt a little bit. "

Please, just take it out, scratch it with your nails if we do not have any other options. It will not sit very deep".

"Well, I am not sure about this. "

"Pleas, just do it." John started to reach his hand to his back. He used his left hand to push his right hand further on his back. He could really reach the spot. If she did not dare to do it, he would have to do it himself. He pointed his nail on the spot and crashed it open. Some blood came along but also a little apparatus.

Lia gave a little yel. She was not very good with blood.

John took the apparatus and smashed it on the ground and stepped on it. The apparatus was cracket.

"Lia, would you please search for another one, you never know. "

"Are you sure?" She asked a little shacky.

"Please?" John asked, "I really will be grateful if you would do this for me."

She started to touch his back sorrowfully.

John felt her touch intensely and found it sensual.

"I do not seem to find something more, but you do have a strong muscled back. I like your back," she smiled softly and gently feeling his back , like a sort of massage.

"Come, "she said, "let us try it again at the mall. I think you are clean now. "

"Just one moment, Last time their also was something about my shoes. I have to test these as well. " He kicked out his shoes and tried to find something. Even a small wire on the side could be of interest. The bottom seemed solid, he did not find anything. Lia looked as well but did not find any suspicious kind of wire either.

They returned to the shoppingcentre and they got in without any more trouble.

John looked around to see if there were persons watching him in particular. He was not convinced but could not spot anyone watching him.

Lia lead him to a small eatcorner at the top of the mall. They eat a lot, also Lia eat far too much, she said. "You have a bad influence on me. Eating with you is fun. Normally I eat alone, all my colleagues envy me, so I am the diva and must eat alone. You are great to be with. Would you like to tell me more about yourself. Why are you dangerous? "

"Lia, I am a problem. I lost my memory in an explosion. So my memory goes not further than two days back. In that period I have been kidnapped several times and I have no idea why. The last kidnapper told me that there were more parties interested to have me. He also wanted to know why but I could not tell him because I have no idea. And I still do not know. These parties wanted to pay for me and he wanted to find out how much money I was worth. I escaped so he shall be very angry and will do his very best to kidnap me again."

He hesitated, what more could he tell. "I am sorry, I have no money so I was very glad that you offered me a meal. I enjoyed being with you very much. Thank you. I suppose you will have to go your own way. I could never forgive myself if you got hurt because of me. You have already done more for me than anyone else in this world and I am very grateful about that. I like you very much. " John sight and wanted to get up.

Lia put her hand on his shoulder. "Oh, no John. I found you and I do not want to let you go. Come , let's go to my place, you will like it. I like it as well. With my balletdancing I do make real money. Come, first of all I want to buy you new cloths. This is not done. Come on, there is a real nice shop in this mall. I know the lady that runs it, I mostly buy my clothes with her. "

Lia paid for the lunch and walked with him some stories down. They entered into a modern looking fashion shop. John bought a double set of clothes including socks and shoes. Lia was enthusiastic. They left the mall and walked through a large park. Lia took his hand and walked towards a modern apartmentsbuilding. She walked in and they took the elevator. On the twelfths stock they left the elevator. There was a small area with four doors. Lia stretched her hand and put it flat on the door. A camera came down from above the door and scanned her eyes and looked at her face. The door opened.

She walked in and John followed. He was totally surprised. He entered a large entrance and looked through a large open area into a giant livingroom. This was a super apartment. She must make really a lot of money with her dancing. He entered the room, all over the place there were dancinglinks, from ashtrays to paintings, from small figurines to large dancers as a groundfloorlight, shining towards the ceiling. A super large balcony was behind the livingroom, at least twelve meters wide and approximately five meters deep. Behind the balcony there was a magnificent look over the town.
John stood flabbergasted in the opening from the livingroom.
"You like it?", Lia smile happily to him. "Please come in." She got to the door of the balcony and opened the door. She walked on. The sun shined fully on the balcony and John saw that she liked the touch of the sun.
John entered the balcony.
Lia made some ballet dancing moves and seemed to feel great. She smiled and made some more moves. She moved extraordinary elegant.
John believed immediately that she was the prima ballerina of her dancing group. She had a small waste and was perfectly formed. John loved her body and her moves. She was a great woman.
She walked back inside and draw him with her.
"Come," she said, let's take a shower. I want to be sure that there are no other marks on your body.

"She smiled naughty at him and draw him to a door on the side of the livingroom. It came out on a small area with four doors. She opened one door . It was a large bathroom, super lux in a modern outfit with some special collars, towels in the same collar, a small math on the floor also in these collars. John looked surprised. This really was extraordinary extravagant beautiful.

Even the lights were indirect and softly collard. John looked around.

"Ok, John, put your clothes on that small table there and come here under the shower. "

John did wat she asked.

Nude he stepped into the walk-in shower. From six sides water jumped upon him. He loved it. He closed his eyes and let the water stream over his body. Suddenly he felt someone touch his left foot. He looked down and saw Lia sitting next to him.

"Ok, please stand still for a moment. I will examine your whole body to look for signalling devices. I would not like your kidnappers to find you here."

John looked surprised but stood still.

Lia started to feel all over his feet and went up his body. She finished with his head. John looked her in the eyes and grabbed her and pushed her against his body. He kissed her and she answered his kiss, happily. John now touched her body, long and strong, small but muscled.

They enjoyed being together. John could not remember such an intense and explosive sexexperience. They could not get enough from each other.

Finally they finished the shower and dried each other.

Lia invited him for a gentle intime dinner at an easy location. John smiled. Everything she proposed was all right for him.

Together they walked, hand in hand, to the restaurant. They mainly talked about her work as a dancer. She loved her job. From her parents she had to learn some medical activity. Her father was an important practice surgeon and her mother doctor in a general hospital. They could not understand that she had no interest in medicine. So in daytime she studied for physiotherapeutic and in the evening she went to the balletschool. She enjoyed the combination because both parties were happy. Her two brothers had specialised themselves in pharmacy. They made a lot of money, just like her parents. She had the apartment from her parents. Of course she could not afford such an expensive apartment from her low budget income as a dancer. She could pay the service-costs and lived perfect from what she made every month.

Tomorrow she had to get to her work again.

Perhaps he would like to come with here, if he had nothing else to do.

John laughed he had nothing else to do but to find out his passed, so he would love to come with her.

They left the restaurant and wanted to walk back to her apartment.

A big taxibus stopped next to them. Three man jumped out of the bus and politely invited them to enter the taxi. They would have the pleasure bringing them home.

John politely thanked them and wanted to walk on. He saw that one of the man push a handkerchief against the mouth and nose of Lia and another tried the same with him. He got angry. Nobody could do this to Lia. He smashed the man that tried to put the handkerchief for his mouth and nose, toughly aside and jumped to the man that was dealing with Lia. He knocked him straight in the face. A big bloodstream jumped out of his nose and with a big bow he rammed backwards on the street.

The third man stepped back and draw a gun. "Stop it and get in the car ! " he commanded.

People in the street saw wat was happening but did not dare to intervene. John draw Lia against his body and tried to calm her.

Lia was flabbergasted about wat was happening. She turned to the man with the gun and yelled at him. "Who are you. What do you think you are doing. What the hell do you think you are doing" she got more and more angry.

The man stared at here. "Get into the car or you will get hurt. He pointed his gun on her legs. Her balletlegs. She cried "No, no, no !!!!!"

Suddenly she stepped forward with her right foot and kicked with her left foot the gun out of the hand of the third bandit. She handy caught the flying gun and pointed it at the legs of the man.

"The hell with you !!"she hysterically yelled and shot the man in his right leg. Both the two other man were coming up again. She quickly turned around and shot them both in their right leg. She was fast and furious. She certainly knew exactly what she did.

John was at this pointy totally flabbergasted. His balletdancer was a qualified fighter and supershooter.

Lia threw the gun in the taxi and draw John to walk with her away from the scene. Some people had filmed the whole action with their phone. She could not help it, it had happened.

She quickly moved away. Once out of the direct scene she started to tremble and John had to help her walking. She was totally out of order. She shaked and trembled. John did not know what to do. He looked around to find a solution. She could not walk anymore. He lifted her and walked towards a taxi.

"Sir", he asked the driver, "could you bring us to a hospital, something has happened to my girlfriend. I do not understand wat but she is totally out of order. "Yes, of course, please get in," he stated immediately.

He opened the backdoor and John stepped in with Lia in his arms.

The taxi drove onlyabout one kilometre and stopped in front of the emergency entrance of the hospital. John got out of the taxi, thanked the driver and walked in with Lia in his arms.

A nurse came up to him and asked what had happened. He had to lay her down on a bed and told that they were attacked by three man and that she totally got mixed in her mind. The nurse looked in her eyes by lifting the closed eyelid. She pushed on some alarm and pushed John aside. She moved the bed through the hallway and disappeared.

John was left alone. He was totally surprised. Wat was happening what did they do with Lia.

He did not knew what to do. He left the hospital and started to walk around again.

He just walked and walked. He walked for hours. He did not knew what to do. It was already dark for more than an hour when he walked into a park. He decided to take a break and sat down on a bank. He looked around. He was in a park with enormous large trees. Presumably an old park.

What had happened. Three man had tried to kidnap them. He had blown two man one by pushing him away and the other, who held Lia, by an aggressive blow in the face. And thereafter, he draw Lia towards him. Lia started to loudly cried out to the third man. Then the third man got a gun and threatened them with it. After that, Lia did a step forward,.. No first the third man told them to get into the taxi, otherwise he had to hurt us by shooting Lia in her legs. That's right that is wat happened. At that moment she got furious, did a step forward and kicked the gun out of his hand. She caught the gun and shot him precisely in his right leg. Yes, she hardly had the time to aim. She knew how to shoot him. She turned around and directly shot the two other man in their right leg. Unbelievable. She must be a well-trained gunshooter. The way she kicked the gun out his hand was masterly. She caught the gun and could shoot at that very instant. Masterclass. He thought. She probably is not a balletdancer but a well-trained secret agent or something like that.

John shaked his head.

"Troubles?"

John shaked. Beside him on the bank an old lady was sitting. He was surprised. There was nothing wrong about his ears but he had not heard the lady approach him and got seated.

She had a really old sounding voice. She sounded wise and warm. John realised that he analysed her voice automatically.

Again somebody that intervened in his life, coming out of nowhere. He was suspicious. He trusted nobody anymore.

"Yes", he answered simply.

"I presume you do not want to be helped?" She said staring to the trees in front of them.

John only sighted. He had no need for this kind of conversation. He got up and wanted to walk away.

"I know who you are," the lady said cool but warm and looked at him.

"He", John reacted and stopped, being busy leaving he already had done a step away from the lady.

She did caught his attention.

John stretch his body out. He turned around and looked at the lady.

She smiled at him.

She got up and started to walk away. The other way as the direction that John would have gone if she had not used the magical words.

She walked away from him.

John did not liked this way of being treated. If she really knew something about him than she had to tell him. Now she expected him to follow her but he did not wanted that. He refused to follow her. She had only used magical words but that was all. It was quite likely that she did not know anything. He decided to get back to the bank, to see if she would come back. She must do more than only using contentless words.

He returned to the bank and sat down. He calmly looked at the leaving lady. He waited.

Nothing happened. The lady kept on walking and turned away.

Chapter 6

John sight and decided to try to find the apartment of Lia. He knew he could not get in but he could wait until she would come back. He started to walk. He must first of all find out where he was and where he had to go to. He smiled when he saw a busstop. A small map gave him the needed information.
He studied the map. Citycentre was quite a long walk away. He looked at the route so he would find his way. He looked back but did not had the impression that someone was watching him.
He thought back at the older lady. How had they found him. There must be a way they could use to locate him.
Who were "they"? Why was he so special. Could there be a link between him being special and the way they could locate him. Was his brain different from the brain of others. Could they locate his brain because of that. One way or the other he found it frustrating not knowing wat was going on. How could he get any idea whether his thoughts were correct or pure nonsense. Why should he be special. Only because "they" tried to get him. There seemed to be more interested parties.
If he could hide his head, than his brain could possibly not be located. Should a helmet work.
He kept on walking to the citycentre.

Perhaps he should find a location where no signals could get in or out. Where was such a location. Should he tried to get in a bank. They had safes where nobody could get in. He did not wanted to be in that position.

What else could he come up with. He walked along a motorshop. All kind of motorcycles were visual. John loved the view of one specially. He was attracted by this motor. A big heavy piece. Blinking and shining. John entered the shop. He could not stay away from that machine. He kneeled down at its site. This was familiar. He felt the seat and the steer.

A young man came into the shop from behind some curtains.

"It's a fantastic machine. Would you like to make a testride? " he is completely ready for it. I have tried him yesterday. Please, take a seat. "

"Thank you," John said but stayed with the motor.

"How does it work such a testride? "he asked.

"Well we do the ride together. First I drive for about a quarter of an hour, than you can ride, back to this showroom. If you would like to buy this model I can inform the delivery time and the price. It depends on the options we select. "

"Ok, first I would like to have that ride. I must have a good feeling by the model. I must admit that at this moment it does give me a good feeling. He again stared at the motor. Somewhere in his memory a bell ringed. He had a kind of feeling he also had when he had that special music-happening. It looked as if he changed. He got a special feeling. The young man picked up two helmets and two pairs of gloves. He went to a desk at the back and picked up the keys.

He came back to John and handed him the gloves and a helmet. John tried the helmet. It actually fitted well. He also found the gloves perfect. The young man rolled the motor out of the showroom down to the street. John followed closely.

The salesman stepped on the frontseat of the motor and John got at the back. They calmly got through the traffic. The young man was an experienced driver. He found his way very easy. He left the citycentre and rolled on the highway. John was really enthusiastic. After a nice ride on the highway, John took over the wheel. He enjoyed the ride extraordinary. He loved it. He decided not to go back to the showroom but stopped at the citycentre. He followed the sines to the centre. He stopped the motor, thanked the young man and promised to be back at the showroom. He handed him the gloves and promised to bring the helmet back and walked away, keeping the helmet on. If the helmet would help, he could not be followed. The young man was quit disappointed. He stared after John not realising wat was happening. John walked quickly to the park and found a suitable spot on a bank from where he could see the entrance of the building where Lia's apartment was.

He calmly waited. Several people went into the building and others left. He realised that he must look funny with the helmet on. He saw people looking at him. Two girls passed by and giggled about him with each other. John understood that he could not go on in this way. He would get too much attention. He saw no solution for the moment. He decided to wait.

Some hours later nobody had talked to him. No one got seated beside him. Everything stayed calm. He looked at the building and estimated where the balcony of Lia was. It looked all dark there.

A taxi stopped before the building. John decided to come closer.

He was really happy to see Lia getting out. There was someone with her. An older lady, probably her mother, John expected.

He crossed the road and came along the taxi. The two ladies went into the building. John followed quickly. The older lady helped Lia walk straight up. They went into the elevator and John went in with them. Lia kept her head down. She had problems to stay right up. She slightly got aside and John caught her.

The older lady looked at him and said "Thank you" and let John hold her.

A mother would not have accepted this, John thought. Who was this lady. How come Lia already had left the hospital. She was not in a very good shape.

The elevator stopped and the lady got out, leaving John to get Lia out of the elevator. The lady walked to the door of Lia and waited until John and Lia were near the door. She lifted the hand of Lia, the camera came down and scanned her face. The lady opened her eyelid and had her eye scanned. The door plopped open. John walked in with Lia and put her in her bedroom on her bed. She was out of notice.

John got back to the livingroom and asked the lady if he could do more. The lady thanked him friendly and picked up her phone out of her bag. She walked him to the door and wanted to let him out. John picked the phone out of her hand, simple pushed her out of the door and closed it behind her. He looked at the phone. This would come later. He went to Lia and undressed her so she could sleep a lot more comfortable. He got to the bathroom and used a small towel that he made wet and refreshed her face with it. He also looked at her hands. They were not very clean so he cleaned those as well. Further he left her alone.

He was hungry and looked in the kitchen for some food. He found some salads and fruit and eat it all. He looked at the phone. It seemed to be owned by a "Marian". The number, she was trying to use, was of a certain "James".

All names did not meant anything to him. He scrolled through the list of names and found a "James". The second name was not mentioned.

John took a shower and decided to have a quick look at the television. He had the idea that it had been a long time since he had looked at the television. He searched for a news program and found one. They were discussing violence in the present society. He was surprised that the way Lia and he were attacked was the example they used. They left out the shooting of Lia. He was curious whether they would discuss this point as well but they did not. He quit the broadcast and went to the other bedroom to catch a sleep as well. He had had a very special day. He was tired and fell asleep quickly.

John slept long and deep. He got awaken and felt great again. He stepped out of his bed and saw through the window that the sun was already shining and coming up really high. He decided to do some exercises and after that he took a shower and got dressed.
He walked into the room and was totally disoriented when at least six persons were there waiting for him, it seemed.
"John!" Lia yelled out and jumped up to him in excitement. John caught her and kissed her.
"He, are you all right?" he was flabbergasted. Last night she could not even walk, now she looked as she was before.
John looked in her eyes. They stood bright and sunny. He felt happy. This was good.

"John, may I introduce you to my mother, " An older lady got up and made a small nix for him. He did not understand that reaction. So he nicked to her.

"And this is my father. "Lia said, sounding proudly. An older gentleman got up and came to him and shaked hands. A firm strong hand , John felt and did the same.

"These two younger guys are my brothers Kole and Steve and beside Steve sits his wife Elenore. So now you know the whole family. And the whole family knows you.

John nicked to them and they nicked back at him.

"So now that you know for certain that I am not kidnapped and disappeared in the night, please tell me what had happened. Dad, you first, What do you know about this case." Lia picked a cup of office and put it in front of John. She also showed him a plate with sandwiches, for his breakfast.

John smiled at her, she did take good care of him. The coffee was perfect and the sandwiches were awfully good and he eat far too much.

Lia's dad told that he yesterday morning had heard about the kidnap-try through a college who thought that he recognised Lia in this affair. The images were shown on the television last night as an example in some dispute about safety in the city. They seemed to have shown only a part of the happening. Lia's father had contacted the police who had the complete film and informed him that in their perspective his daughter had escaped miraculously. She had kicked the gun out of the hands of one of the kidnappers. She and an unknown young man had run away from the scene. That was all the police could tell. Anyway, at the moment the police arrived at the spot of the scene. She and as they had presumed, her boyfriend were gone. All three kidnappers were severely hurt through a shot in their right leg. Peculiarly were all three shots at exactly the same location in the right leg. Also special was that the shots were fired from the gun of the third kidnapper. How things had happened nobody knew.

There are rumours in the city that a new Robin Hood was active and punished criminals if he got the change. Lia 's father looked at Lia. He had called her mother and her two brothers and told them about the kidnapping. Immediately the police had visited the apartment of Lia but nobody answered their call on the door. They informed Lia's father about that. Nobody knew the unknown boyfriend. He was not registered anywhere. For some reason his image was very difficult to catch, the image seemed to have a vase foley on it. He phoned Lia several times but got no reaction on her phone. This morning the police controlled again if somebody was at home. The talked to one of the other inhabitants. He told that he last night had found a lady in the outer hallway. She was pretty groggy but did not wanted any help. After some water she left. There was no workable prescription of the lady, just "an older, white lady".

The police called on the door and Lia was there. She talked to the police and they left again. We were informed by the police and decided to visit you, Lia.

"That is my part of the story. That is all we know. Please tell us more about what happened. You do look all right. So wat happened." Lia's father looked hopefully to her.

John looked at Lia who did not know what she could say. She had no idea what had happened.

"I am afraid that Lia does not know what has happened. "John informed the group, including Lia. "As the police has informed you, we ran away from the scene, for some unclear reason Lia collapsed. She fell on the ground. We had to run, so I picked her up and ran on. I came on a square and stopped a taxi and asked him to bring us to the nearest hospital. He did and I walked with Lia in my arms into the casual-entrance of the hospital.

Immediately a lady came up to me and asked what had happened. I had to put Lia on a bed. While asking me her questions the lady felled Lia 's bloodpressure on her pols and looked in her eyes. She straight away pressed some kind of button and raced away with the bed and Lia. I was left behind. I could not get in the hospital so I left. I walked through the streets, lost in an unknown city. I decided to walk all the way to the park in front of the apartment of Lia to see whether she would come back. Last night, it was already getting dark, a taxi came and stopped in front of the building. I had the feeling that Lia was in that taxi. She felt present but not really, not completely. I do not know how to make this feeling more clear. I walked directly after them into the building. Lia did not recognize me. She had her head down, as if she was not well at all. The lady supported here while she walked. She did not held her as if she was her mother. She was a stranger for Lia. I was sure. I came into the building after them and waited with them at the elevator. We stepped in together. The lady pressed the storebutton. She let Lia to press the button go so she fell aside. I picked her up before she could fall. Lia was totally absent. Her eyes were closed, her breathing a little bit stumpy. I did not liked this. Lia should have stayed in the hospital in this condition. There was something bad going on. The lady let me supporting Lia and went to the frontdoor of Lia's apartment. She used the hand of Lia to touch the door, she lifted her eyelid to have her eye scanned. The door went open and I entered with Lia in my arms. I put her on her bed in her bedroom and returned to the lady as if I would leave the apartment. The older lady was already ticking on her phone. She opened the frontdoor and I picked her phone and pushed her out. That was something she did not expected. I closed the door without looking at the result of my push. I tried to give Lia some water to drink but she was in a sort coma. I made her comfortable, cleaned her face and hands with fresh water and let her sleep. I went to bed as well. I had had no sleep the night before. Therefor I was late this morning. I am sorry." John looked at Lia.

She looked at him. "Thanks John. I know you will always take good care of me but know that I have special crème for my skin, for my face and for my hands," her voice raised when she was talking.

"Oh," John said, "why did not you tell me before. If you do not tell me these things how am I to know this, " he smiled. She smiled.

"Gordius John, I love you. Oh what do I love you. Hopelessly " She stepped up to him and kissed him overdone.

He freed himself. "Calm, girl, calm," John smiled at her.Lia 's father got up. "Thank you for taking care of our daughter, John. She is rather wild and always wanted to go her own way but I am glad that she might find some steadiness with you. She needs it. You can give it to her ,I think", he smiled and shaked hands with John.

"Well, "John said, "I did pick the phone of the lady. Do you know somebody named "Marian", it was her phone. She was busy calling somebody called "James". Does these names ring bells or could this just be anyone. Nobody could combine these names with people they knew. Everybody left, they all went back to their normal life.

Chapter 7

Lia", "John started a difficult conversation. "I did not
tell everything what happened." He looked at her.
She came siting with him on the coach.
"Please, tell me everything. I do want to know all
that happened. "She smiled at him.
"Do you remember what happened when you kicked
the gun out of the hands of the kidnapper?"
"What do you mean. You said that I did it, someone
has even filmed it but I do not remember it. I do not
know, how I did it. "
She looked at John, puzzled.
"Lia, after you kicked the gun out of the hands of the
kidnapper you shot him in his right leg. Perfectly
and precise. One shot only. You turned around and
shot the two other kidnappers also in there right leg
at exactly the same spot. Unbelievably. "John
looked at the reaction of Lia. She looked at him,
shocked. She did not believe him.
"John, I never had a gun in my hand, I never kicked
something out of someone's hand. I am only
scared. I hate guns. I am sorry but it is simply
impossible. "
John understood her problem. "I am sorry. I must be
mistaken, " he reacted to calm her down.

"I am sorry. I do not feel good. Please be so kind to let me alone for a while. I have to get myself under control again," she sight.

She went to the kitchen and did put some money in his jacket.

He did not notice it. He walked to the balcony and looked over the city. He still had no memory about this city. Should he find a city he knew. A city in which he would feel himself comfortable? He did not know. Lia wanted him to leave. She had to live with his strange story. At this moment she could not. It is clear, he better should go. She had to get her life back to normal again.

He walked back to the room he had slept, collected his second set of clothes and his helmet in a plastic bag, so he had at least something to remember Lia and came back to the livingroom.

"I am sorry Lia, I won't bother you with my stupid stories. I am sorry. Please forget me and start your life back up again." He gave her a kiss on her hear, picked up his jacked and walked out the door.

She sniffed but let him go.

John left the building, crossed the street and walked through the park. He kept on walking. He walked for about three hours, ever straight on. He did not care where to go.

He walked on a calm street with hardly any traffic. Suddenly he heard a telephone ring in his bag. He first did not believe it. It must be someone else's phone. The phone kept on ringing. He stopped at a

small wall. Put his bag on it and opened the bag. In his helmet there was indeed a phone. He suddenly realised that it was the phone of the lady that had brought Lia back home. He stole it out of her hand right before he had kicked her out. He picked up the phone and accepted the call. He only said "Hallo".
"Yes, at last. I presume you have found my phone. Would you please give it back to me. I do need it very much. All my addresses and so are in it."
"Ok, "John stated simply. He took up the bag and walked to the end of the street where he was. He looked at a large square with opposite to him a big building. The Archaeological Museum. He asked if it was possible for her to meat in one hour at the Archaeological Museum.
She confirmed and John finished the call.
He put the phone in his bag.
He took it out again. He did remember her trying to contact her boss. "James". He looked for the number she was ticking at the moment that he picked the phone. The phone had anyway completed the number. He activated the number and listened to what would happen. He found a bank on the square and got seated.
The phone rang.
"Marian, do not phone me in daytime, unless it is urgent. "A woman's voice sounded. John had the feeling, that it was a familiar voice. He tried to remember where he had heard the voice before.

"This is an emergency. In two hours this phone will be returned to Marian at the Archaeological Museum." He finished the call.

He was curious how this would end. Probably he could talk with Marian to find out what she knew about him and about Lia.

He put the phone in his jacket and felt the money Lia had put there. He understood what had happened immediately. She really was sweet.

He found a bank in front of the Museum and waited. He tried to remember how Marian looked like. She was an older lady. He just waited. She probably would recognise him when she saw him again.

A good half hour later an older lady walked by. She recognized John.

She stopped right in front of him, stretched her hand out and only stated: "My phone".

"Please, be seated," John asked friendly.

She looked scary around but got seated besides John.

"Please, tell me who gave you the order to collect the girl and bring her to her apartment."

"James did," she answered immediate.

Who is this "James" and in what relation does she stand towards the girl?"

 She was shocked. "How do you know that "James" is a woman?"

"I talked with her. I am going to meet her. Please inform me about her?"

"I better do not say a word. She is extraordinary dangerous. She is the head of a large criminal organisation. She murders and kills regularly, she seems to like that. Sorry, I think I have told you enough. "

"Just one more point? What is the relation between her and the girl?"

"I do not know. I only got the order to bring her home. I got the address and the way to get in. That is it. I am sorry," she again looked around.

John took the phone out of his pocket and gave it to her. He thanked her for the information.

She immediately got up and walked away.

John decided to look around and see if he could find a coffeeshop for some coffee and a small sandwich. He really found one and had a cup of coffee and a sandwich with cheese.

More than an hour later he walked back to the square in front of the Museum. He sat on a bank at the other side of the square. He wanted to see wat would happen. He calmly observed the square.

He saw a big black car entering the square and ride about four times around on the road around the square. He did as if he was calmly sitting and only watched the building of the museum.

Suddenly the black car stopped right in front of the museum and a person got out. John could not good see who it was. The car left and a figure, dressed as a woman stood on the stoop in front of the Museum. She calmly stepped forward towards the entrance of the museum. She looked very comfortably. She knew what she was doing. She controlled it all. Short before the entrance she stopped and quickly turned around. She directly looked at John. John knew her. This was Mindy. The same woman that escaped with him from the prison.

She came straight to him.

John waited for her. He was sure the voice of "James" had sounded different from the voice of Mindy.

How com that just Mindy showed up here. Did she work for "James". Mindy was a dangerous woman, probably just as dangerous as James. He must be careful.

Mindy sat next to him and said: "Hallo John. How are you. Did you already found out more about yourself? This is not easy for you. The world will use you for its own benefit. "

John looked aside to her. What was she saying? She seemed to know more about him.

"I will tell you something about yourself. Your first name is really "John". There are several sources that mention you. The name they use is "John Normal". It is not clear if that is your actual name. You were used as a testperson for medical tests. You did react on these test extraordinary. Only the testers knew all that you could do. The problem is that the two testers were killed with the explosions. You have deliberately been freed by our organisation. You had to be available for our technicians to find out what you could do. We were informed by the testers that you were capable of very special mental actions. You could influence people extremely. We do not know how your mind works. Would you be prepared to come with me freely to help yourself and us to find out what your mind can do? " She looked hopeful at John.

"I am surprised. Did you place the explosives?" John was glad that he at last got some information about himself. He was disappointed that Mindy only told him this in the present situation and not immediately after their escape.

"No, I was also imprisoned at that very moment. I do not know who actually placed the explosives. We, by the way, still do not exactly know what did cause the explosions. As far as we could find out , also the police still have no idea how the explosions occurred. They did not found any prove of any explosive, fascinating in itself. The organisation I am part of, planned my escape. They used the explosions to speed up my escape. The jeep that stood there was placed there by my man. The gate was pulled out by my man, so everybody could get out. You at that moment just happened to be in the group. I did not know anything about you. After I left the apartment of Rosemary I returned to my criminal history. I had too, there was no alternative option for me. The information about you came from them. Please think about my words. We would really

prefer you to cooperate freely. It is, we think, the only way to really find out what you are capable of. "
"Why should I cooperate with a criminal organisation? A criminal organisation will undoubtedly wanted to use me for its own purposes. Why should I be freely wanted to be a part of that?" John looked at her.

Suddenly she looked across the square. She pulled a big thing out of her coat, it looked a large plate and dived behind it under the bank.

John stared totally surprised at her.

A loud heavily tacking sound made him clear that someone was shooting. The bullets ran against the plate Mindy held in front of her. John understood that the shooting was only mend to get her. He was spared. Could this be "James"? Shooting at Mindy. Two different organisations, criminal organisations were killing over him. This was not acceptable. He had no intention to work with any criminal organisation at all.

Now that he knew that he could probably influence people, he tried to influence the chauffeur of the grey shooters car to leave the square by turning away to the right.

He concentrated and tried to influence the chauffeur of the grey car of the shooter. To his big surprise the car moved over and left the square. Did he really influence the chauffeur or was did just coincidence. He could not believe he had this kind of influence.

Mindy come from her lying position up, moved the plate again in her coat and set next to him again, constantly looking around.

"James?" John asked.

"Yes, I presume that he now understands that we have cracked the telephone of Marian. "She smiled. John repeated what he had said to her before.

"Mindy, I can assure you that I will never freely cooperate with ant criminal organisation. Not with your organisation and not with James's organisation. Are there more criminal organisations interested? " John did not thought that it could be the case. He was already surprised that two criminal organisations were involved.

"Oh, yes," Mindy immediately stated. "There are at least two more organisations involved. Peculiarly you were involved with one member of each of the organisations. Rico is from the "Wolves" as they named themselves. Marion is a member of the "Gloves". They both did here about you after our escape and after our return to our organisations. Please reconsider your thoughts. I cannot stay any longer, James might come back. Take care of yourselves. Keep alive and live well. If you want our help against one of the others you just use this phone. She gave him a phone and left. The black car immediately came on the square. She got in and disappeared.

John now finally knew more about himself. He was glad with Mindy 's information. Could he find any source that could confirm this story or did he had to accept it as it was. He sight.

This story could at least partly clear the special actions of Lia. If he had in a way influenced her to kick the gun out of the hand of the third criminal and made her should all three of the kidnappers than he was the shooter and not she. He decided that he had to find out whether he could really get people do what he wanted.

He got up and left the square. He returned to the coffeeshop and ordered a cup of coffee. He influenced the bartender to come with two cups to him.

The bartender actually came with just one cup as he ordered.

So there was no reaction. He should not have believed Mindy. What purpose could they have by telling this story.

What could be of interest for a criminal organisation. What could some people do with your mind that others could not. He puzzled. Mindreading, no nobody could do that. Moving objects. Wat would that help criminals. Could he move money from one place to another? He had never heard of this kind of powers. He could not believe this.

Chapter 8

John left the coffeeshop and wandered around through the city. He passed an internetcafé and decided to go for a search on his history. He could start with the prison, perhaps there was more information on the internet about the kind of research they actually did.
John went in and bought three hours internettime. He started his search with the prison and its information. Almost everything was "classified". He needed to get in. He just gambled to find the inlogcodes. It must be his lucky day. He found the codes almost immediately. He found information about several technical projects. Nothing about tests on people. He sked the system for that information and again he needed a code. He just gambled again and once more he got rather quickly into the system. There were several projects with people. Only one was about a young man of his age. This should be him. He found no name, only a number: PP32-56. No indication what these numbers mend, only the number. The tests were done voluntarily with the permission of the person that did the tests. Because of the special case, the tests were located at the backside of the prisonbuilding. Something had gone wrong with the tests and the prisondoctor had to intervene. He blocked a part of the brain of the volunteer. The

patient had gone in a coma. Nobody understood what had happened. The mind of the patient made untestable blows on the measured signals. They could not understand these signals. The report was dated three days before the explosion on the prison took place.

John read the information again. This could be him but he had no idea about special mental qualities. Also the info about the tests they had done were not there, only that something went wrong. What were they testing. He searched for information about the people that worked on the researchdepartment of the prison.

Again he needed a password and again he found it gambling with letters and numbers. He found four names. The two doctors died in the explosion, two nurses seemed to be alive. He noted the two names with their addresses.

He searched on for information about the explosion. Some eyewitnesses were puzzled by the kind of explosion. One said that there was just a big bang and in that big bang two buildings were blown away, The basic prison and the entrance building. Another mend that there were three different explosions. One at the main building and the last one at the entrance.

The police stated that they did not found parts of residue of explosion material. They were thinking about laserbeams, this could declare the total, uncontrolled collapse of the buildings and the lack of explosion material. There was not yet a better explanation. Laserbeams could be fired from any mobile truck, large trailer or a rebuild bus. There were no pictures that had made clear what had happened. They were only guessing.

John left the internetcafé.

He decided to find both the ladies that had worked for the testdoctors at the prison. He looked at the addresses, walked to a busstop and looked at the map on the wall. The two addresses were quite far away and both on another side of the city. He looked at the names and decided to start with the one on the top. In both cases he had to walk for at least two hours. He did not care. He liked walking through the city. He looked at the route that he had to take and he got on the way.

He passed a large park and followed the great avenue leaving the citycentre. He walked on, passed a large Theatre and two churches. He ended at a superstore, right under the building were his first nurse was living.

He did not wanted to waste time by waiting till it was dark. He entered the building, found the right stock and got up with the stairs. A lot of people were going in and out the three elevators. At the fifth floor he walked to the frontdoor of the housenumber he had written down.

He rang the bell. Nobody seemed to answer. He waited. He rang again and waited again. He was just considering to leave, to come back later when he saw some movement behind a window. He showed himself clearly, so she could see who was at the door. She must know him, she had been present when he did the tests or at least a part of the period.

The curtain that had moved was back at its place. Now he had to wait whether she would open the door or decide not to talk to him.

He was lucky, she opened the door gently, stepped forward, said "Hallo", to John and looked around if she could see somebody else. The coast seemed to be clear so she stepped back and invited him in. John was surprised but did step in. She quickly closed the door behind him.

"Hallo "she now said far more friendly. I am sorry but I am pretty suspicious about unknown people at my frontdoor without appointment. In this part of the city you better be careful. Lately a lot of criminals have tried to get in with all kind of tricks.

She invited him in her livingroom. John got seated and put his bag with clothes and his helmet beside the chair.

"I think I know you, "she said, memorising where she should know him from. 'Do you want something to drink, coffee or do you prefer thee?"

"You are very kind, please some coffee," John answered.

She walked to the kitchen and a few minutes later she came back with a cup of coffee for him and a glass of thee for herself.

She sat down and asked what she could do for him. John thanked her for her kind approach and informed her that he had lost his memory at the explosion on the prison. He could find her name in the personals files, hoping she could tell him more of what happened, who he was and wat kind of tests they did on him."

"That are a lot of questions in one sentence", she remarqued smiling. "Yes I know you. You were in the prison as a volunteer for several tests. You were tested in your hometown in our hospital there and were chosen as most promising volunteer. About a week for the explosion you were the only volunteer left. All the others were send home. Hardly any result with them. You did it extraordinary well. The tests tried to find out whether the human mind could influence its own body, for instant if it was possible to lower your bloodsugarlevel with your mind. You did that. You lowered your bloodsugarlevel just through wanting that in your mind. It did ask quite some concentration but you actually did it. The doctors were very enthusiastic. You could also do that with other things your body does. There are many persons that can regulate their bloodsucker, a limited number of people can willingly regulate there hart beat, even less can regulate their volume of ureum in their extending water. You were the only one that could do that all. Our doctors tried to find out how you did that. They could not find any reason. There was nothing unregular about you while you did it. They desperately tried to find something. At last they tried to stimulate certain mental activities. Unfortunately you did not react as they had expected. You fell in a coma.

They panicked. You were transferred to a section at the end of the building. The doctors were on their way to you, I understood from my colleague, who was there already, when the explosions hit the buildings. I was at home, I was free. My service would start that evening around six o'clock. I am now temporary placed at the police academy for medical services. "

John thanked her for her clear information. He was grateful for her willingness to inform him.

He left her and walked to the other side of the city. He ate a quick small meal on the way. It was already dark when he entered the street where the second nurse lived. As the first nurse had told, she was present at the moment the explosions happened. He was curious about her experiences. He saw that the lights were on in her apartment. He entered the building and ringed the bell at the frontdoor.

He was surprised when an older man opened the door.

"Yes" the man asked.

"I am sorry, My name is John, I am looking for Josefine, she used to work as medical assistant in the prison, " John informed the man.

"That is correct. She lives here. One moment. He stepped back , turned around and called out load "Josefine !!!, a visitor for you. "

A young girl came from behind a door and looked at the door.

"Do not make it too long," the older man said and got through the door where the girl came from.

"Hallo, what can I do for you, "she said. The last word came slowly. She stared at John. John stared at the girl.

"Marion, you are Josefine," John stuttered.

"John", she whispered.

"Now you know I am a medical assistant , but am also connected with a gang. I live with my parents at the moment. How did you found me. Well, that does not matter. Can we meet tomorrow morning. There is a coffeeshop there," she pointed at the corner of the mall." Can we meet at ten o'clock? We can talk than, please?"

John sighed "Ok," he said. She stepped back and closed the door.

John walked away.

He walked backed to a park he had walked through on his way to Marion. He sat on a bank. He puzzled over his special skills towards the regulation of his body. He could not understand why he, with his, so called special skills, should be interesting for criminals.

His luck with finding passwords was far more interesting. That was something. Could that be an option. If he had a special feeling in finding passwords he could easily break in in all bankaccounts or secret internet information. He got up and started to walk again. Such a skill wood be very interesting for criminals. For himself he had proven that he could crack several codes in no time. How would this work. He had no idea. He just had done it. What could he do with this skill. Could he only feel what the codes were or did he change the old code by just thinking about it. He had no idea. He just did it. He got tired from all the walking. He counted the money he had. He had to live a long period with it, so he must be careful with it. He had almost two hundred dollars. He could not effort to rent a hotelroom for a week. Bed and breakfast. He sight. He started to walk again, he saw no better way to spend the night. Tomorrow he would see wat he could do to earn money. He came on a giant square. Several enormous hotels were located here. They all made clear by lightsignals that the all had fantastic casino's with new games. John stopped. Should he be capable to forefeel if he would win or loose on a playtable or a game. Could he take the gamble. He found that he did not had any other options. He walked into the first hotel and went straight on to the casino. He walked around to get a feeling about the games that were played. He looked at the roulettetables. Several people were playing. He did not had the feeling he could predict the next number. He walked to the

game tables. There seemed to be one table that caught him for some reason. He walked to it. There was nobody playing. He decided to spend twenty dollar, playing with one dollar per game. He started. He lost. He played on. He noticed that if he did made a win on the next game he got a kind of tingling in his brain. After it happened three times he started to raise his bet after he felt the tingle. He made a profit of sixhundred dollars. Than he stopped. He collected the win and left the casino. He went to the next hotel and did there the same. He again found a table where he felt the tingling. He visited all the six casino's and made about five thousand dollars. He realised that he had found a way to get money when he needed it.
He decided to stay in a hotel for one night. Tomorrow he would search for a private small apartment. He could stay there the coming period. He had to pay the hotelroom in advance. He did. John slept well. He was tired he had walked a lot the whole day. He thought back at Lia and wandered how she was doing.

Chapter 10

John slept good. He felt good. He took a shower. He left the hotel and got a cup of coffee and a sandwich at a small coffeeshop. He had a very pleasant feeling about the way life had developed. More than a half hour before he had his appointment he entered the area of the mall close to the apartment of the parents of Marion.
 He found a bank where he could watch the entrance of the coffeeshop. He calmly waited. Again it was a beautiful day. He had the impression that the weather was very stable in this city. He must admit that he liked that very much.
John calmly waited. Some people entered the coffeeshop and came out again after about half an hour. No Marion. John calmly waited. He had the impression that Marion would not come. Why should she. He smiled at himself. He was naïf. Suddenly Marion came out of the coffeeshop. She looked around and saw John sitting on the bank. She was angry. She came aggressive walking towards John. She banged on the bank beside him and said "Hallo, you wanted to talk to me, why do you let me waiting. I do not like this. I do not want to be treated like this. Why"
John smiled to her. "Sorry Marion. I though you would not come. So I waited here for you, so I could see you entering the coffeeshop. You did not got in.

So I waited. Sorry. I did not consider the possibility that you could got in through another entrance. I am sorry," John looked at her. She calmed a little bit and sight deeply.

"John, I was part of the medical team that was involved in you. You were a volunteer with special abilities. Officially you were tested on your capability of influencing your internal organs. In reality we , my criminal organisation, thought that you were able to influence people. Unfortunately we could not get results on that point. On the day of the explosion I was in your department of the prison. The doctors were on the way to us. They were hit by the explosion. Peculiarly together with them, one of the major criminals, that was in prison, got killed as well. Nobody understood the impact of that murder. Was it all just meant to kill him or was there another reason. That major criminal was the leader of the group where Rico was part of. They think that the Major, our leader, planned this attack. We know that he did not. We are not very well with explosives or lasers and so. We think James is better in that kind of actions. We still have no idea why it all happened. " She sighted.

"Thank you Marion, or should I call you Josefine?" John asked.

""Marion, please. In my home situation I am Josefine, in my criminal business I am Marion. You are only connected to me through my criminal life."

"Ok, Marion. Do you know who this "James "is?

Do you know where I can find him?"

Marion smiled. "James is a woman."

She waited his reaction.

"Yes, I know. I had her on the phone. I made an appointment with her. She did send someone that only came to shoot my conversationpartner at that moment. "John looked at Marion. "Mindy was with me".

Marion reacted surprised. "You were with Mindy! What were you two doing together. You know Mindy is a big criminal. She is close to the group of the Major." Marion sounded surprised.

"Only talking. I must admit that she came to me. I was surprised but she made me a proposal. They, her group, do still think I can influence people. "John sighed. "I am afraid that everybody is on the wrong path with me. I do not think I can influence people. " John shaked his head.

Marion looked critical at him.

"Well ,John, I have told you what I know. I have to go to my work. Take care. Try to find your way in the world." She left.

John got up. He walked back to the citycentre, passed an internetcafé and got in. He searched for an interesting small, cheap apartment. He found several options. He noted the addresses and walked along al four addresses. He decided to choose one of them. He entered the office of the broker who offered the apartment. They were of course very willing to show the apartment. They were situated at the opposite site of the street, so if he wanted he could get the key so he could look inside himself, alone. John found that a perfect option and accepted the key. He crossed the street and found the entrance of the apartment. It was the topapartment on the fourth stock. There was no elevator so he had to take the stares. The staircase looked clean, that was already a positive point. The apartment was dirty. It looked empty for a long time. He decided to accept the apartment but to negotiate the price. It was reasonably large. A nice livingroom at streetsite, two large bedrooms, a good kitchen with an eatbar. He had to clean the whole apartment, paint it and buy furniture, pots and pans etcetera. He returned to the broker and made a price. He filled in the form with a fake personal statement about the date he was born and the place where. He actually had no identity. "John Normal" that was it. He had to pay the rent for the first month in advance and so on every month. The broker also gave him some forms for asking energy and water. John filled them in and the broker would take care of the formalities. They both, water and energy were already working.

John returned to his new apartment. He went to the shops that were nearby, bought the necessary materials for cleaning and painting. He bought a bank and two chairs and more household materials as a large bed, a refrigerator, a washing machine etc.. The shower and the toilet only needed cleaning. He also painted these walls in a gently soft brown colour.

He needed two whole days to get this all arranged. He decided to buy a television and a tablet. He accepted an abonnement on the network so the television and the internet on his tablet would work. Several things as a cupboard and kitchen machines still had to be bought.

For the next day he wanted to visit some casino's to fill his money supplies. After that he would have to open a bankaccount. It would be better to pay with his creditcard.

John was very happy with the result of his home creating activities. Ok, he still had to learn to use the kitchen for cooking.

John slept well in his new bed. He showered and had breakfast. He tried his tablet and his television. There was news. The four great criminal organisations threatened with a war. One of the leaders was killed with the explosion in the prison. His gang accused the police of the fact that they did not do anything to get the killer. The gang was certain that one of the other gangs was responsible for the murder, as they called it.

The Mayor defended himself and the police. It was a difficult affair. There were no facts that could give an indication about the solution. The proof who did this and why was unanswered. John listened interested. No questions about all the people that had escaped. Nothing about anybody.

He was curious about the persons behind these organisations. Who was "James" and who was "the Major"? Who was now the boss of Rico?
John tried to get information about these figures on the internet but could not find anything. He supposed that he had to break in in secret sites to get more information. He had one big problem. He had no idea what names these secret site had. Without names he had nothing. He went out, opened a bankaccount and visited some casino's. He did won again around six thousand dollars. He bought some clothes and also got some sportclothes.
He found a fitnesscentre just around the corner. He entered that fitnesscentre and a strong looking man advised him on his fitness options. He tried all kind of apparatus. He liked it very much. The adviser was impressed, he said, by Johns physical qualities. He made a kind of program for him to get his body in a better shape.
John followed the program. While he was working as a boxer on a big sack and quick movements around the sack, a big man made trouble at the desk. John's adviser tried to calm the man. He was angry. John just went on with his training. He did not wanted to be part of any problem that others had. He speeded up his reactions and was self surprised about his own speed. He liked it. His adviser came to him and watched his boxing skills. He tried to get John 's attention. John stopped.

There was a problem with one of his clients. He wanted a sparringpartner for his trainingsactivities for his boxing game next weekend. He needed the training now. John's adviser must admit that he had promised to find someone for him but he had nobody. Would John be prepared to help him out. He was a perfect sparringpartner for this man, the adviser tried to pay John. John had no intention. He had just started with training.

The adviser was disappointed but did not pushed him to accept.

The boxer came to them.

He apologised for intruding but he was prepared to pay if John would help him. He was willing to pay John one thousand dollars, if he would help him the next two days in his training and to spar with him in the ring.

John looked at the man. He was calm now. He was big and certainly very strong. John wanted to know what he must expect. The big man looked at the adviser. He explained what it would mean. Every day two hours in the ring.

John accepted. He wanted to find out how this worked. He thought that the man was very strong but not very quick. They decided to start direct todays training.

John entered the ring. His adviser put the boxinggloves on his hands. John had a peculiar feeling with these gloves. He started to move through the ring. He kind of liked it. It felt good. He asked his opponent what skills his opponent had, was he quick, did he block every beat, did he hit hard, how did he move.

"His opponent," the boxer answered," was not to quick but was a superhitter, quick and hard."

"So you have to be quick on your feet," John reacted. He started to move around. He learned the boxer to move around his opponent. The boxer found it very exhausting. That was precisely what John wanted. He told the boxer that he had to train this extra option. They also trained his hits, the speed of his hits and his reaction on a mishit from his opponent. The problem was that John was very fats. He moved very fast and he hit very fast.

The boxer was happy with him. The made an appointment for the next day. John got his thousand dollars and was happy with it.

He took a shower and left the fitnesscentre.

He bought some more clothes and ate at a Chinese restaurant. He was tired when he came home.

He tried to find secret sites on his tablet, searched with the names of the leaders of the criminal organisations and the names of the groups, like "the Wolves". He suddenly had a hit. A site in the list stated that he had "no entrance permission". He looked at the name of the site and wrote it down on a separate paper. "Dark Dimension" was its name. He tried to find out how he could get in the site. He tried something but did not had the feeling that he was on the right line. He stopped. He was tired and went to sleep.

John got up early. He felt well. He had a small breakfast and looked at the "Dark Dimension" site at his tablet.
He did not think about a password but just typed what came in his mind. He typed far longer dan usual but he just did what he thought was right.
He was totally surprised that he actually got in.
The side offered all kind of materials you could buy. Paintings, jewellery, high quality artistic specimens like a chessboard of jade with diamantes, etc. This was not what he was looking for. He looked at the end of the site. There were some comments. He read them but no real information. Disappointed he closed his tablet. He was happy with the fact that he got in the site. He had to look further. He decided to look at the site of the opponent of his boxfriend. Perhaps that could help him with his fight in two days. John found the site. The man really was a very well-known fighter. Even bookmakers were involved in the fight. John saw that the chances of his boxmate were not very good. The bookmakers gave seven to one for his opponent. John understood the problems his boxfriend had. He looked at three fights of his opponent. He really hit super hard. He did indeed not move very well. John found his defends not very strong. He also looked at several fights of his friend. He did not move at all.

He had a good hit but used no show. John knew what he had to learn him. Showboxing. Moving without hitting. Move and hit the other way, or the other hand. John noticed that he liked his analyses. He should bet if his man could learn from him. He closed his tablet and realised that he was well informed about boxing. Could he find something about himself in connection to this sport?

He tried it on his tablet but had no feeling with arena's or playing grounds.

Perhaps he could better try to find something about the criminal activities if he was interested in their products. Drugs. He searched on the internet under "buying drugs". There were plenty people offering drugs on the internet. He wandered which sites would be from the police and which from real criminals. He selected three sited and asked for prices and deleverytime and location. He had to wait for answers. With the answering information he probably could do something. He searched further but without any success. No secret sites. Suddenly he thought that it was possible that in his tablet dubious sites were filtered out. He looked for the sites that were put aside by the system. Most of them were filtered under "spam", some were filtered as "risk sites". He smiled. This is what he was looking for.

The morning had flown away. He got out for a small lunch but was back soon. He was very interested in the risqué sites.

Chapter 11

He immediately found a site where he could not get in. He just typed what came to him and again he was in. This was the site of the Wolves. The site of Rico. They were very "interested" in casino's, bookmakers in sportsgames, gaming and gambling. No names were mentioned, only nicknames John thought. He decided to take a nickname as well. He was "the Dolphin". He asked for gambling on the fight of his boxfriend.

He searched further on the site but found no information about the organisation behind it. There were well hints to some other sites. He quickly looked at these sites but found nothing interesting there. It was time to go to the training of his boxfriend.

John walked to the fitnesscentre. It seemed to be busy. More and more people came to train. His adviser only had a short moment for him. He simply pointed at "Toko" as he called John's boxmate. Toko was already working on his speed. John made him clear that he did not only mend the speed in the move of his hit, but the speed in moving himself. John changed and went with Toko in the ring. He deliberately moved away by Toko. He was always close but always away when Toko tried to hit him. John started to touch Toko on his nose. Toko got angry, he felt bad about this kind of boxing. Suddenly John stopped . He stayed on the same spot. He stopped every punch. Every hit was caught by his gloves. He tried to let Toko move around him. He called at him, all the time, "move, go, come on, move". Toko got hopelessly tired. He could not handle this. He had no walking condition. John made clear to him that he could only box when he had a fantastic condition. He advised him to postpone the fight with two weeks. That was very short for getting him in the right condition but he needed that. John was clear about that. Toko believed him. He had one condition, John had to train him. He was magnificent as trainer.

Toko explained that if he would win that fight, he would make more than four grand. If he lost he would only get fifty thousand. "If you make me win, You will get fifty percent. If I lose you will get only ten percent." Toko smiled.

John looked at the man. "Toko, you will need at least four weeks to get in a shape to by capable to win. You have to train very hard . I will be very tough against you. Four weeks. Postpone the fight four weeks and I will do it, if you will do your part as well." John looked at Toko.

Toko hesitated. "Ok Toko. I wish you all the best. I will be here tomorrow and then our show is over. No problem. See you tomorrow. "

John left. Toko was still hesitating. He could not decide. John went home. Took a shower and looked whether there were reactions on his mails. He really got offers to buy drugs. He found the prices not acceptable. He informed the offerors. He tried to follow the answers and located them through on the location from where they had answered. He noted these addresses on a separate page in his tablet. He also found an answer on the rating of the fight between Toko and his opponent, Big Pinto. The rating even got worse for Toko. It was now twelve against one.

John found the location from where the answers on his mail were send. He wrote the location at the same page as where he had noted the drugsaddresses. He realised that he had to check whether the mailsenders could also locate him. He checked his location but that information was "not available".

John again tried to find more information about the criminal organisations. He had to eat. He walked to a small restaurant and had a quick bite. He slowly walked back home. How could he get information about the criminal organisation. He was convinced that they knew more about wat happened in the prison and how the explosions had taken place. He realised that the police must have a lot of information about these organisations. He must start there. Satisfied about his new thought he went back. He got a strong cup of coffee and sat down on his couch.

He found the website of the police and followed his feeling about the forbidden areas. He found what he was looking for. The new leader of the Wolves , the gamblingsyndicate was Rico. John stared surprised at his picture. There was a name mentioned. Mendoza Price. There was more information. John read the data. Mendoza had a twinbrother, Rico. John corrected his first impression. Rico was really close to the new boss. He was his twinbrother. Could it be the case that Mendoza had freed his brother and killed the old boss in one action. It must have been very convenient that the old boss was killed at the explosions and that his twinbrother got out of the prison safely. According to the vision of the police this organisation had never worked with explosives or laserbeams. They did not found it logical that they would have organised the explosions. The police had a rather explicit picture of the organisation and the way they worked. Also the names and addresses of the major leaders were stated. Very important was the financial man. He was an accountant, a nephew of Mendoza. John noted the address of Rico and his brother.

He continued his search through the policefiles. He found information about "James". The leader of the drugsdealers. Marion's club. Heavy organisation. John was totally disorientated when he saw who "James "really was. It was the mother of Rosemary. !!! The woman he had met in the apartment of Rosemary. He could not believe it. Should not he had felt something? He noted her address. The police thought that her organisation was responsible for the explosions at the prison. There was no proof.

Also unclear was the motif. There did not seem to be any reason why they could profit from such an attack. Through contactpersons they had tried to find out what had happened but there was no information available jet. Collecting this information needed time. In this organisation the finances were in the hands of a runner. The police qualified him as a brutal murderer, who killed everybody that did not pay in time. He was ruthless and emotional. John wrote down his name and address. This was by far the largest organisation in the criminal area in the city. They were a small part of a worldwide organisation, the "Motherorganisation". All the drugs were brought in by the Motherorganisation.
John was enough informed and searched on.
He was a little bit surprised that he could not find information of the organisation of the Major. As far as he remembered the Major was responsible for bankrobbery, kidnapping, thieves, burgling etc. Perhaps he had to find that information on other files. The same would go for the fourth organisation. That organisation was the financial banking centre of the underworld. It was shortly mentioned, he found a hint where to find that file. He also found the link towards the Major's organisation. He linked the files and looked into it. These files seemed less interesting. The leader of the Majors was a man. John noted his address. Mindy was part of this organisation. He suddenly made the link between the organisation and the kidnapping of Rosemary.

Rosemary, being the daughter of the leader of "James", the drugsorganisation. She certainly was worth a lot of money but also hopelessly dangerous with that killingmachine holding the money.
Probably Mindy did know who she was. And most likely, Ross, the kidnapper knew that Mindy would not have agreed with this kidnap, because of the killing risk. The shooting of James on Mindy, also was clear. James daughter had been kidnapped by members of the organisation of Mindy.
That was not acceptable. The police found this all very confusing and was afraid that this could lead to a war between the gangs.
The "Lords" organisation was very low profiled. They were active on buildings, shoppingcentres and offices. They were the bank for all criminal organisations. They made black money white. So all other criminal organisations were very careful with this group because their money was involved as well.
John looked at the clock. It was late. He went to his bed. He slept well. He was glad with the found information.

John got up late. He had been sleeping extraordinary well. His trainingsactivities felt good. He felt very well. He had a simple breakfast . He had found information about the criminal organisation but that had not brought him further on his own history. Where did he came from. Who were his parents, where were they. Did he had brothers and or sisters. His good feeling came down to the ground. He did not even knew why the prison was exploded. He could accept the vision of the police that James, the mother of Rosemary, the drugsorganisation, had coursed the explosions. Could there be an unknown organisation involved? He should change his way of thinking. Wat was the result of the explosions. The prison was destroyed. If that was the purpose, who could have been benefitted with that result? All he could think of was some kind of political organisation? Such an organisation should than have claimed the attack and the reason why they had done it. Just the purpose to damage the government, to hurt the city? He could not really find that a logical solution. He should talk to James. He had her address. He had to find out how she lived and how he could reach her.

John looked at the address and located it on the internet. He zoomed in from above to see how the security was organised. He broke in in the securitysystem through the organisation that, according to a big sign at the frontgate, arranged that. He looked around through the different camera's, so he knew where they were. He could not see much of the inside of the house. He looked at the screens of the camera at the frontgate. The camera looked at the front and turned towards the house. He saw an older, prairie looking, house,

huge and large. He tried to get an impression of the location where the office of James could be. No results. He stopped. He had seen enough.
He left his apartment. He walked through the streets, thinking on a solution how to approach James. He did not know anything about her agenda. Could he try to break in in her agenda, in her computer or tablet. He returned right away. He looked whether the security group had a warninglink from or to the house of James. He actually found one. He had to pass at least three codes but those were no problem for him. He got access to her desktop. He looked around and found her information on the prisonexplosion. They really were not part of the happening. John looked further. They had been approached by the Lord for a possible option to eliminate somebody for them. They had refused. Not because of the impact but because of the financial offer. To get somebody killed in a prison you could have to kill more or to find a special way to escape. John read fascinated. The Lord wanted a job to be done at the prisonsite. He had to break in with the Lord to find out more.
He closed his tablet. He took a quick bite as lunch and went to his, for the time being, last boxing appointment.
Toko was actually talking with John's adviser when he arrived.
Toko waved to him to come to them.
John calmly walked towards the two man.

Toko was not a man of many words. "John, I have tried to postpone the fight but the others did not wanted that. The fight must take place tomorrow." He sight .

"Well, well. So you honestly have tried to postpone the fight. Good. Then now you are ill. Awful, to get ill at such a wrong moment. Did you tell the manager of Big Pinto that you were ill. I hear you are not well. Did you call yourself or do you have somebody else doing your communication with the outside world? " John looked at Toko.

"Well," Toko started", my wife said that she had called Big Pinto 's manager. "

Joh smiled.

"Do you have his number? "

"Well, yes, here in my phone." Toko picked his phone out of his pocket, searched for the number and showed it to John. John took over the number and called it.

"But John, he does not know you. You cannot call in my name. My wife is my manager", Toko looked surprised at John.

John nicked to him, "All right Toko, all right, " he said still smiling.

"Hallo madam, My name is John Normal, I have heard that there might be a problem with tomorrow's fight from Big Pinto against Giant Toko, is that really so ? " he asked.

He was put through to the manager of Big Pinto.
John got a man on the line. The man sounded as an
former boxer himself.

"Hallo sir, "John started with a gentle admiring
voice. "I have heard that Giant Toko has a bad cold.
He seems to be sick. Is the fight going on
tomorrow? I presume that Big Pinto wants to fight a
fresh and top fit opponent , so his victory will give
him the option to go for the world championship, or
does he prefer a not-fit opponent that sacks through
his feet before the fight starts?" John listened. The
manager of Big Pinto made a long story of his
answer. He did not say anything about the possible
postponement of the fight.

John interrupted his stream of non-saying words.
"So, the fight goes on. I will inform the papers and
the tv-station about your vision on this fight. You are
a big man in the boxing world, so your vote counts.
Thank for informing me about your vision. Good
day". John ended the conversation.

"So, you will have to fight tomorrow. They do not
want to postpone. They only want to win. So todays
training will be our last. You will certainly lose
tomorrow. I will learn you some funny tricks that
might help you. May be this will be all you can try.
"They got dressed and went into the ring. John
showed him how Big Pinto boxed. He always came
in with his head forwards, then he placed the
hardest hit you can imagine. So at the moment he

comes in with his head forward you have to step back. Step out of his reach."

They trained it. John made the following trick. After stepping back five times you step forward the sixth time. You blow in your whole body and punch him on his chin. From right under upwards. A real tough uppercut. "

They trained it. Toko got tired of all these moves. His condition was still horrible. John said so. That meant that he had to do this in the very first round. It was time, they had trained enough for today. John thanked him for training with him and left.

He must admit that he was curious about the fight. He returned to his apartment and searched for the location of the fight. It was in one of the hotels in the centre of the city. He bought a ticket to get in. He also decided to throw away thousand dollars and made a bet on Toko. It was more that he had worked for that money with Toko, so he was entitled for some support.

He forgot Toko and tried to get more information of the Lord. The financial centre of the criminal world in this city. His name was seen at several occasions. He sponsored several organisations and was an important man in the city. Everywhere he was called "the Lord", that was special. Why would a criminal using that name and also being well known in the city by that name. No secret criminal name as "James" or as "the Major".

He used the link from the policefiles. He had to break in immediately. He just typed something and got in. The Lord was a financial expert. He had to follow some general pages with all kind of local news. No sign of any criminal activity. He went on. He found something on page 35. There seemed to be a link to another site. He followed that lead . Again a password was needed. He again passed that point. It was a 35 points long code combination. He really was surprised about himself that he got in. The page was clearly not meant to be found by non-members. There were a big number of mails collected here. John started to read them. He followed the mails back in time. After sixhundred mails he knew what had happened. He read the mails again but now from the back in time to the present. It all went clear. He copied the mails to his tablet and to his phone.

The Lord was involved in the prison explosion case. He had used the two doctors of the institute to do experiments with special drugs to get patients mutate into a new form of more qualified human beings. All experiments went wrong. No results. The Lord found out that the Wolves had heard from these experiments, so he had to decide to eliminate these two doctors. He did not wanted to be linked with these experiments. Nobody else, even his own organisation did know about it. He had gently approached James but her price was far out of range. So he contacted an outside party. They were very interested to do a simple job outside their own territory. They could never be located, because they were unknown. This other, external party, using the name "No-one", was experimenting with leaserbeam technology. They got the order for liquidation but did it on their own, in the eyes of the Lord, super stupid way. They did wat he had asked but ruining the whole prison was not his own go. So he got involved in the rebuilding committee to get a new prison on the same location.

Now John had to find out who the Lord in person was and where he could find him. He tried to find the location where the mails had been send from. It was already late and he had not eaten yet. He took some sandwiches and biscuits with coffee and went on. He did not wanted to stop now. He searched for the location on the internet and found a large office. The Lord used his business location as the home address for his criminal activities. John was surprised. On the other hand. This was his business. He tried to find a picture of the Lord or a private address but he could not find it. He located the office and looked at the office from above through the internet. On the topfloor of the building lights were still on. He expected that the bank was active on the job specially at night. John realised that he could not find out whether this was real life or an older picture of the location.

He closed his tablet and went to bed. It was already early in the morning.

John got up late. He slept solid and deep. He took a shower and ate an easy breakfast. He looked in his tablet to find the way to the hotel, where the fight would take place. He better could go because it was a long walk. He preferred to walk. He could take a taxi but he preferred to walk. He confirmed the deal for the fight and paid the thousand dollar at a rate of one against twenty. He put his tablet with his ticket on front and his helmet with the phone of Lia still in it and some cloths, needed if it got rainy, in his backpack and left.

He walked through the city. He liked it. He should get more running activities in his training. He enjoyed walking through this city. He felt more and more at home. He must admit that this was all he knew, so real alternatives were not available.

After more than two hours he arrived at the hotel where the boxing gala would take place. There also was a casino. The fight between Big Pinto and Toko was planned for over about two hours, all kind of other fights were planned before the big fight.

John visited the casino and won five thousand dollars. He found fife machines that gave him the tinting feeling. He made sure he did not win more than nine hundred dollars per visit an a machine. The pay-out could be done direct on the special pay-out apparatus.

After one and a half hour he went to the boxing area. A big exposure about the different fights was making clear where to get in. John showed his ticket on his tablet and got in.

He sat on row ten almost at the side. He had a reasonable good spot. He looked around. There were quite a lot people. He watched three fights between younger and far lighter boxers and one fight between two, quite good boxing ladies. He was enthusiastic about the fight of the ladies.

Then the big fight was to take place. All kind of officials came in the ring and were interviewed by the spokesman. Than a special music was plaid and Toko came in, surrounded by a lot of glamour and waving around. He was followed by a lady that probably was his teacher, manager and wife, John supposed.

Toko happened to come along John's seat. John stood straight up and applauded for him and smiled. Toko grabbed his hand and pulled him over.

"Please help me as my ringassistant, give me hints and water. "

John accepted and followed him. Toko 's wife faced him, surprised of what happened.

"You were his trainer, a young man of almost twenty. " She smiled and shaked her head. She could not believe that this could work out very well for her husband.

Toko got in the blue ring. Then an enormous applause sounded up. The first notes of the hymn of Big Pinto were heard. The speaker announced his entrance. Almost all the public got op and welcomed

the coming champion. Just a couple of fights he had
to win and then he was ready to beat the present
worldchampion.

John talked to Toko, who was impressed by this
performance. He talked to Toko, repeating his
lessons. "If his head goes forwards, you get back or
aside. Out of his reach. And again , and again. After
five times stepping away you go forward and you
blow his chin through his head. With your whole
power, your whole body must fly into that single hit.
John kept on talking. Toko listened to him. He forgot
wat was happening around him.

John tapped him on his shoulder. He had to go to
the referee. Toko got up. The referee talked to the
fighters, explained his instructions and let them
return to their corners. The bell ringed and the two
man came to the middle of the ring. Toko stayed
calm. Big Pinto got furiously into the attack. Still only
boxing with his head up. Toko defended and moved
slowly sidewards. Suddenly Big Pinto got his head
forwards and immediately Toko stepped back.
John called a compliment to Toko.

Toko made a small attack but it was perfectly
defended by Big Pinto. More and more Toko slowly
walked back. Big Pinto was not prepared for that
method. Toko used to fight on the frontline, always
forward. Big Pinto looked at him. He stretched out
he waited for Toko to make one of his famous
attacks. Those attacks were the reason for this fight.
That was how Toko used to win fights. They made

both of them several small attacks without real options to place a big shot. The first round ended. The public did not found this very interesting. These man should have tried to slaughter each other. No real blow had been placed.

Toko 's wife put a kruk in the corner and Toko sat down on it. She cleaned his face and his gloves. John made Toko clear that Big Pinto was afraid of his fists. He could try, carefully to step aside and hit Big Pinto's nose. If that worked he must immediately step forward and swing with the same hand a great circle and blow the man under his chin. From the hit on his nose he would get up a little bit, enough to give his chin open. Be careful, prepare the action by first stepping several times to the other site.

The bell ringed. The two fighters came to the centre of the ring. Toko stepped a little bit back, so Big Pinto had to come to him to fight. He calmly stepped aside and stepped immediately forward, gave a hit on Big Pinto 's head. Big Pinto blocked the hit partly but he got a small crash on his head. Toko stepped back immediately. Always stepping back to the right.

Big Pinto got angry. "Come on, fight, " he called out. Pinto smiled at him. "He Big man, are you hurt, I see blood on your head". Toko smiled at him.

Big Pinto lost control and bowed forwards to hit Toko with a magnificent blow.

Toko simply stepped aside. He again made a small try for Big Pinto 's head.
This time Big Pinto blocked the hit.
Again Toko stepped aside.
Big Pinto had to turn towards him.
And again Toko got away.
"Come on, fight man. Do not turn away all the time, come on, fight." Big Pinto turned again towards the new place where Toko had turned to.
At that moment Toko turned the other way, hit Big Pinto strait on his nose with his right hand. Blood splatted out of the man's nose. He came up. Immediately Toko circled with his right hand and blow Big Pinto, while Toko stepped forwards, on his chin. A fantastic uppercut. Big Pinto stumbled backwards. Fell backwards and did not move anymore. Immediately a doctor came into the ring and put the blown down fighter on his site.
The referee ended the fight.
Toko had don what nobody had believed. He gave a loud and clear yell.
Toko 's wife also cried out loud. The public was still silent, shocked. Their hero was down. Knock out in the second round through a fantastic uppercut. A big applause and a lot of noise exploded. The public had a new hero. John congratulated Toko with his fabulous win and left. Toko was busy with the audience and the referee. The camera's brought him in close up. He was the new big hero. He had beaten Big Pinto, magnificent.

Big Pinto was looked at by the doctor. He woke up. The doctor controlled his status by looking in his eyes. Everything was all right. He got up and was deeply disappointed about the result of this fight. His manager got angry about his fighting. He nicely congratulated Toko with his win. He immediately stated that he wanted a new fight in four weeks. He had the right to get a revanche.
Toko did not know what to say.
Big Pinto's manager raised the fightresults to a higher level. One million for the winner, half of it for the loser. Toko and his wife accepted.
They left the ring and got back to their dressingroom.
John had left the location. He walked into a park and got seated on a bank. He picked up his tablet, and claimed the win on his bet. He got a decent answer. The win was paid on his bankaccount. John looked at his bankaccount and indeed the twenty thousand dollars were there. He was fine. He walked calm and satisfied back to his apartment. He needed more time than he had expected, but he was in no hurry.

Chapter 12

When he entered his street, the street was blocked.
Everybody was kept away. He asked an officer what
was the matter. The officer pointed up into the
street. The firebrigade was busy with a major fire.
John had to step two steps aside to see it. He
looked surprised, even ashtonisched. It was his
apartment where the fire was. Wat had happened.
The officer could not tell more. He only knew about
a fire. John walked around the block and ended at
the opposite site of the road. Here he had a better
view. He looked up. The spot where he had stayed
was totally destroyed. There must have been a
major explosion there. He was lucky that he was not
at home. He hoped that nobody of his neighbours
got hurt.
John walked away. This was becoming dangerous.
His opponent had drastic ways of getting what he
wants. One way or the other John had the
impression that only the Lord could be that
opponent. He probably had made a new
arrangement with the "No-one" group.
He wondered how they had found his location. His
location indication on his tablet was not active.
Could they had activated that signal. He quickly got
his tablet and looked at his location sign. It was on.
They had the option to activate it. He put it out

again. So probably they knew now where he was, or at least where the tablet was. So they knew he was not at home when they shot it down. A warning. For what, from whom. Could he find the computer that had changed his location signal. He looked if he could find who had intervened in his system. The information was available. He tried to identify the information and to follow the burglar back through his own line. He came at the same address as he already had from the Lord. The office.

He closed his tablet and put it out. He walked away from the spot where he had looked in his tablet. About twenty meters further he sat down again. He looked what happened. The Lord knew where he was. His computer was out now, so he could not find him now.

Nothing happened. He looked at the people that walked by. No one seemed to be interested in the spot where he had seated a moment ago.

John searched for indications about what he had to do. He had no home to get back to. He supposed that his opponent, the Lord, must have had a purpose with this blow-away action. If he had wanted to kill him, they would have waited until he had been in, when the light was on, for instance. So what could have been the intention.

Should he visit the Lord, in his own office? Was this an invitation? What other options were there. Just a stay away sign? He did not found it very likely. That did not seem to be the way of thinking of the Lord.

He Lord had taken out the two doctors. These two who knew everything about the special treatment he had had, were brutally killed, heavily overdone of course but just killed.

Something came up in his mind. Could it be the case that these two or at least one of them, had private files about his case. He had to find the private addresses of the two doctors.

He did not wanted to use his own tablet, so he left the park and walked to one of the internetcafe's. He tried to see if he was followed. He thought that that was not the case.

He walked in the café and bought half an hour internet time. He quickly logged in in the policefiles and found the addresses. One of the doctors was married and had two children, the other was single. He decided to first look at the location of the single doctor. There should be nobody at home.

He left the café and walked to the house of the single doctor. He was surprised. He walked through a broad avenue. The address was a broad, great house. He looked at the house from the opposite site of the avenue. On several rooms lights were on. He thought that the doctor lived alone. He saw three young men going to the house and simply walking in. It seemed as if this was a house with several inhabitants. Apartments, but than in a large house. He decided to walk into the house and find the right apartment and see what happened.

He calmly crossed the road and walked in. Direct against the sidewall were a large number of postboxes. John found the name of the doctor and had to look at apartment 2 B. He got up the stairs to the second floor. He expected to find the apartment there. He was right. The apartment was at the back. He walked to the door. All was silent. The frontdoor was locked. He looked around. He felt on the upperpart of the doorstyle. He was lucky. There was a key. He picked it up and tried it on the door. The door opened. He got in and locked the door behind him.

He listened, it was silent. He looked around. From outside came some daylight. He looked around. If he would hide a secret file, where would he had put it away. He felt that he had to look in the kitchen. It was a very small kitchen. Only three meters deep and two meters wide. He looked around. He felt attracted to the refrigerator. He looked in. There was not very much in it. Under in the refrigerator some green vegetables were still available. John got the box with the vegetables and put it on the small table, more or less the eatcorner. He looked in the strongly closed box. He needed quite some power to get it open. No vegetables, they were painted on the inside and on the outside. John smiled about this. He found a file. He was convinced that it was his file. It was rather big, at least seven centimetres. John picked the whole file out of the box, closed the box again and put it back in the refrigerator.

He left the apartment, locked the frontdoor and left the key on the place where he had found it.

He got out on the street and passed a small hotel some streets further. He decided to get a room for the night. He got in, rented a room for one night. He was curious about the file. He wanted to read it first thing once in his room.

He got in on the second floor, locked the door behind him and got his bag from his back, set it besides the chair in the corner, next to the window. He threw his jacket on the bed and sat down in the chair.

He got the file from his bag. It was thick. He expected everything. He opened the file and looked surprised. On the front there was a paper. He had expected everything but not this. There was a text on the paper. The text was directly meant for him. His hears raised to the ceiling. What was this. He read the text. It was in big letters.

"Hallo John." It stated. Who could know that he would use this name. He had no memory so who could know about his choice.

He sight but started to read the text.

"Do not be surprised. Many things are predictable for us. Even more things are different then you think. Of course we cannot and will not put these things on paper.

Probably you cannot read the next line. To be able to understand the text, you will need the second part of your file.
You will find it with my colleges wife. She is great. She knows.

"On the innersite Only if you of this file ask for it you will find explicitly at my our memorystick number colleges' wife, she one. In the will give you other file you a special mixing -plug -in will find number two."

Use it in your tablet to read and see your file. Use all three together. This is essential.

After you have read the file we will contact you. "

That was it. What was going on. The writer was talking about "my colleges wife". The only link he could think of was the two doctors. He had collected this file at the house of the single doctor. How could he have known that he was to break in in his apartment and how did they know he would find the file, while the others, like the police and the Lord would not find it. He could not imagine that the police would not have looked in the refrigerator. He must admit that the house did not looked a mess. It was all need and decent. Perhaps he had to look into the policefiles to find whether they had search the house or that they only had visited it and had not looked for anything. They had not known about a private file, kept secret at home. Perhaps also the Lord had not known.

Maybe he would find that out when he had the meeting with him. He still had his invitation, or was it not?

He got back to reality. He looked into the files. There were all kind of pages about all kind of daily tests they had done on somebody called PP 1257. At the beginning of the file there were some indications of the person, further to be called PP 1257.

PP stood for Private Person. The information mentioned, born 17 February 2000 at Bopol Central Hospital. No further name was mentioned, not the name of his parents, if these were his data.

Very good conditioned sportsman, volunteer for the money. Student, learning law and technics, special combination.

Boxer, motorracer and marathonrunner.

Then all kind of medical information followed, bloodgroup etc, etc.

On each page these personal medical information was measured. It seemed to be the case that this file only had data on every other day. He immediately suggested that the other file would have the other data. He saw that more than a week before the explosion things changed, other medicines were used. The names were explicitly mentioned. John looked at it hopefully. If they had explicitly registered the medicines he had been given, finding a way of removing the memoryblock came closed and became more likeable.

He closed the file. He opened it again. He looked at the innersite of the papers. Indeed there was a small memorystick taped against the downside of the map, right in the middle of the map. He carefully got it out. He did it in his wallet. He did not wanted to loose this.
He felt good. He was on the right track to find himself back. If this were his data, he was a runner. He had to start running again. He used to be a boxer. He could understand that. It could declare his role with Toko. He had not thought of Toko from the day he won the fight. Miraculously. He must admit that Toko had fought a fantastic game. His blow really was killing.
John decided to go and have a dinner somewhere along his trip to the house of the other doctor's wife.

He left the hotel and walked through the city. He picked a quick "fruit and salat" dinner.
While he was eating, he suddenly thought about the last sentence of the first page of the file. Was not there stated something like: After you have read and seen the file we will contact you." But these man are dead. Officially declared dead. Yes, they were. We're not they? Could they have made some arrangement about their death? The peculiar fact of

the files could be declared by this not-being dead position. They simply placed the files later in the refrigerator. He was the only one that would come to look for information later than the police and the Lord. Was that also why the apartment was clean and decent. But this all also could have been planned by the wife of one of the doctors. He would visit her tonight and see what she knew about this all.

He started to walk again. He came through a park and decided to try some running. He had never thought about it but in his file he had read that he could run marathons. He started calmly, he did not wanted to get at the doctors house dumpy and sweating all over. He kind of liked it. He decided to try this out further on the way back.

He did not wanted to come too early at the house of the wife of the married doctor. She had two kids. He wanted to wait until the kids were asleep. He also wanted to find out whether somebody watched the house. He did not wanted to get caught by whoever should want that.

He walked around the block of the address he had. It was a normal flat with apartments. He found the number and the name on the postbox with the right number. He walked another round, looking at others that seemed to be interested in the apartmentblock. He noticed nobody. He calmly waited. He looked at the back of the apartment, waiting for the lights at the sleepingrooms to go out. After that had happened, he calmly walked to the front and looked at the apartment from the opposite site of the street. The light was on in the livingroom. John waited fifteen minutes just to be sure that the kids were asleep.

He walked in and got up the stairs to the third stock. He ringed the doorbell and waited.

The door was not answered. He ringed again. He heard some stumbling. He was surprised. He had not foreseen any problems. At last a woman's voice asked who he was. John stepped forward to show himself for the camera above the door.

"My name is John. I would like to talk to you about your husband," he answered.

The door was opened just a little bit. The chain was still on the door, John saw it clearly.

A big manshand pulled her back.

John put his leg against the door.

Someone tried to hit the door to close it again. Johns' foot kept it open. He pushed immediately strongly against the door. He swept the chain with his hand. The chain broke. John pushed again strongly against the door. The door got open. A young woman and a big man fell together backwards. It was clear that the woman had pushed the big man backwards. John immediately closed the door behind him and helped the woman up.

"I am sorry for breaking in, " John stated.

The big man rolled stewards and tried to get up.

"Look out, be careful, she is the attacker," he shouted.

John was surprised. The woman turned to John and tried to hit him hard on his head.

John got quickly through his knees and jumped immediate after that up and pushed the woman backwards with his right hand.

John did not understood what was happening. What was this. Who was who? The man got up and looked at John with big eyes.

The woman stumbled against the wall of the hall. She looked angry at John, gave a cry and attacked again.

John looked at her, did a step backwards and came against the frontdoor, further back was not possible. The lady was really a fighting machine. She was capable to jump up and tried to kick him on his face. John was surprised but caught her foot with his hand. She immediately turn her body and tried to fulfil her action with the other foot.

John turned her foot, that he had in his hand backwards, against the moving direction of her body. At the same time he stepped forwards and hit the other foot tough with his other hand. He heard the foot crack by his hit. The foot that he had in his hand also cracked. The woman's attackingscry changed into a cry of horror. She banged hard on the ground and rolled on her back, still yelling. She calmed down. Carefully feeling the problems at her feet.

The big man looked at John.

Suddenly he looked aside. The two kids had left their beds, awakened by the yelling lady. They immediately went to the big man. Looking disturbed. The man sussed them and took them to the livingroom.

John understood that the man belonged to the house. He was the connection with the children. He looked at the woman on the floor right in front of him.

What did she do here. She had to tell him.

John kneeled next to her. She was still very busy with her feet.

He sat down. She was laying now between John and the sidewall of the small hall. There was not very much space there.

She looked angry to John. "Who are you!! "she yelled. "What are you doing here. Get lost, get lost", she repeated loud.

"You have a problem," John stated very calm.

"Yeah, you are my problem. How could you do this to me. Who do you think you are?"

"Good question, but that is not an item for this moment. Who are you and what are you doing here." John smiled at her.

She could not believe her eyes. This smiling youngster had beaten her down in just one action. She could not believe her eyes.

She calmed down. She understood that this young man was extraordinary dangerous.

She looked at him. He really looked strong and well trained. He was fast, very fast. She sighted.

"What were your orders?" John asked still smiling at the wounded lady.

"I cannot tell you" she simply reacted.

"Would you tell me to what organisation you belong," John tried to get answers.

She only looked at him. "Sorry".

John did not wanted to hurt her more.

The big man came to look at the two in the hall.

"Sorry for my interruption," John stated, "Would you call an ambulance to collect her, she cannot walk with these feet. "

The man picked up a phone out of his pocket and made an emergency call.

They waited for the ambulance. The lady did not wanted to talk. John asked the man to wait until this lady was moved, so they could talk freely.

Twenty minutes it took for the ambulance to came. Efficiently they put the lady on the stretcher and moved her to their ambulance by the elevator.

John went into the livingroom with the man, he got coffee and they talked.

Chapter 13

The big man informed him what happened. About half an hour ago this lady called on the door. He had just put the kids in and had collected a cup of coffee when she called on the door. She wanted to come in, but he did not wanted that. She just slipped by his site. He had never expected that an unknown lady would force herself into his house. He was so surprised that she was already sitting on his couch in the livingroom before he knew. He followed her to his livingroom. She told him a story about her having lost her memory and that she was appointed to him for answers.

John told him that that was his story. He had found the file about him at the apartment of Paul, the colleague of his husband. He called himself John Normal, because he did not know his own name. The big man introduced himself. "Peter is my husband. My name is Mark. Paul and Peter are already working together for, I think, more than twenty years. They were always interested in the human mind. Peter and I have adopted two kids. We are super happy. I am only informed about a small part of his work. He told me that someone would come to me and ask for a file. I must control certain physical things about the visitor. One thing was your looking. He gave me a photo. If you will permit me, I will collect the tools I need to confirm that you are the one, sorry but that are my instructions."

"All right, please do," John stated. The coffee tasted reasonable. He waited calmly.

Mark came back. He had a box with him. He sat in his chair and opened the box in front of him. He looked in the box and found a tablet. He picked it up and opened it. He looked at the tablet and looked at John.

"You do look like the man, John," he smiled.

He got to the next page and got up. "Your eyes, I have to scan them , please cooperate," he asked. John let him scan his eyes.

"Also correct," Mark noticed. He did the tablet in the box and left again for, as John supposed, their bedroom.

John finished his coffee. He was curious.

Mark came back with a file. This file looked like the other. John smiled at Mark. Mark gave him the file. John wanted to open it, Mark made him clear that that was not intended. He had to take it with him and read it elsewhere.

John accepted. He asked Mark if he could hand him the plug-in device for his tablet.

Mark smiled. He was happy with this question. It confirmed that this was the right man. Mark went back to his bedroom and came again rather quickly into the livingroom. He handed John a small bag with something in it.

John put both things in his bag, he thanked Mark and left.

He did what he had promised himself and started to run, calm and easy. He liked it. He found it even great. He raised his speed regularly. He also looked around if he was followed. He took a big round through town to make it more difficult for followers to keep in touch. He got through great malls and small streets. He partly ren hard and sometimes he sat down on a square and then suddenly he left the spot.

He ended at his hotel. He was curious.

He got to his room. He closed the door behind him and locked it.

He did the lights on and closed the curtains and dropped his bag on the small table.

He left his jacket on his bed and sat down. He opened his bag and took the two files out.

The two files looked the same on the outside. He looked into the file that happened to be on the top. He knew this file. He took the other file and sat back in the chair. On the first page there also was a letter from the auteurs.

"Hallo John,

You now know something about us. The right information is available now on the memorysticks. Read the peculiar lines in the other file with three by three words together, making two different sentences. Use the sticks, put in first the blue one, than the other, than connect them with the system. Good luck and we will meet again."

That was all. The files behind the first paper were indeed the other half of the daily reports of all the tests they had taken from him.
John looked at the inside of the file and found the second memorystick.
He laid the second file on the other one, picked the small bag out of his bag and took his tablet. He decided not to use his own tablet. He found a apparatus to combine several plug-ins in the small bag he got from Mark. He took the two memorysticks and watched if he could find the colours. Well, that was easy. One was red and the other was blue. He put the two sticks in the little apparatus of the plug-in device. He left his big bag in his room but took the small bag with the plug-in device and the two memorysticks and put it all separate in his pocket.
He left his room. He was hungry but also curious. He decided to eat first and then visit the internetcafé.
He just bought a big burger on the hand and walked into a large park. He found the burger very tasteful. He must remember this spot. He walked further to the internetcafé. He bought an hour and got a cup of coffee.

He started the computer up and found his little bag and putted it on the desk. He opened it and entered the plug-in in the computer. Then he put the blue memorystick in the plug-in and then the red one. The computer registered the new device. John activated this one started the combined connection. He waited tensely. He got an image.

A young man, Peter, John supposed, looked at him, his image trembled. He started to talk but John did not here any sound. He tried to find a sound connection but could not find it. Again the image started to vague out. The young man became totally green. The collars mixed again. This could not work. He looked heavily disappointed to the screen. He let the image go on but did not expected anything of it. After ten minutes of bad images and no sound he stopped the contact. He disconnected the plug in and put the whole device in the bag and in his pocket.

He decided to look at some news in the internet. One of the hot items was the winning uppercut from Toko against Big Pinto. John looked interested at the report. Toko talked out loud. He was extremely happy with his victory. He had a problem. His trainingsmate had disappeared. He wanted him to come back. He had learned so much from this guy. He came close to the camera. "John please come back to me. Please?", he really looked as if he was begging. John smiled. He would consider this option. He must admit that he liked this giant boxer.

Toko was a nice guy. He could really became a very good boxer. He was very talented but his physical condition must get far better. He had made big money with his gamble on Toko 's win.

There was also some news about the building of the prison. It was decided to rebuild the prison but in a new and more modern outfit. The police had left the premises and the prison board was now in charge again. They had continued the close down of the area. The whole area would be taken down. In the meantime the new building would be developed. John stopped and left the internetcafé.

He felt that he had too much energy and walked back to the park and started to run around the park. It felt good, this running. He must admit that he was heavily disappointed.

He speeded up. What was happening. Was somebody just joking with him. Making fun with nonsense, empty promises. How did anyone knew about his visiting Mark. Coincidence. He could not believe this. A fightingmachine was no joke. He must admit that the way he handled the attack from the fighting machine gave him a good feeling. He had to find out more about himself. As far as he could believe the information from the testfiles, he was a marathon runner, a boxer and a motorcrosser. He did had helped Toko with boxing technics and tactics. He did liked it very much to run. And he had liked it to ride on the motor. He still had the helmet. He would bring it back or should he buy the motor. He loved the idea. He did have money. If he got back to Toko, he could even make more money. He rase his speed again and started another round through the park. He got back with his thoughts to the case. Himself and all that had happened. How had the fighting machine found out that he would come to Mark. Was it obvious or just coincidence. Did she know why he would visit Mark? What did she had to do. Knock him out and bring him somewhere? Why now, why today. Could it all be a complot. Could Mark be part of it. How come Mark and the fighting machine did not fight. John found this a peculiar affair.

Was the whole filestory a giggle. Was it all fake. Who would create such a complex story and with what purpose? He could not find any logical base. He stopped. He got tired.

He walked into a supermarket, bought some snacks and something to drink and walked back to his hotel. He was really puzzled.

He took a shower. He was really tired. He still was very disappointed about the informationmisfit.

He forgot the snacks and his drank and got to bed.

Chapter 14

John slept badly. He was thinking about almost everything. He knew that there were all kind of things that were different than they looked like. His major problem was that he could not found out what was right and what was wrong. He could not really understand why, whoever was responsible for it, had ruined his apartment. What purpose could it serve? The only good reason he could imagine was that "they" wanted him dead. Not an invitation to talk. That was not logical. If it was "the Lord", what could he have had in mind for this kind of attack. Could it be someone that wants to blame another criminal organisation. Was there someone that was starting a war between the four major gangs? What had he to do with that. Why he, why him. He knew that members of the Majors group had kidnapped the daughter of James. Rosemary was the daughter of lady James. How could they have had the possibility of kidnapping Rosemary. You could expect that Lady James protected her daughter like hell. Nowhere in the news, as far as he could remember, anyone seemed to knew about this kidnapping. What was the roll of the "Wolves". They lost their leader!! Did they? Paul and Peter, the two doctors seemed to live in spite of all the information in the news. Was that so. He had not met anyone of them. He had visited the homes of the two doctors. Anyone could have arranged these files with a more or less dead end. Why had Mark, the father of the two children in Peter's home not fought with the attacking fighting lady machine?

Nothing seemed to fit. The most uncleared part was his own role in this whole affair.

What had he found out about himself? He was not the son of the two people that had lost a son at about the same time as he probably started with the testseries at the prison. Their son was sold to an interested organisation. The next link seemed logical. Sell the kidnapped man to a secret organisation. Was that an idea? Was there another organisation busy to push the present four big ones? Was it logical to kidnap kids from dangerous people like James. Their own boss could not be very happy with such an action. So that would be not very likely. Must it be a new organisation or could it be one of the others. The Lord, no, too much risk. You would not like to get one of your clients in trouble. The Wolves. The club that lost it's boss. Was that so? The doctors might have survived, why not the Big Wolf. That could be an option. If the leader of the Wolves was not dead, he could certainly be the one that pulled on the strings.

He got up late. Took a quick shower and left the hotel. He felt lost. No home, no target to go for. Well he had Toko to take care of. The thought about

Toko gave him a better feeling. That thought made him start running again through a park that he had entered while walking. His bag was heavy on his back. He found it ok to have all his belongings with him. Should he burn the files? No just let them give some weight on his body while running.

It started to rain. John quickly entered a coffeeshop that happened to be next to the park. He found a spot near the window and he looked outside. He ordered coffee and toast. He remembered that he did not had breakfast and got hungry immediately. The waitress brought him a large cup of coffee and a complete breakfast. She smiled at him. "Running before breakfast", she remarked", that is great, sometimes I do it myself. It is an extra from the house". She smiled again and was called by another client.

John eat tasteful. He looked outside, the rain was getting heavier and heavier. The people that were still outside, run to their homes or their cars. John liked the way people were hurrying. He was sitting dry and comfortable.

Suddenly an older woman stood by his table. "Excuse me," she said. "The whole café seems full, may I...."she stuttered and stared at John.

John looked at her. This was the woman that not happened to be his mother. He got up and offered her the seat opposite to him.

She hesitated, but sat down after looking outside to the very tough rain. She sighted and looked at John.

"Thank you," she said with a sigh.

"How are you doing. Oh, I had hoped so much that you were our son. I had that trembling feeling, that I thought I would feel seeing my son back again. I am sorry. I am again only thinking of myself. How are you doing. If I remember well, you had lost all knowledge about yourself. So where do you live? You do look all right, but also a little bit puzzled? "

The waitress came. "Hallo Mrs Friender, what can we do for you? "

"Oh, please a cup of thee with a small toast, not such a complete breakfast, please. " She looked at the last pieces of John 's breakfast.

"Ok," the waitress answered, smiling at John and got away.

John also again felt that good touch for someone you feel close with. He told her so. He also told where he lived. She reacted surprised. She thought that somewhere around that place a big fire had happened. John confirmed that but did not say that it was his room that was burned out. He did say that he was looking for something else to live.

She was glad that he was all right. The tea an toast were put on the table before her. She eat and drank very decent. She offered John to come and live in her porthouse, a small cottage at the front of their house outside town. At the frontgate there was an old little house from origin mend for the gatekeeper. Now they used all kind of electronic securtitytools to protect the area. John said that he would think about it. She wrote down the address and her telephone number so he could call her, when he wanted to contact her.

Just in case he would consider her offer he asked for the rent, so he knew where he would be in for. She mentioned a very low monthly payment. He really considered it. He told her that he was really interested and would probably tomorrow visit the location to see what he found of it. He thanked her for her kind offer and the very pleasant conversation and left. The rain had stopped and the clouds seemed to have left, a shiny sun came through the leaving clouds.

He walked again into the park and started running again. He felt that his condition was getting better. He had to do this every day. He liked it.

He knew that he had to go back to the fitnesscentre in the centre of the city in the afternoon to contact Toko. He calmly ran into that direction. He must admit that meeting Mrs. Friender made him feel good again. He did not understood why. She had told that she had had a special feeling when they met the last time. He also had had that peculiar special feeling. He could not place that feeling.

He entered the citycentre and walked through the park near the fitnesscentre. He gave himself some rest and looked around at the people that walked by. He started to wonder. How come that Mrs Friender coincidentally walked into him. Was it coincidently. Was she tipped by one of the other visitors of the coffeeshop. How come he got a big breakfast, while it got very busy in the cafe? Did they had to make sure he would not leave in the meantime? Or just coincidence? He had it difficult with these unclear happenings.

What did he had to think of the offer to rent the gatehouse. He must admit that he liked the idea. Living in a small house of his own. He got the snacks from last night and the drink he had bought in the supermarket. He ate the snack and took some slocks of the drink. He kept the rest.

It was time to go to the fitnesscentre to meet Toko. John walked to the fitnesscentre. It was very crowdy. John could hardly got in. A long line kept the people for the frontdesk. John looked along the line. He did not wanted to wait before he was entitled to get in. Suddenly the desk lifted a large sign. "Closed" was on it. The whole line started to make noises. Everybody had a reason why he or she should be allowed to get in in spite of the sign. John walked backwards and left the fitnesscentre. This was not what he had expected. Toko must have created a large attention through his win in the fight against Big Pinto. Well he had done his best. He decided to find out where the cottage of Mrs Friender was and take a look there. He got back to the park, sat down and used his tablet to find the location. He found it, a nice route through a large forest made it interesting to run. He got on his way.

It took him more than an hour to get to the forest. There he raised his speed strongly. He loved it. The path moved up and down and curved between big trees and large bossage's. He sprinted several times to see how fast he was. He left the forest behind him and walked on a broad boulevard with giant trees all along the road on both sides. He found the name of the street. He was on the right spot. He had to walk on for the right number. He calmly walked over a small path behind the big trees. He liked the surrounding, the broad road with the enormous trees, the super forest, old and large. He walked on. There were large area's with great houses. Enormous gardens. The third house he walked by had the number of the neighbour. He attended the next house. It was huge. Three wings and four stocks high in the centre part of the building. He looked forward. He saw the entrance of the grounds. A large number of high trees took his view away. He crossed the road to have a better look at the entrance. He was surprised. A large gate accompanied by, on both sides, large trees. Direct behind the frontline of trees a small, old house was visible, almost completely hidden by the trees. The frontdoor of the porthouse was high and broad. He walked by and looked back at the gate. Also from this side the porthouse was hardly visible. In a way he had a fantastic feeling about this small cottage. He crossed the road and tried to see more of the house. He had to walk back along the gate to look backwards to see more of the premises. Here he had the best look. He had the feeling that the porthouse pulled on him. He knew that he could not resist this cottage. He decided to come back tomorrow, he would inform Mrs Frieder this evening. He wanted to see the inner of this porthouse. He started to get back. He took his time, speeded up regularly and got back to the centre of the city. It got dark but he kept on running. He felt good. He decided to enter a house offering a bed and breakfast. He had to pay in advance and did that. He got a room at the backside of the house. It was all decent and clean. He mailed Mrs. Frieder that he would like to visit her tomorrow morning round 10.30 to look at the rental.

He left his bag in the closet and got out. He looked around in a nearby super large shoppingcentre. He got something to eat and was in no hurry. He walked calm to the fitnesscentre. It was all easy now. Nobody in front of the door, no line up. He just walked in and got to the frontdesk. Nobody was there.

He just walked on, changed his dress and got into the training area. He started with some weightlifting and followed with push-ups and arm-power. Nobody had special attention for him.

He did his workout for more than two hours. He found it all ok.

He stopped. Took a shower, got dressed and left the fitnesscentre.

In front of the centre a taxi was parked. The driver stood with the door open direct in front of the door of the fitnesscentre.

"Hallo sir, John Normal, I presume," he said very polite.

John was surprised. "What ? yes," he reacted.

"No I am not going in. I was not invited by anyone. " He started to walk away.

"Please sir, Toko is waiting for you. Please". The man did his best to be convincing.

This was not the way Toko would approach him. He did not believe it. He kept on walking. The driver came after him. Excuse me sir, Hallo, hallo. Please, I have to bring you with me!!"

Suddenly John stopped. Turned around and caught the man at his throat.

"O, you have to bring me with you !! " he repeated the words of the man. "Whom gave you that order? Not Toko, well?"

The man stared at John. "I cannot tell you. That is too dangerous. "

He really looked scared. John smiled at him. He could not hurt this kind of assistants.

He let the man go, turned around and started to run. Calm and comfortable.

He liked it. He tried to look aside to see whether the driver followed him. He saw nobody.

He made a turn, around a tree and run back, got to a site and came back on the road again. He got seated in the park. He seemed to be alone. He looked around. He walked back to his bed and breakfast and went to bed.

Chapter 15

John still did not had any idea what was going on.
He could not sleep. Now again there was this
peculiar meeting with Mrs Friender. He could not
believe that it was a coincident. Then there was the
big business at the fitnesscentre. Toko had become
important. People knew that he used to train there.
He must admit that he did not know whether Toko
still trained in this fitnesscentre.
Then there was this taxidriver. He had his orders.
He was obliged to take John with him. Again why?
He knew that he was at the fitnesscentre. Who
knew that he was there. Who knew that he was at
the fitnesscentre at that time. How could they have
known. Were there camera's. Security camera's?
Quite likely. He had not noticed. Who would have
access to this securitysystem. Probably everybody
that knew how to break the code. He did.
Still no answers. Only new questions.
He got fat up with all this. This had to end. He
decided to get to the office of the Lord. He must at
least have some answers. He got out of his bed.
Searched on his tablet to the location of the office of
the Lord. Found it, looked how he could get there
and left the bed and breakfast.
He quickly ran through town. In an hour he stood for
the huge officebuilding. He was not surprised that
only one window was lighted. He counted, stock
eleven. He tried to get in but he needed a pass to

get through a gate. He simply climbed on and over it. No signal, no alarm as far as he could notice. He simply walked to the frontdoor of the building and got in through that frontdoor. He quickly looked around if he saw camera's. There were camera's almost everywhere. He got aside quickly. He walked all along the wall. If they were looking they could hardly see him. The lights were all out. The offices seemed closed. Again he met a passage with gates, only to be passed with a special card. Again he simply climbed over them.

He decided not to take the elevator. He found the stairs and walked up. Here were no camera's as far as he could see. He found it a good training, getting up the stairs. He kind of liked it.

At stock eleven he carefully opened the stockdoor. He looked into a long hallway. It seemed to go all the way to the other side of the building. The elevator was direct opposite the stockdoor. He saw nobody. He saw a camera above the door he had come through. He got sidewards and got quickly into the hallway, so the camera could not spot him. He estimated how far the office of the Lord would be. It was the third window from the end. He calmly walked through the dark hallway. Indeed he saw light under the door of one of the offices. This office was close to the end but not the last one. This must be the right office.

He stopped in front of the door. He listened. He heard a strong female voice. He was surprised. A woman's voice. Could the Lord be a woman? Why not? He listened again. No other voices. It became silent. No voice anymore. He heard a door slammed. He wanted to step aside, but nothing happened. He carefully listened again at the door. No sound. He got a blow on his head and lost consciousness.

He woke up slowly. His head hurt heavily. He wanted to feel his head but he could not. His hands were tied up together. He looked at his hands by opening his eyes slowly. There was a big light directed in his face. He closed his eyes immediately.

"Hallo, at last you are here," a man's voice sounded calm and controlled. " What brought you here. Why are you here?"

John did not answer. He tried to look again but the light was strong for his eyes.

"I was looking for the Lord. I would like to talk with him. I think he can tell me more about myself."

"Why, do you think that?" the man asked.

"I eliminated the options about the responsibility of the explosions on the prisonsite. The Lord was in my eyes the most obvious criminal organisation leader. "

"So all the others were less likely," the man asked.

"Correct," John answered.

"Sorry, your vision is wrong. How do you know that this office has anything to do with the Lord or his organisation?"

"If I understand you right, you confirm that this office is from the Lord, or his organisation. Good to know. "Do you also confirm that the Lord and his organisation had nothing to do with the attack on the prison and do not know anything about me and my history? " John was surprised about this conversation. Someone of the organisation of the Lord talked with him. He did not say much but they talked. That was already a big plus.

"I am sorry, we have no idea what happened there in that prison. You came out of nowhere. We do have tried to contact you and to talk to you and with you, but you did not accepted our invitations, today for instance we had a taxi ready for you but you did not get in."

John noticed a sigh from the site of the man. Could he believe this man?

"Are you the Lord? "he had to know.

""No," the man smiled by the thought. "No, I am only one of the technicians. This is my office, here we have our information centre. That is most likely how you found this address. The real business is not done here. I even do not know where that actually is. I am sorry. Would you be so kind not to tell outside this office that we have this office. Otherwise we have to move out and that costs money. The alternative is to kill you. We do not like killing, we also do not like to attack prisons. We do not want to be visible anywhere. We like to stay out of the picture. Please?"

John was a bit surprised. Was the move out of this office such a big deal? He promised not to tell anybody about this office.

The man asked him to get up. John raised. He was pushed a little bit aside. The light went out and he was pushed forward. He could not see anything. It was dark, his eyes had to get used to the dark. He was surprised. He felt that his hands were made free. He heard a door got closed.

Slowly his eyes got used at the little light that was on the spot where he was. He recognised the hallway and walked back.

He returned to his back and breakfast and got back to his bed.

Was the Lord really not involved in the prisonaffair? He must admit that it did not fit in the policy of the Lord and his organisation as far as he could interpret the vision of the moneycontroller.

He fell asleep.

He was up early. Again all kind of thoughts spoked through his mind. He had a great breakfast. The service was very good. He would remember this home. He collected his bag, did all his things in it and left. He started to run to get to the house of Mrs Friender. He was curious about the house. In his own way this cottage attracted him.

He enthusiastic ran through the forest. He loved this forest. The last part, along the avenue he walked calm and easy. Just looking around. He had a kind of feeling he indicated as "homecoming". He could not describe it otherwise.

He stopped before the gate. He looked through the big steel ornamented port. The large garden was clearly visible. He found it soft and gentle. Several spots with large roses and other flowers all along the gras. At the back he saw a large greenhouse. He was sure that someone really loved gardening. An older man came along the side of the gras towards the gate. He was dressed as a gardener. He had several tools in his trousers to be used for the garden. The man looked surprised to see someone standing for the gate. He greeted John by a nick with his head and walked calm but steady to the gate.

John greeted him as well. He told that he was John Normal and that he had an appointment with Mrs. Friender.

The man looked at him in surprise. "Are you sure that you should be at this address? " he asked frowning his eyebrows.

John picked up the paper out of his pocket with the name and the address on it. He showed it to the man. John asked whether this was the address mentioned on the paper.

The man hesitated. "It could be," he stumbled.

 "I will inform the lady of the house. Just a moment."

He grabbed in his pocket, got something that looked like a phone. He pushed a button and waited. "Hallo milady. I am at the gate and there is a young man standing here who says that he has an appointment with Mrs Friender. Can I let him in? "He listened to the answer. He looked surprised again. "Ok," he said and finished the contact. He put the phone in his pocket and started to tick on his pockets.

John thought that he was looking for the place where he had hidden the keys. He smiled. This man loved gardening but started to forget things.
He liked him.

The man could not find his keys and felt a little panic coming up.

John spoke to him to calm down. Just search carefully and structurally", he asked with an extremely friendly voice and a sweet smile. The man stopped with his agitated search. Stared at John. Nicked with his head and started his search all over again. He quickly found his keys and with a big smile he got them out of his right pocket.

He opened the gate , let John in and closed it immediately again. He looked up and down the road to see if there was anybody looking at him, opening the gate. He turned around and waved to John to follow him. He started to walk to the house.
John smiled and followed him.

The man did not look up or behind him to see if John followed him. He walked on till short in front of the big and broad entrance of the house. There he saw something in a large area with roses. He stopped. Looked sharp to the roses, caught something out of one of his pockets and stepped into the roses and started to get out the dying flowers. He seemed to have forgotten John completely.

John looked at the man and let him be. He really was the addicted gardener. He calmly walked on to the frontdoor. A large step up area was in front of the door. He stepped on it and stopped there.

Mrs Friender new that he was coming so he waited for her to come to the door. He looked around. The gardener really was completely fascinated by the roses and the other flowers.

He heard the door opened. He turned around. A young lady stood in the door.

"Who are you? What do you want?" her voice was sharp and unpleasant.

John immediately hesitated, this voice was shocking. This was absolutely not what he wanted to be nearby. Everything broke down, the nice atmosphere, the sweet garden the fantastique surrounding, even the very nice old gardener. It all was gone.

He sighted, said "Sorry", turned around and started to walk away.

"He, you !!" the sharp voice quoted loud , "You cannot just walk out of me. He you!!"

John just walked on. This was no option. He had been nice and polite. This monster was not interesting to be around. He simply walked to the gate. He could not get out. The gate was closed. The woman came rushing after him. She came at the gate at the same time as John.

"Why are you walking away?" she asked it as if she did not understood his behaviour.

John looked at her. "Good morning," he started the conversation.

"Yea, hallo?" she stumbled.

"I came for an appointment with Mrs Friender, I must have been mistaken. You are not Mrs Friender. I am sorry, could you please let me out? I want to leave?" John looked at her.

"What is this, yes I do believe that Mrs Friender expected a visitor at this time, but not such a snobby loser as you are." She looked at him probably trying to get a reaction from him.

What was she waiting for. John did not liked this conversation. He also disliked this quite unfriendly lady. He lifted one eyebrow, trying to get her in a better mood. He just wanted the gate to be opened. He looked at the old gardener that calmly came their way.

"But, why do you want to leave. You have an appointment, you must keep that. I will inform Mrs Friender about your arrival, OK?" she tried to convince him to follow her back to the house.

He had enough of it.

"Sorry, your behaviour is too much for me. I want to get out now !!"He started to get angry.
"I am sorry, "the old man come in the conversation. "Sorry, sorry, "he said several times. He got the key from the gate out of his pocket and opened the gate.
John looked at him and then to the young woman, said "Goodbye" and wanted to get through the open gate. He felt relieved.
There was just one small point. The old man stood in the gateopening. John could not get out as long as he stood in his way.
"Sorry sir, would you please let me through, you are in my way," John asked politely and with a smile.
"I am sorry" the older man said and smiled to John. "Thank you, Miriam, " he said to the young lady, "You played your roll extraordinary good, you should consider to go to the performance academy. You really are good."
The girl smiled at the old man, nicked to John with a big smile and left through the gate. The old man waved at her and looked at John. He closed the gate and locked again at John.
"I am sorry, sir," the old man said to John, "My name is Leo Friender, I am the father in law of Mrs Friender. She has asked me to be present when you would come. Unfortunately she was occupied. We will meet her later on. Please be so kind to forgive me our little show. Mrs Friender, my daughter in law, Boseley, as she is called, wanted

me to find out what kind of person you are. I must admit that you do look a lot like her lost son, my grandson. He also happened to be called "John". You are a lot more mature than he was and are far more muscled. You do look very strong, John, my grandson was a kind of week in his muscles. He loved to sport but he was not very good in it. He really was extraordinary intelligent, just like his grandfather and his father. " The old man laughter loudly about his own joke.

John understood that he was tested. Boseley, Mrs Friender, wanted the vision of her father in law about this youngster. He could understand the idea of finding out what kind of type she allowed to live on her, or her husbands, premises.

The fact that this man has informed him about the test made him believe that he succeeded the unfriendly welcometest.

The old man, Leo, smiled at him friendly. "Please John, forgive us our unfriendly welcome. I did not know any other way to test your personality. Boseley gave high up from you as a person, though she had to admit that she really did not know very much about you, except that you had lost your memory and were looking for the possibility to be her son. At the moment your bloodtest made clear that you were not her son, you did not even try to change the outcome. You accepted it blindly and left right away. That is honesty. You really were looking for the truth. I must admit that she let her personal feelings for you play a large roll in her way of thinking. She never, really never has given anybody the option to live in this cottage. Her parents have lived here for about three years. They died about a year ago in a car accident. She kept it clean but recently the cleaning have been optimised. Miriam, the girl you have met, works here as cleaning lady. I must admit that she played her roll fantastic. She is really very nice and friendly. I enjoyed her performance very much. You must also forgive her, she had her orders. She is a good girl. Well I do a lot of talking, please tell me if you can forgive me for testing you?"

Leo looked at John.

John must admit that he still liked the man very much. This new position made the whole affair change again.

He was puzzled. He still felt misused and could not forget that so easy.

"I do not know, sir. I must admit that I am not used to be tested in a way you did. A normal conversation about things could have given you also some idea about me. This way of testing is not the way I liked to be treated.

I have to reconsider all this. Would you please let me out. I have to be alone for a while. When I came in, I felt great, I liked it here. Now my mind is twisted.

Perhaps this kind of testing is normal for you and your familymembers, but not for me. "

He looked at the old man. The man was shaken. He was convinced that his story would clear up the whole affair and that was that. He had not considered for one moment that this young man would have doubts about him and his familymembers.

"But.." he sputtered, I have declared it all for you. It was only a test, no more. Please do not make more of it. Come, please let me first, before you decide, show you the house. It is really magnificent. " He looked hopefully at John.

He picked John's arm and pulled him with hm to the cottage. He got the entrance key out of his pocket and opened the frontdoor.

John liked the entrance. They walked through the house. It was not very large but very intimal. There were two bedrooms, one of them was activated as an office. A nice bathroom was combined with the masterbedroom, the other bedroom.

John liked the cottage.

They walked outside, a small part of the big garden was more or less privatised for the cottage. Leo told that he kept the garden in condition, that included this part of the garden. He spend three days a week for the garden.

He himself lived in the left wing of the house, his son and his family stayed in the rest of the house. Most of the time his son and his wife stayed in town in there house where John had been before.

John calmly walked back through the house and to the gate. He asked Leo to open the gate. He would reconsider the offer. He only wanted to know the price of the rent. Mr Frieder, Leo , told him. It was really a very low price for the whole house. John thanked him and left.

Chapter 17

John walked away. He must admit that he was quite disappointed. He also must admit that he loved the place. If the old man had not planned his stupid way of testing him, he would have been grateful to get this spot to live. He did not wanted to walk through the forest. He got the other way. He wanted to find out where this road lead to. Maybe to nowhere but he would notice if that was the case. He sight. A missed opportunity? Did he now leave his place to live because of an old man that wanted to please his daughter in law through a stupid, wrong calculated test. He remembered the astonished reaction of Leo, the old man, when he declared that he wanted to leave. In a way he felt that he found it now more important to hit the old man back than to forget what he had done. Of course, his reaction was a little childes, just as this way of testing. He must smile because of this conclusion. The old man and he were in a way much more alike than you would expect.

John's humour improved a lot. He more and more liked the idea that he was testing the old man now himself. He was curious about what should happen after this. He decided to walk far out, then return to the city, got after dinner to the fitnesscentre and stay the night at the bed and breakfast where he stayed last night. He found it a good plan. He saw again the sunny side of life. He walked through the broad avenue and came at a small village with several very small shops. He liked it.

In the centre there was a very small square with an huge tree. Of course four banks were situated under the tree. Several very old man were sitting there, talking with each other. John could not resist the atmosphere and asked if he might get seated with the men, there were still three open spots.

He got seated and immediately they asked him all kind of questions. It made him realise that he did not know much about himself.

At a certain moment one of the man asked him if he was the helper of Giant Toko, at least he did look like him.

John was surprised about that question. The man thought to recognise him from the television. Regularly there was a short broadcast in which Toko asked everybody to find this man and inform him about where he was.

John smiled. "That is quite possible," he reacted.
"Would you allow me, may I make such a call?" The old man reacted.

"I will only call with your permission. I must admit that I would love that reward that Toko has promised. I would love to see his rematch against Big Pinto. What a fight that was, highly remarkable. I followed both boxers but they were not really superstars, until Big Pinto started to really use his fists. He blow every opponent away. Magnificent.

And then, out of the bleu he got an uppercut that he would never have felt coming. Unbelievably. "
John smiled at the man. He surely was a lover of the boxsport. He might call. John was going nowhere. He stayed in the comfort of the ease between older man. The man made his call. Another man asked him if he lived around here. Somewhere he got a familiar approach.
John said that he seemed to look a little bit like the lost son of Mrs Friender, but he had other blood. He stayed for more than another hour and listened interested to the local problems told by the men. He liked it, the friendliness, the cooperation between al members of the group. He got hungry. He asked if there was a local pub where he could get a bite. They immediately pointed at "the Saloon" right behind the tree.
John got up, thanked them for the very friendly accompanyship and walked to the Saloon.
He found a seat at the window. He looked at the square with the old men on the banks under the tree. He loved the view. This felt good, very good. The waitress came to him . She made a yell. John was shocked. He immediately looked up to the young lady. It was Miriam, the young woman that had welcomed him at the premises of the Frienders house. He understood her reaction. He smiled at her. She trembled. John tried to calm her down. She had had her orders, who was she to refuse her cooperation. John invited her on his table. She

calmed down a little bit. "Aren't you angry on me?" she asked frightened for his reaction.

"Of course not, You played your roll magnificent. Do you play in the theatre, you are really good." John smiled at her again. She really looked a sweet, nice girl.

I must tell you something, Miriam," John said softly on a secret sounding way. I have left the premises. Leo is thinking that I will not come back, which he certainly did not wanted. He wanted me to stay. "

"So did I, "Miriam declared immediately. "You do remind me of "John", the son of the Frienders. Your way of doing, your attitude, you yourself, yes, just like John would have behaved. Selfish on one hand but very sweet on the other way. He hated this kind of testing, Leo should have known." She stopped talking and got in her memories.

John looked at her. She was a nice girl.

"Well," John woke her out of her thoughts, "what is the speciality of the house for lunch. Could you bring me that?"

Miriam, got back again from her memories , said that she would bring The "saloon coupe" a sandwich special from the house.

She walked away and yelled an order to the kitchen. It became noisy in the pub. Many locals came here for lunch. Also the group older man from under the tree came to the saloon for lunch.

It really was very busy in the saloon. It was clearly the meetingpoint for the people living around this small local centre.

John attacked the big sandwich. He liked it. It was a kind of clubsandwich with salmon, cheese, boiled egg and bacon. He had a double coffee with it. He needed some time to finish it. He was sitting backwards, completely filled when he looked outside. A big black limousine rolled gentle to the square with the big tree and the banks under it. The car stopped near the banks at the other side of the square. A man stepped out and closed the car. He looked around. He noticed the Saloon and walked towards it immediately.

John followed the man smiling. He deliberately kept on looking outside so that he was hard to recognize from the inside of the pub.

The man entered the Saloon and looked around. He raised his voice and told his name. he came in the name of Giant Toko. The older man reacted immediately. He walked to them and the older man that had made the call, walked with him to the table of John.

John was still looking outside, doing as if he had not noticed the commotion. Everybody in the pub was looking at the new man and at John. What had that man to do with Giant Toko, the famous boxer?

The man at John's table, tried to get the attention of John.

"Excuse me sir, My name is Tom Droot, I come in the name of Giant Toko. Are you John Normal? John turned to the man and invited him to sit down on his table opposite to his seat.

The man started to smile, "Really, you really are John Normal," he remarked and got seated with an enormous smile.

He looked at John, got a photo out of his pocket and looked again. "You really are," He smiled optimistically. "Sorry for the interruption sit but Giant Toko would like to see you as soon as possible. He says he need you for the next fight? You really are John, aren't you", the man repeated himself still being surprised that he did found the man he was looking for.

John nicked to the man. "Yes I am the man he is looking for, what does he want from me?" John was teasing the man.

The man, Tom, looked at him, puzzled. "Well, sir, I suppose he wants to talk to you, I must admit that I do not know what he really wants from you. I have the order to find you and to bring you to him. That is it, I do not know more. "

"Do you know where he is training these days?" John wanted to know whether he still was active in the fitnesscentre or not.

Tom did not know. "Please come with me, I know where I can drop you so Giant Toko can find you."

"John frowned his eyebrows, "You are going to drop me somewhere and then I have to wait there until

he is willing to come to me on that spot?" John
sounded very surprised. Toko was looking for him
and he had to wait somewhere, No deal.
John smiled at Tom. "Tom, listen. I will not go with
you. If Toko wants to talk to me he must be tonight
at nine o'clock at the fitnesscentre where we met, if
he is not there, I could be here for lunch tomorrow.
Thank you for your visit, you may go, Tom". John
invited him to leave with his hand, stretched out to
the way out.
Tom looked at him. "Sir, do you know that we have
been looking for you for several days now. I cannot
leave without you. I have to fulfil my order. I only get
paid when you really are the man we are looking for
and bring you with me." Tom looked astonished.
"Sorry, you may go. "John had enough of it. Tom
saw no other way than to leave. He walked out the
door of the pub.
John looked at the man through the window. Tom
was immediately using his phone. He did the only
right thing, talk with his boss.
John had seen enough he wanted to leave. He was
surprised when a man stood next to his table.
"Please John, allow me to talk to you, please."
John looked up. Leo stood at his table. He looked
along Leo and saw Miriam looking at him. She
quickly looked away and got to another table. It was
clear. She was loyal to Leo. He found that really
positive. She found it obviously to inform Leo about
his presence in the pub.

"Hallo sir. I thought we were finished talking. Please be seated." John looked at the old man. He preferred to stay polite. He once again found him a nice man. It was a good thing that he came after him. He also must admit that he loved the cottage and the surroundings, the forest, this local mini-centre. He felt at home, for the first time. But he did not wanted this man to have it all too easy with his decision.

"Thank you, John, you give me hope. Thanks again. I will be honest to you, I am sorry about the testingaction, please try to forget it or to forgive me. What is the case. My daughter in law, Boseley is a very strong woman. I like her very much, she has achieved very much in society. Thanks to her my son, Joseph has a fantastic job and makes a lot of money. Thanks to this situation I can live in a part of the house, you have seen. Also thanks to that I do not have to pay any rent. Further I love the garden. I used to be a good businessman myself. I have created a really good company. My two other sons organise it now. They do it very well. I am retired. I love gardening and that is what I prefer to do. I play cards with a group, I play golf, I love traveling around the world. I can now do that all pure for my pleasure. "

John found it a nice story but did not see where Leo wanted to end.

"John, I would love to please my daughter in law, Boseley by telling her that you will consider the option to come and live with us in the cottage. I know that she wants that very much. I must admit that I do not know why she is so fond of you, but I do know that she is. Further I must admit that I like you very much myself. And I am very surprised about that. This has never happened before. I never have followed anyone with a refused proposal. I just do not do that kind of actions. It is not me. But I really want you around. You are so friendly, also for an old memorylosing gardener. Fantastic. The speed within your acceptance of my change from that gardener to a decision maker, was remarkable. Please reconsider your decision and come to live with us. If the money of the rent is a problem, I am prepared to pay the rent the first year. "

He sat back. He had told his story , he had given all his arguments. Now it was up to John to decide. John looked at Leo.

"Leo, there are some points that I would like to have made clear. One, why are you my contact, why is Boseley not here? "

"Sorry, John, she is occupied with her job. She cannot just leave her company at short notice. She always has many appointments. She is active as an accountant, works in a banking system as financial advisor of many companies and is general manager from a bank, her bank. "

"Ok, I understand, "John reacted. "I can understand that her work is far more important than a completely stranger but it still does not declare her good feelings about me. Could you tell me the name of her bank and the location of her office?"

Leo looked at John. He did not seemed to feel comfortable with these questions.

He tried to talk around it but John only looked at him.

"Ok, Leo. Thank you for coming. Please give me any idea when I could talk to Boseley in person. She invited me, I want to speak with her. I will be here for lunch tomorrow. Maybe I will be here for lunch in three weeks from today. She may choose. " John smiled at Leo. "Yes," John continued." This might mean that I will reconsider your offer."

John got up, walked to Miriam and asked for the bill. She said that his bill was already paid for by Leo. John smiled to her and left. He walked to the banks under the tree. The large limousine was gone.

Chapter 17

John felt good. He walked back along the broad avenue, walked along the cottage and started to run through the forest. He did several movements options while running. He almost fell by one of his special moves on one leg with both hands on his head. He had fun again. He raced through the forest and did it again, he was in a good mood again. He took the time to go to the centre of the city. He bought some snacks and water so he always had something to eat. He sat on the bank in the park near the fitnesscentre. He had used this bank before. He found it interesting to look at people going by. Asking himself who the passengers were, what they did for a living, where they were going. Suddenly he heard someone whisper, close to the back of his head. He automatically started to turn around.

"Please sit still. We cannot talk now", the voice hastily asked. "You are being watched from the bankbuilding straight in front of you. I do not know why but I know more about you. We may not been seen together. That would be my end. Can we meet somewhere in the night. Do you see the bank on the left in front of you. I will be there tonight at one o'clock sharp. "

John did not know whether he had heard it all clearly. One way or the other again something unexpected happened. Obviously everybody seemed to know where he was. Why would he be observed from the bank straight ahead of him. He looked forward and indeed there was a large, you may say huge, bankbuilding. John looked at the building but could not see anybody looking out of the window. The bank was too far away. Why should anyone from a bank being extra interested in him. He quickly thought of Boseley, but she would not have time to stare out of the window. Being the bankboss means that you kept occupied by your personnel all the time.

He looked at the bank on the opposite side of the square where he sat now. Those banks were hidden from the bank by a number of small trees. He could not understand why the bank was so important. He did not liked the thought that everybody knew where he was. He started to walk again. He regularly looked around if he found anyone looking at him or following him. He did not. He got out of the citycentre and walked into a new area with al lot of small houses. He passed a small local shoppingcentre and walked towards these shops. He decided to have a coffee at the coffeeshop. All the tables near the windows were taken so he decided to take a table against the wall. He ordered coffee, the young man, that took the order, tried to sell him some drugs but he wanted just coffee.

The coffee tasted well, strong and tasteful.

Suddenly a man got on the chair on the other side of his table.

"Ok, I know that you have recognised me, but just tell me how you did it. " The man stayed with his head down, looking from below towards John with a staring view. He obviously was wearing a large wig, to cover his face as much as possible. He also wore glasses, as far as John could see there was no glass in it.

John had no idea where the man was talking about. "I am sorry sir, I do not think I know you," John simply reacted and looked away.

The man smiled. "I understand your approach. We have met at the apartment with Lia. I am one of her brothers. Now perhaps you can let go the" I do not know" part. Lia was worried about your health. She said that she gave you a phone. She has send you a lot of messages but you never answered. I shall inform her that you are well and alive. May I ask you what your problem is. My sister is a fantastic girl. She can have every man she wants. In spite of all advised she falls for an absolute stranger, an outsider. Awful but no problem. Then he leaves and she does not hear from him anymore. She is capable of killing us all for this. But she is my sister, so please react to her. She might do crazy things to get your attention. Please?"

John was surprised. He really had not thought about her very much the last days and yes she really was a magnificant woman.

"I must admit that she really is a fantastic woman. My problem is that she did not tell me that she was a killing machine. She did not tell me that she was part of a drugssyndicate. There, those are my problems. I do not know if I can cope with that. Your organisation is very well known as the most dangerous, they shot at people that were talking to me. I do not like that at all. Perhaps I have to forget her. She was the finest woman I have ever met. Just tell her I love her but I cannot and will not be part of a criminal organisation. I am sorry."

"Thank you for your honest answer, you are exactly as she predicted and what she feared. I have to be the riskfull informer. She certainly will try to hurt me, but I get used to that. " He got up and disappeared. John stayed behind, disillusioned. He knew this was the trough. He really loved Lia. He really wanted her by his site. But he could not live in a criminal organisation. He saw no solution. It would be almost impossible for her to leave the family for him, he could not ask that from her. He felt sad. He had known this problem all the time since he left her or since she send him away. He did not wanted to think about it. Now it was out in the open and it was the trough. He dried his eyes that had gone wet. He got up, paid for his coffee and walked back to the citycentre. He was in no hurry. He walked calm and easy, even slow. What did he wanted from life? He asked himself. Yes he wanted Lia, but she was out of range. Could he create a circumstance that would solve the criminal problem? He had no idea how such a situation would look like. Leave for another city? That meant for Lisa: leaving the family. He must keep on looking for a solution. He was not hungry. He walked through the park close to the fitnesscentre where he would go round nine. It was still early. He got at the other end of the park to a bank and eat his cold snacks and drank the water he had in his bag.

He went early to the fitnesscentre. He wanted to start with some fitness actions before he might meet Toko. He could get in easy. It was crowded inside. He more or less forced himself through a busy group. He left his clothes and bag in one of the last lockers. He had to wait until he could start with his session. Once started he worked hard for an hour. He enjoyed it. He came a little bit to his rest. He stopped at nine o'clock sharp. He walked to the entrance. Nobody. He looked around. He might have missed Toko. The big man was not very easy to miss but it was still possible. He did not saw Toko. He waited three minutes and left. He made another round with trainingsessions. It had become calmer in the centre. He completed the second session, took a hot shower and got dressed. He found it comfortable to have trained well again. It had been some time ago. He said goodbye to the manager of the centre and left.

He calmly walked to the citycentre. He entered a large hotel that had a casino. He walked around and looked at several games. He could not really felt any excitement for one game. He turned to the bar and ordered a warm snack and coffee. He got seated with his snack at a high seat and looked into the large casino. Many people were playing. He looked at the expressions on the faces. You could see how things were going. He loved it to study those expressions. Suddenly someone got on the seat next to him. He quickly looked at the man, hocked and looked to the players again. It did not took long before he realised that the man next to him was Rico. So he turned to him and welcomed him.

"Hallo Rico," he stated and accepted the hand Rico stretched out to him. He smiled. Rico did look good. John told him so. Rico thanked him for it. He was doing well but wanted to know how John was doing. John told him that he was still puzzling about his past. He had not reached anything. He even was puzzled about his present.

John wanted to know from Rico, how it was possible to stay out of the hands of the police. He was a convicted criminal and had escaped from the prison. Did the police made problems or not? John looked at Rico puzzled.

Rico said that the police was no problem. They were in good compliance with the police. He was safe.

John asked how the promotion in the organisation had come to him.

Rico looked shocked at John. He wanted to know what he knew about that. John told him that the internet gave many information's about criminal organisations. It had stated that Rico's twinbrother was in charge now.

Again Rico quickly looked around. "That is incorrect", was all he said. He had to go. He left, leaving John surprised behind. He must have asked the wrong questions, he supposed. Wat could be wrong about all this. The only thing he could think of was that if the information was not correct about his promotion and about his twinbrother being in charge then the old leader might still be the leader. That made it logic that he was not killed by the explosion in the prison. That indicated that he could have been the one to instruct the gang that fixed the explosions. He must have organised three bodies to be found. His body and the bodies of the two doctors. This could declare very many things that had happened. This did not declare why his apartment was burned down. Could the two affairs be separate actions. Two different goals? One to free the boss of the Wolves. Two to get him leave his apartment. That was a very aggressive way of getting him out. He hoped that the owner had a good insurance to pay for the damage. Why would anyone wanted him out of his apartment. Why could it not be discussed by a cup of coffee? He could not find a good reason why his apartment had to be destroyed in such an extreme way. The other option had been that they really had wanted to kill him and that they were too stupid to notice whether he was inn or not. If that was the case, it still could be a connected case. The destruction of the prison also was completely out of order. The whole complex was destroyed while all they wanted was three man to escape, or actually one man to escape and the other two to be evacuated.

Why had the doctors to die as well. They had no reason, as far as he knew to start a new life. Especially Peter with his two kids. What if they had done things that were not allowed and these things would come out after the liberation of the leader of the Wolves. How could these points be connected. What could the doctors have done in connection to the leader of the Wolves. They were experimenting. Could they have developed something for the leader of the Wolves and had they with the good results created a shot for the leader of the Wolves? That sounded logical. The leader of the Wolves of course first had to test whether the shot really worked as predicted by the doctors. That also mend that if he found that it worked the leader of the Wolves would kill both doctors. They had to be eliminated so they could not create another superman? Were they still alive? Suddenly another thought shocked him. What would have happened with the persons that had been used testing. Of course they had to got lost as well. This would declare a lot. He, or his apartment was shot at to kill him. Rico got away to be sure that he was not involved with him, he was, or had been one of the testpersons. He looked around. This surrounding could be dangerous for him. He got up and walked calmly to the door and left the casino. He sharply looked around if he saw any special attention for him. He could not notice anything of it all. He walked out of the hotel and got back to the park. It was almost twelve o'clock. He still had an hour until his visitor would come to the park. He got seated on the bank as instructed by the secret speaker.

Chapter 18

John waited on the bank in the park. He expected that one of the other prisoners, or perhaps even one of the doctors was his informer. Perhaps he should get more out of sight. Whoever should wanted to hurt him could do so easily. On the other hand, everybody could have killed him if they really wanted to. He stayed on the bank.
In what way the doctors would have changed the Wolf. In what way had he been changed?
Suppose that he was the son of Boseley. He looked like him but had explosively grown muscles. How about other points. Was his mind sharper? Was his reactionspeed better? Could he run longer and faster? Could he raise more weight.
His problem was that he did not knew how these points were before he lost his memory. Good question?
Did the Wolf lost his memory or not. If not than he may have had a later version. If he got a better shot was always the question.
John realised that his whole affair was based on the hint that Rico gave about his position within the Wolves. But just that point was essential for the reconsidering of the whole situation. He wished he knew the facts.
He heard some leaves move behind him. He wanted to look but a gentle voice said not to move.

"Hallo, thank you for coming. You know me, I know you. I am Marion. I could not tell you anything in the presence of my father. Even in the coffeeshop he was nearby. I know that the doctors have not been killed. They have done experiments with more than ten people. Some of them died, some of them had to be killed because they got crazy. You were one of the last testpersons that survived the chemical implants and "medicines" as they called it. I have no idea of the content of the medicines but there were many drugs and forbidden pills in it. These medicines made your muscles grow wildly but had impact on your brain. I think that it was all mend to have a medicine for the person that gave the orders. I do not know him, but he was very wild and strong but more brutal than intelligent. I have not seen him since the attack and our escape. Please never say anything about this ever. I would be killed. Thank you for listening. I have to go."
John heard again some leaves being moved. She still was a murdermachine and extraordinary dangerous if she was against you. But even she was not as fast as a bullet.
His suggestion were very close to the reality, he concluded. He was a person, changed through all kind of experiments.
What could he do with this information. He could better try to find out who the Wolf was and where he was now. He had to be careful. The Wolf was dangerous. He must be a big fighter with all these

new medicines. The Wolves were involved in the casino's, bet offices, bookmakers and al kind of paying games. Perhaps he had to find out something more about remarkable profits. Who were the competition. What big losses had they made lately. He thought about his own win through the fight of Toko. Were there more profits made on boxingfights, or carraces.

Still all these wins would not give him any information about the place where the Wolf would stay at the moment. He looked in his bag for his tablet. He got the helmet out that was in the way. The phone from Lia fell out of the helmet on the ground.

He picked it up. He stared at it. Lia. His hart bonked. She was really the love of his life. He could not forget her. He had pushed her away, far away. She was out of reach for him. She was deep involved in the worst criminal organisation of them all, drugs. He stared at the phone again. It would not harm to activate the phone and to see what she had to say to him. He activated the phone. He had about twenty calls missed. He found ten mails. He started to read them. She regretted that she had send him away. She could not mis him. She got honest in her sixth mail. She was a killingmachine. She really could fight as the best. She had automatically used her abilities when they were attacked by the kidnappers. She could not let them kidnap him.

She understood that he did not wanted any contact with her, now that he knew that she was dangerous. In a bad moment she could easily kill him. Of course she never would do that. She loved him far too much for that. She hoped that the one night together might change his mind. She was willing to leave her family for him. " Please contact me", she finished each of the mails with that sentence.
He decided to let her know that he missed her too. "Hallo Lia, I miss you. I am also afraid of you. I do not know if I can leave you again when I meet you. I know I hopelessly love you but I do not know if I can ask from you to leave your present world and start all over somewhere else with me. I am puzzled"
He did send the mail away. What had he done. He had created a problem. For himself but also for Lia. Why did he had to do this. Just try to forget her. He tried to print himself in. That was the best way. Forget her.
He tried to get his thoughts on other objects but that was difficult. He had to think about his meetings today. He had a double lunchappointment. One with Toko, the other with Boseley. They probably would not come, either of them. He felt tired and wanted to sleep. He would try to find a hotel. He had to be up in time tomorrow.
Suddenly a loud noise was heard. A kind of heavy motor was crossing through the park. John listened to the sound. This really was a strong motor with a magnificent sound. He did not know why but he

loved the sound. He had the idea that he felt the wind blow through his hair. He sat back and enjoyed the sound. Suddenly the sound came towards him. He looked and got sitting right up. A big motor really come around the corner of the park. A rider completely dressed in a hard yellow motorsuit, came full speed his way. He got careful. Before he could do something the motor was at him and stopped with peeping brakes and slipping tyres. The speed was too high to stop in front of him but two meters further the motor stopped.

John prepared himself to defend his life. The driver looked at him, made a horrible cry, jumped of the motor that immediately fell aside and jumped on John. He was not prepared for someone to jump at him so he catch him carefully but strongly.

"John," the driver cried out. It was a woman.

"Lia" he recognised her. He grabbed her, got her helmet of and kissed her.

Oooh, he felt good. This was worth everything.

Lia crawled close to him and kissed him back furiously. It was a long and intense kiss.

Lia only said "Come", picked up her helmet and got her motor right up again. John got his helmet out of his bag, hang his bag on his back, did his helmet on and jumped at the back of the motor.

He moved against her back and grabbed her and pressed himself against her body.

"Aah, yeeeh," she grumped , started the motor and raced away.

John loved the wind through his hair. He loved feeling her body pressing backwards against his body. This might last forever.

John had the impression that Lia loved motorriding as much as he did. He did not know why but he loved it. Because of the full speed Lia was driving, they quickly completed the ride to her apartment, in spite of the fact that she had been riding on a big broad boulevard several times up and down that road.

She parked the motor in a special private box. They got up to her apartment and loved each other almost the whole night. They could not get enough of each other.

In the morning they got up late. Lia had to go to her ballettraining and John remembered that he had two appointments at the Saloon. John had to promise that he would be back the end of the afternoon. John promised and said that they had to talk with each other about their future.

Lia left and John walked happy and in a good mood to the Saloon. He ran the whole distance, took an extra round through the forest and finished on one of the banks under the tree in the centre of the small community just along the road.

Everybody welcomed him. They were curious if Toko had contact him. John had to deny that. He had made an option to meet him yesterdayevening or today at the Saloon for lunch. He had not seen him yesterday, so the second option was that he would come to the saloon for lunch.

All man were very interested to see whether Toko would come. They did not believe he would show up.

John stayed with the group until he found it time to enter the Saloon for his lunch. He went to the same table where he had been the day before. From there he could look out of the window and overlook the whole square. He loved the view. He felt welcome in this neighbourhood.

Miriam had no duty, so another girl took his order and brought him a little later a large fruit salat, as he had ordered. It tasted good. He finished with a cup of coffee. He looked at his watch. It was almost half past one. Almost end of lunchtime. He decided to wait till two o'clock. That was really for him the end of the lunchtime.

He looked out of the window and saw a motorrider, all in black, entering the square. Could Toko drive a motor? The driver actually stopped close to the big tree in the centre of the square. He looked around and saw the Saloon. He turned and parked his motor in front of the saloon. He got in and did his helmet of. Indeed it was Toko.

The old men-group immediately yelled at him. He stepped towards them, asked who had given the call and handed the man a small package. He turned around and came to John.

He had seen him when he came in. He got seated opposite to John and shaked hands.

"Hallo John, here I am. I am a little bit late but here I am. Good to see you again. Thanks for your perfect assistance during my last fight. You really hit the bonus. He did not saw that uppercut coming. Whoooo what an experience. I owe you one. Well than, why I have tried to contact you is that we had a deal. I would pay you half the profit when I would win or lose. So I owe you € 200.000. Please give me your bankaccount so I can decently pay you. Of course," he went on direct " I would like to make the same deal with you for the next fight. I really need you, your way of boxing is what I want to learn. This Big Pinto is not the end but only the beginning. If you learn me how to approach boxers, opponents, I can maybe even became worldchampion. "

John saw him explode in glory with the idea of becoming worldchampion.

"Toko, Nice try. We only made a deal about the first fight if I would help you out for a few days. If you could postpone the fight with four weeks, then the proposal was to pay me half the prizemoney. You have already paid me for the first days. The two grand are yours, " he looked at Toko. This was what they had discussed and approved.

"That is right John but," Toko looked at John "we did not made a deal about you helping me during the fight. You couched me during the fight without a deal. So I want to reward you for that. I must admit, honestly, that it would help you to help me with the next fight and perhaps even the fights after that under the same conditions. Please".

John smiled at Toko. He really was a good negotiator to go for his really wanted goals.

""Sorry Toko, I cannot accept the two grand for just assisting you during your first fight in my presence. I am willing to accept your second part of the deal, but you may only give me a bonus for my role in the first fight of € 50.000. That is really very well paid. "

Toko almost jumped up. "You do it, you accept. John you are fantastic. Please give me your bankaccountnumber so I can pay you your bonus." John showed him his bankcard and Toko caught his phone and typed in all kind of things.

Toko glanced. He passed the bankcard back to John and informed him about the location where he did train nowadays. The fitnesscentre was far too crowdy. He now trained at a private location. He asked John his phonenumber so he could send him the address. John gave him a paper and a pen, so he could write it down. Toko looked at him surprised. No phone? I will get you one, no problem."

"Wrong, Toko. No phone. I will stay free when I am not on the job. We will keep it this way for the time being. "

Toko shaked his head. "You must come along with all these new things, be modern, young man." He looked at John, smiled and wrote down the address.

He handed over the paper and the pen.

"Normally I start my trainings at nine in the morning. I do first some fitness on trainingstools, than I have a lunch. In the afternoon I have my boxtraining on the sack and the small ball. After that I train in the ring. At night I stay calm and visit what disco's for dancing." He smiled broadly by the last words.

"Ok, Toko. As you know I think you have to train on other actions. I will be in your trainingsarea, every afternoon. When is your next fight, against Big Pinto, I presume?"

"My next fight is in three weeks at the SuperArena, here in town. There is a large starting programme. Our fight is planned for 10.30 in the evening and will run for twelve rounds. That is extraordinary lang. I have never had a fight over twelve rounds."

John heard some hopelessness in his voice.

"Really John you must help me to overcame such a fight. This is outrageous. I do not understand that my wife accepted that. She is my manager. Why don't you became my manager? I think you would not have accepted such a long fight."

John smiled. "Toko. We will make it a short fight. If needed you will need an extraordinary condition. Big Pinto, if he still is up after five rounds, will be surprised. "

John felt that Toko needed this kind of words. He must get convinced of his own qualities. Of course he needed a lot of conditiontraining.

They shaked hands and John promised to be at the trainingsarea round two o'clock tomorrow. Toko left enthusiastic. Waved to the group older man and left the Saloon, climbed on his motor and raced away. John felt good with this deal. He controlled his bankaccount. The € 50.000 really was paid on his account. He must be honest. He was happy with Toko and the luck he had being so close to this man.

Chapter 19

John had to smile. For the time being he found that
he had done it all very well. He must admit that he
was a bit surprised about his knowledge of boxing.
He must find out what he could do himself in boxing.
He was still thinking about Toko when he saw a
very old woman on a very old bike coming down the
road. John had the idea that the lady could fall of
the bike any moment. Not that the bike was broken
but the speed the lady used to come forward was
extreme low. He looked at the moves of the old
lady. She really seemed to have problems in getting
the wheels go round. Suddenly she fell aside.
Immediately, surprisingly quick she got up. She
brushed her coat with her hand to get the dust of
and looked around to see if anyone had noticed
what had happened. She did not seem to see John
sitting behind the window in the Saloon.
She took the bike by the hand and walked to the
Saloon. John smiled. He found it brave for such an
old lady to try to use a bike for transport. Walking
would certainly be a lot safer for her.
John was surprised to see the lady putting her bike
on the standard and entering the Saloon. The bike
was not locked now, so everybody could take it
away. The lady walked with a big curve in her back.
She walked into the Saloon. Because she had the
curve in her back and she was wearing a really big

hat her face was hardly visible. She suddenly stretched out. Looked around in the saloon, saw were John was, got back in her curve and walked to John.

The group older man got up, greeted everybody and walked out with a lot of noise, talking among each other about their meeting with Giant Toko.

The older lady sat down opposite to John on his table.

"Hallo John, here I am. You wanted to see me Leo stated. "

John had already expected to see Boseley in the older lady. Who else would be hiding herself as she did, just to visit him without being recognised.

"Hallo Boseley, may I call you Boseley?" John started intime but formal.

"Ok, John," she smiled.

"Thank you Boseley, also thank you for coming. Please do not be angry with me but I had expected to meet you when I was to visit the location. I must admit that I do not like it to be left as a not interesting piece. That is how I felt. You were not there. I thought You, yourself had made the offer to let me rent the cottage. Therefor I would like to hear from you how you see the future in connection to the cottage. What are the conditions, how long is the rental period, is water and electricity included, who pays the costs for repair if something is wrong at the cottage?"

Boseley sight, "I must admit that I have never thought about these things. Just let us say that if there are major things wrong, you tell me or Leo about it. We will always solve the problem. Your cottage will be part of the cleaning of the premises. That means that we will keep the house clean. Once a week Miriam or someone else will be there for a whole day to clean the cottage, do the wash, the ironing if necessary etc. etc.. You must pay the rent. Leo will give you the payment details. Ok?" She looked at John.

John still had a fabless feeling about her. She must be special. He thanked her for coming and wanted to know when he could get in.

She smiled wide out at him. She touched his hand and said: "Welcome, I am very glad that you have accepted my invitation. It feels good to have you as our new user of the cottage."

"Well, I have to go back. Thank you. As soon as you feel settled please come to the house for a dinner or lunch. Leo will always be around. My husband and I are very busy people, Leo will be your contact. "

She got up stretched her hand out to John. He also got up, shacked her hand and smiled to her.

She walked out in het curved way of moving. Once outside she got on the bike and moved speedily up the road. No sign of slow riding, she really made a race out of it.

John had to smile. He got up and paid his meal and left. He speeded his ran up and came quickly at the cottage. He walked to it and felt on the large trees right in front of the cottage. The parts between the trees were filled with wooden poles. He could not see or feel the house. He walked to the gate and saw Boseley biking to the back of the big house. Here he could see the cottage. He really loved it. Enthusiastic he started to run again through the forest, and back to the apartment of Lia. He had no key, so he called at her number. She was not yet in, so he walked to the park on the other side of the street. He got seated on a bank and picked up his bag from his back. He found that he had the option to buy a motor now. On the other hand, he preferred to have Lia ride, so he could hold her against his own body, really far more likable than each on his or her own motor.

He got the paper out of his pocket where Toko had noted the address of his gym and looked where it was. It was quickly found. The street was completely on the outside of the city. An area where John had not yet been before, as far as he did remember. He would look around there early in the morning.

He looked around in the park. It was calm in the park. He heard a motor coming his way. He got up and walked to the border of the park. Indeed Lia came on her motor and got into the parking area of the building. She saw him and waved enthusiastic at him. She parked the motor and came to the front of the complex. John was there waiting for her. They kissed and got into the building.

They drank a glass of wine together. John liked it. They had to talk. He told Lia that he loved her very much but that he had one problem. She was a killing machine member of a criminal organisation. He did not wanted to know how many man and/or woman she had already killed for the good of the company. He did not know whether he could live with a wife with that occupation now and in the past. He was honest about himself. He did not know where he came from or who he was. He was really muscled and he could run rather long in a high speed. He could not compare these things because he had never measured it or compared it with himself out of the past or with others in the present. He found it difficult to force her to leave her family, he also did not know whether the family would accept her stepping out of the organisation.

Lia said clearly that she was willing to let her family go. She of course had to bring this very carefully so there would not exist any trouble out of it. They had to realise that the organisation was capable of solving the situation by killing John. That could not be the solution.

John told that he had accepted a job as trainer for a boxer and that he had found a home for himself. It was a cottage just outside town.

Lia congratulated him with both successes. They decided to live together in the weekends and separate during the week. So they could still be together regularly but they would not be disturbed by each other's work.

Lia found this workable for the time being. Luckily it was Friday today so the weekend was there, only she had to work tomorrow she had a last try out in the afternoon and a real performance that evening. They both had to laugh about the situation. John told that he had made also an appointment for tomorrow afternoon and that he wanted to clean up his new home and to see whether he needed extra furniture or that everything was available jet. He anyway had to fill his refrigerator. There would be nothing in it now.

So they would see each other again tomorrow night around midnight.

They went out for a big pizza, got to the cinema for a lousy movie and got home round midnight. They made love and slept well.

It was late before they had finished their breakfast. Lia had to go, so she could be in time for the try out. John also left and walked to the other side of the city. He walked along the building in which the trainingscentre of Toko would be. There was no sign outside. John was a little surprized and puzzled. He stepped in and asked at the reception whether there was a sportingcentre in the building. The receptionist had no idea. He had never heard of it. John found that he looked as if he was not allowed to say that there was such a centre. He understood such a position, if it was the case.

It was early, so he got out and walked around. This was a different area. Many high officebuildings made the basic view one of a big city. The high buildings were surrounded by a lot very small, old-fashioned looking, but newly built small houses. There were several small shoppingcentres. He had the impression that all of these centres looked alike. Modern and with no special looks. Concrete and concrete. He found it a little bit depressive. He ate a small lunch at a sober coffeeshop. The surrounding did not promoted his appetite.

By the time that he was expected by Toko he returned at the building where Toko should be. He got in, looked at the number where he was expected and took the elevator. He had to go to the sixteenth floor, almost at the top. He stepped out of the elevator. There was a large open area. He looked around. The right housenumber was on the right side of the square. He walked to the frontdoor and ringed the bel.

The door was opened by a young lady. She looked at him, waiting for him to tell why he called at her door.

"Hallo, my name is John Normal, I was supposed to be here at this moment. " He looked at his watch to notice the time.

"Yes, Mr Normal, I will accompany you to the right place. Please wait a moment, I will come back to you. "She closed the door.

John did not liked this. He was supposed to go to his job in a normal way, no unexpected happenings. Indeed she came back at him. She wore a leather suite.

"Please follow me. The first time you need to know the rules to get in. "

John did not liked this way of secrecy. The young lady walked to the other side of the square. She stopped at the opposite door. She asked John to come closer. She tapped in a special order on the door and a small camera came down from above the door. She showed his face to the camera, moving the camera manual. She scanned both his eyes and returned the camera up. A small panel appeared on the door. She had John place his right hand on it. He felt a little tickling on his hand. She let him move his hand away from the panel. He had to step back and then return again to the door. The camera came down, looked at his face, scanned his eyes and again the panel appeared on the door. He placed his right hand on it and the door gave a click and moved sidewards away.

The young lady invited him in but stayed outside herself. She wished him luck and left.

John was surprised. He expected a motorride because she was wearing a leather motorsuite. He walked through the door. He entered a small room.

The door closed immediately after him. In front of him another door opened. He walked to the door. Behind the door he saw a large office. He walked further. The door closed direct behind him. It was very silent in the office. Only two of the ten computer workspots were occupied. The two did not look at him, they kept on working on the computer. He had no idea what he was doing here. He looked aside. He noticed another door. On the door was a large sign. "Sportscentre" it said.

He expected to find something there, so he walked to that door and opened it. He came in a small corridor. To the right was the dressingroom for men, to the left for women. The signs were clear. He got through the door on the right. He did not liked this kind of games. He came in an empty dressingroom. He went to the door at the opposite side. As he more or less expected this door gave entrance to the training area.

A large but low gym was in front of him. Toko was busy cycling. He yelled at John. He stopped and came to him. He gratulated him with his appearance. It was good that he was here. John did not found this very attractive. This way of isolate training was not what he had in mind.

Toko smiled happy at him. "Welcome, in my little trainingscentre. I have rented the whole space for a month, so we can do what we want. All needed attributes are available, as you can see. Shall we begin with your way of training/"

He looked hopeful at John.

John asked him for his trainingsschema as Toko would have trained without John.

Toko looked surprised at him. He had no schema, he would train al the normal things, the big bag, the small bag, the ball all to strength his fightingspeed and to strength his blow. "What more was there to do?"

"Your condition, your moves, how about those?" John asked.

"Well, John, that is why you are here. How do we train that?

"Well I think we should start immediately. In the morning you train in here, for the time being we will go outside. Running and learning how to move. "

"Outside?, no John, I stay inside. This area is where it all must happen. " He found it clear. Toko stayed inside.

John looked surprised at Toko.

"Why?" he simply asked.

"I do not want all the people staring and following me. That is heavy enough if I go shopping, I do not want them around all the time. I want to train as we want and I think we do that the best here in our own territory. "

John did not agree but had no real alternatives. He started to run around the area. Toko had to follow. He moved sidewards, right and left, he moved with two feet together and on one foot, first left than right. Toko followed. John speeded up. Toko could not follow. They trained moving by standing opposite each other and stretching one hand at the time. Toko had to touch Johns hand as he stretch it. Then they trained it with two hands. Suddenly John moved both his hands at one time. Toko missed it completely. They trained these options until Toko was to tired.

They took a rest.

John also tried to learn Toko to move his feet faster. He had to train all the moves and handtouches together.

John found that Toko had to learn a lot. His fists were really very strong. His hits on the big bag were impressive. Now he had to learn to create the options to get space at the defence of his opponent. Toko found it enough for today.

Toko informed John that he normally did not train in the weekend, just a little running and hitting the bag. They agreed that Saturdays and Sundays were days of.

John left. He took a shower and walked back to the apartment of Lia.

Chapter 20

He still did not wanted to get in. He tried in the park to find out where the balletperformance would be held. He found what he was looking for. A local theatre, "the Performance" had a balletshow tonight. He looked where this theatre was, found the address and the location on his tablet. He walked to the theatre, ate a large Chinese meal and took some time to give his stomach rest. He was early. He looked at the promotionsigns for the ballet but did not saw any recognisable figures, Lia was not mentioned and not visible at the faces shown. He walked back to a small park nearby.

How logical was his thought that she really was a balletdanser. Had she not meant that she had to go to her work as killingmachine.

He must have been very naive to think that a killer could work as a balletdanser. Why was he so stupid to not understand what she did for her work. She also must keep her body in condition. She must train. He had to keep up with her and with Toko. He should be more clear to activate his own body. He did not know what he could do. He started to make , in the park a number of boxing moves. He liked it. Toko had a magnificent hard blow. He had to train it as well. Toko had to learn to take blows from Big Pinto. He had to train that as well. He also started to swing his arms and his legs, moved his feet and his hands. He liked it. He took a short brake and sat on one of the banks.

He was no longer interested in a balletperformance. He decided to visit his new home. He could see if he needed things for in the house if he was allowed to use it anyway.

He started to run, got through the forest and ended in front of the gate. It was getting dark. He tried to see how he could get the attention of anyone so they could let him in. He found something that he indicated as a sort of bellbutten. He pressed the button and waited. No reaction as far as he could see. Well, he had to come back on daylight. There must be a way to get the attention of anybody. Suddenly he saw a movement on the right side of the garden, close to the trees on the side. He recognised Leo. He was glad that Leo was his contact. Leo reacted enthusiastic. He got through the gate and closed it behind him.

John looked surprised at him.

Leo smiled at him. He embraced John to his surprise.

'Welcome, John. I am so glad that you accepted the offer. I have been waiting for you. Come, I will show you your way in."

Leo got along the gate and walked to the second tree on the side of the cottage. He stopped, smiled at John and got in his pocket. He got a key out of his pocket and put it in a small hole in one of the broad poles between the two trees. He turned the key and pushed against the pole.

John looked surprised at Leo's actions.

Leo had opened an invisible door, or a visible number of poles that formed a door. Leo stepped through the door and invited John to follow him. They came right in front of the frontdoor of the cottage. John noticed that the fence of the gate was enlarged to the wall of the cottage right behind the frontdoor. He could not get to the premises that route was closed by the fence.

"Yes John, Boseley found it better that your guests could not just ren around on her premises. So she already had ordered all the material and I had to make this fence yesterday. It is not very strong, so just see it as a visual border. Here this is the key for your outdoor between the trees, were we just came through. The same key is for the frontdoor of the cottage, try it yourself. I will only enter the area of the cottage on your invitation. I must admit that Miriam and her team does have entrence permission to keep the internal clean. I will keep the garden decent, if you do not mind. I love to see the garden in the right condition, so also here around the cottage."

John found it all perfect. He thanked Leo and invited him to visit him regularly. He would light the frontlamp at the frontdoor, also at daylight, if anyone was welcome.

John let Leo out through the outdoor, closed the door again and entered his cottage. The lights were working ok. He calmly walked around. It was outside already dark now, so he did not enter the garden. He looked in the refrigerator. Empty. So he had to buy all foot and other things, like coffee, thee, wine etc. he better make himself a list. He looked at the sleepingroom. There was a large bed. It looked great. He like it all. Also the bathroom was great. He even had a bath and a large walk-in shower. He thought he did not had to buy any furniture. He was glad with this cottage. Monday morning he would be back with food. He got out, put the key in his pocket and started to run back to Lia's apartment. Tomorrow was a whole day free. Sunday. He already enjoyed the idea.

He spend more time on special moves. If he wanted Toko to learn these moves he had to control them himself perfectly. He made the moves more and more complicated. He found that he really was very well in condition. He also could make these complex moves easy. He tried to combine the various moves, make a complete turnaround in the air and make a roll over his head at the same time. Quite complex but he knew how to do it. He got very fast through the rather dark forest, only at the beginning with enough light and at the end he made these special trainingsactions. He walked out of the forest. He felt good. He ran through town towards the apartment of Lia. He kept on making moves in the park opposite to her flat. There was rather much light in the park. He only regularly looked whether the light in the apartment of Lia went on.

It became later and later. Round midnight he went to the apartment, although it was still dark in the apartment, he rang but no one answered. She was not in. He left again.

He tried it again at two o'clock in the night. Still no light on and no answer.

There must have gone something wrong. Her balletperformance might have had a not-planned end. He got worried. She could have got badly heard. He got to a bank, picked up his tablet and looked if there was news in the city about something with a bad result. He found something about a fight in the northern part of the city. Several people were badly wounded. The newsbulletin insinuated that there might be a problem between two large criminal organisations.

This was new. Normally the big four kept all the others under control together. If they got problems with each other, there could easily grow a war. That would be a disaster for the city.

John read it with a growing bad feeling. If Lea was involved in this fight. She could be badly hurt. That could explain why she was not back. It really was the only declaration for her not being here. Of course she could also have had a trafficaccident but that was not her style.

He searched for trafficaccidents but found nothing
of the kind.
He really got worried. He did not know what to do.
He tried to find a policereports of the fight, but there
was nothing yet.
At three o'clock he decided that she would not get in
this night. He walked back to his cottage and went
to bed there.

Chapter 21

John slept bad. He had expected his first night in his cottage to be a pleasant one, for instance together with Lia. Now he had to fear the worst. If Lia had been involved in a fight. In a real heavy fight, she could have been badly injured, maybe even worse. He could not sleep. Over and over again he thought back at her, at her laugh, at her jumping lifestyle, her enthusiasm. He missed her already.
He had bad dreams.
He got up early. He felt bad. He had nothing to eat, so he left. He walked back to town, bought some crackers and water in the sundayshop and ate it without tasting it.
He went to Lia's apartment and called on the door. No response. He tried it again. Again no reaction. He walked away. What could he do.
He walked back to the park at the opposite side of the apartment of Lia.
He again got to a bank and sat down. He grabbed his tablet and looked whether there was more information available about the fight from last night. On local social media was a large story about the problems from last night. It all happened in a large entertainment centre, called "the boxing match". This was a meeting centre for all boxing fans. Half way the night a well-known boxer was mentioned a small fighter. Half an hour later the young girl did

this again. The boxer got very angry and hit her straight on her face. She had not expected that he would hit her. She was knocked down completely. One of her group got so angry that he tried to hit this boxer himself. In no time the whole centre was one big fighting crowd. The barman immediately called the police and an ambulance. It took the police about twenty minutes to get there and only five minutes to get the whole crowd down with their teasers. At least twenty persons were brought away per ambulance. Most people got out as soon as they could. It was not clear who were the wounded people or how bad they were hurt.

From the police there was no information.

John tried to find out where the ambulances had brought the patients. He could not get that information. Then he tried to collect information about the hospitals around the spot where the fights had taken place. There were two hospitals in that part of the city. He tried to find information about patients. He really had to break in in the systems. He first tried to search under unknown patients. In one hospital he found three patients, only one was brought in last night. He found the personal information. It was a man. In the other hospital there were even seven patients with no name yet. Three of them were woman. He decided to bring a visit at that hospital. He collected the roomnumbers where these three female patients were.

He found the hospital at his tablet and walked towards it. He took a quick bite during his walk. He started to feel better now he could do something.

He found the hospital. It was very crowdy. It was Sundays visithour. John just walked in and got to the first patient on his list. It was an older lady. The second was a young woman but not Lia.

The third patient was Lia. He looked at her. She was still unconscious. John looked through the window in the door. He looked around and got in. He sat down at the chair next to her bed. He looked at her. Her face was partly covered with a bandage. At the side of the bandage her skin looked blue. John got up and looked a little bit closer. She must have been the one that had had the first blow. What was she doing there. Why was she there. Was this her balletperformance. He did not feel well. It was clear she had fun with her friends. He did not belong to that group. He was only her lover. He felt hopeless. He decided that he did not belong in her life. She had a complete other interest. He put her phone, the phone that she had given him, on the table next to her bed.

He left the room. A nurse noticed him and asked him if he knew the patient. John told her her name and address. He did not know more.

He left the hospital and walked back to the forest close to his cottage.

He sat down on a bank at the entrance of the forest.

He realised that he had to say good bye to Lia. She was far too different. She had to live her life. He had to start his own life. What did he expected of his future. What did he know about his past. He still had found nothing about himself. Where should he possibly find something. The doctors. They must know more. They knew everything about his past. Where had they gone. They would contact him. Was that so? Could they contact him?

Suppose that also the leader of the Wolves really was not dead, what could that mean. Suppose that he was the man that had organised the explosions at the prison. What could have been his purpose. What could he have tried to achieve with those explosions. Must he be dead for the world, or for his own people or only for the government? He remembered that Rico gave the impression that someone else than his brother was in charge of the Wolves. Who else than the old leader could be that. Suppose that that was the case. Suppose that the old Wolf had arranged the whole explosion at the prison to have himself declared dead. Suppose that had worked, what then. What could he gain by that position. If he was declared dead, than he could not be made responsible for things that would happen. So what could he tried to achieve. He could take over other criminal organisations? He was active in the gambling world. Could he take over the banks, the business of the Lord? Not very likely. Could he take over the world of James, the drugs? Also not

very likely. The major, kidnapping, the black market? He could not believe it. No that was not what was very likely as target. He could not find another argument. Without a target it was difficult to make it logical to get yourself declared dead. What could be the roll of the doctors? In the earlier suggestions the doctors had no roll. The doctors had made all kind of forbidden experimental chemicals to be tested on people. They had given him all kind of chemicals. What could these "medicines " have done with him. He remembered what Marion had told him. They had given him all kind of "medicines". He was the result. He was the only one that survived al the tests. What had it changed. His body, his mind, his physical options, his knowledge? He could believe that it did something with his body. He was a good fighter, he had a remarkable condition and was very flexible. He had tested that with his moves, yesterday. He knew much about boxing. He maybe should try to find out whether he really was a good boxer. He never had seriously thought about fighting himself. He did not know whether he would like that.
On the other hand a very good boxer could make a lot of money. Toko had made four grand with his win. When he would win the next game against Big Pinto, he would even win a million. That really was a lot of money.

He had to find out if he wanted a boxingcareer or not. He would visit a boxingschool to ask their opinion.

It was getting dark. Sunday was coming to an end. He had to eat something. He went back to the sundayshop, bought some bread, milk and filling. He walked back home at his cottage. He must admit that he really felt as coming home. He kept the frontlight out, he needed no visitor now.

He ate and watched television. During the late night news there was a small item about the fight of last night. No details, only the scene was shown. The police did not give any information in the interest of the investigation.

John went to bed. He needed rest. His mind was not very restful. He slept bad, again, just like last night. He did had rest now that he knew that Lia indeed had been involved in the fight. She was in a coma in hospital. The whole affair was awful, but he felt left outside. He had to learn to accept it. That was difficult, very difficult.

John got up early. He felt bad. He tried to get himself in a better shape by doing difficult training activities. He had a sandwich and started a heavy run through the forest, several times over. He had no rest. He started going to town early. He must be at Toko 's training at two, so he went to his trainingscentre and ate a bite in the neighbourhood.

Two o'clock sharp he got in. Again two spots at the computercentre were occupied. The rest was empty. He went into the trainingscentre and Toko greeted him enthusiastic. He had great news. John was surprised. Great news, What could that be?

"John, have you heard about the fight last night in the boxing club?" Toko asked, still very enthusiast. John looked at Toko. What could Toko had to do with that affair? Was he there as well? Was he one of the "well known boxers" that had been involved in the fight?

"Do you know what has happened there? My opponent, Big Pinto was there. He was the well-known boxer, where everybody talks about, that was insulted by some young girl. He blow her away and was hit himself badly. He is in hospital. This means that our fight in almost three weeks cannot go on. The fight is off"

John was surprised. If the fight was of, than that was no good news. Their trainingsagreement might be off. This was an option they had not talked about.

"But..."John started to say.

"No, wait, there is more. " Toko continued still extreme enthusiastic. "Next week there would be a fight between Big Buster, the worldchampion and Great Grover, his opponent. Well, Great Grover was also involved in the fight last night. He is seriously hurt and cannot fight next week. Isn't that great, at last my time has come". Toko kept on talking.

John could not follow Toko 's enthusiasm.

"I am going to fight against Big Buster next week. Com on we have to train, we only have one and a half week, ten days left. I have to be ready. This is it, this is where it was all about. My wife is fixing the last details, come on we have to prepare me. Come on"

John stared at Toko. Toko was going to fight for the worldchampionship in ten days!!! He was not ready, with his condition being the same as last time.

He asked Toko, Toko confirmed. He was pure enthusiastic, he could not think about anything else. Slowly the new situation got into his brain. He did not quite found a place for the remark "This is where it was all about", but a fight against the worldchampion, that really was something.

He realised that he did not knew the present champion so he asked Toko whether he had movies of the fights from the present champion. Toko confirmed and told him that the two men at the computers where collecting that information at the moment. At that very moment one of the young men came in and told that he had made a compilation of the fights of Big Buster. He wanted to play these on the big screen on the wall in the trainingscentre. Toko found it "perfect" and started to look at the wall even before the young man had started the programme. The movie was played. John and Toko looked interested at the moving pictures, gave their comments on the way of boxing. The man was strong and great. He had the same size as Toko, in a way they looked like each other. They found that he was not very quick on his feet. Training the moves could be important. The left blow was even heavier than his right one. He always first moved his head and then his body, that gave his opponent time to get him. His chin was always good covered so the eyes most be closed down, by repeated blows on his face. Because of the heavy beats Toko had to be away extra fast. They decided to train on Toko 's condition because he had to be quick in and out and on the fast blow to the head.

John tried to hit the big sack and the ball as well. He felt comfortable. With this activity. He really hit the sack hard. He also trained with Toko, to learn him to get fast in and out and still give a hard beat on the head. He moved his head quickly away, he did not wanted to catch a blow for his head. He trained Toko also with his speed. He was very much faster than Toko. So he ticked Toko on his head and on his body and moved away. Toko was just far too slow to follow John's moves. Then they trained just to block the blows from his opponent. Toko has to be fast enough to get his glove for the blow from his opponent or to move away, or forwards but away from the glove from the opponent. Especially the step or the bodymove forward could be very surprising for his opponent and very threatening if he combined it with a blow from himself. The uppercut was a willing activity. He had beaten Big Pinto with it therefore Toko liked that move very much.

John trained him to make showmoves, to find out how the opponent reacts on them. He had to notice this all very closely.

John also trained himself. He wanted to be a lot faster than Toko. Toko had a very tough blow but he was a little bit slow. You could see every beat coming. He blocked them all easy.

He started to move around Toko to activate him to move as well. Then they ran around the room to increase the condition of Toko.

Toko was very active and certainly motivated to do his best to improve his fightingcapacity.

At the end of the day John took a shower and said goodbye and left. He had the impression that Toko had no part in the fight at the boxingcentre the night before. He had been very quick in his reaction to take over the fight with the worldchampion. Still he had no reason to think he was involved. He must admit that it was very peculiar that both these boxers were involved and injured.

He ran through the city, promoting his condition. He also trained the boxing and fighting speed. He felt surprised that he liked it. He thought that he was against violence but must admit that he really felt good if he tried to get Toko in the corner. He never hit him hard as he did the sack and the ball but he liked it all. He bought a lot of snacks and cheese. He intended to watch television all evening. He felt a little bit tired after two nights of bad sleep.

He came home at the cottage and started to eat from the snacks. He watched television.

At the news broadcast there was more information about the boxers that were hurt. The story from Toko was confirmed. Also the fact that both boxers now would fight each other, newt week Saturday. There also was a short item about the girl that was hit in the fight. She was awakened out of her coma but it seemed that she had a light form of brain damage. She seemed to have lost her memory. This was really a serious problem for her and for her family.

John looked astonished at the television.

Memoryproblems! Could it be the case that he also had had his memoryproblem through a heavy blow on his head.

Could it have happened through the explosion. He could not remember that he had a sorrow spot on his head. Lia certainly had a hurtingspot on her head. He had seen her with a bandage on her head. It was good that she was out of the coma. It was a problem that she had problems with her memory. Perhaps he should visit her, maybe that would help her getting her memory back.

Maybe she was at the boxingclub to make problems with the two boxers.

Mission completed but personally damaged.

He sight. Well, he must be honest. It could have been her mission. Of course it was not the idea to get hurt herself but these things happen.

Suppose it was her mission, from whom would they have got this order. Who could be involved in such a way that he got what he wants?

He could only think of one person. He was astonished about his way of analysing the fighting incident. Only Toko could be the ordering party. Only he wanted to have these two boxers set aside. Probably he found it the highest option to fight for the worldchampionship. He, Toko, had been fighting for the title. Of course he will win, so he will be the legendary worldchampion heavy weight.

John found it all together quite likely. But who could Toko be, to get Lia and the organisation of James, involved in a fight in a bar in his favour, on his demand or request ? Who had enough position to cooperate with James to arrange a fight in a bar with certain persons getting injured? Not just an innocent boxer who just happened to have one, very surprisingly, win on his name. Ok, his opponent was expected to be the easy winner but got down. One perfect uppercut made the show. There was no reason to have expected such a victory. How come did the present world champion accept a fight against an unknown fighter?

For the money? Of course, no fight, no money. That also goes for Toko.

How were all these options combinable. Was Toko in another way an important person. Was he the brother of the Wolf?

John was surprised about this thought Was he himself the Wolf. John got a feeling by this thought. This could be the missing link. This would declare why the Wolf had to be declared dead in the explosion of the prison. He did not exist anymore. Now he was Toko. Toko was the Wolf. Only the Wolf himself could get two doctors so far to create the physical possibility to get the body extreme muscled. He himself was a possible example through the "medicines" tested on him. The final results was used to get Toko, as he was mentioned now, in condition. He, Toko, was only focussed on winning games. That was where his organisation stood for. He must win the game, any game.

Only the Wolf could have requested from James to make a problem at such a short notice in a boxingcentre.

John remembered that he had found some information about the Wolves. A location of their headquarters. He looked in his tablet and found the address. It was the address of the boxing location where he was training with Toko !!

He knew that there was something acquainted on the address but he had not taken any notice of it. He also found the photo of the leader of the Wolves. He could see that the man did look like Toko but that he was a lot less muscled. He now found the whole affair logical. It made also clear why he and the doctors had to die. The doctors could lose their licence to work as a doctor after all these wrong and forbidden tests. The official leader of the Wolves had to die so that Toko could get born. It al made sense now. He supposed that the doctors, just as Toko, had survived the explosions. They probably had some bodies of unknown testing patients that had died, as far as necessary changed for identification, and left them behind to be found as victims of the explosions.

Where would the doctors be now. Probably they were kept somewhere in the building of the Wolves. That was logical. But how and where? He wanted them to tell him the whole story and to see if they could solve the problem of his memory.

Chapter 22

John was stopped eating the snacks. He had to get used to his thoughts. Was it realistic. Could Toko really be the leader of the Wolves? John did not had the feeling for one moment that Toko was capable of leading an organisation. Certainly not an organisation as the Wolves.
He thought back to the start of their relationship. It was in the fitnesscentre in the city. Toko was looking for a trainingmate. Was not that peculiar for somebody who was supposed to be a well-known boxer. John was the only one he had met as a trainer. John supposed that Toko must have been a good amateur boxer with no expectations about a future boxingcareer. Perhaps someone approached him with a suggestion that his muscles could be increased firmly or that he has approached the doctors to develop a " medicine " that would create such a muscle grow and condition raise as the Wolf had made trough to became Toko.
How could he get a confirmation of his thoughts. He had made a gamble on Toko for his fight. If Toko was convinced of his win, he would have done the same. If he also was the Wolf, than he would have put his money at a competitive booking office.
John tried to find out which bookingoffices did not belong to the Wolves organisation. He found on the cracked Wolvessite the information he was looking

for. Three offices of the competition were mentioned. Also mentioned was the glorious win of Toko on Big Pinto.

John cracked the three sites of the mentioned bookmakers. In all cases large amounts of about fifty thousand each were put in on Toko. His gain was enormous. He made at each office twelve times his input. John had the conformation that he was looking for. He closed all the sites and put his tablet away.

What now. Could he find the doctors somewhere in the Wolfbuilding, if so, where?

The cellar was the most likely place, but he had thought that also for the sportsdepartment.

Did the Wolves use the whole building or only the upper stocks.

What would he have done. The wolves owned several buildings. Only the head office, including the small sportscentre was in the building John knew. The other buildings were casino's, racetracks for horses, dogs and everything else that could race, further bookingoffices and rentaloffices. They owned a lot of houses. The receiver the rent from these buildings. They had only one officebuilding and there they had their main office, their headquarters. They also ran many casino's in grand hotels. John saw also the hotel where he had met Rico the other day.

He made signs on the citymap on his tablet to identify the locations of all of these buildings. He had an interesting feeling about one casino. He trusted his feelings for this kind of guesses. He could play in the casino and find a way up to the higher areas in the building.

He found that he had to go now. He had no rest. He took some snacks in his hand and left. He knew where the building was.

It was dark and John sprinted to the location. He was surprised that the building was next to the hospital where Lia was.

John got straight on to the casino. He could not get Lia out of his mind. He walked through the casino and found rather quick a friendly feeling machine. He did make a quick win. He went on and was lucky. He had four machines that gave him each thousand dollars win. He almost forgot where he came for. Many times his thoughts got to Lia sleeping in the next building.

He looked around in the casino but there was no way up. Probably was the elevator in the offices. He walked around the building and found an entrance for the people that lived in the building or for the people that worked there. He simply walked in. No obstacles or gates. The elevator got as high as stock eleven. John thought that that was the topstock. He got up to the eleventh stock and left the elevator there.

He looked around on the floor. He saw several doors, he counted eight of them. On one of the doors he saw a plate. He got closer. It was a wolf on

the sign. He was sure this was the place. He saw a
bell but decided to knock on the door.
Rather quick, he heard a voice calling "Coming !"
"Just a moment."
John was surprised to hear the voice. Somewhere
this voice sounded familiar He was sure. He could
not place the voice. He had no face or name with it.
The door was opened and a young man stood
there. John looked at the man and tried to tell him
where he came for.
The man stared astonished at him. He quickly came
to himself and made same unregular arm moves.
"Sssttt," he whispered and looked around, also into
his own apartment. "Careful. Please come back
tomorrow late at night. I have company, I am sorry,
see you tomorrow, " and closed the door right in
John's nose. He tensed backwards. What was this.
The man seemed to know him and wanted to talk to
him tomorrow. Ok, he had to accept this. He left the
building.
He could not help himself. He was busy with the
man that had let him come back tomorrow, but all
his attention was to the building next door. The
hospital where Lia was. He looked at the building.
Almost everywhere the lights were out. Only in a
few rooms was light. He thought also in her room.
He tried to resist himself to go there but he could
not. He entered the hospital and went to the floor
where Lia's room was.

He saw that there came light trough from under the door. A curtain made it impossible to see something in the room. He walked to the door and listened. He heard voices, or one voice. He carefully opened the door and stepped inside. He also closed the door behind him. A woman was sitting on a chair beside the bed. She held the hand of the patient, Lia.
Lia was awaken but looked tired.
"Why do not you let her sleep. She needs it", John simply quoted.
The woman jumped up out of her chair, as if someone had hit her on the head. She super speeded around and made a move as if she was going to hit the speaker.
John looked completely surprised at her. This was the mother of Rosemary !
She shaked her head. She swept her hand through her hair. Her total looks changed.
At once, in a way, she did look like the mother of Lia. Where these two the same person? Then she also was the leader of the drugssyndicate.
Were these two the same person? John looked again. It was just as if she was changing regularly. The woman came to a controlled position. She smiled at John, now looking like Lia's mother.
"Hallo John," she said friendly.
"Hallo James," John reacted and smiled. "Fabulous how you can change your physical in seconds, magnificent." He looked flattering at her.

"Thank you John. Please will you help me. I found your phone and tried to call you but you were not in the records. I tried to talk to her but she remembers nothing. " She turned around and looked at her daughter.

"Did you asked her to go to that bar and to make trouble with those boxers?" John asked because he had to know.

"Yes, and I regret it. I thought that she was untouchable. She was such a fantastic fighter. I still cannot believe that she is here now without any memory." She sniffed and went back to her chair.

John came closer to her. "I think you better leave. You need sleep, Lia needs sleep. I will stay with her until she sleeps. She is tired, very tired. Please give her the time to recover. "John helped James up and leaded her out of the room.

He sat down on the bedside of the bed of Lia. She looked at him and said," He handsome, do I happen to know you? "

"Hallo Lia, I am John. We have met before. Now it is your time to go to sleep. Be calm, get rest. You will see that it is all better tomorrow. Come, lay backwards. How is your face doing. "

"Ooh, ok, they gave me something to sleep. I feel that it is good that you are here. Thank you for coming" She was already asleep.

John got one pillow away so she would be more comfortable while sleeping.

He closed the light and left. He did not saw James, so he left the hospital and went home. He felt a lot better. Some pieces of the puzzle were cleared, still a long way to go.

He used the way back to eat the last snacks that he had in his bag and trained his reactionspeed and his runningspeed.

He bought some more snacks and got home.

He was tired. He took some of the cheese because he had not eaten very much the last few days. He promised himself a great meal tomorrow. He went to bed. He fell asleep quickly.

Chapter 23

John got up late. He felt alright. He was glad that he had visited Lia in the hospital. He now realised that he had never thought about the fact that Lia and Rosemary were sisters or halfsisters. Did they had the same parents. No, anyway he thought he had seen two different man. One as the father of Rosemary and another as father of Lia. He must admit that he had also thought that it were two different mothers. How did she do it? Changing her looks in a split second. Ok, she changed her hair. Hanging completely on the left to hanging completely to the right. But then also her face must have two different looks. He found it very special. Well, being the big boss of a large drugssyndicate made her also extreme dangerous. He must be careful. He certainly would like to take care of Lia. She had to get used to her new way of living. No memory, no information about your own history. All normal things like eating and going to the toilet will be learned almost automatically. All the other things, like social behaviour cannot be teached by someone like her mother. Maybe he should take her in his cottage. He had to think about that option.
He started, after a simple breakfast with training his moves. He found that he needed that more than a running condition. That condition was already good. He went to the city. He had to train with Toko for his

big fight in nine days. Why was Toko so busy with boxing. Did he set up the whole chemical test for the option to get world champion heavy weight boxing? If he found that so important than this all fits. The tests, Toko himself, becoming a superboxer overnight. His muscles had grown enormous since the photo in the file of the Wolves was made. He looked in the mirror. He must admit that he himself also had grown large muscles. He did not know how his own history was, but he found it logically that he was the person that had survived all the tests. Did Toko know, that he was the result of the same "medicine" as he had taken? He had to talk to the doctor tonight.

He wondered what could be in it for him. Was the offer from Toko to share the profit his reward or would he not survive the next round. Would Toko get rid of him after he had become the world champion. It would be worth it. He would not have to share the win of the fight. He must be honest. This was the way criminals do think. How could he escape out of this mess. He had the advantage that he knew everything about Toko while he did not know that John knew that.

He started a website in which he promoted a new superboxer that found that he had to fight the wold champion boxing. He wanted to create a possible problem for Toko.

Perhaps he had to get Toko so far that he, after he had won from the present champion would fight an unknown boxer to defend his worldtitle. He would calmly bring this to the publicity. He made a statement to some newspapers and a televisionstation.

He made it sound like a great well-known boxer from another country. The text made it sound that he should be the opponent for the present champion.

He got on his way to help Toko with his training. He took a small bite on the way to the traininglocation of Toko.

They trained and John mentioned the new story about the fighter from another country.

Toko reacted furious. His wife had finished the negotiations. The winner would gain five million dollar, the looser only one. John confirmed that Toko had to win. He would love to get half the wining money.

Toko did not react on that.

John activated Toko 's lack of moving speed. He more and more trained himself on that speed.

They finished the training for today. John did not ask whether Toko had done its morning training and let it this way.

He left and got to the hospital. He walked in and visited the room of Lia.

Lia's mother was again in the room.

John found that a positive situation. James was clearly also a mother. He just went in very gentle.

Lia was sitting straight up in her bed. She looked reasonably clear out of her eyes. The big bandage around one side of her head was gone. A small wound was visible. No coverage on it, probably it would heal the best way in the open air.

She immediately looked at John when he came in, A big smile ran over her face.

Her mother saw her smiling over her head, so she quickly turned around. She saw John and nicked to him.

John greeted both ladies and asked how things were going.

Lia reacted. "I feel good but still no memory. I should get out of my bed. Walking is far better than just laying down. She at that very moment slipped out of her bed and walked, a little bit shacky to one of the chairs at the table next to the window. She quickly got seated. This was far enough for now.

Her mother quickly followed her and got seated next to her.

John also walked to the table and got seated opposite to Lia. He looked at her. She did look a lot better than yesterday. He told her so. He also asked whether her mother had been with her all day.

Her mother confirmed that.

John suggested that she better leave now. He would stay until Lia would go to sleep. She was still tired and needed to sleep a lot.

Lia's mother thanked him, kissed her daughter and left.

John tried to talk with Lia about her day. The things she had done and experienced. They walked together a little bit through the room, so she could train her muscles. He also shacked hands, let her move her arms and her body. She used to be extreme flexible. Now she was stiff. She really had to train her muscles.

He contacted one of the nurses and asked for a massage for her during the day, tomorrow. She would pass the question on to her colleagues for tomorrow.

Lia got something to eat. She liked it. Shortly after that the nurse came to tell John that he had to leave because Lia had to go to sleep.

John left.

John walked into town to get a good and big meal. He was hungry. He felt good being with Lia, even in her present condition. He had talked with her about herself, what she felt and where it did hurt and what moves were easy and where the opposite reaction was felt. No problems, no disputes about anything. Just being helpful together.

He entered a no-limit foot restaurant and eat far too much. He calmly walked back. He wanted to visit the apartment of the doctors, as far as he could understand the short contact from yesterday. He simply went into the building at the backside of the casino and got to the right stock and the right frontdoor. He waited a moment so they could see who was calling. Then he ringed the doorbell. The

door was opened quickly and he was more or less
drawn inside. He looked surprised. He stood with
the frontdoor, closed in his back. The man in front of
him looked at him very angry. John did not knew
who he was. The man looked aggressive.
"What do you want", the man yelled at him. He held
his arm in front of John's throat, holding his head
against the door. He had spread John's legs with
his feet.
John was completely surprised. He did not liked this
position, so he shaked his head, as if he could not
talk in this position. Again he looked at the man.
This man did not looked familiar. The man that
opened the door yesterday did. Somewhere,
somehow he had met that man before.
The man loosened his arm against John's throat.
John could breathe normally now. He took a good
breath and looked at the man.
"Please stand back, I do not want to hurt you", he
said with a small smile.
The man laughed loudly. He had a heavy voice.
"Do not be afraid , just hurt me if you can." Again he
laughed loudly. He obviously found the situation
funny.
John grabbed the hand from the arm with witch the
man blocked his throat. Pulled it down. The man
came forward, losing his balance. John simply
stepped aside and at the same time, knocked the
head of the man against the frontdoor. He stepped
behind the man and kicked his right foot away to the

side. The man could not stay up and again knocked with his head against the door and immediately after that, he fell on the ground.

John stepped back, giving the man enough space to go all the way to the ground.

The man tried to kick him with his right foot. John stepped backwards, so he missed. Immediately he stepped his foot on the leg of the man. John heard a bad sound. There might have been something wrong with the man's leg.

Behind John a door was opened. John turned around. The man that had opened the door yesterday stood there, completely surprised about what he saw.

He certainly had thought that it all would be the other way around. He came to help the innocent visitor. He looked at John and then again to the yelling man on the ground.

"I will call for an ambulance," he said and grabbed a phone out of his pocket and made a helpcall for an ambulance.

The man on the ground started to call names. John looked at him and then to the man of whom he was convinced that he was one of the two doctors.

Remarkably quick the ambulanceman came to the frontdoor. They had a waitingpoint at the side of the casino, being a high risqué location, therefor they were her fast.

They controlled the leg of the man, who was still making angry noises. The leg was broken. They blocked the leg temporary and took the man on a stretcher with them.

The doctor invited John in. They sat on a sofa. The small room was almost empty.

"How is your memory?" the doctor started to ask.

"My memory starts at the moment of the explosion in the prison. From the period before that I do not remember anything." He looked at the doctor, expecting a good story about what had happened before.

"Hallo John," the man began." I am Peter. You just knocked out our guard. He must make sure that we could not go out without permission. They are holding my wife and kids and Pauls mother, somewhere. So we cannot do what we would like to do. We do not want any trouble. I will inform you quickly, because a new guard will be her soon. Your story, as far as we know it. You volunteered on an advertisement from us about testing the possibility of having muscles grow through "medicines". We told you that it was all very experimental and that we had no idea about the actual physical risks. You told us that your name was John Normal and that you lived at Sommerville, that is a small village far away from the city, high up at the opposite side of the great mountains. You said that you were 24 years old and wanted something new. We had no reason to doubt your words and, I must admit, were happy to have more than three candidates. We had the order from the group that called themselves

"The Wolves". They would pay all the costs. We, my college Paul and I, worked at the medical staff of the prison. We found it a perfect location for our experiments. Nobody knew about it, except of course the Wolves. We have given you and three others several chemical combinations. We made fakefiles to make it look legal, but it was not. You made good progress. With the last test it went wrong with you. You lost your memory. We prepared a antidope to get rid of the block in your memory but it did not work. We were busy to find another solution when the explosion destroyed it all, everything including our own registrations got burned away. We are still trying to find out who did it but we have no idea. "

"So the Wolves gave you the order. They are also the ones that keep you here, away from your wife and kids?" John wanted to know. He found the information very simple and with an enormous lack of details.

"As far as we have understand it we are kept here by the group of the Major. I understood that they had an order from the Wolves to do this. But I do not know whether this is the truth."

"Does the leader of the Wolves know about these experiments and the persons on who experiments were done?"

"Most certainly. He was the big motor behind it all. He also wanted to have your medicines to have his muscles grow. He had seen the results at your body. He knows you very well. He followed every step. He only got scared about the possibility to lose his memory, so he took his precautions regarding that point. I do not know which, but he at last got the same medicines as you did. We also gave him the solution that had failed with you but we do not know whether he took that or not. We also do not know whether he has lost his memory. He was totally focussed on becoming a magnificent boxinglegend." Peter looked at his watch.

"John, I think you better leave, before the new guard is coming in. If he find you here that might be a problem. What can I tell him about your presence her?"

"Ok, Peter, just tell him that I am a salesman, I sell insurances. Do not you want to buy some? " John smiled about his own suggestions. He now knew the main story of his experiments, No details but these might come in later. He said goodbye and left. He did not meet anybody in the elevator or in the building.

One thing was clear. He had to talk to Mindy about the part of the major and her group.

Chapter 24

John walked into the city. He tried to remember where the apartment of Mindy was. The apartment where they found Rosemary.

He took his tablet. They had made a ride with the jeep, than they had walked around a church. He looked at the map. He found the prison, the likely route of the jeep. The church and the location short behind the church. He decided to go there and see whether Mindy was still using that location. He walked to the church he had in mind. He remembered that Mindy also was escaped from the prison. She must have been convicted of something, just like Rico.

He must keep in mind that these were real criminals. Not just small thieves but main figures in criminal organisations. He saw them as co-fugitives but that was a wrong idea. Marion was a nurse, so she was not a criminal, but she was because she was part of the organisation of James of the drugssyndicate. The wursted criminals, the easy killers. Was that correct or were kidnappers the worst. They were bad both, he decided.

He found the church and remembered the streets to follow from that point on. Ten minutes later he stood in front of the door of the apartment of Mindy. There was light in the apartment. John simply knocked on the door. At the same moment he realised that it was almost midnight. No normal hour for a regular visitor. Well, he was not a regular visitor and he found that criminals were more used to having visitors around midnight than around noon.

He heard someone walk to the door. A small window was opened. John made a small step back, so the person that looked could see him clearly. In the light of the hall.

"John?" a voice asked.

"Correct Mindy, could I say you for a moment? Please?" he asked.

"Well, yes, ok, a moment than I will open the door. " she said.

It still took her some time to find the key, John supposed. At last he heard the doorkey being turned around and the door got open.

Mindy looked at him. She invited him in. He got in and she after looking in the hallway immediately closed the door and locked it.

Mindy got in front of him to her livingroom. She pointed out where he could sit and immediately started with an attack in words.

"Hallo John, how did you know I was here?" She looked at him as a punishing mother to her child.

John could not help himself. He had to laugh about her behaviour.

"Sorry, "he said, I am not used to be looked at by someone making a statement as an angry mother.

I had no idea you were here. This is the only address I have from you and I wanted to talk with you. "

"Why?" Mindy was obviously not amused with his visit.

John looked at her. She seemed changed. She was involved in kidnapping. She was a thief, active in steeling and all other kind of criminal affairs. She probably did not had too much fun in her life. Always scared about something or someone. He pitied her.

"Mindy, are you involved in the mission for the Wolves to hold two doctors in prison and their families somewhere hidden? "

Mindy looked surprised at John.

"What more do you know about our businesses? "

"I am interested in my own case. These doctors are part of my history. As you know my memory is gone and I want to find out how I can get it back. These doctors made it disappear, maybe they also can bring it back to me." He looked at Mindy.

She nicked. She understood his approach.

"Well John, I must admit that I am in the middle of it. I was just ordered to go to Peter to keep him better under control. Our man is brought to the hospital with a broken leg. I have to take his job for a few days. " Mindy got up.

"And I do not like this !!!"she yelled. As if John had supposed something.

"I feel treated like a schoolgirl. I never get orders in this kind of work. " Mindy really was angry.

John looked at her with a smile. Why do you accept this order?" He smiled friendly to her.

"I cannot refuse. It came from the Major self."

"Do you have to fill the job in in person, or could you send somebody else?' John got curious.

She looked at him. A big smile broke her angry face. "Right, I refuse the order but make sure that the spot is filled. So the task is organised. " She smiled at John.

"Good thinking, John," she said in a far better humour then a moment ago.

"May I offer myself for a part of the job?" John proposed.

"Just one more question. Do you know where the family of Peter and the mother of Paul is hold prison. I would like to see them free. " John looked at Mindy.

She smiled. She did know where they were.

"You found all those beautiful papers about your history. Did you buy that story? Also the family at the right addresses, Mark and his kids? It was worth trying. It gave the Wolf some extra time. We know this would not hold very long because they promised to contact you, but they did not, of course not. Now that his fight for the worldtitel is next week Friday, all these points are no longer of interest. If you like it, we will let them go tomorrow morning. If you will take over my place in the present apartment

of the doctors, then I will be there tomorrow at nine o'clock to bring them back to their families. "
Mindy looked at John. Well everything solved? "
Just one more thing. Can we talk about that tomorrow after you have brought the families back together in freedom. I could be here at eleven, all right?" John looked at Mindy.
She smiled. "OK," she quoted. John shaked her hand and left. He had to walk back to the apartment of Peter and Paul.
At the moment he arrived Paul got back on the apartment as well.
John informed the two man about his new function and a possible surprise for tomorrow morning.
They took a drink on a possible coming happy end and went to bed. John slept on the couch in the livingroom.

John got up early. He could not really sleep. The couch was too small and too short. He looked for some food in the small kitchen, found some crackers and eat them. He made coffee and waited for Mindy to come and collect the two man.
Paul got up as the next one and Peter was a lot later. He had no breakfast and found a cup of coffee enough for this morning. His stomach was totally twisted.
John told them that Mindy would be in their apartment at nine o'clock to bring them to their family, everybody was free to go home.

Peter and Paul were quite emotional about this fantastic solution.

Indeed Mindy was at the door at nine o'clock sharp. John was happy with her. He said goodbye to both man and left himself as well.

He was in no hurry to go to Mindy's apartment. He walked through town. He found the attention form Mindy for the welfare of the kidnapped families promising. Maybe he could get her for his other plans. He also wanted to know whether she would inform Toko about her new vision about letting the doctors and their families free.

He wandered why Toko found it necessaire to kidnap these families. Did the doctors not wanted to cooperate with Toko. There seemed to be more than Peter had told him. He did not say a word about being forced to do the tests for Toko. He also did not gave any indication how they had succeeded in Toko not having lost his memory. Further he must admit that Mindy had been extremely cooperative in realising this quick solution. He wandered why. Ok, she had something very urgent to do. That other matter was so urgent that she was willing to cooperate even against the probable wishes of the client. How serious were these crooks regarding jobs for each other? Did they cooperate at all?

In his case the Wolves cooperate with the Major. Why did the Major accepted this job. What was in it for them ? He could not find any reason why or what. Just money? Possibly. Were the Wolves extreme rich. The casinos were a good business. The other gambling affairs also made good money. So they were rich, he supposed. Perhaps that was the only reason why Mindy could let this happen so easy. Perhaps they even already had been paid. Mindy had another case going on, that was more important. He could only guess what that could be. It was not his business to interfere in her private or business affairs, as far as he was not involved.

He still had the idea that there were all kind of things happening that he ought to know but was not informed about.

He arrived at Mindy's apartment just at the moment that she walked in. They got in together.

Mindy offered him coffee and asked him what they had to talk about.

John made clear that he had made a deal with Toko about helping and coaching him for his boxinggame against the worldchampion. He was afraid that Toko would not take the deal seriously. He could be interested to have him, after the fight, disappear.

Mindy wanted to know the content of the deal.

John told him fifty percent of the win or loose premium.

Mindy looked surprised. That was a lot of money for this short period of work. She understood his concern. She promised to find out if there was anything planned against John in connection to the fight or the period direct after. She also would try to get information from James, normally killing is there business, in connection to drugs. But she must be careful.

They made an appointment for over two days, but at another location. Mindy wrote down the address of a restaurant, they would eat there in a separate room. He was expected at eight o'clock in the evening.

John left, thanking Mindy for her input.

He walked to the Toko 's trainingcentre. In the park nearby he got an a bank and tried to find information about the city called "Sommerville". Peter had said that he had declared to have lived there. He took some snacks from a sales boot and eat them tasteful. He was surprised about the fine taste.

Sommerville was a small village, deep in the mountains. There was not very much on the internet about the village. There lived only sixthousand people, including the people that lived in the area around the village. There were pictures of the villagecentre. It reminded him of the square near his cottage. A square with a big old tree and some banks under it. Several older inhabitants were sitting there. He loved the atmosphere of the village. He could not say that he recognized anything else than the atmosphere.

It was time to go to the training of Toko.

They trained hard. Toko really was doing his very best. John tried to hit him more and more, so Toko had to defend himself against a fastmoving opponent. He was really more attend. Toko even began to move himself. He stepped more aside, forward, backward, faster. John promoted these actions, more than just a tough blow.

He promised that the next step would be to coordinate the moves with blind tough blows. He showed Toko same samples for his training with the big sack. He had to roll over his feet, forward and backwards and hit the sack when he got forward. He learned Toko to change his foot upfront. Not only the right foot forward, but regularly change it to left foot forward. Toko got confused. He always only boxed with his right foot forward. John showed him the great advantage of being capable to change. Toko was a very good student. He learned fast. He had to understand the background and the advantage of the action. If he did he could do it very quick. He also tried to train these moves on the big bag and the ball.

John found him really very good. He had to move faster and faster to stay away from the tough blows of Toko. He even saw Toko in their final trainingsmatch change his footposition three times. Toko really learned fast.

John took a shower and got dressed. He told Toko that he was very good today. If they could go on like this the coming week, he even might win the match. He did it very well today.

Toko was happy with John's words. He himself also found that he was making great progress.

John left and walked straight to the hospital to see Lia.

Lia was sitting at her table. She looked a little bit tired. She welcomed him with a big smile. She immediately started to talk.

The old Lia seemed to come back a little bit. She had just finished her eveningmeal. Before that she had a massage. It had taken more than two hours. A young girl was her physical therapist and she really knew what had to be done. They had found out that they had been to the same primaryschool. She was a couple of years younger but they must have met there.

John was happy for her. The nurse came. Lia had to go back to bed. She had a very busy day and must go to sleep now.

John said goodbye end left.

This was all he could do. He deliberately had not asked the states of her memory. If she had her memory back, she would have approached him in another way. Words were not necessary to determine that.

He left the hospital. He found an "all you can eat" restaurant and spend a large part of the evening eating.

He thought about Summerville. Was it useful to go there ? Could he have lived there? Should not he had more feelings about that part of his memory. He decided to find out. He looked how he could get there. There were roads but no train or bus came near the village. Should he buy a car?

Chapter 25

No he would buy a motor. He had promised the
salesman to be back with the helmet. He was glad
with his decision. He loved to ride on a bike. He
walked back to the city and found the motor sales
centre. Indeed the same young man was in the
showroom. John came in. The young man looked at
him surprised. He started to smile and came to
John with his hand forward.
"Yes, I knew it. My boss was certain that you had
fooled me and simply had taken the helmet for your
own benefit. What can I do for you." He was most
helpful.
John greeted him also very friendly. He showed the
helmet and told that he was looking for a motor that
would be capable of riding long distances and a
quality to ride in the mountains.
The young man new the right motor for him. A
Harley Davisson. He showed the motor. A real
heavy motor, very good for long distances and very
good in the mountains. They made a small trip with
the motor.
John found it ok. The made a price and John took
the motor with him. He drove through the city.
Distances were of no importance anymore. He got
back to his cottage and went to bed.

The next morning he took a small breakfast and looked at his tablet to find the road to Sommerville. He had to go through the city and follow the road to another city. He planned the route and informed the navigationsystem on the motor.

John found it a fantastic experience. He calmly drove through town but on the highway he made speed. The motor did it great. It did not go extraordinary fast but a good speed it had. He followed the route, crossed a larger town and several smaller towns. He got into the mountains. The road became smaller and smaller. At the end he only had a small path, two cars could not pass there. There were special spots for passing. The motor had no problems, even cars meeting him could pass easily. He really enjoyed the ride. He, after two hours, finally entered the village of Somerville. On the central square with the old tree in the middle, he stopped.

He found a small lunchroom and got in, the motor parked in front of it. He found the surrounding very warm and friendly. This was a good place, but he felt no connection. No memorial points. It was clear, or his memory could not get connected or he had never been here before. He ate a quick sandwich with coffee and got back. He was glad that he had done it. On one side he now knew that he could not feel any connection with his present memory and he had gloriously toured around on his new motor.

He was right in time for the trainingsession with Toko.

Again it all got better and better with Toko. He really started to become a very dangerous, mobile boxer. They trained the combination between moves and fast hits, enormous blows by extra weight with his body and his feet.

Feints were introduced. First with only the body language, than with the hand but without a blow, then with a soft blow, only to take away the sight on the other hand that really hits.

At the end of the day even six feints were trained to give the opponent the idea that he could not foresee which hand would really blow. A footchange in between made it even worse.

John was very satisfied. He started to believe in the realisation of the worldtitel for Toko.

Even Toko himself started to get more and more enthusiastic.

After the training John visited Lia. She was still on her eveningmeal. She welcomed him and pointed to the chair in front of her. She finished her meal and smiled happily to him. She seemed to get better by the day. She started to get small pieces of memory back. She remembered being with him. She remembered him as "John". They were together but something had come between them. She did not remember what it was but they got partly separated? She did not understood the impact and the consequences. She was convinced that it would all come back in due course. She was glad to see him. Then there was also something with a phone. She did not remember anything about that at all. John changed the subject and asked how her muscles were doing.

Lia told about the massages and the strongly improvement of her muscles. If it all goes as planned she could get home in two or three days. John asked if she remembered her own apartment. She conformed, not all the details but a fantastic view from the balcony over the park, she remembered.

John was glad for her. Again the nurse came in to end the conversation.

John had to leave promising to come back the next day.

John got back to his motor. He found the paper with the address of the restaurant for the meeting with Mindy on it in his bag. He noted it in on the navigator on his motor. He looked surprised at the result. It needed a 30 minutes ride with the motor. Almost deep in the woods outside the city. He picked up his tablet and found the same location there. He looked a little bit around the spot but it seemed almost only forest. What could this mean. Not a restaurant but a countryclub, perhaps for members only. Members of the Major, of course. He still had almost an hour to get there. Anyway, with the motor he had time to look around there. He started the motor and left.

After half an hour he was very close to the address. He found a large sign. "Virginia's Home restaurant". John looked around the corner. It was dark but the entrance was brightly lighted with many lights. At the end of a broad road an enormous building was located after a big parking place opposite to the large entrance. He saw several people walking in the park around it. He decided to simply go there. He started his motor again and drove to the parking area. He parked the motor, put his helmet and gloves in his bag and looked around.

This really was a lux hotel. He first walked around the huge building. At the back, there was a huge swimmingpool, large terraces and a great field of grass. Several people where on the grass, playing games by the lights that were all around the field. Further backwards was a small lake with a beach on front of it. Behind the lake there was the forest. It all looked very lux and innocent. He returned to the front and walked to the reception. He told that he came for "Mindy".

"Of course, Sir", was the decent reaction. He ringed a bel and a young bellboy came to him.

John would be brought to his appointment, if he, please, would follow the boy.

John found it all a little bit overdone, but he followed the boy.

The boy lead him to the side of the large hall. A large door was opened by the boy and he followed. Behind the door was a small hallway with three doors. He walked to the door in the middle and nocked three times. A heavy ladies voice called "enter" and the boy opened the door. He did one step inside, called gentle "Your appointment", turned around and closed the door behind John who had entered the room.

John looked around. This was really a lux office. Large curtains where all over, making a super impression. In the middle of the room stood a large officetable. Behind the table two women were sitting. They both got up.

John approached the table. From the left side another woman came to them.

"Hallo John," this lady said. John had to look again. Mindy was totally changed. She had her hair long and loose, she used to have it in a knot behind her head. She wore make up, also new for John and she was dressed as if she was going to an important ball. She did look dressy. He noticed that also the other ladies where dressed in the same style. Different collars and different outlooks but the same luxe performance.

"Hallo Mindy", John reacted a little bit surprised.

"Hallo John" the lady on the left said.

Obviously John was supposed to know this lady. He looked again. He was surprised, This was James, the mother of Lia. What was going on.

"Hallo James", he said, meanwhile looking at the third lady. She was nodding, hearing that the other two knew this young man and he knew them.

"Welcome John, I am Major."

John smiled at her. At last he met the big boss of the kidnappers and thieves. Mindy's boss.

"Thank you, Major", he said.

"Please be seated," Mindy came to John and pointed at a chair opposite to the two ladies. She took the chair next to him.

"I "Mindy started the conversation "have asked you all to meet here because the interests of the different large organisation are more and more getting mixed. I think we need to make clear to each other how we see the future. The point is that if we accept orders from other criminal organisations instead of only from noncriminal organisations, we might get problems with each other. We have accepted missions for the Wolves. The same goes for James. James accepted a mission to shoot on me. I do not know who ordered it, but it did happen. John is my witness. He was there when it happened. The shooting was only mend to kill me, not to hurt John. I would like to create an independent organisation, small but loyal, that judges all the missions that might involve one of the other organisations. John is important in this matter. He is afraid that the Wolves will kill him, or have him killed, for instant by someone of James-organisation direct or very short after the boxingmatch next Saturday. I think his fear is realistic. The wolves have promised him 50 % of the premium of the game. That is an interesting amount, worth to be

killed for or to be disappeared. First I would like to ask James if they have had a call to have John killed after the game. If you do not want to answer, please do not. This is not mend to create a problem. This is mend to clear our vision in the future. "
Mindy nodded to James.

"I understand the problem," James answered, "Yes we do have had an order to kill John after the match. In fact it is only an order to have him disappear. It pays us about two hundred grand. That is a high amount. We cannot just refuse such an order. It means money and it means that no external killer will be introduced. We have to protect our market." She was honest and direct. Her vision was also very clear. She cannot limit her market because otherwise new competition will be involved in her market.

"Further," she continued her answer, "is only our business competition vulnerable. Drugs and killing are sensitive activities. If anybody else would take an order in our aria we want to know. We only give warnings once. " She again was very clear.

"If I may ask something" John started. He had no idea why he was involved. They could have had this conversation without him. "Would you like to have an organisation that makes clear that the market of each of your organisations is unique and exclusive?" John looked at James and Major. He wanted to know how both managers thought about it. If they wanted to protect their market a protectionistic way of doing business was necessary.

Major was less direct. In her branch many small players were active, so a real exclusive position was never realisable. For the Wolves and James, she could understand but she had no need for such a strong line. Regarding the Lord and her position a similar situation was the case. Many banks were involved in financial affairs. The black money market was immense large. Small financers could not kept away, " Major said.

"May I ask who was responsible for the explosions at the prison?" John wanted to know.

No one reacted.

"May I ask who blow away the apartment in the centre of the city?" Again no answer.

Are there special arrangements between the four largest criminal organisations?" Again no answer.

"Ok, thank you for the information. I understand that I will be killed by your organisation, James, I will tell Lia about your vision in this case. Maybe you can ask Lia to do the job. You do not care, do you? " John moved his chair backwards.

He got up and left.

Nobody reacted. He left the building and got on his motor. He speeded fast over the roads. He was worried. If Lia and her mother were going to kill him he really had a problem. He got straight home. He parked the motor behind the outside door, next to his cottage and the trees.

He got in and took something to eat. He was not hungry. The meeting was not very helpful. He at least knew now that Toko had given the order to get him killed. Why should he help him. He had been fouled all the time by Toko. Now it was time to change the position. He had to think about his own interest.

Should he became a criminal. Should he kidnap Lia. Should he kill Toko. It was certainly a way to get a solution. He did had an advantage. He knew about his position. He expected that Toko did not know that he knew. How could he get the best results for himself. To have a future he needed money. To get money he needed Toko to win the fight. He had again and again looked at the worldchampion. He was convinced that Toko would win. So he had to put all the money he had on Toko. He looked how the bookmakers were quoting him. He now knew who was part of the organisation of Toko and who not. To hurt Toko he would put his money on one of his bookmakers. He made a search. The best deal was at a large bookmaker. The score was one to ten. Really interesting. He looked at the amount on his account. He still had more than fiftyfive thousand on his account. He had to buy the motor with a loan, so that had not lowered his account.

He put the bet in and paid the amount. That was that. If Toko won, he would have through this bet a lot of money to live from. Even without his part of the money for the win.

What more should he do. Could he find out who would be the killer. Could he brake in in the account of James. The side of James would not mention the orders, because all the members could get in. The bankaccount was the central information for payments. Would Toko already had paid for this order. Would James already have paid the killer? There was only one way to find out.

First he had to find the bankaccounts.

He got some more snacks. He felt better now that he had a target. He still had to find a way to prevent the killing. He got in the general website of James. The bankaccount was clearly mentioned. He searched for other numbers and found three more accounts. He left the site and got in the first account. He had to concentrate three times before he really got in. He was relieved. He looked at the information. He was surprised about the number of cases. Of course almost all cases were drugsdeals. He tried to find a payment of two grand. The last week, no such deal was paid. He looked at the other accounts. He did not found any amount in this hight. He decided to control the account of the Wolves. He found three accounts but on none of these accounts a payment looked to be done in this hight.

What could this mean. Had James made up this order. That was very good possible. She did not wanted her daughter to have intime contact with an unreliable outsider. Understandable. But not very

professional. Had she expected her daughter to find a mate in the business? Of course. The drugsworld was a super dangerous surrounding. Bad luck for her. What could he do with this. It was therefore possible that no murderattack was planned. How could he get more clearance on this point. Would the deal be completed after a successful disappearance ? Quite possible. Even very likely. No payment in advance. He had no proof of any of the options, only the word from James for what that was worth. Was it decent to betray your client by telling the target that he was to be killed.
No, of course not.
Were drugsdealers decent ? No, of course not.
He did not know how to find out the trough.
He went to bed. He had a lot to think about.
Somerville had not ringed a bell.

Chapter 26

John did not sleep well. He found again and again new items where he had no answer for. Was it really the main goal for Toko to get worldchampion boxing. Was that it. Ok it was really something. You would be on the list forever. He could feel something for that goal. Would such a target justify illegal practises? Kidnapping, forbidden chemical tests, forbidden injections all criminal activities that were not usual for the gambling area. Did the other Wolves knew about this all? Was he responsible for the explosions at the prison. He was convinced on that point. He seemed the only one that could have a goal involved there. What would the authorities say about the two doctors that out of the bleu and alive got home. Who would they declare the found death bodies.

He was more concerned about his own status. Should he get to Peter to ask how he solved the problem with the memoryblock with Toko?

He found this point so intrigant that he decided to go to Peter.

He stepped on his motor and raced to the apartment where he had found Mark with two kids the last time. The fake story.

He called on the door. Peter opened the door and reacted enthusiastic to John. He thanked him. Also his family was safe and back at home. They were very grateful. John accepted their thanks. He would not bother them long. He got a cup of coffee and asked Peter about his memoryblock. How had they solve the problem for Toko.

Peter got a little bit unsecure. He admitted that they had not understand how John had had a problem with his memory. They had not changed anything for Toko. Toko seemed very convinced of the fact that he would not have any problems with his memory. He even stated that he had prepared all kind of information in case he would lose his memory. So he could not say anything about that. John asked him the info of the used chemical injections and other information.

Peter secured him that he would not have any negative effect of the tests. All that had happened was that the muscles had grown strongly without a problem to the rest of the body, including bones, skin and bloodvanes. Everything stayed in full function. If he would ever get a problem he would like to hear about it. They had not found anything that could course a negative result.

He still was convinced that they had nothing to do with his loss of his memory. Peter suggested that it could have had something to do with the explosions but he corrected himself immediately. They knew the problem already before the explosions in the prison took place. Maybe the problem was only temporary but got heavier through the explosions. Peter could not declare that.

John thanked him and left.
He had his answer. There must have happened
something outside the vision of Peter and Paul.
Who could have been involved there. The only one
he could think of was Toko. How come that he was
so positive about his options, not to lose his
memory, unless he knew more about this.
He would try to get Toko to talk to him about this all.

He returned to town. He parked his motor in the
parking under the building. He did not feel very
good about that. He locked the motor and got a big
chain to secure the motor at a solid concrete pillar.
He walked to a coffeeshop, ate some snacks that
tasted great. He was surprised. At the right time he
got to the trainingsarea of Toko. He did not yet
knew how he could make it clear to Toko that he did
not wanted to get killed. He could easily had
connected a killer from elsewhere. He could ask
Rico. How likely was it that the other Wolves did
know about this whole affair. If you really tried to be
objective than you had to conclude that this whole
affair was far away from the normal business of the
Wolves. Ok, betting on boxfights was within their
business but that was all. That was completely
legal. He thought about his own bet. If he wanted a
future, he should make it sure that Toko would win
the fight. He really had to. No win, almost no more
money. How did he looked at Toko. Was he a
murderliking type? Actually No, he did not found

Toko a person that liked murders. Ok, gambling was great but that was no problem. How had he come so far that he got involved in this whole affair. Ok, he got stimulated to became worldchampion. He had a very good business in the casino's and bookingoffices, plenty of money. He wanted more. He was a former boxing amateur. Perhaps he should look at his former performances. His boxing qualities certainly must have helped him getting up in the organisation of the Wolves. Maybe he even started the organisation. Was he very smart? Was he capable of running such an organisation? John must admit that he had no idea. He never noticed Toko being involved in other things than his coming worldchampion. He even never looked at him as the manager of the Wolves. Not even as the boss of one casino. Was he really the big boss of the Wolves? Others had confirmed it to him but based on his suggestion. They had confirmed more points that did not fit. He felt lost. He did not know what to believe. One thing was clear. If he wanted a future with enough money to be free from others, Toko had to win this fight. So he forced himself to make that point come through.

He focussed with Toko on his footchanges. Right for, left for. They controlled which blow was the toughest. The opponent fought always with his right foot in front of him. That made him vulnerable for somebody standing with his left foot in front of him. The right arm had more space to a blow than with the other foot in front. John made the fight more and more looking like a real fight. They boxed for over an hour in one ongoing fight. In practise the rounds would be short. John wanted Toko to be capable of fighting more rounds super active. His condition should be superior. They together looked for more than an hour to the fights from the worldchampion. Every time again John pointed at the knowledge points of the way the champion moved. He always betrayed his next move. That was what Toko had to see. He could react on it before the action actually took place. The last hour they trained what they had seen.

Toko thanked him for his lessons. It was Friday so they had two days of rest in front of them. Next week would be a week of calm training, keeping the condition on the right level and relax.

John left. He could not talk with Toko about his suspicions against him. He had no real point against him. It was not realistic to tell him that he had spoken the leader of the James organisation, so actually James herself, and that she had told him that she had a contract on his head for two grand. This did not sound very likely. His behaviour could influence their very good relation seriously in a negative way. It did not feel right to mention this point at all. He just had no good feeling about such an action. He could not understand why not. Ok it could influence his money but that was all. He never

had been thinking about money being a problem.
He could always visit a casino. Problem solved.
He got on his motor and drove to the hospital. He
realised that he did not really had the intention to
visit Lia. Lia was part of the organisation of James,
her mother. Drugsbusiness. He had a very negative
feeling about that kind of business. He now knew
that James did not wanted to have him near her
daughter. He decide to get in and say goodbye to
Lia. She probably could get home tomorrow so
there was no need to continue the relation.
He went into the hospital. He walked to the room of
Lia. She was sitting on the table, just finishing her
dinner.
John smiled at her. She did look good, she was
fantastic, he must admit. He felt that it would be
difficult to forget her. He would always keep on
comparing another girl with her. He sat down with
her. He smiled.
"How are you doing. Your facewound is almost
healed, great. How are your physics, does the
massage work? How is your memory, better?"
She raised her hand. "Yes, yes, it is all going well.
My memory is almost completely back. I remember
everything between us. You have to understand that
I was ordered to go to that club to make trouble.
Nobody expected that I would get hurt. My father is
furious, my mother is awfully concerned. She comes
here every day. In a way she feels responsible for
what happened. I think we just did not understood

enough what it must mean for a boxer to lose a fight that he should have won easily. His total ego was splashed and I crabbed that wound open. Now I can understand his reaction. I should have realised this point before. I did not. You are working together with Toko, the fighter that beat Big Pinto, don't you?"

She looked interested at John.

He realised that she had changed the subject from her to him.

John confirmed that.

"What kind of man is he? How was it possible for him to hit Big Pinto all at once to get him down? "

She really looked interested.

John found it a peculiar conversation. No word about herself, no word about him, just talking about somebody she did not know.

"Why are you so interested in this boxer? Do you want to bet on the result of the fight? "

John looked at her. What would she say?

She said nothing. She stared out of the window, her thoughts were floating away. John looked surprised at her. There was something very wrong. Her mother, James had been here today. Lia 's memory was coming back. She knew about the different lives they lived and the new deal they had made about being together during the weekend. The first evening she had other plans and was gone to the boxingcentre. So it was clear that she could not hold the appointment they made.

"Your mother gave you back your phone. I was here the night after you had the problems. I had to see you. I missed you. I wanted to know how you were doing. I understood our problems. Unfortunately we had no future as long as I am who I am and you are who you are. Our worlds and our views are too different. I came that night to say goodbye and left the phone. I came back later to help you because you had lost your memory, something that is not easy to cope with. I know it through my own experiences. Now your memory is back and you know everything about us. You probably even know that your mother has told me that she has accepted a contract on me. I must disappear after the fight of Toko for the worldchampionship. So it could be possible that she will ask you to fill in this contract. I love you but I cannot sacrifice myself for that. I am sorry, I will never forget you."

John got up. Lia looked at him the tears stood in her eyes. She completely understood his words. She knew it all.

John kissed her on the top of her head and left. He also could hardly hold his tears inside.

He felt awful.

He had a whole weekend in front of him. Alone. No family he could talk to, no friend to go to. Nobody in the world cared about him.

He bought two bottles of rum and a big bag of snacks and got home on his motor.

Chapter 27

He woke up slowly. His head aced. He was laying on the ground on the carpet in his livingroom. This was not good. He got seated on the sofa. He saw the two bottles of rum lying on the ground. Empty. He had a bad hangover. He looked outside it was dark. He tried to remember the time. He left Lia, got home and had started on the rum. It tasted awful but it gave him rest. His head protested. He got to the kitchen and took a cup of coffee. He returned to the living and activated the television. The speaker announced the Saturday late night news. He was lucky. So it was Saturday late night. The coffee worked, he started to feel better. He even took a small snack. He slowly started to feel better.
He found that he had pity himself enough. A young man of his age should do more than just having pity with himself. He should go out, he should be dancing and having fun with other people. With nice young girls. He could go to a movie. He found that a wise idea. He left his motor at the cottage and left on foot. He ran through the very dark forest but did not feel obstacle by that. He got into town. He knew a square with a theatre, a moviecentre and a big hotel with a casino. He walked there.
It was beautiful whether, soft and gentle with a small wind. He liked it and felt better and better. He had a goal to amuse himself. He realised that he had

never done something like this before. He must let
go the past. He would help Toko win his fight and
then he would be free. He first got to the casino. He
liked the idea to gain some money.
John realised that he had bought good bottles of
rum. His hangover was hardly present. He started to
feel better and better. He searched for the right
machine to play at the casino. He won his first
eighthundred dollar and went on to the next. He
stopped after four wins. He left the casino and the
hotel and got to a movie. He just picked one. He did
not really care. He had bought some candies and
took them during the movie.
A group youngsters left the movie together with
John. One of the girls looked at John.
"All alone?" she asked and smiled at him.
"Yeah," John reacted and smiled at her. She was
really beautiful but totally different from Lia.
"I am Rodina, what is your name?"
"I am John."
"Common come with us. We are going to a fine
club, just around the corner.
John found that ok. He got introduced to the other
members of the group.
It was a long and happy night.

John got awaken on a large bed with three girls
around him. They jumped at him immediately and
they had fun till late in the afternoon.

John searched for his clothes and got dressed. He said goodbye and left.

He felt great. He stopped at the "all you can eat"-restaurant and ate all he could.

He went home and got to bed early.

He slept long and deep.

He got up late. He took a late breakfast and got by foot to the city. He found it better to get his condition on level again. The motor was great, of course, but very bad for your condition.

John had tasted from the fun in the city. He trained mainly on keeping the condition of Toko on the high level he was, looked regularly at the moves from the champion and made the moves to block and beat.

The week changed John's life completely. He danced many nights, met many different girls and had fun with them. He did not bother about who Toko was and what he did for a living. Toko was his boxer and that was it.

He visited several casino's in different hotels. He gambled extra money on the win of Toko. He made a list of the bets he had made, so he could control the payments after the game.

He was a good dancer in style and in freestyle. The girls started to know him.

Fridaynight he came to the point that he should be prepared for the big fight the next day. Toko 's fight would start at eleven in the night. He was expected to be there at seven, to prepare Toko for his fight.

He felt calm. Toko was in a perfect shape. He felt great. John made him clear to defend the blows of his opponent in the first round. That would mislead him completely. In the second round he would start to move, circle around him. Than in the third round he really have to start to fight. Move your feet, move the feet position regularly, he will get confused. Than you hit him, hard and fast. Toko smiled. He had the feeling that this was his day. They held a light training to warm up his muscles.

Indeed close to eleven o'clock they got into the arena. A special music, belonging to the presentation of Toko, made clear that they were coming in. The public made a lot of noise. The televisioncamera's were running.

Toko got in. He kept his hands high in the sky. The noise even got louder. It was a real spectacle. The speaker announced him and Toko got into the ring. The same procedure was held for the champion, the speaker even made it extra noise by making a big story of the presence of the worldchampion.

Then everything calmed down. The speaker left his position and the referee came into the ring.

The two boxers were spoken to by the referee. They got back to their corners and the fight began. It was a calm start. The champion started careful specially noticing the right uppercut options from Toko. The blow that finished Big Pinto.

Toko just blocked the soft blows of the Champion. He once or twice made a hit at the face of his

opponent. The champ got even more careful. The public found that there should be more activity.
In the second round Toko started to move more. The champion regularly lost his opponent out of his site. Toko noticed. He already started to hit the champion. The public saw what happened. They got more and more on the hand of Toko. The unexpected for almost everybody started to happen. The champion got worried. He could not follow the moving Toko. Toko even, just once changed his forefoot, he changed from his right foot to his left foot. At once the super strong blow from his right hand could hardly reach the opponent.
The third round started. Toko started this round by getting his two hands in the ar. The public found it glorious. Immediate the champion tried to hit Toko. But Toko was already away. He made a show of it. He started to dance. The champion got angry. He even started to yel. Toko should not run away from him. Toko stepped in and hit the man full at his nose. A really tough blow, This was totally unexpected. The champion started to lose his balance. Immediately Toko hit him again and again. The public got wild. The champion was about to be blown away. Unbelievable but it was happening. Toko stepped back and got to the neutral corner. The referee looked at Toko. Toko smiled at him. He raised his hands in triumph. The referee looked at the champion. The man stood still on his legs but had his hands down, hanging along his body. This

was unique. He found that he had to count the champion out in spite of the fact that he was not actually "down".

The referee touched the champion with one finger to get his attention. The champion fell backwards on the arenafloor. The referee ended the game and called the doctor in the ring.

Toko stretched his hands up. His victory was fabulous. He was the new worldchampion. He really had won the title. His goal was reached. He had made his dream come true.

John looked around. From this moment on he could be killed. He could not find any threat. Of course if he did he would be dead at the same moment.

John was happy too. The power of Toko was really fabulous. He was the new Worldchampion.

A great applause from the audience was his reward. Toko got the belt. He showed himself with the belt. John applauded for him as well.

Toko shined. He could hardly believe it. He did it. He really was the new worldchampion.

The speaker announced it once more. The audience could not get enough of it. Finally the speaker ended the show and Toko and John went back to their quarters.

Toko embraced John. He thanked him. He wanted John to stay with him as his trainer. He would like to defend his throne. He wanted to stay the champion for a couple of years. He was really happy. John smiled. He was happy too. He really had made a big smack of money.

Toko declared that they earned a vacation of two weeks, than they had to get ready for the replay of this match. Approximately in six weeks. The old champion would need at least those six weeks.

Toko 's wife came in. She was glorious. She embraces Toko. She was extraordinary proud of him.

She asked Toko also when he would be ready for his next fight, probably a rematch, that was usual for the loosing champion. Toko told her that it could not take longer than six weeks from today.

He looked at John. He looked serious.

"John, we have to talk. I have to tell you a lot of things you do not know yet. Of course you are entitled to find out everything about yourself before we start up the training again in two weeks. Therefor we have to talk tomorrow. Please, come to the traininglocation at the normal time, two o'clock in the afternoon. I will bring some things with me."

John looked surprised. He was prepared to look around to find out how he would get killed. He was not prepared to have a special talk with Toko about himself. What was this? He also had not thought about a continuation of the job with Toko. He just had not thought about that. He would get killed for the money. What had he missed. Or was this only to mislead him. He still stayed suspicious. He accepted the offer from Toko. There was no problem to continue the trainingsystem. They congratulated each other again and John left. He got into town. He controlled his bankaccount. He must admit that the bookmakers payed out really fast. He was surprised about the total amount. Than he realised that also his part of the fightwin was already on his account. He was rich.

He really was rich. If he would have same more of these fights, he would have even enough money for the rest of his life. Ok, he still was not killed. How come? What had he missed. Did he misjudged Toko.

Toko was the leader of the Wolves. Was that not true? John walked through the city. He still looked around to find a possible killer. The later it became, the less he believed his own story. Or actually the story of James. She just wanted to get rid of him. She wanted to have her daughter back. Well she had what she wanted. He searched for an "all you can eat"-restaurant and got in. He calmed down , ate slowly and with small portions. He again tried to reconsider all arguments for all his solutions. He did not come to new ideas. He really had no idea about the whole situation. He decided to let it go. He could not live thinking all the time that there was something wrong somewhere. It was already late at night when he left the restaurant. He found a movie cinema and looked at a fightingfilm.

Again he came in a group young people and partied with them the whole night. It was Saturdaynight so a lot of people were partying.

John forgot his problems. He also wanted to forget it. He danced and partied along with a lot of others. Suddenly he got caught by a young girl. She just jumped up to him and kissed him. He swopped his arms around her in an automatic reaction.

"Hallo John," she simply stated, still hanging in his arms. She smiled at him. At last I have the opportunity to touch you. I always wanted to hold you. Ooooh you are so cool," she crawled closer against him, keeping her arms around his neck.

John stared at the girl. He had no idea who she was. He looked again. This girl, this was Marion. She looked a lot older than before.

"Marion," he reacted. "Marion, wait a moment, how old are you, girls under 18 are not allowed here. "

She smiled at him. "perfectly correct John. So now you have found my secret, I am already 18. They are always controlling me but I always have my driverslicence with me, so I can prove my age. "

She smiled at him and started to wrap her breasts against his body. He looked at her. She really was beautiful. She looked good.

She kissed him again. She really was experienced. He got under her influence. She got down, took his hand and dragged him with her.

She entered a sidespace. They came in a kind of cleaningroom. She immediately started to get her clothes off and jumped on John. He was astonished. She kissed him and started calmly to undress him. They made love. John really found her attractive. She seemed very willingfull and took almost all the initiatives. John accepted that. He found it attractive.

They both got satisfied. They got dressed again. Marion kissed him and asked whether she could meet him more often. She was in love with him from the moment they had met at the prisonside.

John came to his senses. He realised that again he had made love to a murdermachine. Did he wanted to start the problem over again after his experiences with Lia. He promised to come to this place again tomorrow at this hour. She looked gladly at him. She kissed him and left.

John did not know what he had to do with this situation. He on one hand did not wanted to have a girl with her background. On the other hand these two girls were really beauties. Also physical, their super bodies, were extreme attractive for him.

He decided to go home. He had had a special day. He was still alive and rich. He left the partycentre and ren home.

Chapter 28

He felt good being back home. He took some
snacks and watched the television to see whether
there was any comments on the boxing
championship. Indeed there was very much
comment. Large analysis about the different way of
boxing. The fantastic development Toko had made.
In only six fights worldchampion was at least
special. They found him a fantastic complete fighter.
He moved extraordinary fast. John was happy with
these comments. It anyway was not just a bought
fight. Toko really was seen as a candidate that
could hold the championship for a longer period.
It was late and went to bed.
He slept deep and long.

He got up late. He felt good. He had a nice
breakfast. He had to get more of these, he liked
them. He also had to think more about the food he
ate. He must get more fruits and more vegetables.
He made a note for his groceries, so he would not
forget it. He had to be with Toko at two o'clock. So
he had enough time to go there running.
Just at that moment his doorbell ringed. He looked
surprised at the doorbell. Then he looked at his
frontdoor. A visitor?
He got to the door, but saw nobody, looking through
the small window. He opened the door but still there

was nobody. He looked if he saw the doorbell. He pushed the bel and got a totally other sound. He was even more surprised. Behind him somebody bonked at his outside door. He forgot that he also had a ring at the outside door between the trees. He opened the outside door.

Leo stood in front of him.

He was surprised. "Hallo Leo," he smiled at him.

"Hallo John, is everything all right? I more or less missed you several times. Yesterday I saw your motor here but you were not, is that all right?"

"Yee, Leo, everything is fine. As you see I did buy me a motor, but I often want to go to town running to stay in a good condition."

"Ok," Leo reacted, "sorry for disturbing you, I just was a little bit concerned. See you."

John smiled at him and closed the outside door. He collected his bag, left the helmet at home and left. He got to town through the forest and took a quick snack with coffee near the trainingslocation of Toko.

He got in at the right time.

He was surprised to see that the computercentre was occupied by more than ten persons. No one reacted on his entrance. He got to the trainingsarea. In the middle of the room stood a large table with two chairs. Toko came from the backside and welcomed him enthusiastic.

"John, you are a miracle. I knew it but I had my doubts. You proved your rightness. Perhaps you did not understand what I mend. "

Toko invited John to sit down. He got back to the place where he came from and picked up a big envelope. He put the envelope on the table. On the envelope his name, "John Normal" was written. He looked at Toko.

"John first this. My manager is not my wife. She is my manager. She makes the arrangements for the boxingfights. I started to box in my young years but only as an amateur. I needed more musclepower and more moving quality. Keep that in mind when you learn more about yourself.

I will be out of side for the next two weeks. I will be on a cruise, so I do only have contact with my organisation. You know in the meantime that I am the leader of the Wolves. In the evening and the night I managed my organisation. There were not really large problems but in principle you always have to be close to your organisation. Physically I will not be around, mentally my organisation feels that I am near. This means that our next training will be in sixteen days, on a Friday we will start. The date for the next fight will be cleared by then.

There is, as the last information I give you, one more point that is important for you."

Toko looked serious at John. He got up.

"John, I am your father. I have to go, we will meet again. Good luck." He ticked John on his head and left. He was gone before it all came to Johns mind. What did he say. What? "I am your father?" What was this? Toko his father? Impossible. Really impossible. He sat there. He did not move. He was completely flabbergasted. This was beyond his mindset. How, what, who? He did not know what to think. This was completely new. He even had never thought about that possibility. But why? What was the purpose of this all. Getting Worldchampion. Right. That was the purpose. They succeeded but why through this way. Why all this secrecy. How fitted his memoryblock in this or was that only a unfortunate incident?

He kept on asking questions, knowing that there were no answers yet. He looked at the envelope. What could be in there? He did not wanted to stay. He propped the envelope in his bag and left.

He now knew that his father was the leader of the Wolves. Did he had to doubt his word? Why should he have made up such a confession?

He was the son of a criminal. Was he a criminal as well ? Who was his mother? Where had he lived? The questions kept on flashing up. He did not run. He walked calm and controlled. Maybe even afraid to find out what was in the envelope. What could he expect. Which questions would be answered, which not? How did he know that this was real.

He got into the market to buy all kind of food ingredients. Also fruit and snacks. He left the market with two big bags filled with food. He walked back to his cottage. He was free for the next two and a half week. There was more than enough time to get the envelop opened.

He knew he could not wait. He ate on his way back in a simple restaurant and walked further. It was almost dark by the time that he got at the cottage. He got in and laid the envelope at his bureau.

He made coffee but could not wait any longer.

He sat at his bureau and opened the envelope. A letter fell out, a small very long box and a memorystick.

He picked up the letter and started to read, sipping on his coffee.

"Hallo John, the letter started. I am you. You, I, wrote this letter. Toko is your father. He might have told you already.

The letter pointed at the memorystick. On the stick he himself had made a statement. It would declare the whole position and the whole entourage.

That was all.

He did not know what to think of it. He got himself another cup of coffee. He picked up the memorystick, got his tablet out of his bag and decided to first serve all the things he had bought. He kept two snacks but placed the rest in the refrigerator and in the cupboard in the kitchen. He returned to his chair. He connected the memorystick and activated the information on it.

"Hallo John, "a vague figure spoke. The picture got sharper. He looked at himself.

"If you see this image, then there must have gone something wrong. This information would only made available if this injection."

He showed a big syringe.

"In this syringe is a non-tested nanogryte, as the creators called it. It is a kind of minirobot. It is injected through the skin, therefor there is no real needle on top but only a sprayhead. It spreads the nano's through your skin. It comes in your blood and is manoeuvred to the right spot in your body. In this case the right place is in the brain. It has to function so that it will make your memory stronger. You should get a photographic memory. The risk might be that our memory get blocked. If you see this information, something has gone wrong. In the envelope is a syringe with the antidote. It will activate the nano's to leave the body. It will be leaving your body with the urine. It could be useful to catch them when they leave your body.

As you may have suggested I have made a deal with Toko. He could get injected with all these medicines I have taken the last five months to find out whether it really worked to be qualified to have your body moved into a fighting machine, a boxingmachine. What I always did good was moving in the ring. Toko misses that completely.

Further the musclestructure will became massive. Both capacities are necessary to have Toko be capable to box on the level needed to get worldchampion. I have taken all these medicines and I am really a lot stronger than before. Toko is build a lot bigger than I am. He always have wanted to become a world famous boxing champion. I have promised that he will be qualified to became one.
If you really have trained him you have learned him how to move. You , I , were highly qualified in that part of the boxing arena. I just could not hit hard enough. I had no knock down, Toko does.
If you want the nano-problem solved, you only have to put the syringe against your leg, press on it and the nano's will be forced to leave your body. If that has happened your problem will be solved. It might take four to seven days to recover but it will. I can assure you that.
During the last weeks some unexpected problems have arisen. The families of the doctors, you undoubtedly have met them now, have been kidnapped by the Major. Please try to get them free. They are completely innocent. The Major is angry because she was not involved in this whole affair. Be careful. The Major and James are regularly working together in certain cases. They are really dangerous. The Major wanted money for the kidnapping but Toko refused. It is a difficult situation. Please try to solve all this. Good luck."
That was it. The screen got dark.

Well, he already got Peter and Pauls family free. So the Major and James were more or less working together. The two ladies against the two man, the Wolf, Toko, and the Lord, finances. Could they work without the positive cooperation of the Lord?

He doubted that. Who controls the money, controls every business. Every business needed money. He realised that indeed the Lord was the man with the central power. He could pull any string to have things done. How come that he never had tried to find out who he was? How did he control these criminal organisations? He remembered that he tried to break in at the financial centre of the Lord. He was simply worked out of the building. They knew one way or the other that he was coming. He must admit that he was treated decently.

Who was he, this financial masterbrain. Most likely he must be part of the financial world already. That anyway had the easiest way of handling white and black money. He had to think this over again. Now he had to decide whether he wanted his memory back.

Of course. The explanations that he had offered himself on the benefit of his father was not complete enough. Why this illegal way of acting. Why not out in the open. Why this nano-option? Through this information he would have been informed about everything. He actually did not know anything, except that he might get his memory back if he used the syringe with sprayhead.

He grabbed the box and opened it. Indeed some kind of syringe was in it. Indeed it had a sprayhead. He put it in front of him on his bureau.

He sighted, took the syringe and opened his trousers, got his pants down and spread the content of the syringe in his upperleg. It took more time than he had expected to get the whole content in his leg. He was standing a little bit curled. He had to smile about his position. He was bended a bit forward with his back far to the back. Finally the syringe was empty and it gave a click as a signal that it was empty. He put the syringe on his bureau and looked at his leg. He did not saw anything special. He pulled up his trousers and sat down.

Suddenly he remembered his appointment with Marion. He had promised to be on the same spot as last night again tonight.

He actually did not wanted to go. Marion was, just as Lia a murdermachine. Beautiful woman but dangerous. He realised that he found it a problem not to go. He liked keeping his promises. He had to face the problem.

He did not wanted to use the motor. Only if he was in a real hurry he would use it. It was getting late but he decided to run all the way to the dancingcentre. He arrived deep in the night. He got in and calmly walked around. He would not have to look for her. She would find him most likely if she was here.

He was leaning against a big pillar when Marion embraced him. She kissed him direct on his mouth.

She was a beautiful young girl. He got influenced again in her presence. She happily smiled at him. "Thank you for coming John.

"Marion, I have to say something to you," John started.

Marion looked at him, sadly. "You have another girl, you have already cheated on her once, yesterdayevening and you do not want to do this again. I understand, but can we at least be friends, perhaps just for the sex? I love your body. It makes me hot, wanting to have you, to feel you in me. I already am hot now. Ok, can we be friends?"

"Marion, you are a fighting machine and a good one. I am afraid of fightingmachines. They indefinitely get angry and might hurt you from one moment to the other. That is dangerous. That danger takes the passion away."

"She stared at him. "Yesterday there was no such problem," she said with a smile.

She grabbed him between his legs. "And now also, no problem, I feel your passion. This is enough passion for me. Please, forget my profession, just enjoy life. Live!!"

She dragged him again to the room where they had been the day before. He must admit that there was nothing wrong with his passion. They made love and enjoyed it both. He knew he would regret it later but now he enjoyed it.

They got dressed and suddenly, without any ground he found that he should ask her if she knew who the Lord was and where he lived?

He asked her. She looked surprised at him.

"You mean you don't know? Everybody knows."

He looked at her hoping that she would inform him. She saw possibilities here. She came close to him. I will tell you, if you tell me where you live. I can visit you in a more private surrounding. My parents don't like it when I take friends with me in their home.

John stared at her. Could he still escape from this trap. Did he wanted to escape? He did had enough money to get another location to live if he wanted that. He told her where he lived.

Marion looked astonished at him.

"But,…. "she started and then she laughed laud.

John stared at her. He did not understand. He could not understand because he did not know what she knew.

"John, Boseley Friender is the Lord. You live on her nose. Straight under her eyes. That is here house address just outside the city." Magnificent. What have you done with her that she gives you such a protected place to live. Oh, I surely want to visit you there. May I visit you tomorrow evening late at night, will you be home? Please?"

I must admit that I Might be very late because I have another appointment with my father somewhere. I do not know how that will go. Ok, see you tomorrow. Thank you, there was nothing wrong with your passion. Love you, " she waved at him and left the room.

John found himself a softy. He could not resist a beautiful girl, even if he wanted that.

He ran back to his cottage. On the way back he had to think about Lia. Also involved in brutal attacks. He got caught by the thought that Boseley was the Lord. Again a woman in power. He had never thought at her as the financial boss. Yes she was the boss of a bank organisation.

Chapter 29

John got home but had no rest. Wat was this again. Boseley was the Lord. Yes she was good in finance. Yes she already had a bank to combine black and white money with each other. The banks were rich because of the ownership of many buildings. How come he had never thought of a woman to be in the lead. He had the information right under his nose. He wandered why she did not cooperate with the other ladies or with the Wolves. Of course she was the friend of everybody. They all needed a reliable bank to arrange their financial needs. She must be reliable otherwise she would not have become the Lord. He thought back on her visit at the Saloon. She was the housewife of a businessman, that was it. She had no reason to offer him the cottage. Or was there more. Being the Lord, she would not do things without a good reason. Ok, he was the son of Toko, the leader of the Wolves. An important customer. Good for a lot of money. Would Toko have asked her to offer this? What had Leo said? She thinks that she has warm feelings for him. Peculiar. Why would a financial tough lady have warm feelings for a total stranger. It was all still very unclear for John. He would visit her tomorrow and ask her. The answers could be so simple.
John felt tired and went to bed.

He could not sleep. Al the things happened with
Marion. The trap that he could not resist. Boseley
being the Lord, surprisingly. Also surprisingly was
that Toko got a vacation of more than two weeks.
Ok he was rich. With all his bets he had made more
than half a million dollar, together with hit part of the
gamewin he had more than a million, unbelievable.
A huge amount for a beginner. He had just started.

John woke up late. He decided to stay at home
today, he did some exercises and run through the
forest. He did the light at the frontdoor on. If Leo
saw it he was invited to get in. Only through Leo he
could make an appointment with Boseley. Leo was
his contact.
Indeed Leo called on him half way the afternoon. He
was not alone. Miriam, the girl from the cleaning
and the waitress from the Saloon came with him.
She wanted to clean up the cottage. She
immediately started in the bathroom.
John offered Leo a cup of coffee and asked him if
he could get an appointment with Boseley.
Leo did a bit difficult about that. After some
stumbling open remarks, he came to the point.
Boseley was last Saturday divorced from her
husband. Her husband was his sun. As he had
informed John, they already lived separate, each in
their own part of the house, with its own bedroom
and office. He himself often slept in the greenhouse,
his comfort zone. Last Saturday it had come to a

climax and Boseley had kicked his sun out of the premises. It mend that also he had left the premises. He was here to introduce Miriam and to hand him the entrancekeys of the total premises. He had another place to live nowadays, with his sun. He already had taken all his belongings as well as those of his sun. So the contacts would stop with this.

Leo got up, greeted Miriam and went to the door. There he remembered something that he had to tell. Boseley had given them ten days to leave. She was, probably with some new lover, on a kind of partytour. She would be back in two weeks from today. If John wanted he could take the greenhouse, because he was out there.

John was surprised about all these new developments. It meant that he could not talk to Boseley for the next two weeks.

Awful but he could not change that. What was going on. Was it coincident that and Toko and Boseley were out of sight for the next two weeks? Strange but for the time being he had no lead for any connection between the two.

Leo left.

John found the situation puzzling. Now he had nobody to talk to. Even Leo was no longer evaluable.

Miriam started to clean the livingroom, so John got outside to his garden. He must accept that it was most likely that Boseley would leave this place now that she was no longer married to Mr Friender. He thought, surprised that this would mean that her name would change. He wandered how she wanted to be called now that she was divorced.

Miriam came outside and told him that she was ready. The coming two days she would be busy in the house and the greenhouse. She had keys of her own to get in, so he did not had to open the door for her. John looked at her, she was really beautiful. He smiled, his thoughts were very directed on the outlooks of the young ladies. Miriam, noticing his looks, moved a little extra with her hips and said goodbye with an inviting smile.

She left, closing the door and the outside door between the trees with her own keys.

John was alone again. Again he thought about the consequences of the divorce of Boseley. If she also would move out, he had to leave as well. He would be prepared for that. He would be looking around to find another home. He noticed that he already called this place his home. He really felt at home. He decided that he would walk around the house of Boseley now that he had the keys. She would not know, she was on her loverstour.

He got out and took the keys from Leo to go through the frontgate. He had never been on the premises itself. It felt as if he was burgling. He smiled while he closed the gate behind him. He calmly looked around, walked over the grass, all the way around the house. It really was big. All around there were plants, having flowers all around. He found it very domestic. It gave him a good feeling. He realised that he loved flowers. He walked at the back of the house up the terrace. It was huge, having two places to sit on couches and an area with a large table with eight chairs around it. Huge and beautiful. He followed the path to the back of the garden. It came at the lake, a large beach was in front of the water of the lake. He walked over the beach to the greenhouse totally on the left. He found it more a rosarium. The whole greenery was surrounded by roses. He looked again. He found all kind of collars not really separated though they were probably started completely separated and kept away from the other collars. Now it all got through each other. It had its own charm. He opened the frontdoor of the greenhouse. It was all glass, thick and double, so very strong, but you could see through it all over. Because also on the inside the walls were covered with roses the inlook was very limited. He was very impressed on the inside.

A meandering path walked through the very large greenhouse. Extraordinary high plants with enormous leaves dominated the overview. At the back there was an area more or less covered by small and high plants. All with large green leaves and without flowers. John walked around further. On several locations small fountains had waterfun. A small part of the water was directed through small pipes to the plants, another part was blown in the air. John was impressed. He could understand why Leo had lived here, in this warm feeling area. He found a door into the backspace behind the green leaves. The door was not locked. He got in. It was rather dark inside. While opening the door some small lights went on. A soft glow spread through the small livingroom. Six large chairs filled the space almost completely. In the corner a small desk was places with an officechair in front. No computer or tablet was there. Of course Leo had taken his tablet and/or computer with him.

John walked on through the living. A large curtain closed the space behind it. He push it aside. Behind the curtain a large bedroom was visible. A large bed, filling half the room looked extra big because of that. A curtain on the side seemed to be the entrance to the bathroom. John looked quickly. A small shower, a toilet and a one person fountain was all there was. He left the greenhouse. Because of the watercyclus he had the impression that the greenhouse would take care of itself. He wandered what Leo had done with it. He walked back around the other side of the house. He was surprised to find there a great barn. At least ten by twenty meters, with an extra stock on it. He walked around it. There was a large door on the front, a real stabledoor, large and high. He tried the door but it was locked. This was bigger than many houses. He searched for a key on his ring but did not find one that fitted. He thought that there was a key on the inside. That was peculiar. How do you get out when the door was locked. There must be something that had to be done to get the key turn. Or was the keylock just fake. This could easy be an electronic lock, that looked like a classic lock. To be opened at distance. Remote control. To open it he needed such an remote control. He wondered whether Miriam had one. If she had to clean this she must have it. He probably would come back tomorrow, Miriam would be busy cleaning al these spaces.

He followed his tour. The garage was large enough for four cars. He did not wanted to get in. This did not seemed interesting. He walked back. He anyway had a good impression of the house on the outside.

He got back to his home. It was already getting dark. He was surprised to find a note behind the outerdoor. It was bound on a stone. Someone must have thrown it over the door. He was not in so he had not answered the door. He picked up the stone and unwrapped the paper. It was sealed in a plastic cover. He got in and opened the plastic and laid the small envelope, still closed on the table. He throwed the plastic away. And sat down at the envelope. Who would deliver an envelope? It should have been someone that knew that there was an entrance behind those wooden poles. Further it must be someone that he knew. He opened the envelope. There was a short note, handwritten in it.

"Sorry I must work today and tomorrow. See you soon! ". Signed Marion.

Ok, clear, she would not come tonight. He got the time for himself.

He prepared a meal with a lot of vegetables. He tried several ingredients with it and some sauces. He finished it with a big pudding. That was of course not done but he loved it.

He put on the television and looked at the different programmes. He did not found one of them interesting.

He took his tablet and started to search. Now that he knew that Boseley was the Lord, he tried to find more information about her and her bank. She was prominently shown at the site of her bank. She was not only the chairman of the board but also the by far largest shareholder. He tried to find more information about her and her bank but he only found that she was not using the name of her ex-husband but another name. Boseley Groundfort, probably her maidenname. He searched further under that name but found nothing on the internet. He tried to find her bankaccount numbers but the bank blocked that completely.

He took a cup of coffee. Did he wanted to break in in the accounts of the bank. He was very curious about the information on her accounts. He decided to do it.

He needed more than seven tries to finally get in. He searched for the accounts on her name and found seventeen hits. He followed the information. The accounts were really enormous. The total was far over the one hundred million. She was really rich. He for the time being did not do anything with it. He tried to get more information. He searched for accounts in the total bankinformation that had money on it but were not used in the last ten years. He found more than sixhundred hits. He was surprised. The total amount of all these accounts was over twenty million. He selected the fifty larges accounts. He was still surprised. The total was more than fifteen million.

He got to a small bank, by far the smallest. He actually bought thirty percent of its shares on the financial market. It gave a sudden hit in the market, he supposed. He opened an account and started to pass money from the twentyfive not-used accounts to his new account. He used this account to pay the twelve million that he needed to get the shares he bought. He got back to the bank of Boseley. He looked for accounts that had not been used in the last five years and had an amount on it above one million dollars. He found ten businessaccounts. Probably secret accounts from illegal activities. He decided for all these ten accounts to change the entrancecode. He wrote them down. He did the same for the three other big banks in the city. He really needed his concentration to be able to crack the entrance codes. It were often six or seven codes behind each other, each had to be cracket. He opened on each of these banks several accounts and searched for the forgotten accounts. He emptied them all. His total account was over hundred and fifty million dollars. He bought more shares of the little bank so that he had fiftyfive percent of the shares.

Of course the bank would feel this as a brutal take over. John did not had the intention to be involved in the management of the bank. They should go on as they did.

It was starting to get light outside. John had been busy all night. He realised that he had been working as a crook. He worked at night, breaking in on bankaccounts and stealing money from there.

He smiled at himself and his honesty. He was a criminal himself. Ok he only emptied accounts that were probably only existing because the bank had not informed the owners or their legatees on the inheritance. They kept the money for their own good. The same would work for the businessaccounts. If the owner died and the legatees did not came to the bank. The accounts staid unused.

Of course he owed the families of the died people if they existed. No family, no legatees.

He was tired and got to bed.

Chapter 30

John did not sleep too long. He got up by noon. He had a brunch and started to train. He ran through the forest, made a lot of balance moves and felt better after all the activities. He must keep this up, now that he did not train with Toko.

He looked at the news and did not found it very interesting. Suddenly a man announced a big change in the bank market. One small bank, always stayed small. Now somebody had taken thirty percent of the shares. An enormous buy. The shares had gone up about twelve percent. The bank itself announced that their total bankreserves had grown with sixty percent. This had given the shares another push. Everybody was surprised about this announcement from this small bank. This new reserves made it in a very short period to a middle bank. Not a big one but a middle one. The buyer of the shares had done a big deal. Nobody knew who he or she was. Nobody had called as a new shareholder. The bank itself did not know either. The shareholdersmeeting that will be in about a month regarding the yearresults of last year would possibly make this clear.

John smiled. He had not thought about this consequence. It was not important. He controlled the accounts and everything was as he had let it behind this morning.

He got interested in the present accounts of Toko and the other leaders of the criminal organisation. He found several bankaccounts in the name of the Wolves. He was surprised to see that the last two days large amounts were paid to an account that looked like a private account. He wrote down name and address of the owner. He tried to find more information on the internet about this person. He was shocked. It was an account in the name of the brother of Rico. This was not good. He tried to find the reason for these payments, but could not find anything. He did found large amounts on the bets on the fight from Toko. Great wins for the organisation, so for the Wolves gambled by competitive bookmakers. John smiled. Toko also had used his abilities to get extra money with the bets. He also found some private accounts from Toko. He found the payment from winning the fight and the immediate payment of half of the amount to his account.

He decided also to look at the private accounts of James, the Major and Boseley. He wrote down the special payments to the accounts and the special payments from the accounts. He was surprised about the amounts that were going on in these accounts. He could understand that in the casinoaccounts a lot of money came in and got out also. Many people worked in those establishments. Looking at the accounts and there payments on the last week, he found it peculiar that there seemed to be a connection between the payments and the private relation between the receiver and the member of the organisation.

John had his thoughts about the payment to the wife of the brother of Rico. He had his address. He decided to bring this man a visit to see if he could declare wat had happened. He also had made a search on the same kind of transfers to each of the members of the other three organisations.

He located the four addresses, looked for a photo of the four activators and found it a good idea to go running to these addresses.

He tried to find out whether his memory was coming back. His name, the name of his father from the past, the name of his mother. Nothing, still no memory.

He realised that visiting these four persons was very risky. These four cheated on their bosses. If they knew who he was, they would easily locate him. He decided to make a nice show of his visits. He ran to the city. Found a masquerade shop and selected a large number of materials to colour his face, change his hair, wear non-usual clothes. He must admit that he liked it. He got back to his cottage and unpacked the big assortment. He tried the different options and combinations. He selected four different combinations and redressed himself several times. He made a picture of himself in the four different outfits. He also changed his profile and his altitude.

Again he made a serial pictures of himself. He used one of his separate tablets for each file. He copied the pictures to the file that belonged to the contact he was going to make, so with the brother of Rico, he was an old badly dressed man. For the man from James he was a middle-aged lady a little bit fatty, for the lady from the Major he was an old lady, for the man from the Lord he was a fat young boy.

He put a W in paper on the Wolves file, an J on the James file, an M on the Majors file and an L on the Lords file, so he would know which file belonged to whose organisation.

He was really satisfied about his transfers.

He made a broad dinner for himself, took some coffee and decided to first visit the brother of Rico, The second man in the organisation of the Wolves. He first made a letter with the information about the transfers of the money involved.

He made this for all four cases. On front was the name and the address of the person involved.

He got dressed as a very old man with a stick and the envelope in his pocket. He walked through the forest and got to the first address. Only right before the house he stopped. He bowed deeply forward and slowly started to shuffle to the front door. He bend deeply and leaned seriously on the stick. His head was far over his ears, so his face was hardly visible. He wore grey lenses so his eyes were of another colour than his own.

John shuffled to the front door. He ringed the bel. It was getting dark outside. The frontdoorlight went on and the door was opened. John saw kidslegs.

A young boy said "Hallo sir, what can we do for you?"

John let his voice sound a little bit crispy and asked for his father. The boy went back, let the door open and called loud out for his father.

A tall man, a little fatty, came to the door.

"Yes?" the man said a little bit disturbed.

John asked if he was the man mentioned on the letter he had in his hand.

He recognized him from his picture.

The man looked surprised at the old bended figure in front of him.

He was not very patient. John was not quick enough in his vision. He tried to give John a big push and at the same time tried to grab the letter out of his hand.

John saw it coming because the feet of the man moved forwards. He quickly bent backwards and moved the letter to his site. He directly jumped a little bit up and grabbed the man at his throat. He immediately draw him to the ground. The man lost his balance and fell hard on the stones in front of his frontdoor.

"Oh, I am sorry, sir. I hope you did not hurt yourself."

He showed the man on the floor the letter. "Sir, in this letter a number of financial transactions are mentioned in which you transfer money from the Wolesaccount to the account of your wife. Please confirm that these are transactions in compliance with the Wolves interest and not only in your private interest. If these transactions are not in the interests of the Wolves, than please transfer the transactions back to the Wolves. I expect your immediate attention for this case. Thank you."

John put the letter in the man's hand and walked away.

Once on the street again he looked back. The man was still on the ground, staring at the old man that walked away from him. He was totally flabbergasted that he was surprised by such an old man.

John got out of his sight and started to run. Three blocs later he tempered his speed.

He got back home and changed. He was now an older lady, middle-aged, he would say. He had a big wig on and a comic little hat on it. He made up his face with green eyeshadow and green contactlenses. He made his skin look a little bit more rosy and wore long pants with a big coat above it. He wore flat shoes. He did not feel happy with high heels. He made his eyebrows deep dark in great contrast with the grey-white wig. His nose, he made extra red.

He got on his way. He had a little lady's bag with the envelope in it. Now he had to get up with an elevator. No restrictions at the entrance so he got in by just walking in. He looked at the sign for the right stock with the housenumber and got up with the elevator.

He came in a small square with only four doors. He looked at the apartment with the right number. He called on the door. He heard the bell ringing inside. A man came at the door.

"Hallo, I am looking for,… "John looked at the envelope and mentioned the name of the man involved. The man looked surprised at the lady in front of him.

"You have an envelope for him. That is ok, you can give it to me. I will give it to him."

The man stretched his hand out to the letter.

John hide it behind him. "I am sorry," he reacted friendly. "I do have to hand it over to him personally and preferably in private." He smiled looking apologising.

"Oh, nonsense, just give it to me!". The man looked irritated. John did a small step backwards. Looking a little bit intimidated.

Immediately the man took a step forward and tried to grab the lady in front of him.

John did a big step aside. The man had not expected that and stumbled forward. John did another step aside, looking at the stumbling man. The man was very noisy and called out. "What are you doing!!!" What.. "

Another man came to the door. He looked questioning. He simply pointed his thump inside and the stumbling man disappeared in the apartment.

John found it interesting how these drugsbosses were dealing with each other.

John asked if he was the man from the name on the envelope. He also recognized him from the picture. The man confirmed.

John told him that there had been several transactions to his sister. If these transactions were in the interest of James than there was nothing the matter. If they were not, he better transferred the amounts back immediately. John gave him the letter, made a nick and turned around to enter the elevator. He nicked again while the doors of the elevator were closing and he got down with the elevator.

He left the building and got away. He made some extra runs to be sure he did not got followed. He got into a hotel, went to the toilet and changed back to himself as good as possible. He should do that the next time better planned than this time, he found it not very professional from himself.

He ran through the forest. He knew where he was going, for somebody not familiar with these woods it should be difficult to follow him without being seen. He got back in his cottage. He put his clothes and make up together with the second tablet in one drawer of the cabinet in his bedroom. The used materials for the first visit were in the first drawer. The third and fourth drawer would be use for the other two visits.

He closed it all, went back to his livingroom and activated the television. He would visit the two other persons tomorrow.

On television there was a dispute about who had to pay for the cost of the rebuilding of the prison. All local politicians found it to be the task of the government to raise the money, the government found it a problem for the local authorities, there was the ground for the destruction. There was also a lot of critic on the police and the justice department because they had not yet found the responsible people that ruined the prison. The police said that nobody was cooperating with them. They were sure that people knew more about those that had ruined the prison.

John found it amusing. He knew that Toko was involved and as far as he could find out the Major, James and the Lord were involved. Of course they did not wanted to pay but would probably make money out of this position. For the time being there even had not been given an order to pull down and remove the rests of the prison as it was.

Further news was that the criminality was growing. More and more fights in bars and pubs took place. More aggressive robberies were happening and two kidnappings. Also on that site the police was heavily under pressure. There also seemed to be a big internal battle going on in the drugsorganisations. There seemed to be four groups that were busy to enlarge their territory. That always gave pressure on the neighbours. Three killings had taken place. This was new for John. He remembered how easy the members of James took their weapons to arrange a solution for a possible problem. He remembered the shooting on Mindy when she was with him. He also realised that Marion could have been involved in these killings. She even could have been one of the victims. He got worried. He tried to let go. He knew that Lia as well as Marion were killers. Dangerous woman with whom you never wanted to be involved in a fight. They were dangerous and awfully good fighters. He should not wanted to be involved. He should not think about them. They made their own decisions.

Chapter 31

John did not sleep very well. He got up early. He had a quick breakfast and created the old lady for his visit to the third person in power of the organisation of James. This also was a woman. Her specialities were gold, jewellery and art. Especial art was her area of interest. She had transferred half the profit of a painting to her private account instead of to the companies account.

There might be something wrong about that transfer.

John prepared her letter and got on his way. She lived nearby. He needed only half an hour walk to get at her house. A big villa with a large entrance road in front of the house.

John started his act at the beginning of the private path. No big gate, only an open road towards the house. This all made it easier than trying to find a way through a heavily guarded gate. He used the stick to lean on with every step. It took a lot of time to get to the door. He located a big black limousine in front of the house. He saw nobody in it.

At last he was at the door. He ringed the bell. An older man, the butler, opened the door.

John asked for the lady of the house. The butler had clear instruction not to disturb the lady this morning.

John made clear that this was an emergency. If the lady of the house was not willing to come to the door, she would regret it for the rest of her life.

The butler was not impressed.

"It is your problem now, sir. Your lady lives in a dangerous world. I am trying to help her. I do not know what it would mean for your position if the lady is no more available, "John simply stated.

The butler stayed calm and smiled at him.

"I am sorry but you are probably signing her death sentence. I have done my best, Good Bye". John made a small nick and turned around.

The butler looked at him and closed the door. John calm and slowly left the premises through the entrance road.

He was almost back at the street when a load call from the house made him stand still and slowly turn around.

In front of the house the butler was waving at him. John waved back at him, turned around and went on to the street.

The butler then started to run to him. He calmly walked on. The butler stopped right in front of him.

"Hallo, madam, I am sorry. The lady of the house is willing to make an exception for you this time. Would you please follow me, she can receive you now."

John looked at the man. He was learning, but he had to learn a lot more. He would not follow him.

The lady could come here if she wanted to talk with him.
The butler was convinced that the old lady was gladly willing to follow him now that her wish to talk to the lady, against all earlier instructions, would be realised. So he turned around and started to walk back, even before John could say anything.
So, John turned back and followed his walk away from the house. He only wanted to talk to the lady of the house. She got scared and also was used to be listened at. John chuckled. She would not come to him. She was too arrogant for that. He would have to approach her by another action. He would break in in her tablet. He smiled about the idea. He calmly walked on. The butler did not came back to him.
John left the street and looked back. Nobody was following him. He quickly ran through the next four streets, entered on a square in a large hotel and changed in the toilet. He put all his cloths in his bag and left the hotel.
He got back home. He was convinced that nobody had followed him.
John took a cup of coffee, looked up her emailaddress in her file and approached her with an e-mail.
"Dear Mrs Chaimber,
Today I tried to inform you about your problems with the transaction of the painting of Mr Stronghold, sold for two million dollars. You did not yet transferred the whole amount to the company. If this

is correct in your eyes, than you certainly will not have any problem with me, telling the Major about this action. Now that you did not wanted to come to the door, I see no other option than to inform the Major, unless I see that you have made corrections within the next 24 hours.

Thank you,

The old lady."

John looked at his mail and send it away. He used the email address of a televisoncompany as stand between so that it would seem as if the mail came from there.
He took a small candy with his coffee and got redressed as a young fatty boy. He had big glasses and large gardentrousers, filled with extra pillows. He wore a wig with longer hair and fillings in his mouth to let his cheeks look fat. He tried to talk and it sounded a little bit special, with a certain accent. He got on his way, the letter and his own clothes in his bag on his back.
The man he was about to visit had a position high in the organisation of the Lord. It was not clear how high he was. His speciality was the accounts of highplaced persons. He regularly arranged the problems, he talked about with his "clients", himself. Sometimes his clients created these themselves. He always made a nice arrangement to solve the

financial problem. Later the man used the contact for the benefit of the organisation of the Lord. Now he had bought a house that was too expensive for himself, so he arranged an extra financial injection in his houseproject with money from the company. This man lived in a big apartment in the centre of the city. Also a very expensive place.

John walked into the complex, he greeted the man at the service desk and walked to the elevator. The man from the service desk, called his attention and came after him. Just at that moment the elevator opened, a gentle lady came out and greeted the man from the desk. He suddenly had no interest in John anymore and paid extra attention at the lady. John went into the elevator, controlled the right stock, based on the housenumber and pressed the twelfth stock button.

He got up. Nobody got in. He left the elevator. He was at a square with three doors. The door on the right was the correct door. He walked to the door and ringed the doorbell. John picked the envelope from his bag and hanged the bag on his back again. The door was opened. A middle-aged man stared at John. He obviously expected someone else. John asked if he was the man mentioned on the envelope. The man confirmed that. John did recognized him from the photo on the website of the Lords organisation.

John did as if he had quoted the next sentence from his memory. "This letter tells you wat your problem is. It also gives you the possibility for a solution, "he quoted and gave the letter to the man.

The man looked surprised at him, but accepted the letter. "What do you mean. Are you threatening me? Who do you think you are? " The man became more and more angry.

John heard the doors from the elevator opening. The man in front of him, heard it too. He looked over the shoulder of John and yelled immediately to the two man that came out of the elevator. John turned around and looked at the two man. He stepped aside to see what the man would do. They indeed came towards John. It was only a few steps. John looked behind him. The door to the staircase was there.

"Be careful !!" he said to the man in the door and stepped back to the staircase door.

Quickly he went through the door and got to the staircase. He ran up the stairs and waited on the next stock. The two man came after him but thought that he got down, not up the stairs. They speeded down the stairs. John followed them but got through the door, back to the stock where the man he had visited still waited in his dooropening.

He saw John coming through the door and stepped forward to catch him. John stopped straight for the man.

"Beware," John said, very calm and not to laud, more a dangerous sounding whisper.

The man tried to hit him. John easily stepped aside and knocked the man down in one blow. His left hand was not as strong as his right hand but more than enough to hit the man heavily on his left eye. John saw the eyes of the man get surprised and the one, touched by his hand got red and after that bleu. The man sacked through his knees.

John stepped over the man. The man got down on the ground, he still had the letter in his hand. John walked to the elevator. The elevator was still on the stock, he opened the door and stepped in. He heard the two man coming back from the staircase. They saw the man on the ground and immediately kneeled at his body. The elevatordoors closed and John got down.

He left the building and walked away. He changed again in a large hotel and walked home.

He made a couple of sandwiches and sat down to find out what he had done and what the results were. All four were guilty, he thought. He did not expected one reaction from either one of them. He had done what he could. He gave them a warning and a solutionoption. He would wait two days. They could use the period to reconsider their position. John put all the clothes and tablets away in the cupboarddrawers and locked the doors.

He tried to find information from his memory but still without any result. He went to the toilet and pied, as usual nowadays in the sieve. He hoped to catch the nano's as he actually pied them out. He thought

that at the moment he had done so, his memory
would come back. He had no idea how small these
nano's were so he had put a towel in the sieve, he
renewed it every time after he had used the toilet.
He cleaned the towels every day again. He now
also controlled the towel. He expected to find
nothing again. He was surprised to find something.
He carefully searched the towel. Indeed he found a
very small strange looking small thing. Once he had
found one he recognized more of them. He actually
found seven. He collected them and put them
together in a glass. He put the glass in the cupboard
in the kitchen.
He immediately tried his memory. He was a little bit
disappointed. He found it time to get his memory
back. He had to wait. The found nano's gave him
hope that it was happening.
What would he do with the information about the
four cheaters within their own organisations. What
would each of the four large criminal organisations
do with this information?
Perhaps he should look at more identical points
within these organisations? Is that what he wanted.
Did he wanted to be a watchdog within these
organisations? What should be in it for him.
What would he gain with that. What would happen if
he blocked all the accounts of these organisations.
He had all the accounts. He could easily change the
accountcodes. Would he make himself the boss of
all these organisations? By blocking there accounts

they had a big problem. Of course they would all try to find out who this new criminal was and kill him as soon as possible. Boseley, the Lord, had certainly options to change the codes again. The others did not had this option, that was why she was the most powerful criminal leader. So in principle it would be enough if he controlled the Lord. Did he wanted that or did he only wanted to have fun, play in the casino's, dance, play with the girls?

He sight. Did he know what he wanted? Perhaps he would know more about this after he got his memory back.

He was a little bit surprised about his thoughts. Did he actually wanted to be a criminal? He did not had that feeling but in practice he already had been very busy as a criminal. He had cracked the bankaccounts of a lot of organisations. He had blackmailed individuals in the criminal organisations. Well, blackmail was a big word for his action to make them correct their possible misbehaviour. He used his ability to feel the machines in the casino where he could win. He could not really spot this ability. He had the ability to crack codes on the internet. What more could he do with those abilities? He did not know.

Could he use it as an inventor. What could he invent. New products? Perhaps he could forefeel options for solutions in the chemical sector, or even better in the medical sector. That was something that could catch his interest. Finding new medicines for existing illnesses. The more he thought about this, the more he liked it. He had no idea how the world of medicines was organised and how it worked to create medicines.

John got out to run through the forest and tried to get used to the idea of creating medicines.

Chapter 32

He dined at the Saloon. He loved the sphere. He liked a combination meal with al kind of small snacks. He started to feel better and better. The idea of becoming an expert in creating new medicines liked him more and more.

He took a kop of coffee after a big ice-cream and looked outside to the big tree on the square. Miriam was not present, she did not had to work here today. Three big motorcyclists came into the square, circled around the tree and discovered the Saloon. They were very loudly. They parked their motors right in front of the Saloon and got in.

John did not wanted to stay. He got up, paid for his meal and wanted to get out.

The three motorcyclists were still standing near the bar. One of them stepped forwards to get in the walk of John. John did not wanted a confrontation and simply stepped aside.

One of the others stepped along the first figure and got in front of John.

"Well, well, sir. Please be more polite to the lady. You do not just step aside. Please make your apologise to the lady."

John looked at the man, then to the college, surprised that it was a lady.

""Are you a lady? "he simply asked.

A loud lough came from aside. The three old man had fun. They also were surprised about the first person, being a lady. They smiled at John. They also wanted the proof for the suggestion.
The first person put her helmet of and a her long, blond hear fell out of the helmet. It really was a girl.
"Is there more proof that you are a girl?" John asked with a big smile.
The old men found it all very comic. They laughed again loudly.
John also smiled to the girl. The second person, the man that had told him that she was a lady, stepped forward.
John looked at him and asked him politely to step aside so he could look at this very beautiful person and to give her the opportunity to prove that she was a lady.
The man got angry. He clearly wanted to play the strong defender of the lady.
"Are you sure you want a fight?" John asked him with a smile.
"Who do you think you are, to match me?" The man asked surprised.
"Well," John started to say." I am the trainer of the new worldchampion boxing. Who are you?".
The man looked surprised at John, than he started to laugh.
The old man group got silent. They did not know what to think of this statement.

"Even if you are a trainer, that does not mean that you can box, yourselves, " the man stated with a big smile.

"Are you sure about this?" John asked again. "Do not say that I did not warned you !"John continued his discussion.

"Com' on, let us get outside. We do not want to break anything in here, don't we?"

"Ok," the man said smiling.

"I will be right back, " he quoted to his mates and stepped outside.

John followed him and stepped outside behind the motorman.

He stepped aside so that he stood in front of the window of the Saloon. Everybody could see what was happening.

The motorman started active and tried to hit John. After three tries that all missed. John stepped forward and simply hit the man on his right eye. Beating with his bare hands made the eye more than just blue. The man fell aside and was groggy. John picked him up and brought him inside the Saloon.

He got a big applause from the older men. He asked for a wet towel and helped the eye of the man to get softened.

The two colleagues of the man looked surprised. They were not used to the fact that there hero got hit and certainly not that he got hit badly.

John apologised but he had warned them. He said goodbye and left.

The old men applauded for him.

John went back to his cottage.

He smiled thinking back on his action with the motorman. Should not he be more confident about his own behaviour. He was a good fighter, boxing was ok. Fighting with his feet and hands and elbows was a new idea. He should find a club where he could learn that. Ok on the internet there was probably more than enough to find about these sports. He searched and found three different sportschools in the city. He found all kind of information about their technics. Even some movies made clear how their sports were trained. He found it very interesting. He would visit them all three to see which club he liked most.

He got to the toilet and pied some nano's. He collected them. Three more. In total ten now. He had no idea how many there were from the beginning. Ten, maybe twelve. He should be good in guessing. He concentrated and found that twelve would be the right answer. So he needed two more to catch or he had missed them already. Again he guessed the first option. Two more to go. He cleaned the toilet and his materials again and put the nano's with the other seven in the glass in the kitchen.

Suddenly he heard someone stumbling at his frontdoor, not the outerdoor between the trees but

his housedoor. He was surprised. Since he had the keys from Leo, only Miriam had the keys of the outerdoor for the cleaning activities in the house.
He calmly walked to the door.
The door was kicked open and swapped around to the wall beside it.
John made a step backwards. Wat was going on. Who would break in with such a noise and obviously with keys???
Three man in black with guns came in and pointed their guns at him.
"Back up " the man in the front commanded, pointing with his gun into the livingroom.
John looked totally flabbergasted. What was this. What was going on.
He looked at the guns of the three man. They really looked original. It were no normal guns but more specials. He got suspicious.
He stopped, looked at the guns and then again to the three man. Behind the three man more people came through the outerdoor.
"Get back to your livingroom," the same man quoted again.
John looked at the guns.
"Careful," the man quoted. He touched his gun, turned on a button and fired on John 's left leg.
John shivered. He felt a burning spot on his leg. He looked at it. The man had a kind of lasergun and had blown his pants to peace's and left a big red spot of about ten centimetres on his leg. The spot

burned like hell. He yelled and stumbled back to his livingroom. He had understood the order. He got seated on his sofa and waited what was going to happen further. Who were they, what did they want. Had one of the criminals found out who he was and where he lived? Not very likely. They certainly did not had keys from the cottage. Who then? Boseley? She was on holidays. She certainly had keys. Where these her assistants from her organisation? The three man came in. They all pointed their guns at John. He again looked at the guns. Very special guns, the power could be limited by turning a button as he had seen. The shot was done in a low position. Now the guns were in a much higher stand. He looked at his leg.

This was not funny. He got a little bit angry but he had no choice. This really was dangerous. The three man stepped back with the outerwall in their back. One man took a quick look in the other rooms and came back.

"All clear "he announced.

Some people came through the frontdoor.

John looked surprised. Boseley got in first. John looked surprised at her.

She smiled at him, saw his leg, immediately turned to the man that had shot him and beat him with a firm blow on his head. "You had to do this, did not you. Be careful with your other eye", she said cryptic.

Could this be the man he had hit this evening at the Saloon? John understood his behaviour. This was the price he had to pay for his blow on his eye. He smiled and nicked at the man. He smiled back. They understood each other.

Behind Boseley the Major got into the room.

John looked surprised again. The Major here, on the premises of the Lord, of Boseley? What was going on. He knew that they worked together regularly but what had he to do with their cooperation. The last time he had left the meeting. This time that was a little bit more difficult.

He even got more surprised when James got in. She was James all right, not the mother of Lia or of Rosemary. She always had been the most dangerous one of them all. Drugs and murder were her business. In a way he had been confronted with them all. He only missed Toko, who's casino he had plundered, probably, or most likely without his notice.

He had hardly thought of it or Toko came in. He closed the door behind him and handed the keys to Boseley.

"Hallo John, I see that you have already started to misbehave. You now know this is serious. I must admit that I am very curious how you are doing with your memory. "

Toko looked around to the others. Everybody waited on the reaction of John.

"Sorry, no memory back yet. What do you all know about this?" John wanted to know.

"Sorry, I got to go," James intervened. She did not seemed to be very interested. "Thomas you stay with him, Moga you will follow over twelve hours. " She simply nicked to the others and left, followed by Moga and the other man.

Boseley also nicked to Toko and followed James, Major immediately did the same. They got the information where they had come for. John's memory was not yet back. Toko would arrange everything with assistance of Thomas. Thomas with the blue eye and the lasergun.

John looked at him. He smiled at him. This poor man had to guard him, even when he was running around and doing his exercises. He felt pity already. John got up. I would like to have a cup of coffee. You too, he asked Toko and Thomas.

"John, sit down!!" Toko did not sound friendly at all. He stretched his hand to Thomas.

Thomas looked surprised at Toko. Toko pointed at his gun and claimed it arrogantly. Thomas gave him the gun and looked surprised ad Toko and then to John.

"Thomas will get us coffee." Toko claimed. He pointed the gun to John, turned the button back to soft and shot at Johns right leg.

John looked shocked. First to his right leg and then to Toko.

"What the hell are you doing!!" John screamed.

Toko did not even looked at him but looked at Thomas who also looked surprised.

"Thomas, how about coffee!!" Toko shouted.

Thomas looked shocked at Toko, nicked and went to the kitchen to make coffee.

John looked at his right leg. His trousers were partly burned away. Now he had two big burned holes in his trousers and two big, bloody red spots on his legs. He rubbed carefully over the new red spot. It did hurt. He looked at Toko. What was the matter. It was clear that they no longer were friends.

"John," Toko started. "First of all I have to thank you. You have done a lot for me. You have made my dreams come through. You do not remember yet what has happened but you will in a few days. "

John looked at Toko. He did not understood what had changed the attitude between them.

"Did you already started to pie nano's? "

John confirmed. "So far, ten."

"Two more will follow. Twelve in total. Then all of a sudden your whole memory will be back. I think we are exactly in time to give you some information, before it will all come to you in one shocking moment." Toko looked at John.

"First of all, you are not my son. You were a very talented young man from another city. We invited you here for some experiments. You invented the laserguns. You also invented the lasercanon."

John stared at Toko. Laserguns, lasercanons. He had not even thought about these things. It must have been another me, he thought. He was not the kind of man that would try to invent guns. So if he understood it all, he was threatened with his own weapons. He stared at Toko. Did he made this up or was he serious?

John tried to say something. Toko lifted his hand, to prevent him from talking.

Thomas came in with coffee. He put the coffee on the table, took a cup and asked Toko for his gun by stretching out his hand.

Toko smiled at him and handed him the gun. He also took a cup and tasted the coffee.

"Perfect Thomas, you are good in this. Toko sat back and looked at John.

John also took a cup, carefully moving. He did not needed another laserhole in his pence.

He must admit, the coffee tasted ok.

"I must admit, that Thomas and his mates trained with the guns and the canon but they made several big mistakes. With the canon they blew the whole prison away which was not even close to the purpose we had damaging the prison. They also blundered with your apartment. It should have been only a blow through the window to make you nervous, nothing more. Again they blew the whole apartment away. Stupid, but your lasers were really extraordinary good. You did built a minimaliser in it but they had not discovered that option until I told them so. He looked at Thomas shaking his head. Tomas simply lifted up his shoulders.

"Sorry , for all those mistakes, they were not really meant against you. "

John did not understand what this was all about. Wat was Toko telling him, that he was a gunman, creating guns? He could not believe that. He did not thought that he was interested in guns, violence, criminality. No that was not him. That was not the person he thought he was. He did not had the interest in guns, he was interested in medicines. He must admit that he had found that only a short while ago, but he did miss his history.

"John," Toko started again . "There are some other things you have to know. I thank you for your way of learning me how to box. How to move. Your input is a lot bigger. You invented a way to have someone's body improve extraordinary. You proved it by doing it at your own body. You used to be a long but very skinny nerd, sorry to say so, but that is the truth. You became what you are now. You made me believe that I could improve my body in the same way as you had done. You also told me about the nano's and their function. I must admit that I did not understood a word of it but you had proven that it worked. You also knew that the nano's organised themselves to a memoryblock. You created a way to get them out of your body again. They could be used again and again. You did it. Four times over. Your body improved enormous. I did it also and used your way of getting back the memory as well. It worked. To give you the time to learn me more about this new body. You did not wanted to have the medicines to get the nano's out before I had won the worldtitle. We, of course, accepted your condition. So now it is time to get your memory back, so you will remember everything again. "

Toko smiled at John. "John , we would like to work with you in the future. You really are a good man. We want you to be part of our cooperation. With "our cooperation" I mean the way the four largest criminal organisations are working together in this project. We now know who can do what for the others to have a mutual benefit. You actually brought us together. Thank you for that. "

John looked at Toko. He still could not understand why they had shot him in the legs, why they had shot his apartment, why Thomas was here now. He asked Toko.

Toko smiled at him.

"You missed the basis. You will remember when your memory will be back. That is all for now. I will be off. Be prepared for the memory shock, because it will come, you will see."

Toko got up and left.

The keys from the frontdoor and the outerdoor were handed to Thomas, so they could get out and in together.

Toko left, he would come back when Thomas would give the signal that that was useful.

It was already getting dark.

John had problems with the two burnspots on his legs. He changed his trousers but found it heavy to get them over the spots. He searched in the cupboard in the bathroom and found some cream against burned skin. He put it on the spots, it seemed to burn because of the cream. Thomas came into the bathroom to see why he stayed away so long. He saw the burnspots and the cream on it and the heavily drown away face of John.
He understood. He also saw that there was no window to get out in another way than through the door. He left again.
Thomas was not so bad to live with. He cooked a meal for them both and made coffee later at the night.
John was surprised to notice that Thomas had brought along his own clothes, and nightneeds in a bag that stood inside the house right behind the frontdoor.
John went to bed early, his day had been long enough. He had to think about the words of Toko. Thomas locked the outerdoor and the frontdoor for all security and also went to sleep but in the other bedroom.

Chapter 33

John could not sleep. What was all this about him.
All four primary criminals were involved in the whole
situation around him. He must admit. He did
underestimated them. They were topcriminals, of
course they knew each other, of course they worked
together, that is why they were the top. How did he
fit in this crimescene. He, only based on his feeling,
did not fit at all.
What more had Toko said? He was not his father.
Who was his father than? How about his mother?
Brothers, sisters? Grandparents? He did not knew if
he had them.
What more? He had developed the laserguns and
canons. How come? He must have known about all
these things. He had no good feelings about guns
and violence at all. He trusted his feelings. That was
his basis nowadays. His feeling was terribly good.
A new development? He could only guess.
What did Toko wanted him to know before he got
his memory back? He was the one doing the
experiments with the nano's. His invention? What
exactly did those nano's do. They had stimulated
the body to became far stronger and more flexible
than before. This worked. He used to be a nerd,
almost without muscles. Now he was strong and
very flexible. Now he liked to run and do exercises.
Being a nerd, this probably was not the case before

or was he wrong about that. He could understand the feeling that he did liked it but did not made much of it. That could have been the reason to develop this kind of nano's. He still had no idea how these nano's worked and absolutely no idea how you could tell a nano what to do. If he really was the nerd that developed these nano's than it was highly necessary to get his memory back. He wanted this knowledge badly. To develop better and more efficient medicines, these nano's could do miracles. He must have been very good in this matter.

He had foreseen that using the nano's would block your memory at a certain moment. He even developed an antidote. Toko must have known all this. He had taken the nano's, so he had lost his memory too. Being the brain behind this plan to make him the worldchampion boxing, he of course had made sure that the whole trick would work, inclusive the antidote. He probably had it all tested by John himself. How did he say it? It was tested several times. So it was clear that Toko made sure that he could take the antidote immediately after he lost his memory because of the nano's. He met Toko only a few days after he had left the prison. It was almost three days now since he took the medicine, and yet without having his memory back. Perhaps it took a little bit longer for him because he already did it several times before? It sounded logically but he had no idea if it was correct. He remembered that it could take four to seven days to get his memory back. It did gave him a good feeling. All this did not clear why he needed a guard. Toko and the others thought it necessary to take this precaution. So it was a necessary act. He needed to be secured. This could only mean that if he got his memory back he did not wanted to cooperate with them.

The idea hit him !!! It made it all clear. He had developed a lot of things, like the laserguns against his will. He did not wanted to help these criminals with these things but one way or the other they forced him to do so. No wonder why the leaders were not happy with his contacts with Lia and Marion. They were far too close to their private circumstances, their own families !!!

He was kidnapped and did not know. It was clear that he had to mis his memory for a while. So he could help Toko and prove that it would all work. He must have done it first, Toko would follow, taking the nano's.

How would they have him under control? Had they kidnapped his parents, his brothers and sisters? Perhaps they had only threatened to catch them. He knew that they could do it easily. It also was a lot cheaper and they could make any move on any moment. How could he defend himself against this all. He just could not. He ultimately fell asleep. He had found several solutions for many questions. He still did not know what Toko had not told him. He had to know who his parents were and what they had done with them. Could he disappear with his parents? He could not get his parents involved.

John got up early.
Thomas, being a member of the organisation of James, so active in drugs and killing, that made him dangerous, came direct after him out of his room. He greeted John and they took a simple breakfast together.
John asked what his orders were. He wanted to do his early morning running and exercises. Thomas found that no problem, he would go with him.
This was what John had hoped for. He would make an explosive run today. Thomas had to do his best to catch up with him. He had Thomas open the frontdoor and the outerdoor and they started to run together.
John did speeded up his running. He must admit that Thomas had an excellent condition. They ran through the forest, two times. Thomas did it easily. John ran to the Saloon, made a turn around the tree and ran back. Thomas followed him and ran next to him. It seemed to go easy. He even gave the impression that he liked it. John started to do several moving exercises. Thomas followed. He was also extreme good in these movements. John was surprised and he honestly informed Thomas about his vision. He wanted to know at what

trainingscentre he kept his condition and
movements on this level.

Thomas told him so and they decided to go there
and see how it looked like.

So they ran to the city, through the streets until,
already against the end of the morning, they
entered the sportsschool.

They walked around and Thomas said that he
trained here every other day for four hours. He
loved it. John had a very positive feeling about this
school. He asked Thomas of this school had
anything to do with James, but that was not the
case. This school was specialised in
bodymovements, not in fighting as such, more a
kind of gymfighting.

John liked this way of thinking. He asked Thomas
whether he could make an appointment here for the
next day.

Thomas made a small and quick phonecall and said
that it was all right. He also introduced a middle-
aged lady. He called her Moga.

John realised that this lady was in his house
yesterday as well. They had to take care of him for
the time being. He wandered how long this would
take. Probably until he remembered what they could
do to his family. He shivered about the idea.

Thomas felt that there was something wrong and
asked him about his shivering.

John said that there was nothing the matter. He only
was not used to this kind of control.

Thomas said goodbye and should take over the job from Moga again the next day towards noon.
John got a membership of the school and got a personal trainer. A very strong and well trained young man made him at home with the different apparatus in the school. Moga followed him, doing other trainingswork close by.
They left and had a lunch in a small coffeeshop. John tried to find out things about her and the organisation of James. Moga did not got into that. She told that she had two kids that she had to take care of and that was why she worked. This work made good money, now she could give her kids everything that she wanted, not what they wanted , because they always wanted more. She said it with a motherly smile. She obviously loved her children. Their father unfortunately died in an action for the Major, five years ago. John asked about the kids, what school they went, what they were good at, what sports they did. He noticed that she really was very close with her kids.
He kind of liked her. She was not so good trained as Thomas but she did come along. They ran back to the cottage and she did it really good.
At the cottage John pied another six nano's. he was surprised but at the same time happy that he had taken the precaution to kept on peeing through the sieve. There were now eighteen nano's. Should that be it, or were there more to come. He could only guess.

They sat a while in John's small garden behind his house. John tried to control the bankaccounts of the four members of the criminal organisations that he had visited the other day. He could not see any backpayments from anyone of them.

Perhaps he had to do this himself, but only after tomorrow. He had given them time to get it done themselves.

They got to the Saloon for a dinner. They talked with Miriam that was working today. She felt good. She had quitted the cleaningjob. She did not liked it. She preferred to serve in the restaurant.

John and Moga got back to the cottage and they watched television.

John got to bed early. He had done a lot in physical training and had slept very short last night. Moga staid up longer.

Chapter 34

In the middle of the night John woke up. He got
straight up in his bed. His memory was back.
He remembered. His mother, a sweet and friendly
woman, nurse in the operatingroom of a private
hospital, just around the corner. His father, bio-
chemist. A great guy. Always busy with his work. He
had been extraordinary proud when John promoted
with a script about laserbeam technology to be used
in the creation of new and smaller medicines.
His elder brother, George and his two younger
sisters Gloria and Julia were a bit on their own, or
actually he was more on his own. He was the nerd.
He had a photographic memory and a super
combination ability. He already had studied
medicines, biology and chemistry. He had many
discussions with his father about bio-chemical
points. They all lived in the outskirts of the city
Bopol. That was where he was now. So this was his
hometown. They lived in a beautiful house near the
forest on the opposite side of town. He remembered
that he got in contact with Peter and Paul. He was
looking for a location to start tests with his new
created mini-medicine. He called them nano's. Very
small, miniaturised drops of gel in a mix of
biochemical material with a small centre of heavy
iron. Using a liner, as he called it, he could situate

the nano to a certain spot in the body. You had to place the liner on forehead, changing the location was not yet possible. The nano first had to be washed out. After having located the nano, it would stay there for a certain period, depending on the location and the number of nano's that were concentrated on that spot. The more there were, the longer they hold. After a while they, one by one started to float through the body. With a simple extra ureum the nano's were spoiled through the waterloosingsystem, so in principle with the urine. It was all clear for him.

The present situation was that he was approached by Boseley to come and work for her organisation. In those days he had no idea who she was and what she expected from him.

He, enthusiast as he was about his experiments with the nano's, explained to her what he was doing. Peter and Paul had their own work and were not very involved in his project. He used their territory but that was it. He sometimes, when they lunched together informed them about his project but they had no idea what he was doing.

He principally worked alone. All the tests were done on himself. He never wanted anyone else to be involved and perhaps got a problem because of his tests. So he needed a lot of time to be sure about the consequences of any test. He predicted the consequences and was extreme good at that, he found himself. He did foresee the problem with the memoryblock. The nano's had the urge to connect to that point in the brain. He had not yet found out why but he had accepted it as a fact. After three tries he had proven that that was what happened. The last time he had visited his parents was a month before the explosion in the prison.

About three weeks before the explosion he was visited by Toko. He demanded to be treated as he had treated himself. He had made him clear that he had grown his muscles extraordinary. Until than he had not really noticed that. He had noticed that his regular trainingsessions went better and better. He had not realised that his muscles had grown this big. He took that point along in his analysis. This on itself was very naïf from himself. He should have noticed. He should have registered this grow. He had intended the nano's to qualify the body at a higher level. He had not realised that this could bring a musclegrowth with it. He had thought more about the hart and the lunges, the kidneys etc. Peculiar but true.

Toko wanted the same treatment. Further he claimed that John had to create a lasergun from his laserexperiences as was mentioned in his promotionscript. He had refused. First of all did he not wanted to make weapons, secondly he did not wanted to do tests on others.

Toko had made clear that that was his risk and his responsibility. He accepted the risks.

John had refused.

Than the real Toko came in. He showed movies of his father and mother, his brother and sisters. He only asked if he wanted anyone of them to be kidnapped or only, the first time, being hurt.

He could not believe this was happening to him. Toko showed him a "almost accident" with his father on his bike. A cardriver almost hit him. Of course the driver apologised. Toko made clear that the next time it could end differently. This threat was always in his mind. And from now on would stay in his mind. He would never again trust Toko.

How could he hit Toko back. There were two options. There was a reason why he was in prison at the time of the explosion. He must have been convicted for something. He had to look into the policefiles. He also had to prove that Toko was the same man as the leader of the Wolves. So he had not died in the prisonexplosion. He was changed and came out as another man. The growth of his muscles could only have taken a week of three. This was really heavy. His muscles had grown for more than four months. He surely came from far behind but still had grown a good set of muscles. Would this be possible for everybody or must there be a certain physical presumption.

He had to find out.

Suddenly he remembered that he had built in in the laserwapens a stop. He must try to find his blocker back. With this blocker he could stop the lasers to work. He must try to get to the prison and to collect his things from his room in the building. The area was isolated but not really guarded.

He got dressed. It was two o'clock in the night. He had not slept very much. He looked at the window of his sleepingroom. An alarm was connected on the outside. He went to the gardendoor. Here he also saw an alarmwire. He opened the upperwindow of the door. It was difficult to get out but he pushed himself through it. It did hurt his shoulder and his back. He got out. He walked through his garden, climbed a tree and jumped into the garden of Boseley. There, a bit back along the large garden he found a tree that bent over the fence. He climbed it and jumped over the fence. He quickly ren to the city. It still took him a whole hour to get to the prisonpremises. There was no guard. Only a red and white wire made clear that this was a forbidden area. John simply got under the wire and ren to the building. He climbed into the building through the broken part. The laserbeam had don a terrible good job to damage the building so heavily. He got in and walked fast to his room, all the way to the other outerpoint of the building, but on the same level as where he climbed into the building, the first floor.

The door to his room was not locked. He looked in, it was a mess. Everything was damaged and lying on the floor. He looked at his bed. The legs seemed to be in order. He put the bed on his side and made the cap from the leg of the bed. It was all still intact. The blocker was still there. He was lucky to have it hide so well. He knew that if they had known about this he would have been punished. He looked if his paperwork was still here but nothing was left. He turned the bed again and looked at the other leg of the bed and opened it as well. Three memorysticks came out. He put these in his pocket. He had to leave now, he had to get back before Moga would notice.

He returned quickly. Found his way back in through the fence by climbing in the fence and through the tree back to his own garden and again through the small window above the door back in the house. He felt good and went to bed again.

He deliberately got up early and simply walked into the garden. Just proposing that he had not noticed the alarmwiring.

He calmly walked in again and started to make breakfast.

Moga came running out of her room, noticing that the gardendoor was still open and that John was in the kitchen.

John felt confident. He had the feeling that at last he had things under control. He only had to go to the sportsschool this afternoon and control the four criminals this evening to see if they had paid the amounts back again. He expected Toko to come in this morning once he knew that he had his memory back. Moga had to inform Toko about that.

John invited Moga at his table. They had breakfast together and John informed Moga that his memory was coming back.

Moga stared at him, then she crumbled on her clothes, picked up a phone and started to type on it. John smiled. Many persons were predictable. That was good. It meant that they were straight forward.

They finished their breakfast and Moga informed John that Toko had informed her that he would be here in a moment. Her job was done, she would, at the moment that Toko was here get back home to see how her kids were doing.

John smiled at her. This was allright.

John walked a bit through his garden and waited for Toko to come in.

He loved to see Toko 's face when he would come in. he was not yet sure if he would inform Toko about the block in his lasergun. Maybe later.

He took a cup of coffee and made one also for Moga. He got out in the garden and heard Toko coming. He was not alone.

John gave the signal to Moga that Toko was coming in. The outerdoor was opened and the alarm of Moga went on.

She stopped it immediately, also stopped all the other alarms. The alarm for the kitchengardendoor was already out, because John had moved that wire earlier and Moga had stopped the alarm then.

Toko came in, Boseley followed immediately. It was clear that Toko tried to be the boss but that Boseley was not used to that. In this project Toko was in the lead. Normally Boseley had all the strings in her hand, finance controlled everything.

They let the door open. They happen to expect more visitors. John did not.

Toko said good bye to Moga, got the keys and her lasergun. She greeted John and Boseley and left. At the outerdoor she greeted someone else. John knew that there would be two more visitors, James and Major.

The big four were present again for him. Ok, he had the lasers created but further there was nothing. He was curious what they had in mind for him.

Toko asked him to come in. John came in and got seated on his traditional chair. Indeed James and Major came in through the frontdoor. Toko locked all the doors and got seated in the last empty chair. John had no intention to offer them coffee.

"John," Toko started his part of the show " now that you do remember everything I will not bother you with things you perhaps even know better than we do. You now know how things have gone. You understand our position. You do can do a lot but your input regarding the nano's has been very unsatisfactory. All our technicians have looked at it but they all came to the conclusion that it could impossibly work, " he looked at John.

John looked surprised at Toko. He had expected them to come to a new order for him to create something they would need. For instance a laserbeam melting safedoors in a minute or something like that. This approach could run into a complete other direction.

His end.

They did not know where he could be of any use. So now he had become a dangerous, too much knowing enemy.

John felt in his sack and activated the blocker. This could only go the wrong way. He had to be careful.

"It may sound curious for you," Toko went on, "but I think they are right. " he raised his hand , stopping John to react.

"Yes, I know, you think you have proven that what you did really worked, but I am not so very sure about that. Of course you know that I have started a new trainingprogramme in which my muscles have grown really good. I always have been a well-trained amateurboxer but never tried to get higher up into the professional world. Now I have done this. Nano's do not exist. "

He looked at John. John smiled at him. He knew that this was only the start of his death sentence.

James took over. "What you have don with Lia is unforgivable. You gave her the feeling that she meant something for you. Then, at a bad moment in her life, you again killed her. She is crying all day, calling for you. You never let her hear anything from you since she got hurt. You are bad, you should be ashamed. " She really looked angry, though she knew better.

Major followed. "You, you forced Mindy to let the families of the doctors go free. No consent from me, no good reason to do so. All totally against all the appointments we made. You have a bad influence on the people around you."

"So, now you have heard the vision about you and your behaviour, " Toko proclaimed. "Do you have to say anything useful at this point. Of course not," he smiled.

"Well," John started, "are there no complaints of Boseley? "He looked at her.

Boseley looked a little bit surprised. "Should there be complaints from me. Is this not more than enough ?"

"Well, "John smiled", thank you all for being here. You all know better. You Toko have cheated on me by threatening to heart my family. You forced me to develop weapons, explicitly against my will.

You, James are a very bad mother and dishonest. I informed your daughter regularly about my problem with her being a murdermachine. You made her to become that. No good mother wants that for her daughter.

You, Major are responsible for the actual kidnapping and unnecessary treatment of the families of Peter and Paul. You are wicked.

The only one that has a view is Boseley. She always stays at the background but really pulls the strings. Finance is the centre of every organisation.

Now that we all know how the situation is, I think it clear that you all four together are responsible for the ruining of the prison. I think I will offer the Lordmayor to rebuilt the prison, on the same spot, paid by you four. What do you think of it.?
John smiled.
All four looked at him fully surprised by the guts that he showed now that his deathsentence was about to be completed.
James got up. "Ok, Toko, time to go. Finished it. "
John did as if he was afraid of the lasergun. He jumped away from his chair. Looked at the group. Went towards the gardendoor.
"Sorry John, " Toko called and pulled the trigger. Nothing happened.
"Sorry, you, "John smiled at the four top criminals. He grabbed his bag and swinged it on his back.
"You will not hear from me but if anyone of my family might get hurt in any way, I personally will ruin you all. You would wish yourselves a better end."
He jumped through the garden door, ran through the garden, got in the tree, jumped into the garden of Boseley, got in the tree hanging over the fence and left the garden. By the time they all were back from their astonishment John was gone. Toko looked at the lasergun. It did not work.

Chapter 35

John was glad that he had left a lot of information in a locker at the railwaystation. He had in the past rent an electronic locked locker. On his memorystick with the red head the code was electronically available. He ran to the city. He must admit that he had not expected this communication with the big four. He expected a new order, without payment. He again underestimated the criminal minds. He thought that he had a future value for them but that was a mistake. They had only used him because Toko had wanted that. In principle for the laserguns but on the way also for his, Toko 's, physical needs. He had been lucky. He escaped from the attack on the prison. There would have been no problem if he had not survived. Toko already had his physical development and he knew how to solve the memoryblock. The laserguns worked, so there was no need for him anymore.

Toko must have been extraordinary surprised to meet him in the sportscentre. Or not. Was he tipped that John was there. He must became less naïf. Nothing happened by incident. Of course he was tipped. He just had wanted to have John close. John new too much. His apartment was not only meant to be blown away. It was also meant to blow him away. He was dangerous. He escaped again.

He happened to meat Lia. She saved him. Nobody would make problems with the boyfriend of the daughter of James. Not even James herself. No wonder she was not happy with him. How come he was caught by Marion. Did she really only had interest in sex. It seemed so. After the two meetings it was over. Perhaps she got instructions about him and therefor did not wanted to be seen with him. Had Boseley deliberately offered him to live next to her house. Of course she did. So he was under control. She was not the murdering type. She stayed at the background but controlled the business from them all through their finances. He now knew that they all four together were responsible for the damage He would like to build a new prison and have the four pay all the cost. John arrived at the railwaystation. He got the memorystick with the red head out of his pocket and walked slowly along the lockers. Almost at the end a locker reacted on his memorystick. The door went open and John took out a large suitcase. He left the station and went to the "bed and breakfast" he had been before. He booked two nights, so he could take some rest. He opened the suitcase. He knew what was in it but more than clothes and toiletware was not really in. He opened the underlayer, there was his laptop. That was the option it was all about. He opened the laptop and found it dead. He connected it with the contact right next to his bed and waited until the connection was strong enough and the computer could be activated. It took far longer than he had thought. The laptop really lost all his energy. He could have known.

He left the laptop in the drawer beside his bed, still connected to get it loaded. He filled his bag with the sportscloths and his tablet and left the rest in the room. He kept the three memorysticks in his pocket. He preferred to keep them with him.

He walked into town and took a small lunch at a coffeeshop. He realised that Thomas and Moga new about his appointment at the sportsschool. Shoot he find another one? How long would it take them to find him again? Not very long he presumed. Their connections were all over town.

So he just went to the school where he had been the day before with Thomas.

His sportscoach, Roderic, was very enthusiastic about his startresults. He was "well-equipped "as he called it. First of all Roderic wanted him to start dancing. Lifting his feet high up, even jumping up and again and then combining those jumps with making a circle, turning his total body around horizontally. Then he had to make loops and handstands and flickflacks. John had to train al these physical movements. Roderic was very satisfied about the flexibility of John. He really was impressed. He let John jump higher and higher, at the same time train to move his legs and arms, make loops in the air. John learned fast. He felt good with this way of moving.

The second part of his training today he had to learn to kick with his feet. High in the sky, hit the head of his opponent. His doll-opponent was more than two meters tall, so he had to jump extra hight to get to the head. He learned fast. He really could jump very high up. Even Roderic was impressed. He noted the results in his notebook for clients and asked John when he would be back. John thought about it. This way of moving was highly satisfying. He did not yet knew how the rest of the week would go, so he decided for next week, same day, same time.
He took a shower and got dressed again. He walked out. Right behind the frontdoor a young man came up to him.
John did remember him. He was the brother of Lia. He had informed him before. John smiled at him. He moved sidewards , more or less inviting the young man to walk with him. The man understood it and walked with him. He did look around. John asked him if he was looking whether his colleagues followed him or whether there was competition on the streets.
He smiled, He said that he was looking for competition. It was there but he could not locate them. He only came along, knowing from Thomas that John had an appointment here, to ask him to visit Lia. She desperately needed to see him.
"She is totally out of line. She threats to kill mother because she caused her to be a killingmachine and through that she was missing the love of her life.

She really is desperate. Please help us." At that very moment, the young man stepped aside and walked away. John stopped and looked how the young man was getting away. He brought his message. That was enough for him. John walked on. He did not wanted to return to his room now. He first had to get rid of the followers. He went into a large shopping mall. He walked around and tried to find out who was following him. He just was not good enough to locate the follower. He believed the brother of Lia. He certainly would be followed. How would he be dressed if he would wanted to follow somebody, he wandered. Just blue jeans and a grey blouse, how old? Very old or very young. He got to a small coffee shop in the cellar of the building. He bought some snacks and found a spot far in the back in a corner. He could overlook the whole area in front of him.

He calm and slowly ate his snacks, he kept on looking around. He could not identify any follower. He got out of the mall, walked through the city, got through three more malls and though two big hotels, walked through the casino and left again.

If anyone had followed him, he or she was good. He had not seen anybody. He ran through a park and back again. He quickly entered the street of his room and got in.

He got surprised. In the entrance, Lia's brother was sitting, waiting for him to return. John looked surprised at him.

"Sorry," the man said. "We really would like you to see my sister." He smiled friendly to John and left the bed-and-breakfast.

John almost fell of his feet. He could not believe this. They knew all the time where he would sleep tonight. He was flabbergasted. How could they know?? Did he wear some location device? He slowly got up to his room.

He remembered that he had to control the payments of the four criminals.

He tried to calm down. He was badly frustrated. He had his tablet to control the bankaccounts. He looked at the accounts. The amounts were not payed back. He controlled his own accounts. He could easily lent these four the money they needed. He first booked the amounts from the accounts of the four back to their mother-organisations. Than he booked the same amounts on their account as a loan from "The old man".

He had solved the problems. Tomorrow he would collect the four tablets and the redress packages from his cottage. He now knew how to get in and out, through the kitchen-entrance.

The laptop was fully loaded, so he could make a search on it. He remembered Lia.

He found that he had to help her. He left his bag under the bed and got out.

It was already midnight but he did not care. He walked to Lia's apartment. It was not far.

He called on the outdoor. His call was not answered. He called again, a little bit longer this time. He was surprised to get a reaction.

"John here," he simply quoted.

"John , John, is that really you. You came to me, oh, oh yea, please come up, please. "

The door was opened and John entered the building. He took the elevator and got out on the right stock. She already was waiting for him.

He must admit that she was a special woman. He also had to admit that his burning flame from last time was tempered. She jumped up to him. He caught her and walked with her in his arms to her apartment.

The door was open. John walked in. To his surprise the brother of Lia got up, nicked to him and left the apartment.

Lia was really happy to see him again. John calmed her down. He wanted to talk to her seriously.

She could not calm down, she was totally out of her senses. John got up and did as if he got to the door. "Lia, if you do not calm down, I will go." He thought that he was clear but she did not hear what he was saying.

He picked her up, she wrangled herself all the way around him, and walked to the bathroom. He opened the coldwatershower and put her there, stepping back in time so he would not get too wet.

She stared at him. She calmed down. He looked back. He sat down on the floor and looked at her through the glassboard at the side of the shower. She really calmed down. The coldwateraction worked. He got up, finished the waterfall and handed her a towel.

"I will wait for you in the livingroom. Please get dry and dressed."

He left for the livingroom. He made himself a cup of coffee and waited calm for her.

Lia needed a long time to get back to the livingroom. John was still sitting in the big chair opposite the giant sofa. He looked at her.

She sat down at his feet, hanged against his legs with her hands on his knees. She started to cry.

"I am sorry John. I am going crazy. Thank you for coming. Thank you. I do not know it anymore. I miss you and I know I cannot have you. This drives me crazy. I know that you are willing but my family, my mother would not allow me to be with you. I know that she is capable of taking you away from me. "

She started to cry again.

" Lia? " John tried to get her attention. She was far too deep in her own sorrow to listen.

"Lia!!"he tried to make her look at him. She did not. He got up.

She looked shocked up at him.

He shaked his head. He stepped away from her.

"Lia," he got her attention now. "Have you ever thought about me. How I had to live with you.

Fearing every minute that you might be killed or badly hurt, as already did happen? Have you ever thought about me? " He started to talk louder and louder.

She looked surprised at him. She tried to understand what he meant.

"I might be killed by your mother, I, not you, You could only loose a lover. I was to lose my life. Over and out. I ought to be pitied, not you. Stop your egoistic jam. Try to be more honest about yourself. Whom wanted to became a superfighter. You. You. You are so used to get what you want, that you have forgotten to think about the other. Do you understand what I am saying? Do you?"

He looked at her. She could not follow his words. He tried another approach. She must be activated.

"You know that you are a good fighter. The very first time you got a mission you got blown away just by one simple blow of an even more simple boxer. You are not a very good fightingmachine. Even I can beat you on all areas. You just name it. "

He looked at her. This made more impression. He now was attacking her. This is what she could understand.

He walked to the table, sat down and stretched his arm in front of him, put his elbow on the table and looked at her.

"Come on, are you scared already!! We have not even started and you are quitting. Prove that you are a good fightingmachine. Only a good fightingmachine can do the job you wanted to have. Your mother gave it to you, only because she is your mother."

Lia did not realised the content of his words but he was hitting her on her own decisions, her own battle for her ambitions. He challenged her.

It worked. She got up. Looking provoked. No more tears. This challenge she wanted to win. She was her mother's best killingmachine. She would prove it with ease.

She sat down opposite to John and put her elbow on the table. She grabbed his hand and they started to push.

John was a lot bigger and had far more muscles but Lia was very tough and strong in her hands. John really had to be alert. She used several tricks to let go and then push again. She decently let her elbow on the table, just as John did.

Suddenly John pushed with all his power and Lia got down. She looked at him totally surprised. This had never been happened before. She had never lost this game.

John got up. "Come here. We are testing your actionspeed. You seemed pretty slow to me but you may prove the opposite.

John stood a little bit bowed up front. She must try to hit him and he had to catch her hands to prevent her from hitting him.

They moved through the room. Lia started to like the challenge. She did hit John several times on his face. Than it would not work anymore. It seemed as if John got faster and faster. John even started to try to hit her in between her hits. Suddenly he hit her three times after each other, while she was missing him. He moved away extra quick and also changed his upfront foot, from left in front to his right leg up front. She had never learned that.

John stopped. "You have lost again," he stated.

Lia was standing back and stared at him.

"John, what are you doing. How is it possible that you seemed to be an even better fighter than I am. Who are you John?" she suddenly realised what she just had said. He, who did not wanted her because she was a fighting machine, was a better fighting machine than she was. For which organisation would he work?

"Next test Lia. "She stared at him.

"More?

He grabbed the standing lamp, caught a hat from the hallstand and put it up the lamp. The top of the lamp was now about the hight of Lia's head.

"Please kick the hat of the lamp without tatching the lamp. "

He looked at Lia. She stared at him.

"O no, you won't tell me that you can do that. I have never trained that. I can kick but not at that hight.

John raised the lamp to about a good end above his head.

Lia stared at him.

"No, you cannot," she stammered.

John made some trainingsjumps, got ready and jumped up to the head. He really kicked the head high against the wall.

Lia got enthusiastic.

"Yes, please learn me that. Whow, you are really dangerously good. Where did you learn this all. For whom do you work?"

John turned around to her. This was how her mind was working. To be able to do these things always must be linked to using your abilities for others.

"Wrong question, Lia. I work for myself. And I only use my abilities to help myself and my family."

John looked at Lia. She nicked. She started to understand his vision. Using violence against other people was not the right way to use your abilities, certainly not when used for the benefit of a third party.

"Lia, try to understand that my problem is not your physical abilities but your mindset to use violence as the basis for your existence. Start a sportsschool. That could be an useful activity with your abilities. Shall I buy you a sportsschool? "

She looked at him. She just had never thought about this kind of options. Using your abilities as a sport. Not as a killingmachine but as a sport.

"Thank you John, "she said. She walked to the table and sat down there. Looking at John.

John looked at Lia. She was beautiful. He had to go now that she was back in the normal world of the living people. "Lia, I have to go now. Think about what has happened this night. Look at your future. If you like sex, try others. We are still very young. We need more time and experience to be ready for a future. Perhaps for both of us. "

Lia nicked, she had understand what he had said. He came to her, kissed her on the head and left.

"Thank you , John, thank you. I will always remember you. Thank you."

John left. It was deep in the night. He got back to his room and went to sleep.

Chapter 36

John got up late. He took a shower and had a late breakfast. He had to see his family. Now that he knew where they lived, he had to see whether they were all right. He walked through the city. He recognized all the places also from the time before the explosion. He remembered also that he had to get back to the cottage to collect his clothes and the materials for his disguiseaction towards the members of the four organisations.

He at the same time realised that all of these organisations knew exactly where he was. The brother of Lia had made that clear to him. How was that possible?

He could not figure it out. Did they had a connection with his telephone or his tablet, quite possible. Even very likely, they had had plenty of opportunities to made such a connection. He got to a bank in a park and controlled his tablet and his phone. They indeed both had a registration signal that indicated the location of the apparatus. He locked both signals. Now he felt better. He thought about finding another spot to stay. On the other hand, the cottage did have a good feeling of its own. He liked the place. Back to a place as he had in the prison was not what he wanted. He just needed new locks to install on the cottage, on the front-, the outer- and the backdoor. He would do that this afternoon or this evening. He would sleep at the bed and breakfast and go back to install himself at the cottage again.

He arrived at his parents' house. His mother was at home. She enthusiastically embraced him. He loved this. This is what he had missed the last period. The warm hands of his mother embracing him.

Also his father was at home. He had not realised that it was a Sunday, they were free today. His brother and sister were out, sporting but would be back the end of the afternoon.

They lunched together. John told them about his experience at the prison and his memoryloss. He apologised for staying away for more than four weeks. The reason was his memory. He got it back last night.

John's father talked about his work. He tried to find a solution for a problem in the brain of certain patients. John told him about his invention, the nano's. His father could not follow John's explanation. He was not specialist in the electric world of the human brain. That was John's expertise. They went to the garden and continued their discussion. John's mother followed the stream of information with big interest. She had seen many operations in the human brain because of all kind of missing spots in the brain. She wanted to know whether this "nano" stuff could also trace bad spots in the brain. They had with the three of them a deep working discussion about the options and possibilities of John's invention.

John's brother and two sisters came back from there sportsactivities and were all very interested in his daily work. They all three had in their studies something to do with the human brain. They had a large dinner together and the dispute was continued until after the coffee after dinner. John wished them all the best and had to promise to come back at least within two weeks from now. John promised. He again realised why he could not had Toko allowed to harm his family. He promised himself that he would punish Toko for that. He got even more angry the more he thought about the way he was treated by the criminal four.

He had to punish them all. How could he do this. While running back to the citycentre he thought about this. He stopped at the great mall and bought four locks all working with the same key. He got four of these keys.

He got to the cottage. He was very surprised when he discovered that nobody had taken the precaution to lock the outer- and the innerdoor of the cottage. His motor still stood behind the outerdoor. He changed the locks and looked around in and outside the cottage whether he could find camera's or sound connectors. He found nothing.

He went away again. He was curious whether anyone would control the entrance of the cottage the coming night.

He went back to his bed and breakfast and went to sleep early. He had a good feeling about his family. He should certainly get back in two weeks.

John got up early. He took a heavy breakfast and left the location, he had his suitcase and his bag with him. He walked to the cottage. On the way he did as much exercises as he could.
The cottage seemed untouched. He expected that the daily business had taken over the attention of the four criminal managers. That was a good sign. He controlled the cabinet with the drawers and the tablets with the disguiseclothes. It still was there, it seemed untouched. He felt good.
He controlled the tablets. He really had a reaction from all of them. They all asked what had happened. They had the whole amount from "the old man", what did he wanted in return. They wanted to meet. John made no appointment. He informed that they would never meet "the old man". He only wanted information about their organisation. About the members, the projects, the money they made. This information would never be used against the organisation. The old man was only interested in the continuity of the organisation. They all promised to cooperate. They also realised that if this information would ever be a problem, they would have a big problem. They also realised that they already had a big problem because of the money they had stolen from the company.

John realised that in a way he was blackmailing these four members of their criminal organisation. They all four gave regularly their signals about their organisations activities. John knew where the most important members lived, how they worked and what money they made with their criminal activity. He found the information very acceptable.

He thanked them all four and would contact them again if necessary. They did not yet had to pay any amount till further notice.

John thought about his other action. Should he block the accounts of the four organisations? Paying to the accounts should stay possible. It only should not be possible to transfer any money. Or should he simply inform them that they were responsible for the damage of the prison so they had to pay for the new prison. He found that a better idea. He could transfer any money at any moment from all of the accounts. He tried to let this get to him.

He had to create a buildingplan. He needed the seize of the total location. Why was it build there. Should it not be a huge building with a special vision. For instance a great mall at the basic eight stocks, four stocks into the ground for parking and three above it for parking. Than ten stocks for the new prison, than again three stocks for parking for the people that lived above it and ten stocks with apartments. John started with the location. The exact size was easy to find and to be controlled from above through internet. There were many high buildings around so a building of almost forty stocks. He made a simple drawing and printed it out, he had created a nice park and walking areas around the building, so nothing showed that there was a prison in the building. He made separate entrances for the mall, the prison and the apartments, each with its own elevators. He did not made further details.

John got to the area and looked around. Almost all the buildings around were higher than his building so he had to raise his building. That meant extra apartments. So also an extra deck for parking cars. He walked back and tried to make an appointment with the Mayor. He got his secretary and made her clear that he would make a suggestion to rebuild the prison without costs for the community. She let him wait a moment and he got the Mayor himself on the phone. John explained his proposal and asked the Mayor his consent. The Mayor made clear that he needed to see him to find out how reliable the statement was. They made an appointment for that evening at the Cityhall.

John made a new plan, the total building was now sixtyfive stocks high. About the same hight as the largest buildings in the city. He wanted to know from the Mayer how many stocks the prison needed, so he could get the right financial structure for the plan.

He used a separate tablet for his plans. He made a copy on a memorystick and projected his special e-mailaddress, coupled on this tablet.

He took a small bite for lunch and started to run around through the forest. He liked it. He must be honest about himself.

Toko had misused him horribly. He did activate him to stimulate his own body to became in a far better shape. He was a nerd, he almost never came outside.

Girls were difficult creatures just like his sisters. He was always busy with his computer, creating things like at last, the nano's.

He had a photographic memory. He learned everything easy. Therefor he was always busy looking for knowledge. He only studied. He never got out to play with schoolfriends. He just did not had them.

Of course he had dreams about a beautiful muscled body. But he had never thought that that would became reality. He liked his present way of life very much. He was a soleganger.

He really was very fond of Lia but also found of Marion a fantastic girl. He liked more girls. He was still very young. He did not yet wanted to be tied by anyone. He liked to have contacts but preferred everyone to be and stay free.

He had to think about the nano's. If he could build the prisontower, perhaps he should take an apartment for himself. Maybe he should also use a

part for offices. He would like to have an area for his nano experiments. He would work this out.
He bought a new set of clothes and got back to the cottage. He took a shower and got in his new clothes.

Chapter 37

John thought about his presentation to the Mayor. Would he be himself or would he use a disguise. He decided to go as the fatty young boy. Convincing the mayor would perhaps becoming more difficult than to be presented as a mature older man. He called himself "Tom". He did not wanted any link with himself. The criminals would find this link instantly. He took his materials for the disguise with him and got into town.

He had his proposals with his tablet and the memorystick in his bag. He ate at a big hotel. He liked it but did not found it special.

He got dressed as the fatty young man and walked to the Cityhall and was nice in time for his appointment with the Mayor.

The Mayor clearly was surprised about the very young guy that came to the appointment. He was looking for possible other people following the young man and looked a little bit disappointed when nobody followed.

He listened to the proposal of John. His concern was about the financing of the project. John made the Mayor clear that there was one condition. The financing of the tower was based on the condition that the rent for the prison was just as high as the price for the use of the ground. John did not know who owned the ground but it would probably be the government that also owned the prison. He also made clear that he did not wanted to be identified out in the open. He would like to stay out of site. The Mayor might take all the credits for the deal. The Mayor looked still a bit uncertain. He did not know what to think of it. This young man. How could he ever finance this project?

John showed him his first design. The project looked good.

John understood the problem of the mayor. He asked permission to start the project by removing the present building. He would ask the buildingpermit with an official architect. He asked the Mayor if he would prefer him to use a specific architect ?

The Mayor did. He got a businesscard out of his pocket and gave it to John. John thanked him and got permission to start to tear down the present ruin. The Mayor laughed at him.

He did gave his permission. He repeated that he would not pay a penny.

John thanked him for his confidence. He left the memorystick and told the Mayor that he could always contact him through the e-mailaddress mentioned in the memorystick.

The Mayor made clear that he still had his doubts but John could prove his proposition.

John thanked him and left.

He now had to get in contact with the architect.

Of course that could only happen tomorrow. He walked back to his cottage.

He now had to decide about the information he would give to the four organisations that had to pay for the rebuilt of the prison. He had to talk with the architect to get a price-indication for the total project. He would have to find out what the sales of the apartments and the mall and the parkingstocks would pay. The rest plus a nice bonus for him had to be paid by the four criminal organisations.

He took a new tablet of the last three he had bought as a package a view days ago and started to make a first mail to the criminal organisations.

"Hallo Wolves", he started.

"Since you, together with three other criminal organisations, are responsible for the damage of the prison in our city, we herewith inform you that we will collect the cost for the rebuilding of the prison from your accounts. We will do the same from your involved colleagues.

Further information will follow.

Sincerely yours

The old man"

He made an identical mail for James, Major and Lord. He decided to use a special a mailaddress and noted that under the letter. He decided not to use the tablet. He would go into town the next morning and use the computers of the internetcafé.

He also would use this location for reading the reactions and to transfer money to the account that he would open tomorrow on the small bank, he had bought shares of. He felt good about the decisions he had made.

He went to sleep. Tomorrow would be an interesting day.

He slept well. He got up, took a light breakfast and made a lot of exercises. In town he first called the architect. He expected that the Mayor had already informed him about him and the mission that had to be realised. His expectations were correct. He could come for an appointment that same morning.

John got back to his cottage and collected his disguise-outfit. He got changed in a nearby hotel. John had a bad feeling about this hurry of the architect. He would probably have a problem with this man about money. The architect had a big office and was very convinced of the fact that John was a charlatan. He made clear that he needed an upfront downpayment of five million dollar to make a first indication drawing of the building. John had heard enough. He must admit that he did not coped with that strategy and got out.

He went to a big hotel and changed back to himself again.

He got to the internetcafé and searched for another architect. He first looked by which architect the buildings around the prison were realised. He looked at the offices on the internet. He had a good feeling with an office in a normal building, led by an extreme young but very ambitious woman. A photo and a simple movie made her personality clear. Street forward and not easy to get rid of if she wanted something from you.

John liked her. She really was very young. He called her office and ask for an appointment with her. She was very busy the young man on the phone made clear. She might have time tomorrow early in the morning but he had to ask her if this was allright. He asked and she found it ok.

John was still in the internetcafé and send away the mails to the four criminal organisations. He was curious about their reaction, if any.

He went to the sportsschool where he had been a week before. He trained the whole afternoon. His trainingscoach was very impressed about his condition and status. They sparred together using the legs as basic movementcentre. No boxing, only feet actions. They decided to wind bandages on their legs otherwise their skin might get hurt unneeded for the training.

John looked around in the trainingsarea. He caught a glance from a young woman that looked familiar to him. He could not place her. He did not remember to have seen her ever before. Perhaps he had seen her on television. He took a shower and got out. He calmly walked around and got in at a simple restaurant to get something to eat. He decided otherwise and wanted to leave the restaurant again. Just at that moment that he stepped out, the young lady from the sportsschool stood in front of the restaurant, obviously hesitating whether she should get in or not.

She looked surprised to John. "You again? Are you following me?"

John had to laugh. " I was coming out the restaurant, are you following me?" he had to laugh about the joke.

To his surprise she answered "To be honest, yes, I did follow you. I saw you in the sportsschool. You are good, man. Fantastic. Are you a professional fighter, Roderic is training with you, he only trains with the very best !!" She came standing right in front of John.

Suddenly John recognised her. This was the ambitious architect. In reality she did look even better than on screen.

"You like what you see, "she laughed at him.

"To be honest, Yes, very much. "

John became honest as well. She was a few years older than he was but he was a free young man. He smiled at her, a bit surprised about his own confession. He was not very used to this kind of conversations.

"Come. Let's go somewhere together and eat. I know this fine little restaurant just around the corner. I like you, " She immediately took his arm and walked with him into the direction she wanted. John let her take the lead.

She smiled to him. Indeed there was a small and cosy restaurant just around the corner. She moved in and walked straight away to a certain rather dark spot at the back.

John smiled. She really was an expert in this kind of work. She really did what she wanted. He liked it. He realised that he liked woman taken action. He was not very used to be in the lead in connection to good looking woman. She asked what he wanted to eat but he let her decide. He tried to get the conversation about her work but she again and again moved it very ingenious to his activities. He first told her that he was busy in a sort of medical world. She told that she was working in the construction world. So they informed each other very basically. John played the game with her. He waited for the right moment. By the end of the simple but good meal, he suddenly told her that he was an inventor of medical, biochemical structures. She looked at him, completely surprised. This sounded quite complicated and very exclusive.

He looked at her with a enjoying smile. She just had not expected a very young good muscled student type, to be a highly educated inventor, active in an extraordinary complicated kind of work. He liked her reaction very much. Suddenly he was no longer just a kind of a bundle of muscles with a beautiful body but he was a lot more. He even was intelligent.

She looked at him again. She could not believe it. He smiled at her.

They took a small extra and John paid. She had not expected him to pay, still the poor student in her eyes.

They got to a large hotel, spend a couple of hours in the casino of the hotel and danced in a dancing nearby. It was late when John said good night to her. She was completely surprised. She had not expected him to leave her. She wanted him to come with her. He asked if she was sure about that. She was a lot older than he. She was almost thirty.

John pulled her against his body and kissed her. By that time she immediately kissed him back. This was where she had been waiting for the whole evening, since she had admired his body in the sportsschool.

John accompanied her to her apartment. It was really extravagant. Very large and open. Super elegant and really a living from a woman alone. She really was very experienced in making love. John learned a lot about the things she liked and how to touch her and where. It was a busy night. She loved his body. She was very good in making love. She got up early, she was a working girl and had to be at her office in time.

They had a simple breakfast and John left as the first one. He walked back to his cottage. He had an appointment with Sonja, the woman he had spent the night with. She did not know. He decided to visit her in the fatty boy outfit. He was certain that she would not recognise him. He got redressed, did the brown contactlenses in, changed the colour of his hair and eyebrows into deep black, Filled his cheeks and his shirt so he would certainly not look like a well-trained young man. He controlled it all in the mirror and got out. He was Tom again. He walked into town. He was a little bid late for his appointment and he apologised for it. He happened to be very busy. His apologies were accepted, there was no other way with a potential new order.

John explained his wishes. Sonja looked completely surprised at this fatty looking young man, talking to her about a giant project as if it was his normal business. She had a peculiar feeling about this guy. She short ago also had made a wrong decision about a young man and his abilities. Peculiar but this guy also had something she could not fit in the outlook.

She staid very businesswise involved in the information he gave her. He left the memorystick with the basic outlines of the building, formed in the sign of "Infinity", a kind of a lying eight. She did found the outlook very stimulating. He seemed to know that she had built a high tower before.

John wanted an indication of the building- and architectcosts for the realisation of the finances. He also wanted a first principle drawing of one of the apartments to get in contact with a broker for the sale of the apartments. Also an important point for the finances. About the content of the prison the board of the prison and the governmental deciders had to be part of the informationgroup for the realisation of the prison. She did understood al he told her. A college of her was present at the meeting. John also indicated the costs of removing the present buildingmaterials. Sonja found that a part of the materials could be used again, all the stones and other materials as well, the concrete should be crumbled and used in the walking paths in the garden. The iron would be used again after being melted and so on.

John also wanted the drawings for an official permit to build this tower. The Mayor already was informed about his proposals and had advised another architect. Unfortunately this architect was not good enough to do the job in Tom's eyes. He also asked her to indicate the costs her office would make to do all this and inform him about the conditions for doing this all. He left his e-mailaddress for questions and made clear that he wanted no publicity around his person. They could do with this what they wanted but he could not be mentioned, never, during the whole building period. The only contact between the architect and him would go through the email.

John left. Of course the office had a problem to find this all realistic.

They decided to contact the Mayor. He really was known about the project. They informed John by email about their contact with the Mayor and gave an indication of the startingcosts to clear the site and the costs to ask a building permit from the Community. They wanted to make a big show of this with the Mayor as central figure, taking all the credits.

John made the payment for the startingcosts. He informed the four organisations about the amount that was transferred from witch of their accounts, to pay for the first costs in this case.

He was certain that the four organisations would go crazy through this action. He had to be very careful with all this. They really were extreme dangerous once you got to their accounts. They of course would start new accounts in due course.

Chapter 38

John looked for a workspot for his medical experimental area. He found a location at the first stock of a chemical factory. They had a part of the building they did not use. They were glad to have someone to use it for a reasonable low rent. The area had an entrance of its own through a broad stairway. John ordered a lot of technical and electronical appliances for his nano's. He wanted four testpersons to train nano's for them. He first had to clear his targets. He thought that he could use the nano's to stimulate in a certain route several parts of the brain, depending on the problems of the patient. The problems must be so that the involved organs were only partly damaged. He had to find out where the limits were on this point.
He named his research laboratory "Normal Nano's". He painted it on the outside wall of his new working area. He found himself happy. This was where it was all about. He still had to find patients that were willing to accept the nano's.
He contacted one of the local hospitals. He told his ambitions and the hospital was willing to make suggestions to four of their patients to try to make them his patients. John was very happy with the positive indication of the hospital. He got the four bloodsamples from the four patients and got to work, making nano's for these four patients.

He made acquaintance with these four patients and told them what he was trying to do. Two of the patients, an older woman and an older man were already far out. He could see that they did not understood what he was telling. He informed the hospital contact that he expected no results by these two patients, simply because their bodies and their minds were already unrepairable damaged. He would still go on with his experiments. The other two patients were a woman and a man.

The young woman of about thirty five had big problems with her kidneys and her lever. A familyproblem for generations.

The man of about fortyfive had problems with his blood and his lungs.

John concentrated with these two patients on their specific two points, with the two older patients he made a more general way of working so it was directed to all the organs, shorter periods in time but more sessions to move the nano's.

He spend a lot of time to make the maps of the brains of each of the patients. He had to know where the nano's had to be placed and concentrated.

John waited to create the nano's until he had the brains of all four patients. He used mainly soundwaves to get the right information. He controlled it all and found it satisfying.

He suddenly was attended by his television that
that evening a second fight for the worldtitel boxing
would take place. John had it all forgotten.
He also had given no attention to his family. He
went there immediately.
He had a great evening. He loved his family, even
his sisters were nice girls. He did not remember
them as nice but nowadays they changed and he
liked them. Also his brother was very friendly. He
left with a great feeling.
He got right on to the location of the fight of Toko.
He could got in easy. At this time there was no
longer a control at the entrance. John found that
absurd but he just walked in.
The fight had already started. It was round three.
John had no seat so he stayed in the lane and
looked how things were going. Toko had a difficult
fight. He stood far too much still so his opponent
could blow his enormous fists against Toko 's body
and arms.
John looked at the coach from Toko. The man just
stood aside. He gave no advises.
John sneaked forward and got without any problem
close to the ring. He came to the ring and started to
yel to Toko.
"Come on Toko, move, get around, go. "
He repeated his yell. He saw that Toko stretch
himself out. Got aside. Stepped aside again. He
quickly looked at the side of the ring to be sure from
whom the advises came. It was John as he already

thought. He nicked to John, Stretched out further and started to dance. The bell ringed.

The coach from Toko put the crutch in the corner for Toko. Toko looked at John. "Please help me, coach me,"

Toko called to John. John nicked and came to Toko. "You are losing Toko. John simply stated.

"Yeah, help me, what should I do. "

"Come on, Toko. I learned you everything. Did not you train it?"

John did not waited for an answer. "This man has a hard blow, stay away from his right hand, change your frontfoot more often, and dance, circle around him and then blow him away. You better do it quick in this round. Do not think, just do it !!"

The bell ringed, The coach from Toko looked furious at John. Who did he think he was to take his task away. He was the coach of the worldchampion !! John looked at Toko. Toko immediately started to change his frontfoot. His opponent looked surprised and got a blow against his head. Toko started to dance around the man. Again and again he hit the man against his head. John saw what happened. "Now, he yelled. " Toko stood still , looked at his opponent and hit him brutally with a heavy uppercut, he jumped upwards with that blow, as he had learned from John. Toko immediately got to the neutral corner. His opponent simply got down. He really was totally knocked out. The referee called in the doctor and the fight was over.

John left and got out of the arena area. He felt good. Now Toko would know that boxing is not only fighting, it is also tactics. He wandered whether Toko would call for him again, maybe even in the media if he could not find him, though he should know where he lived. Toko had been in his cottage. He walked back to his cottage. He had enjoyed his visit to his family .

He got back to his cottage and got to bed. It had been a long day.

John got up late. He had a quick breakfast and went to his laboratory. He controlled the maps he had made from the brains of his four patients and started to create the eighteen nano's for each of them. It was an intensive job. He needed the whole day. He called the hospital to inform them that he wanted to give the medicines to the patients tomorrow in the morning. The cooperation of the hospital was good and they would prepare the patients. They were very curious about this project. John was tired. He had been busy very intense. He bought something to aet and got back to his cottage. He took a calm and rest period. He sat in his garden and was resting on the bench in the sun. He stayed there for an hour. He made himself a dinner and picked up his tablets for his contacts with his four individuals with the criminal organisations. He ran through the forest. He felt good doing so. He got to a park in town in looked at his four informants. They had nothing to tell. Nothing special he was to be informed about.

He got to an internetcafé he had never been before. He contacted his a-mailaddress with each of the four criminal organisations. There was one reaction. Only Lord had made clear that she did not accepted his terms. She had nothing to do with the whole prisonaffair and did not wanted to pay. John simply answered that she was completely involved. He wished everybody to be honest against him, therefor she had to pay an extra amount the next time. "Honesty is needed in this case. If the leaders cannot be honest in connection to their own organisation, they better stop."

John was curious about her reaction. Probably she would not answer at all.

He also looked at the emailaddress for the buildingactivity.

The college of Sonja had a couple of questions. John answered them. He did not wanted to be present at the contacts with third parties as the prisonmanagement or the community about the buildingpermit. John would stay completely out of site. He was curious about the drawings for the apartments.

He closed all the sites carefully. He even deleted the memorysystem of the computer at the internetcafé.

He left the internetcafé. He walked back to his cottage. It was late. He ran through the forest. He should do more about his condition. He neglected it since he was busy with his nano-project. He knew that this was his future. The other affairs were all temporary happenings. He stopped coming out of the forest. In front of his cottage stood a big limousine.

"Toko", he though immediately. He smiled. Toko started to learn. He had damaged his tryst with the lasergun. He carefully approached the car. A big strong man was sitting behind the wheel. John did not knew him. He slipped around the car and suddenly got up right in front of the sidewindow of the car. The man dreaded. He shaked with his head and put his arm in front of his face for the window. He looked scared.

John smiled at him. Slowly the man lowered his arm. He looked at John. He saw the smiling face. He calmed down. He put his arm down and started to lower the window.

"Hallo sir," the man started with a very deep voice. "My name is William Scrowfort. Mr Toko is my boss. He would like to talk to you. Would you please get in the car, I will ride you to him and also will bring you back to this point after the meeting".

It was as John had expected. Unfortunately he had no time today. Tomorrow was also a busy day.

"Hallo William, unfortunately I have to go to sleep now. I have a very intense day tomorrow. Please tell Toko that he may visit me the day after tomorrow round ten o'clock in the morning. I will be here. I will leave at five minutes past ten if he is not here at that time. Good luck. "John made a step back as signal that William could leave.

"But sir," William tried it again.

John walked around the car and walked away towards the forest.

William left the car, called him again and started to follow him. John ran to the forest and got into the forest. An extra training, no problem, John thought. He looked back. William stopped at the forest. He sight and started to walk back.

John looked from the forest and saw William getting back to his car and picking up his phone. He made a call and left. John saw the car disappear. He got back to his cottage and got in. He looked for a moment to the latest news on the television. He saw Toko winning his fight against the former worldchampion and an item about the new developments round the rebuilding of the prison. The Mayor stated that he was in discussion with a big investor. This investor was probably willing to rebuild the prison as part of a far larger tower. He probably would bear the costs for the prison by selling a great number of apartments in the building. He was in contact with an architect that was approached by this investor and had the order to start the activities to get a buildingpermit and to remove the present ruin. After some other questions about this mysterious investor the name of the architect was asked. The Mayor gave the name of

the office of Sonja. The next shot was an interview with the college of Sonja. He confirmed the order. The following questions to the Mayor were shown in the next shot. The Mayor answered that in the present proposals the city did not had to pay one penny. That was the perfect solution. He showed the pictures John had given to him on the memorystick. John was satisfied about the information.
He got to his bed.

John slept well.
He collected his nano's in his laboratory and went to the hospital. The hospital had prepared the patients. He talked with each of the patients to tell what was going to happen. They would not notice anything from what he did. Only the injection of the nano's into the bloodstream could hurt a little bit. The patients took it all very calm.
John located the nano's to the right place in the brain of each of the patients. He activated them and now they had to wait. He asked the nurses to inform him if they noticed something special. The nano's needed time to get results.
He left and took a simple lunch.
He got to his sportsschool. His coach was waiting for him. They trained very intense. The speed in combination with a turn in the air to kick was difficult for John. He had to jump higher than he was used to. He learned to move his body before he really

jumped up. So he could make a better turn. For an eventual opponent this would betray the coming action. So they also trainer other options from the move to make the turn.

A jump sidewards combined with a straight forward jump worked good as alternative. John also trained his coach. The speed in action was to slow and John gave him hints to react on the behaviour of his opponent.

He trained also the change with different feet up front. He found it difficult to get used to standing with his wrong foot upfront. He therefor trained it more and more. His coach was surprised about this option.

John left the sportsschool and ran through the parks in the city. He liked this also. He finished by running through the forest and came home at the cottage.

He took a shower and got dressed up.

He walked to the square of the Saloon and got seated on the bank around the tree in the centre of the square.

The old man group was discussing the new project of the prison.

John only listened. Some found it a great prove of a good vision to combine the building with expensive apartments and a big mall. So the costs for building the prison could be compensated by the profit from the sales of the apartments and perhaps the sale of the mall.

Others found it wrong and unacceptable. They would never wanted to buy an apartment, knowing that the prison was in the same building. The criminals were right under you. Horrible.
John took a large dinner at the Saloon and got back home to the cottage.
He slept well that night.

Chapter 39

John got up early. He felt good. He had no special things today, only a possible visit of Toko.
He called with the hospital to find out how the patients were doing. As far as it was noted, there was no change in the condition of the patients. He promised to call again in a week. The nano's needed time.
He waited calm till five minutes after ten. No Toko. He left. He took his tablets with him and ran through the forest, twice. He got into town, bought himself a new outfit and kept it on. He got to a new park at the other side of town close to the spot where his parents lived. He controlled the mailadresses for the four informants. One of them, the person from James, noted that there was more activity in the internet area, because four new young persons were rented to get more and better information's from the internet. The three boys and one girl were discussing about the options to get into the tablets and computers of others. They were specialist in cracking computers and telephones.
John understood it. James made the most money with drugs and kept her market closed through murders if needed. She had realised that the computers were a new threat. Costumers could buy drugs through the internet, so to protect her market she had introduced this extra team. She probably

also had changed her bankaccounts and was busy transferring the money to these new accounts.

John noticed the remark. He thanked his contact for this useful information.

He controlled his contacts with the accounts of James. It all seemed the same, nothing was changed. Was it a trick, was his contact caught by her boss?

He left it as it was. He first needed proof that James actually did what his informant had insinuated. He looked at the mailaddress of Sonja. The college of Sonja had read his reaction on his questions. He understood the position of the client. He made clear that this needed an extra person to be involved in the negotiations with the Community and the potential builders.

John understood the point. It would all be visible when he got informed about the costs.

There also was a drawing available of one of the apartments. John copied it to one of his memorysticks and had it printed out at a printshop. He took the print and got back to his cottage.

He called the largest broker in town. He wanted to speak with somebody that could give an indication about the sale of apartments. He got an appointment that afternoon. John also took the memorystick with the total building on it and copied the apartmentmap into the memory of the building on the stick.

He ate a simple lunch and got himself in the outfit of the fat young boy.

He walked into town. He was used to this kind of transport. The weather was always very stable and sunny. He felt good with that.

He looked around in the city and got to the broker by the time of his appointment.

He found the person he had to talk to very young and he was very uncertain about every question John asked. He finished the conversation, thanked him for his time but made clear that all the contacts were over.

He got back to the citycentre. He just happened to pass along a small real estate brokeroffice. He just got in. He asked to talk to somebody that could give direct information about new buildings and new apartments. The young girl at the counter smiled at him and immediately asked him to take a seat and wanted to know if he wished coffee or that he preferred thee. John preferred coffee and the girl activated a coffeemachine, right behind her. She put a coffeecup under the tap and got into a door, beside the coffeemachine. She immediately came back with a young man.

She introduced him as Jo Baker the broker, officially recognized as taxation expert and qualified broker. John liked the way she promoted the quality of this very young man.

He got his coffee and Jo asked him to come into his office so they could talk without disturbance.

Jo listened to John's story. He was very surprised that he had come to his very small office. He would love to cooperate in this case. He looked at the seizes of the map of the apartment. He found the seize extreme large. This apartment could bring an amount of more than a million dollar. If he would lower the seize, he could sell more apartments with a higher total amount on the sales. For instant four of these large apartments would bring all together perhaps five million dollar, while seven smaller apartments would bring six million dollar. Of course the costs for smaller balconies but two more might also give lower buildingcosts.

John discussed about different options on different levels.

Jo suggested a top restaurant on the highest stock and the roof and perhaps four stocks direct under that for a luxe hotel. Perhaps the building could be these four stocks higher, than the hotel was a complete extra with limited extra building costs.

John thanked him for the good advice. He wanted to know under what conditions he would do the sales , including the possible sale of the hotel, the restaurant, the parkingarea's and the mall. They came to a deal and John promised to contact the architect with the new ideas. He would come back with the drawings of the building as soon as the final buildingpermit was available.

Jo thanked him for the order and accompanied him to the door.

John was glad with this broker. Young and enthusiastic. That was what he needed. He got to a park and informed Sonja about the new view about the hotel on top of the building and the smaller apartments. He got a positive reaction from the college of Sonja. He expected that it would take another week to get the principal drawings, needed for the permitrequest, ready. John would like to see the request upfront.

He felt good. It started to get a body, this new prison. He got into a big hotel, change from Tom to John and walked out again.

He looked for another internetcafé in the city and found one in a hotel around the next park. He realised that he could also use the businesscentre from hotels. He could use every time another location. He walked to the hotel, got into the businesscentre, payed for the use of the internet for one hour and made a search on the sites of the four criminal organisations. The bankaccounts of James were empty. He controlled the others, there nothing was changed. He Immediately made a search on the banktransfer-informationsystem, found the inlogcodes, seven in total to get in, found the transfers and the new numbers of the accounts. He logged in on these accounts. There were extreme high amounts on these accounts. He decided to transfer extreme much from these accounts except from two. He kept those as reserve. He took six million from each of the other six accounts. If you punish you must punish strongly against an organisation as James had. He also transferred from the thirtysix million on his building account to a new account in his name on his bank.

He send a small mail to James telling that she got punished because of a lack of honesty. He informed her that he had transferred thirtysix million to the account of the prisonbuilding.

He was glad that he had secured this accounts by his eyescan and fingerprints. He was the only one that could ever get in. In the organisations the administrators had to get in, so they had to use another system.

John felt even better now. He started to run again and got back to his cottage.

He put all his tablets away, again in his special cabinet.

He also left his outlooks in the cabinet and took a shower and cleaned his face and hair. He got hungry and walked to the Saloon.

Miriam was at the Saloon. She immediately came to John and advised him a special dinner from the chef. John found it ok and ate with taste. He left an hour later.

He walked back to his cottage. He was thinking about his nano's and the working of it. He now had experience with the nano's about stimulating the growth of muscles by stimulating the brain. Could it work the same with the liver. What would it do. Would it stimulate the growth of the liver or would it stimulate the working of the liver. The brain did not really stimulated the working of the liver. The liver itself reacted on the conditions in the blood and the watercyclus in the body. He stopped. He now had given the patients only nano's that stimulated the brainfunctions. Did not he needed to stimulate the organ itself?

His deduction seemed correct. Could he combine the two functions, stimulating the organ itself and stimulating the brain to let the organ grow. Did the organ needed to grow or were they large enough. He had to think this through again. He looked at his cottage and stopped. The big limousine of Toko 's assistant was again standing in front of his cottage. John stopped and looked at the limousine. He calmly walked to the big car. The chauffeur stepped out. It was the same man as the day before yesterday.

"Hallo sir, please help me, "he sounded sad. "Mr Toko offers you his apologise, he could not come this morning. He asks you to come to him if possible today and preferable now, so he can offer you a great proposal in person."

"Why should I help you?" John asked with a smile. "What is in it for you?" he wanted to know.

"Sir, I must be honest. If I may bring you to Mr Toko, I earn a great bonus. That will help me enormously to pay a part of the costs for my new house. It would be my day. " He beamed a big smile.

John liked the big giant with a great inner sweetness.

He got in the car. He almost heard the chauffeur enjoying his cooperation.

The man drove away. He got out of town and ended at a large house about ten kilometres out of town. He had to wait for a big, strong gate. He got out of the car and announced his present and his guest. The big gate opened and he drove the limousine to the house. John got out and looked at the house. An old looking great country estate.

The chauffeur walked with him to the door. There a young lady opened the door and invited John in. The chauffeur got back to the limousine. He would wait there for John.

John got in. The young lady brought him to a large room, the office of Toko. Toko was waiting for him He enthusiastically received John.

As John had expected he offered him a permanent job as his coach for his boxing career. He wanted to continue that for another three years but he needed a coach that new what he had to do. And John knew that. John asked about the conditions. Toko looked at him. The new fight was already in three weeks. He offered 30 percent of his win. John asked about his last win. That win was included. He would pay it immediately. John only wanted to be available for two afternoons per week. In the last four days before a fight he would have one whole day extra to be available. He had also several other activities that he had to take care of. Toko accepted the conditions. They made appointments about the day of the week, and the location. He had a great trainingsarea in his barn, right behind his house. John accepted that location.

He was brought home by the chauffeur, who was very glad about the willing cooperation of John. John got in the cottage and made a planning for his daily activities. He did have enough time to serve Toko and to help the patients. He wanted to see how the patients were doing and if he had to do something more with the nano's.

He hoped that James would never find out that he was the one that "stole" millions of her account. He knew that these kind of amounts were really heavy, but the total accounts were more dan ten times this amount, so James would not feel any pain by missing this amount. She had to feel it, yes, that was necessary.

He fell asleep with that thought.

Chapter 40

John got up feeling good. He after his breakfast went to the hospital. He would like to find out how his patients were doing. He did found that the nano's did work. The way they sensed made it clear. The brains did react. He decided to change the nano's with the two younger patients. He transported, very careful nine of the nano's to the organ that needed to be activated in his way of functioning. The nano's that staid in the brain activated the same organ to grow. The new placed nano's activated the organ to do more in his way of making all kind of specific matter needed in one's body. He wandered how he could measure the results. He made some soundpictures of the organs and the brains. He also looked at the two older patients. He wandered whether he should spread out the nano's so they would altogether have a function for a great part of the brain. He decided to do so. The total brain could be better activated as a whole. He made sound pictures before the changes and after. He put the information in the files of the patients. He looked at the pictures he made before and had the impression that the nano's already had activated the brainpart where they had functioned. He also looked at the stimulated part in the body and found a very little positive reaction. It was only a few days since the nano's were activated so he could not expect too much from it. He decided to come back in a week. Perhaps the results could be visualised then.

He walked into town. He found that he had to learn more about the way to stimulate muscles, for instance with a massage. What were the effects of massage. Why was that so good for the body to function. He got into a park and searched for more information on the internet regarding this subject. There were many different views about this. It seemed as if everybody had his own view. He wandered if the nano's could play a role in this matter. He again looked for the vision behind all of these massages. He had the impression that the movement of the muscles made them transfer the waste removal quicker. Heavily used muscles got problems in removing their waste, the restproducts born as result of the use of the muscles. He was convinced that his nano's could be of interest here. That could result in a longer use of the muscles before the problems with the restproducts would start. Acidification might be reduced sincerely. He liked the idea. He would see what he could do with that. Perhaps he could use this on himself. He should get himself activated so he would get problems with his arms. He got back to his cottage, got his trainingscloths and went to another trainingsschool than where he trained the kickboxingactivities. He informed the coach that he wanted to strengthen his arms. He got a number of attributes he had to use for his arms. The coach told him not to do too much the first time because he would get trouble with his muscles. Acidification was a problem than. John thanked him and did deliberately too much. He did the same training for more than an hour. The coach warned him after half an hour. John continued. After an hour the coach stopped him. He had to leave the attribute. John thanked the coach and really felt his muscles. He now knew how he could measure the working of nano's in his muscles. He must admit that he did not liked the pain in his arms. He got back to his laboratory. He injected his own nano's and brought them to the painplaces in both his arms. He activated the nano's. He got back home. He ran through the forest and was curious about the results of the working of the nano's.

He took a shower and got redressed. He walked into town. He ate at one of the "all you can eat"-restaurants. He was hungry and was busy eating till late at night. He walked to a cinema and enjoyed a movie about some active fighting guys. They used their feet as well as their hands. John was impressed about their fighting method. He got out and visited a casino at a big hotel. He started to win at a specific machine. He was surprised. He did not had a good feeling about this machine. He qualified it as just luck. He walked around and left. His arms felt ok already. He got back home. He got to bed and slept well.

John got up early. He had no problems with his arms. It felt good. After his lunch he direct got back to the same trainingsschool as where he had been yesterday afternoon. He did the same training with the same attribute as the day before. He actually trained for more than two hours. He had no problem with his arms. The nano's worked fantastic. He was very satisfied with the results.

He got back to his laboratory and transported the nano's to his legs, divided all over the muscles of his legs, even one in each of his feet. Eight in each of the rest of his legs. He started to run right outside his laboratory and as fast as he could. He tried to keep on running as fast as he could on the road. The traffic made it difficult for him, so he decided to leave the city and started to run out of town. He ran as fast as he could for three hours. He returned the same way and ran again three hours. He was surprised, it seemed to have perfect results.

He at last returned to his laboratory and started to feel his legs hurt badly once he had stopped. He was not surprised. It would have been too beautiful. He was again very happy. Who could run for six hours at his fastest. He decided to start with athletics. He tried to find information about this but he only found an athletic organisation at a small location with no facilities. Everybody ran on the streets. They organised streetruns and that was it.

John did not found that very interesting. Could he jump higher, could he jump further? He had no idea. How fast could he run? He had no idea. He had learned to jump with his sportschoolcoach.

He got back to his cottage. He made a bar in his garden and tried to jump over it. He collected some pillows so he would land on a soft place. He had not enough pillows. He had to buy them first. He started to train without a bar. It was not very satisfying. He got inside and realised that he had not eaten after his breakfast. He made himself a meal with many small snacks and enjoyed his dinner. He put the television on and looked at a kickboxfight. He found it very intriguing. The fighters were all the time jumping around, trying to hit the opponent with their feet or knee or elbow and also with their hands, boxing. He understood his coach. He was also involved in this kind of sports. Perhaps he should accompany his coach once to get a better feeling about this sport. He still did not liked to be involved in a sport in which the target was to hit another human being.

He realised that he was more or less cheating on the other fighter, using his extra options through his nano's.

He got back to his laboratory and removed his nano's.

He got back to his cottage. His legs hurt but he wanted to recover in a natural way. He had to think about what he wanted with his nano's. Did he only wanted to use them for others having a problem to be solved or also for sportsactivists to be better during a fight or only during a training. He had to make up his mind. Should he be involved in anything else than his medical view with his nano's? He got to bed to sleep over it. It was a difficult decision.

John found it difficult to catch his sleep. The question about the use of nano's kept on dancing through his brain. He could not decide. Toko misused his extra possibilities by using them to box. Toko needed someone to tell him what to do, how to fight. Without this information he could not win. So it was not only the extra power that made him win, tactics were just as important. He was curious whether Toko still had his nano's in his brain or that he had taken them out and collected them. He would ask him. Tomorrow afternoon he would be at Toko 's traininglocation. At last he fell asleep. He was tired of his runningactivities.

John got up late. He had slept bad. He had troubles with his legs. He still had pain there. Cramps followed each other regularly. He took a very warm bath to ease his legs. It helped a bit. He took a breakfast and got to his laboratory. Should he use the nano's to get rid of the pain. He decided not to do that. He had to recover without nano's. He had the feeling that using the nano's for this kind of reasons was not really all fair play. What had been done was done. That could not be changed. Nano's should only be used for medical reasons. That was why he had developed them, that was where they should be used for. He felt good with his decision. He walked calm and carefully to the park nearby. He looked at the four informers but they had nothing to tell. The architect had send a first map of the total building having the restaurant at the top and the mal at the bottom. Parking-areas were situated as John had suggested. There were four different types of apartments. One very big, one a smaller version and two smaller ones. John looked at the maps. They all looked alike but differed in the seize. He liked it. There was a list of the number of apartments to be realised in the total building. John gave his consent and walked immediately to the broker in the centre of the city. He stopped, turned back and simply send the mail through to the broker Jo Baker. He promised to drop by the next morning. John got back to his cottage. He took a simple lunch and wanted to get on his motor. He was not interested to walk to the house of Toko far out of town with his sore legs. It was already getting better but it was far from good yet.

The bell ringed. John was surprised. He looked at the outerdoor. The driver smiled at him, the back door of the limousine was open and the driver invited him to get in.

John got his tablet and his bag, locked his housedoor and the outerdoor and got in the limousine.

He was glad with this solution. He would have taken his motor to go to Toko 's house. He still had trouble with his legs.

Toko showed very proud his private trainingscentre. John was impressed. This barn was a total gym, including a fightingring and all trainingsoptions for the boxingsport.

John explained his problem with his legs.

Toko immediate took action. He gave John a card from a massageinstitute. He needed a good sportsmassage. This institute was the best, in the vision of Toko.

They trained although John did not train along. Toko had to do it alone this time. John asked information from Toko about his opponent. Together they looked at four fights of this very good and active moving fighter.

He did not had a tough blow but he was fast. He had a quick hit and moved around his opponent. This was a hard job. John made Toko train to box with his left foot on front. The opponent had his right foot on front. Toko had to train to suddenly change his front foot and got back again quickly. The idea was that the opponent would be surprised by these changes and stand still for a short while. That moment was Toko 's moment. He had to use his jumping uppercut.

Toko understood. He also had to train his condition. He had to move along with his opponent. He even ought to move faster and turn around and away and back again.

Again they looked at the fights from the opponent and John showed him where he had to take action, the moment and the right blow in that situation.

Toko felt good. He really had been afraid for this opponent but he now already felt better and better. John was good in his advises.

Toko let John, after the training directly delivered at the massagecentre. He wanted John as soon as possible in the right condition to be his sparringpartner in the ring.

John entered the massagecentre. He stumbled in. He really had more problems than before the training. The man behind the desk understood his problem. He brought him to a special chamber and asked him to undress, take a shower and lay back on the massagetable.

John did so and kept the towel around his waist. He got on the table and waited.

A young woman came in almost immediately after he had climbed the table. The table made a contact as soon as a weight came on it, so the masseur would know that his client was ready.

The woman introduced herself as "Mary". John found her a little bid skinny for a massage but did not say a word.

Mary smiled, she knew this kind of reaction from her clients when they saw her for the first time. After that they never thought about her in that way. John introduced himself as "John" and told her about the problems with his muscles in his legs. Mary found it a very unlikely story, running for six hours without real training upfront. Nobody could run for six hours, even marathonrunners did not train that way. She started carefully and felt that the muscles were indeed thick and strong and enormous hard. Even she had to be careful with these overused mussels. She carefully started to move the muscles. John had to push his cheeks firm together not to scream. She started to believe him. This extreme position was almost impossible to bear. How could he have run with these mussels. She asked him and got an even more stupid reaction about an invention he had done through which he could run for six hours the fastest he could. He also had removed his invention after the running and he regretted that almost a whole night and day now. Perhaps he should use it again to get rid of the musclepain faster.

She massaged his muscles carefully. After an hour of massage John asked her to stop. This was tiring enough for her although she was used to this. John got up. Took again a shower and got home with a taxi.

This was unacceptable. He got with his motor to his laboratory, took his nano's with him and got back to his cottage. He loaded his nano's, took his nano's and directed them again to his muscles. He activated them with soundbeems. He immediately felt his muscles relax. They softened right away. He took a simple meal and stayed at home the rest of the evening. He had learned something again. His nano's were good, but he had to use them also for the care afterwards. He went to bed early. He was tired and had a bad night behind him.

Chapter 41

John slept good. He got up late. He felt a lot better and decided to keep the nano's for another day. He walked calm and enjoyed the walk, through the forest and got into town. He entered a hotel and rented the internet for an hour in the businesscentre. He looked at all his emails and was not surprised to see that James reacted that she found her punishment out of order. She regularly changed her accountnumbers, so this was nothing special. She expected him to book the amount back at her account.

John did not even reacted. He had to learn fast, just as Lord. She still had her punishment to receive. He waited until the next payment would be needed for the project.

There was an enthusiastic mail from Jo Baker, the real estate broker. He found the solutions about the apartments good, really good.

He proposed the salesprices, based upon a buildingperiod of 30 months from the day the permit was delivered. The architect should make his statement in this matter. The deliverydate must be a hard date, that would improve the salesoptions.

John looked at the contact with the architect and found a confirmation from the city that a buildingpermit was asked for. This was a big project so the decision would take some time. The architect had made contact with the board of the prison to

discuss their wishes on their part of the building.
The seize was already accepted, now the map must
be discussed and the needs.
John found it all ok and closed the contact.
He left the businesscentre and walked into a great
park. Kids were playing and a lot of families walked
around. It was beautiful whether.
He walked back to his laboratory. He felt good. He
tried to get a better feeling about the status of his
legsmuscles and pushed against them. It did feel
good. The nano's really were miracles. These
nano's worked fantastic for muscles. He hoped they
did the same for all other organs. He had to wait to
measure the results with the four patients.
Perhaps he should think about alternative nano's.
Why were these nano's so good for the muscles. He
had to wait. The four patients would give him an
idea about their conditions and the working of the
nano's as they were.
He moved his legs more expressive. No problems.
He decided to remove the nano's. He tried to use
another method by first deactivating them and then
by drinking far more water than normal. He had
thought that the waterdisposel would be more active
though that. Possibly the nano's were moving more
because of the extra watertransport through the
body.
He used his filter to catch the nano's. It of course
needed some time. He started to look whether he
could create nano's on another basis. For instance

with water from the body instead of blood. Could the waste being used for it or did he had to get the water from the lymph's. He tried both options. It took more time than he had expected. It was already dark when he finished his first four testunits. He found it enough for today. He left the units in the refrigerator of the laboratory and left.

He still had to eat and so he did. He found an open restaurant just around the corner and he ate a big steak. He asked for extra sauce because he liked it very much.

He walked over the square in front of the restaurant and saw a big hotel with a casino and a dancing area. He first visited the casino. He again played, deliberately on machines with which he had no feeling at all. He won a little bit and lost it all right after the first little profit. He smiled. He found it all right. He searched for a machine where he had a special titling and won one thousand dollar. He right away spend half if it again on a machine where he had no feeling with. He liked this. He one way or another still had the feeling that he was cheating using his titling by playing on a machine. He had to find out how it worked and why.

He left the casino and stopped by at the dancing. It was a crowded happening. It was large but there was a lot of young people. Most of them were dancing. A number was just standing and sitting along the side or at the bar, right opposite to him. He walked through the crowd to the bar, ordered a beer and looked at the people moving on the dancefloor. Many of them danced alone and just around. Still a lot of couples were active, often close to each other.

Suddenly he got caught by his arm.

"John, you here? I am surprised. I do not believe I have ever seen you here before?" A woman's voice sounded from behind him.

John turned around. Mary, the masseuse from yesterday stood right behind him.

"Hallo Mary, correct, I have never been here before. I do not come often in dancing's. This is just a coincidental case. I was curious how this kind of places look like. You come here often ?" he asked.

"Yes, I love to dance, come on, finish your beer and let's dance, ". She suddenly remembered his problem with his muscles.

" How are you doing, how are your muscles doing?" she wanted to know.

"Oh, they are ok now. I told you about my invention. I have decided to use it, so I think they are all completely recovered already."

She stared at him. "John, come on, that is impossible. Yesterday you could hardly walk. There is not something like a miracle available to solve that in one day! "

John only smiled. He finished his beer and walked to the dancefloor. He calm and easy started to move on the loud and rhythmic music.

Mary followed him and danced as well, looking at his moves with astonishment.

John smiled and made even more complicated moves. She tried to follow his moves but that was not easy. John calmed down and returned to the bar. Mary followed him immediately. John got seated on a high barstool, Mary came standing right in front of him.

"John" she said . This is really a miracle. I know how hard your muscles were yesterday. I still do not understand how it worked. " She looked at him and touched his leg. She felt. Indeed the strong muscles felt great and flexible. Totally different from yesterday. She stared at him. "How is this possible", she stumbled again.

"I told you, my nano's."

She did not understand.

She came close to John.

She really was a beautiful girl with her big brown eyes and her light brown, almost golden skin.

John smiled at her and looked her in her eyes. She came closer and toughed his body with both her hands and softy moved her lips along his face.

She kissed him on his mouth, softly and gentle. John answered her kiss, also very calm and easy. She put her hands on his head and looked him in his eyes. Then she kissed him strongly on his mouth. She pressed her body against his chest. John automatically closed her in his arms and kissed her.

"John," she said, will you come with me. I live nearby. I want you. "

"You are very beautiful Mary."

"I think I would like to inspect your muscles, I have to control them," she said with a big smile, got up and pulled him along with his hand in her hand. John followed willingly. He liked her, she really was a beautiful woman.

John spend the night with her. She learned him things about massage he did not knew. He liked her touch. They said goodbye in the morning and John returned to his cottage.

He needed again extra time to catch the nano's if they already would come out. There should have been a faster and more efficient method. He knew how to bring the nano's to the right place, then it must also be possible to bring the nano's to the urine, direct ready for disposal.

He walked to his laboratory and used the method he had just found. It worked perfectly. He actually was surprised that he had not use this before. He collected al the nano's and put them back on their spot in the refrigerator.

He had to go to Toko this afternoon, so he returned to the cottage.

He had a simple lunch and the driver came on the door again.

John trained with Toko, mainly in the ring. After each half hour they took a short break to look at the actions of the opponent. They found that Toko should train ten rounds of each four instead of three minutes. They would do so next time. John made Toko sweat, he had to keep on running around in the ring. In the last half hour John continuously beat Toko from another corner. Toko had a problem with Johns movement speed. He was a lot faster than the opponent from Toko, but John found that he should not only being prepared for the speed of the opponent but also for faster opponents. John also let him change his frontfoot far more often than till then. Toko got better in these moves. John also trained him his uppercut. This jumpshot was his superblow.

John took a shower and was brought home by the driver.

John stayed at home. He had to think about his nano's. Tomorrow he wanted to have a solution for all the questions he still had over the new nano's. Did he needed another way through the body to bring the new nano's to their right spot. He first had to test them on their reaction on the soundbeams. Could he activate them on the same way as the bloodnano's or did he needed another method. What would that be for a solution? He tried to create some options. He also thought about the compact of the nano's. Should they be smaller? He already needed specified apparatus to realise the present form. Smaller could only by computersensed apparatus. Could the whole nano be in one drop of water? He kept on thinking about options and alternatives. He again and again noted each of his questions in his tablet. The options as answers he noted as well.

He went late to his bed.

He slept well. He had a heavy night behind him . He had some sleep to catch up.

He got up late. He had a breakfast and took his tablets with him. He ran again through the forest and calmly walked into the city. He entered a new hotel and got to the businesscentre. He bought an hour internettime and looked at the different emails. There was not much news. Only James complained that he had not reacted.

He did react, stating that actions needed from his site could be expensive.

The architect gave information about the cost made until that moment. There was still a remarkable amount available.

John left and returned to his laboratory. He started to work on his new nano visions.

He realised that these experiments would take a lot of time. Testing and testing was the coming months his daily work.

He tried to use his special feeling by his research to a smaller nano and with a nano with other materials, such as bodywater, lungmoist etc. .

The four patients were doing good. He was surprised about the older patients. They did recover, very slowly but there really was a progression visible on the organs that he had stimulated in the brain and later on both places, in the brain and on location of the organ.

He realised that it would certainly take a lot of time to really get his patients recovered. The two younger patients also recovered but only on the organs he was treating. The problems with the other organs did not improve. He had to reconsider his methods. Should he always use a more general method in combination with a gentle and softly promotion of one or at the most two weaker organs? Would it work at all. It did work with the older patients why should it not work on the younger ones. Should he try to use more nano's? He was afraid that it would take too much energy from the body. The older patient already had a problem with their own energy regulation. He had advised the nurses to make sure they got enough energy in their food and if needed extra's beside the normal food. There were a lot of complications he had to think about and to solve.

Chapter 42

John visited his parents and told them about his experiments at the hospital. They really were enthusiastic. He did make progress with these patients. That was extraordinary good news. His father advised him to ask for a governmental financial support so he would have no financial problems.

John told him that he did not had to worry about his finances. Through the coaching of the worldchampion boxing he made more than enough money for a lifetime. His parents had not known that he was the coach of a boxing person and certainly not a world champion. They knew how John always had hated all kind of violence, including all fightingsports.

He told them that he had read a lot about these sports and through an incident had been involved in a boxer that wanted to improve his boxing qualities through him. He had learned this man a lot and still did.

He told them about the next fight coming week. He had to be at the traininglocation to get the champion ready for this fight.

His parents found that he had changed. He did not wanted to have anything to do with boxing.

John smiled. I make a lot of money, each time he wins. I have more than enough to live from.

John's brother wanted to know more about his activities with the boxing area.

Their parents stopped the dispute. They came back to John's experiments with his nano's.

John told them that he had made great progress with his nano's to the growth of muscles. He also told that he had done experiments on himself.

They had already expected that because of the growth of his muscles.

John's father wanted to know if he was thinking about a productionmethod for his nano's. if they really did what he had told them he should try to sell it to other hospitals, learn the personnel to work with them and to gather all available information about this new revolutionary medicine.

John had not thought about such an option. He realised that he was very closed about his invention. Only the hospital and the four patient knew about it. Of course Toko knew as well.

He promised to think about it.

He left them again and walked through town through the centre because he lived at the opposite site of the centre. He liked his cottage, even though it was owned by Boseley. He felt at home there.

He walked through a large park and decided to look at his emailaddresses.

He had already looked at them this morning so he did not expected anything new.

There was a new massage from the architect. The office wrote that they had had contact with four potential builders. Because they did not know who the client was they asked, all four, for a bank guarantee for fifty percent of the total buildingcosts, estimated by the architect on an amount of around fourhundred million dollars.

John stared at the mail. He closed the contact and stared out in front of him. How was that. Terribly logical but he had not thought about it for a moment. He would take money from the criminal organisations when the money was needed. No bank could give a guarantee if there was nothing available to hold that amount.

He had to think about this. Taking such a large amount from the criminal organisations would certainly give problems. They probably already were busy trying to find him.

He started to walk again. This could make his whole plan fall down. Of course he could put a part of his own money in it but he did not wanted that. He had only money to loose in that position.

Ok, Lord still owed him a penalty but that could not be more than ten million. That was already an extreme amount. The penalty for major had been extreme, he knew that. These two organisations had by far the most money. Perhaps he would first of all find out the amount of their total bankaccounts. He could then see in what part each had to be involved in the project.

He walked back to his cottage.

He thought about the problem again. He also realised that he only had the bankaccounts from the organisations. He did not know anything about their properties, their real estates, businesses, shares they owed etc. Also their legal businesses were not really visualised in his information.

He actually did not know whether the accounts he had cracked were filled with criminal money or regular money.

He saw no other option than to clear the punishment for the Lord with an amount of ten million dollar and to divide the rest, so beside the two penalties, among the four organisations.

John slept bad. He had gone to his bed early. He could not sleep. He was restless about this guarantee affair.

 Of course the criminal organisations would be furious. The four managers were tough criminals, certainly James. One more murder should be no problem at all. She would even be happy that John would no longer exist. Lia did no longer had to long for him.

Would Toko try to defend him? He already was worldchampion. He had to stop but that was all. How bad did he wanted to stay worldchampion? It was a very insecure position to put your life on.

John got up early. He had not slept at all. He felt broken. He got dressed and ate just one cracker. It

did not taste. He even left half a cup of coffee behind. He did not wanted to run. Nobody was waiting for him at his laboratory so he was not in a hurry. He shuffled through the park. At the end of the park he got seated on a bank, along the road. The sky became darker. Black clouds came together and the rain started to fall down. It rained really hard. Even a bang of the thunderstorm and a sweeping lightning came along. John staid all the time on the bank. He got sockeye wet. In a way he did not care. It all belonged to his bad mood for today. It all took more than an hour.
The sky cleared and the sun came in again.
It took John another half hour to get up and another fifteen minutes to get back to his cottage. He got redresses after a warm shower and got out again. He took his bag with him this time. The warm shower had made him feel a little better and he walked straight to his laboratory.
He tried to forget the threatening of the guarantee and to concentrate on his nano's. What had his father asked ? A nano factory. He had not yet thought about that. Could that be the future. How did such a factory had to work, how would it look like? The way he did it himself was a one man show. He needed a microscope and a computer that could follow his instructions to build the nano's. In itself it was not very complex. It was the result of very many tests and new alternatives. Once the working nano was created it was a matter of

reproducing it. He tried to instruct his tablet to control the handling of the tools that would build the nano. Because it was so small he needed an enlarged seize on the screen to follow the several steps to be taken.

It al did not work at once. He had to improvise several times because the tools were too big for the seize of the nano.

He stopped. He first of all needed smaller tools. With these it could not work.

He searched on the internet for smaller tools, found them and ordered them It would take three working days for delivery as soon as he would have paid the order. John paid and could only wait for the tools.

It was already the end of the day. Time had flown. He had had a bad start this morning so the day was extra short. Tomorrow he had to go to Toko for his trainingsactivity. The end of the week was his next fight so he would not only the day after tomorrow being busy with Toko but also the day after that, the day before the fight. It would be a busy week.

John walked into a park and looked at his emails on his tablet. He got in his emailaddress with the architect and found a new story. The architect expected the building permit in a week, the permitinformation was now available for the civilians for comments. Nobody expected a problem from that site. The architects were starting to make a bidbook for the whole building. They thought that it would be wise and sufficient to make a rolling guarantee for fifty million dollar. So there would always be money before the next payment would be needed. Each time any amount should be paid, the guarantee should be recovered. The bank that will give the guarantee will only give it when the amount of the guarantee is always available on the account. So any payment can only be done from an amount above the guarantee.

John felt relieved. This amount could he get from the four organisations plus the punishment for the Lord. He would make it available tomorrowmorning. He gave his ok to the architects and closed the mail. He felt a lot better. This was a realistic option. He would tell the organisations how it would work so they would understand.

John also send a mail to the broker and asked him to contact the architect about all the details of the building, needed for the sales of the apartments, the parkingarea's, the restaurant and the mall.

John walked home. He would stay at home tonight, tomorrow he would go on with Toko.

He ate at home, watched television and went to bed early.

The next three days he was busy with Toko. They trained what John had shown Toko before. John was reasonable satisfied. He told Toko basically to watch very carefully what his opponent did, his moves his bodylanguage and his eyes were basic.

On Saturday Toko had to box his next fight. John was there as well. Toko made it a great fight. He was superior to his opponent. If his opponent started to walk around Toko did it twice as fast and right in the opposite direction. His opponent did not understand what Toko did but he deliberately changed his stand by putting the left foot on front. His opponent did not discover that. He did not understand why he could no longer reach the champion. Toko was good. He used this extra as an active tool. He made his opponent mis often. In the third round he found it enough. He stopped. His opponent looked at him completely surprised and Toko hit him with his famous jump uppercut. The man got flat out.

Toko smiled at John and nicked to him. He took the applause and the congratulations from the audience and all the thousands fans that were standing outside, looking at large screens. The noise from outside was so enormous that it could be heard inside.

John waved at Toko and made him clear that he got home. Toko understood and waved him good bye. As they had decided after each fight they would have a whole week free. Than the same circle would start again. Training twice a week on Tuesday and Thunderday in the afternoon.

John found it all fine. He had made again a great amount of money. Toko would pay him his share as he had always done.

Toko had told John that his manager, who arranged al the fights only got five percent of the fee he won with the fights. John was satisfied with his thirty percent. The amounts involved were enormous.
He walked back to his cottage. He thought about all of the different tablets and all of the different outfits in which he only incidentally had dressed. Only the fat youngster was actually active for the architect and the real estate broker. The others were actually inactive. The use of a whole tablet for each e-mailaddress also looked extreme.
He came home late and went straight to his bed. It had been intensive days with Toko.

John got up late. He had a whole week off from Toko. He also did not wanted to go to his office, although he had not looked at his mails for more than three days.
He walked into town with all his tablets in his bag. He entered into a big hotel and got internet in the businesscentre. There were reactions from the architect and the broker.
The architect declared that they were about to finish the bidbook for the builders. They wanted John to look at the totaltekst in their office to give his personal consent to the total buildingplan. They expected the permit in just a few days. The builders would need about a week to clear their price and conditions. After they had decide who would get the order all the details would be cleared. John was not

needed for that unless he wanted that. Of course he was always welcome.

In the meantime a specialist was already started to get rid of the present ruins and to reuse almost all the materials. He was happy with the order for zero dollars. He could keep the materials.

The architects asked him if he could come to their office Mondaymorning nine o'clock to go through the bidbook.

John accepted the invitation.

He also made an appointment with the broker for Monday, the end of the morning. They had to decide about the salesprices of all the objects he could sel.

There were no other mails.

He closed them all and left the hotel.

The whether was changing. He felt a cold wind starting to blow. Some dark clouds were driving in from the horizon. He decided to go home. He took the rest of the day of. It was Sunday so he did not had to work, though he never thought about workingdays. He was his own boss and he decided when he worked.

He played games on his tablet. He liked it.

He ate at the Saloon, talked with the group old man and got back. He got to bed early, he had to get up early on mondaymorning.

Chapter 43

John got up early. He took a quick breakfast, collected his tablets in case he might need one and got redressed as the fat youngster.
It rained heavily, so he took an umbrella and walked to the office of the architect.
Sonja was present and welcomed him friendly. She did not seem to recognize him. The college of Sonja, the projectleader, as Sonja stated, was present as well. He told wat was going on. Sonja listened with John about his explanation.
In the bidbook a passage was there about the guarantee for the money to pay. An onrolling amount of fifty million dollar would be available on a bankaccount specific and only to be used for payments to the builder until the builder agrees that he had been paid in full. Misuse by the builder was punishable. Misuse by the client was also punishable. Sonja had several questions about the ground under the building, the way the cars could get to the upperparking decks, the use of sunpanels on the roof at the part that the restaurant did not use, about several materials, kitchenfinish in the apartments, the number of elevators and the access to the prisonarea. She seemed satisfied about the answers. It was all cleared.
John signed the bidbook for "agreed" and congratulated the projectmanager and Sonja. He asked a copy of the signed version and same extra

copies of the apartments, the parkingarea's, the mall and the restaurant and hotel areas.

He got it all, said goodbye and left.

He had the impression that Sonja started to get a special feeling about the difference between his face and his body.

John went on to the broker. They made a plan to get the attention of the potential buyers for the project. John would never be in the picture, so Jo, the broker and his assistant should do the job. They decided about all the apartments except one. That was mend for a good friend of the client. The price for the mall and the restaurant was very difficult. Jo wanted to talk to several investors to find out what they thought it was worth and the question was raised if a rental position could be an option?

John would consider such an option as well. For the parking areas there were already several investors interested. They had already asked for the price. Jo had put the question back to them, two were already starting to mention there prices. They had time to get these prices up, sincerely.

John found it all ok and left.

On his way back to his laboratory he entered a hotel with a businesscentre. He decided to transfer the amounts from the criminal organisations to his central account for the buildingproject. Each of them paid fifteen million and Lord as a penalty an extra ten million. He immediately transferred the ten million to a third account and from there to his account.

He finished it by finishing the internet contact and left. He got into the toilets and changed. He washed his head and hear and came out as John again. He found it more than enough redressing and hoped it would not be needed ever again. He had collected the clothes and the lenses and decided in a controversial mood to throw it all away. He did so. He dropped it all in a container that he happened to pass on the street. He had enough of it.

Walking back to his laboratory, he found it unnecessarily overdone to use so many different tablet.

Once he was in his laboratory he collected all the emailadresses in one tablet but gave them al a special code for entrance from the opening of the tablet. He cleaned all the other tablets from everything. He made his own tablet so that the basic start up position was his own standard tablet. Nothing could be linked to other activities than his nano's and private searches on that matter. All other searches were deleted, so nobody could find out that he had cracked the files of others. He picked five tablets, controlled whether they were all clean and placed back into the position as delivered by the producer. He made five nice packages in golden paper. He would surprise his family with a tablet. He new they all had one but they were all pretty old and needed to be replaced.

The other tablets, also cleaned, he put in the drawer of his bureau. He might need them in his research. He looked at his prototype of his productionmachine to see if this really could be used.

The new handles were delivered. He unpacked them. They were extraordinary fine. He tested them. They seemed strong enough as well. He picked up his safetyglasses and put them in front of his head, not yet for his eyes but on his forehead. He opened the machine and unfastened the old arms. He put them away and fastened the new arms. He close the machine and looked at the tablet from the machine how it al seemed to work. He was very satisfied. He put away his glasses and sat down to make instructions for his machine to let it work.

Suddenly the frontdoor of his laboratory was blown away. John was totally flabbergasted. What was this. Wat happened.

A couple of masked man in black came fast at him and he got shot before he knew what was happening. He lost consciousness.

John came to. He wanted to feel on his head but his arms were tied toughly. He opened his eyes. It was dark. On his left side he saw a small window. Something black had covered it, so he could not see if there was light outside.

He was in a room. He seemed to be right in the middle. There was only a small line of light coming under through the door. He now saw that he was sitting on a small kitchenchair. His arms, his legs and his breast were tide on the chair. The chair did not seem too strong. He moved his body a little bid forward and back again. He felt that it moved. He pushed hard with his foot and the whole chair fall backwards on the floor.

John immediately tried to give the chair an extra boost by hitting the ground with extra speed. He pressed his legs against the legs of the chair. The chair broke in pieces. His legs were free immediately, For his arms he needed to break the armrest. He used his elbow to made more pressure. It worked. He rolled away from the sitting of the chair and was free. He got up, walked to the window and tried carefully to look behind the black cover of the window. It was stuck. He saw nothing. It seemed all dark outside. He looked around in the room. There was not much to see. It all seemed as a forgotten, empty room in an apartment. No other window, so only the door was left to get out.

John first searched on his body if he had any damage from the hit that got him down. Nothing. Who were these men? What did they want? What did they want from him. They wanted him alive otherwise he would not be here. Blowing the frontdoor from his laboratory was ridiculous. Why?

Could James and or Major suspect him from something. He could not believe it.

John tried the door. Closed !, as he could have expected. Could he use the chair to spoil the window. It was worth trying.

Just at that moment he heard voices. The voices came to the door of his room.

He picked a piece of the chair and hit the window. No chance. This was a solid strong window.

The door was opened. He heard bolts move and a key turning in a lock. He got backwards to the end of the room. He sat down on the ground. He felt again his body. He was shot down. He must have been hit by something. Suddenly he remembered. His own laserguns. They could hit your body all together. They must have trained with these guns to know how they had to be regulated.

The door went open. Four men in black, masked, came in. One stepped forward.

"Come," was all he said, moving his lasergun to wave him to the door. The man stepped aside and the other three left the room through the door. John had no alternative than to follow.

The man looked at the window and smiled.

"It always works," he chuckled. John looked at him. The man knocked on the window. "No window," was all he said, "solid wall with a painting as a window", he really smiled now wide out. John looked at the window. Just a painting . He immediately looked at the other side of the room.

The man smiled at him again and grumbled "go", pointing his lasergun to the door.

John nicked and walked through the door. The three other man in black were waiting for him. They turned around and one man started to walk through a long hallway. The two other came shortly after him and the third man followed them all. They must find him extreme dangerous to have him escorted by four laserguns. He still did not understand what was happening.

The first man moved around a corner and stopped ten meters further. It must be a large building to have these kind of hallways.

The group came together and they entered a large broad room. Right in front of John stood a large table with about ten seats on the opposite side. Only one seat was taken.

"James !!"John screamed.

"John???"James reacted.

"What is this !!" James got up. Looking angry to the men around John. She grabbed a picture and showed it to the four man.

"Is this the same man? Is this the man on this photo? "

"Get out you , move, get out, now." She was really pissed. She even looked mean. John stared at her. Was she behind all this. Had she kidnapped him, was not that the job for Major and her team. Wait, he remembered that she had activated extra computerfreaks to get behind his identity. They must have found a link. She had a photo from the fatty young man. How was that possible. He had to find a story about this. What did she know. She would probably tell him. He must admit that he had met this man. He even had sold him the five tablets he was going to give to his familymembers. Where had he meet him the first time. In the days after the prisonbreak. He was just walking around through the parks of the city. So was he it seemed. He had not seen him the last time, until today. He had needed money and had sold him the five tablets. Were these stolen?

That would be his story.

He deliberately stared at the picture she had in her hand.

"Are you looking for Tom, James ," he asked as if he knew Tom.

"What?," she reacted, "do you know him?" she asked surprised.

"Well knowing, no but I have met him, twice I think. Some weeks ago after the prison explosion I walked through town for a couple of days. I met him in one of the parks. The second time today", he stated as if he reminded that surprised.

"He sold me the five tablets I was going to give as presents to my family. They were in my laboratory." He looked at James, surprised that he had met him after such a long period.

"How do you got his picture? What is wrong with this man?" John wanted to know.

"Sorry John, please come and sit with me."
John walked around the table and took a chair.
"We have a problem. We think that this young man
has cracked our bankaccounts. He seems to think
that four organisations are responsible for the
damage of the prison so they have to pay for the
rebuilding of the prison. Nonsense of course, but he
is plundering our accounts to pay for the costs."
"That is that superhigh new building on the same
spot as the prison was?" John wanted to know.
"Correct. This man," she ticked on the portrait, "has
instructed an architect to ask for the buildingpermit,
all totally legal, but he pays it all from our money.
We have activated an internet squad. Yesterday he
contacted us again and grabbed a lot of money,
millions, from our accounts. Our internetsquad had
coupled our accounts on a special app with what
they could look through the camera of the inlogger
from outside our location. That was how we got this
picture. "
"You mean he broke in in your system and you
broke in in his computer," he smiled, he found this a
nice way to cheat among each other. He now
understood what had happened. Tom did no longer
exist. He could only talk to the architect and the
broker by email.
"So, you mean that he is the client for building the
huge tower. He pays the prison with your money but
how does he pay the rest?" John started to laugh.

"You know what. Tom promised me a very large apartment in that building. I thought he was talking about a prisoncel, not a real apartment. I think I have to talk to the broker, I suppose. Perhaps he even told him." He laughed again. He really enjoyed this conversation.

James got up.

"Sorry John, this guy as incredibly brilliant. He must have noticed our app. He cleaned the tablets, sold them to you and disappeared. You got the blame. We will renew your entrance. I will order it right now."

She grabbed her phone, made a clear and not disputable statement and nicked to John. "The door is renewed now. They have to get the materials but it will happen today."

John asked for his tablets and James smiled. She walked to a small cupboard against the wall and collected the five tablets.

She gave them to John. He looked at her. "Are they clean ? he asked.

"I do not know John. I have not touched them."

John shaked his head. "Trust", was all he said.

"Should you not pay me for your kidnapping ? he asked.

"Wrong, I ordered to kidnap Tom, as you call him, not you and certainly not with this kind of violence. Major organised this. I will contact her about this. You will hear about this. "she had to smile. She seemed to like it to point Major on her mistakes.

"James, how is Lia doing?" John wanted to know . He must admit that he more or less had forgotten about her. As great as she was.

"John. It is unbelievable what you have done with her. She understood that not only you but almost no interesting man would stay long with her as long as she was a killingmachine. She stopped overnight. You left and she stopped. I do not know what had happened but she quitted. She wants to start a sportsschool. That had been your advice, she said. John, what has happened that night. I know that my youngest sun had approached you and asked you to visit her. She was totally down and broken. After that night she knew exactly what she wanted. She was totally changed, an other woman, really a woman. Please, I think as her mother I have to know, I have to understand her and what you did to her. Please?'

John looked at her. "James, you cannot understand what happened because you would not want to believe what I would tell you. "

"Please, John, try me."

"Ok James. First I told her that she was far too young to find herself bound by one man without a broad experience with other man."

James looked surprised, she wanted to say something but John stopped her by getting his hand up.

"Secondly, I told her that she was not a very good killing machine. "

Again James wanted to interrupt him.

John wend on. " Of course she was angry about my statement, so I challenged her in several experiences. She lost them all. She agreed with me that I would be a better murdermachine than she was. I also stated that I hate violence, even if I happen to be the trainercoach of the worldchampion boxing, Toko. She understood my vision and promised to think about one of my suggestions to start a sportsschool. Is she? Please I would like to know. Maybe I will start training there." He looked at James to find out whether she believed his story.

"Yes , yes," she tried to win time to get the through into her mind. John would be a better fighter than her daughter. She found that unbelievable. Would his story be untrue, would her daughter than have changed so radically, No. So it was unbelievable but it was most probably the reality.

This John was a dangerous fighter. She also realised that she was not. This man had invented nano's, she had no idea what these things did but it had very complicated medical consequences, this man combined that with being a great fighter. Unbelievably, she could not make anything else from this. She told that Lia was looking around if she would take over an existing school or became a partner in an existing school or that she would start a complete new school for herself.

John asked what she had advised but she had not. She did not wanted to get involved in this kind of choices, she had her own business.

John made her clear, very clear that a mother should use more time on her children and their interests. "Help her to decide, advise her. You are suppost to be her mother, you know," John got a little bid angry.

He tempered his voice, apologised and wanted to get back to his laboratory.

James told him that they were out of town. She would have him brought back to his laboratory.

John was glad to be back in his laboratory with his tablets. There were three man working on a new door. The wall was also partly destroyed. They corrected it all. They already had cleaned the floor in the laboratory. John was happy with that. He offered them coffee and they finished the job in half an hour. John got the new keys and thanked them again.

John was glad that the kidnapping had finished without being unmasked. He had to let Tom disappear as person. He could only have contact with the architect and the broker by mail. Even that should be done as less as possible. The money was his largest concern. The sales should be speeded up so that the buyers had to pay all along the building was growing, so they would pay for the needed amounts above the guaranteed amount.

He went to an internetcafé. He posted a mail to the broker, Jo Baker, making him clear how the units should be sold. He informed him about the bankaccount and the name with witch it was identified.

He also marked the apartment fixed for his friend with a photo an eyescan and a fingerprint from John himself.

He searched on the internet to a sportsschool that had financial problems. He actually found one. He noted the address and looked at the location in the map on the computer. He found it, left the internetcafé and walked to the school.

It was getting dark so he took a simple dinner in an restaurant that looked very colourful. For John's taste too colourful.

He ate quickly. The foot was good but he did not feel happy in the mood of the house.

He walked out and followed his route to the sportsschool. He was not familiar with this sportsschool. He walked by and looked in. He could not see anything special. It looked a dark and sober location. The walls were brown, the ceiling was rather low and lighter brown. No he did not found this an interesting school. This one would not survive.

He walked back to his laboratory. He had to see whether he could help Lia. He would advise her another school to be interested in for her future.

He knew three schools but these were all too much coupled on the criminal organisations. Perhaps a new location should be the best option. He would wait for her decision. On the internet the opening of a new sportsschool would very likely be an item of interest.

Chapter 44

John visited his parents regularly. They even visited his laboratory but even his father could not really follow his nano development.
John found out that nano's also worked as a waternano. The soundbeams had more direct influence on these nano's. These nano's were better for organs, the bloodnano's were better for vanes, brains, muscles and the skin.
John trained the four first patients how they could use the nano's themselves to vary the input with the different organs and the brain. It took longer than he had expected. The two old patient got better but very slowly. The two younger ones recovered but, still needed almost a whole year to get better.
They found it all remarkable. John found that it took too much time. He kept on searching too faster and better recovery methods.
Toko made fourteen fights in the next two years. John stopped after that period and also Toko stopped. Without John he had no change, was his idea. They had made a lot of money with all the fights Toko won. John was through this money a wealthy man.
The building with the prison took almost three years to be completed. All the apartments, the parking areas, the mall and the restaurants were sold in time so that the finances gave no problem.

John kept one big apartment for himself, the gift from Tom. He had made himself known to the broker. He knew all the details, because Tom had told him these. The criminal organisations never found out who "the old man" was. John kept the punishment money for himself, the four criminal organisations paid for the costs for the new prison. The costs for a parking area was partly directed to the cost of the prison. All the other costs, including the garden, the architect and the real estate broker were pay from the sales. John even kept a result of more than enough money for a lifetime.
He closed the four emailadresses for his contacts with the four managers of the four criminal organisations. He also finished the contacts with the four informers and told them that they could keep the money from their loan.
John started a project to produce nano's for a lot of people. He caused a revolution in the medical world. It took a lot of time to convince the opponents but in the end he was loudly and enthusiastic approached.
He won a lot of prices for his nano's.

THE END

www.ingramcontent.com/pod-product-compliance
Lightning Source LLC
Chambersburg PA
CBHW060804030726
47503CB00002B/324